CHAINS: BOOK ONE IN THE BOUND SERIES

SHANDI BOYES

By: Shandi Boyes
Editing: Mountains Wanted Publishing
Photographs: Shutterstock Account
Cover Designer: SSB Designs

❀ Created with Vellum

DEDICATION

To the readers who inspire my every day to write.
Shandi xx

ALSO BY SHANDI BOYES

Perception Series - New Adult Rock Star Romance

Saving Noah

Fighting Jacob

Taming Nick

Redeeming Slater

Wrapped up with Rise Up

Enigma Series - Steamy Contemporary Romance

Enigma of Life - (Isaac)

Unraveling an Enigma - (Isaac)

Enigma: The Mystery Unmasked - (Isaac)

Enigma: The Final Chapter - (Isaac)

Beneath the Secrets - (Hugo - Part 1)

Beneath the Sheets - (Hugo Conclusion)

Spy Thy Neighbor (Hunter - standalone)

The Opposite Effect - (Brax & Clara)

I Married a Mob Boss - (Rico - Nikolai's Brother)

Second Shot (Hawke's Story)

The Way We Are (Ryan Pt 1)

The Way We Were (Ryan Pt 2)

Sugar and Spice (Cormack)

Bound Series - Steamy Romance & BDSM

Chains (Marcus and Cleo)

Links (Marcus and Cleo)

Bound (Marcus and Cleo)

Restrained (Marcus and Cleo)

Psycho (Dexter)

Russian Mob Chronicles

Nikolai: A Mafia Prince Romance

Nikolai: Taking Back What's Mine

Nikolai: What's Left of Me

Nikolai: Mine to Protect

Asher: My Russian Revenge

Infinite Time Trilogy

Lady In Waiting (Regan)

Man in Queue (Regan)

Couple on Hold (Regan)

Standalones

Just Playin' (Presley and Willow)

COMING SOON:

Skitzo

Colby

PROLOGUE

"Hold the elevator," I shout at the top of my lungs. My words are weak, hampered by the sob sitting at the back of my throat dying to break free.

Through a clog of people standing in the bustling foyer, I notice a black suit-covered arm shooting out to hold the elevator doors open for me. Gratitude replaces some of the panic scorching my veins, thankful I won't be stuck bawling my eyes out in a crowded space.

I run my hands across my cheeks to ensure my tears haven't spilled before pushing through the people gawking at me with sympathy. I'm sure I look like a total wreck. The well-presented package I put together every day has been decimated, replaced with an ashen face and desolate eyes. I don't need to look in the mirror to know my eyes are red and brimming with tears, and that my natural tan coloring is faded and washed out. I felt the blood drain from my face the moment I took the call that broke my heart.

Forty minutes ago, I took a call no woman ever wants to receive—a call that shattered my world with four little words, "There's been an accident."

Everything blurred in an instant. My entire world was upended. I can't remember how I made it to Jamaica Hospital in Queens. I think I drove here, but if I was asked to place my hand on a Bible and swear to it, I wouldn't be able to testify that was what happened. My mind is shut down, my heart beyond shattered. The only reason my legs are moving is because they're being encouraged by hope, a hope that not every nightmare I've had is coming to fruition at once. A hope that was also delivered with four short words: "Tate is in ICU."

More tears threaten to trickle down my cheeks as the words spoken to me forty minutes ago play on repeat. They add unfixable cracks to my already shattered heart, drowning out the doctor calls being announced over the hospital paging system.

With my mind distracted on keeping my body upright, I neglect to notice the lip at the entrance of the elevator. I fall forward at a faster rate than my heartbroken mind can register, sending me and my Manolo Blahnik shoes ungracefully tumbling into the elevator car.

"Oh, careful," says a deep and manly voice from above.

His warning comes too late. My fall is so brutal, the stranger's firm clutch on my arms doesn't stop me hitting the tiled floor with an almighty bang. Pain rockets through my knees, producing a whimper of protest from my parched lips and adding more tears to my already drenched eyes.

Ignoring my grazed knees, I crawl forward so I can hide my face in the corner. I need a few minutes to gather my composure before I face the next heartbreaking chapter of my story.

Through the shrilling of the pulse in my ears, I hear the stranger ask, "What floor?"

"Trauma unit, please." My voice is as low as my heart rate.

The elevator chugs to life, launching my stomach into my throat. I suck in deep breaths as I fight through the torrent of pain silently asphyxiating me.

This is by far the worst day of my life.

My manic breaths have me stumbling onto a unique scent not often registered in a hospital: freshly laundered linen. After running my hand under my nose to remove the contents spilling from it, I drift my eyes to the refreshing scent.

Through a volley of tears threatening to drop, my eyes scan a handsome African-American man wearing dark trousers and a buttoned-up shirt. He is standing near the elevator panel, eyeing me through a set of unbelievably thick lashes. Although my vision is blurred by my teary eyes, I can't miss the concern pumping from his alluring green gaze.

"Are you okay?"

The simplicity of his question breaks the dam of moisture in my eyes. My head flops forward as a broken howl tears through my quivering lips. I gave it my best shot to hold in my devastation, but I'm not strong enough anymore. I'm beyond broken.

Before I can register what's happening, I'm thrust off the floor and surrounded by warmth. As I hiccup through an infinite number of tears, the unnamed man holds me to his firm chest and whispers into my hairline.

With my pulse ringing in my ears, I can't hear a word he's speaking, but I know he's comforting me. His whole composure impels reassurance. His breath on my temple and his body curved around mine, simmers the shakes hampering my petite frame. He makes me completely forget I'm trapped in the depths of hell.

The whole scenario is something you'd expect to see in a sappy 90s romantic movie starring Tom Hanks and Meg Ryan. It's cringeworthy and unoriginal, but heartfelt and endearing at the same time. I'm not usually into clichés, but I'm willing to set aside my idiosyncrasy to accept the comfort of a stranger on my darkest day.

When the ding of the elevator announces its arrival to the trauma unit, disappointment registers on my face. I bite on the inside of my cheek, hoping it will stop my tears long enough to thank the stranger for his comfort. After running my hand across my cheeks, I pull back from his chest. I take a minute so my rattled brain can contemplate an appropriate response. While staring at his slow-thrusting chest, I notice two wet patches on his shirt. I cried so hard the lightweight material clings to his skin, exposing more of his rich chocolate skin.

My hunched posture straightens when he cups my jaw. His hand swallows half of my face as he uses the pad of his thumb to remove my tears. His touch scorches my cheek, and for a fraction of a second, he makes me forget where I am. He's standing so close, the sweetness of his breath fans my dry lips. I want to look at him, but I won't. I've always been a hideously ugly crier. I'm sure today is no different.

Once my tears are cleared, the stranger raises my downcast head. A sharp gasp expels from his lips when my head is lifted high enough that my long, dark brown locks fall from my face, fully exposing me. I bounce my eyes around the interior of the elevator, seeking anything but his gaze. Clearly, my concerns about my appearance are warranted by his gasping-in-shock response.

"Look at me." His deep voice breaks through the pain clouding me.

He keeps his hand hovering just under my chin. He's not quite touching me, but is close enough my body is on high alert. My chest rises and falls three times before my eyes follow the prompts of my blurry brain. Just as his razor-sharp jawline, decadent plump lips, and the tip of his straight, defined nose come into view, my name is called.

Snapping my head to the side, I locate my younger sister, Lexi, standing in the corridor. Tears are flooding her cheeks, and her eyes look lifeless and hollow. She's shaking so much, I'm confident she's on the verge of collapse. I rush to her and scoop her into my arms. Her tears trickling down my neck are absorbed by the collar of my cashmere jumper when she burrows her head under my chin.

"They're gone." Her low voice breaks my heart even more.

"It's okay. It will be okay," I assure her as the ghastliness of the situation slams back into me, hammering me enough I struggle to breathe.

I run my trembling hand down Lexi's hair in a soothing manner. "We will always have each other. No matter what happens, we'll get through this."

While pressing a kiss to her temple, her freshly washed hair triggers the briefest memory. As my heart rate climbs, I swing my eyes to the left. My breath hitches in my throat when I catch the quickest glimpse of a pair of unique green eyes peering at me.

"*Thank you,*" I mouth to the blurred man standing in the elevator.

Even with my nearsightedness hindering my vision, I don't miss the curt nod of his head before the elevator doors snap shut.

1

Four Years Later...

"Calm your farm; they don't have legs, so they haven't just up and left town. They have to be here somewhere."

I stop digging my hand into our lumpy two-seater couch and swing my eyes to my sister, Lexi. She wears the *we're about to be homeless if I turn up to work late again* look better than me. Her long brown locks are twisted in a sideways French braid, and her hours of coughing this morning have given her cheeks a vibrant red hue. Her fluffy pink pig slippers and Ms. Sunshine pajamas don't give any indication to the gauntlet of pain her weary body ran through this weekend.

Lexi is sick. I don't mean she drank too much on the weekend and is feeling the effects of it sick, I mean sick-sick. She has cystic fibrosis, the one sickness that can be easily hidden by her bright smile and gorgeous face. Even though we have a five-year age gap, people often mistake us as twins. We have the same dark, stormy eyes from our mother, thick, wavy hair from our father, and the wit of our youngest brother, Tate.

If you were to scroll back through generations of records of the

Garcias from Montclair, New Jersey, locate a photo of any female within the 20-25 year age category, you will find a replica of Lexi and me. We are the very epitome of the Garcia genes.

I crank my neck to our family portrait hanging above the brick and mortar fireplace. Heat blooms across my chest when my eyes lock with my mom sitting in the middle of the painting. She's surrounded by her three children.

If I disregard the faded edges of the oil paint my father used to create his masterpiece that's been hanging on the wall the past fifteen years, I could pretend I was looking in the mirror. That's how similar I look to my mother.

I take a moment to remember a lady who smelled like fresh flowers and had a heart bigger than my daddy's boots before I continue to hunt for my felonious keys. My breathing halts when the coolness of metal graces my fingers.

Screwing up my nose, I slip my hand deeper into the badly-in-need-of-an-upgrade couch. From the crazy beat of my heart and the beading of sweat mottling Lexi's forehead, anyone would swear I was searching for Blackbeard's treasure, not keys for a family sedan that is as old as me.

"Ah ha!" I squeal in excitement when my finger loops around an icy metal material.

Agitation spurs on my annoyance when a broken spring is the only thing that emerges from my in-depth frisk of the saggy couch. Gritting my teeth, I throw my head back and close my eyes, stifling the scream bubbling up my chest.

My efforts are utterly pointless when Lexi asks, "Are these what you're looking for?"

Cracking my eyes open, I snap my head to the side. An ear-piercing squeal emits my lips when I discover my car keys dangling on Lexi's finger.

"If I find out you were hiding them this entire time, I'll forget my detour to the pharmacy this afternoon."

I aim for my tone to come out playful, but it has an edge of bitchiness to it. I've never been a morning person, so a Monday following a long weekend is the worst of the worst.

"Forget the pharmacy; you need to visit the optometrist." An angry snarl mars her beautiful face. "They were sitting in the exact spot you put them Friday night: on the entranceway table."

Grumbling about my annoying nearsightedness, I tug on my coat, sling my satchel over my shoulder, then twist a thin scarf around my neck. I hate winter in general, but I hate it even more since its early arrival gave Lexi a bad case of pneumonia three weeks ago. She was so sick, I was certain she'd end up in the hospital. Considering that is an expense neither of us can afford, I'm being extra cautious to ensure I don't get the slightest sniffle. Something as simple as a mild cold could be catastrophic for Lexi.

"Thank you." I accept a travel mug of steaming hot chocolate from Lexi. "I'll be home a little late tonight, so don't worry about dinner for me. I'll grab a soup on my way past Donovan's."

She nods while pacing to the front door. I increase my already brisk pace when chilly air blasts into our cozy three-bedroom home. October always brings windy conditions to our hometown, but with a drastic drop in temperatures this month, it's brisker than normal. Locals are so wary we'll be hit by another freak snowstorm like we did in October 2011 that the hardware store sold out of rock salt this weekend.

I'm just about to gallop down the front stairs of our patio when I remember I need to remind Lexi about the special parcel arriving today. She's as forgetful as I am nearsighted.

Being cautious not to slip on the warped wood lining our patio, I spin around to face Lexi. "I know, the courier is arriving at 10 AM, electrician will be here by 11." White air from the crisp fall morning puffs out of her blue-tinged lips.

My mouth twitches as I prepare to speak, but Lexi beats me. "I know, Cleo. It's cheaper to run than our last system." She peers down at me with her big chocolate eyes, tears welling in them. "I promise I won't hesitate to use it if I'm feeling cold."

She hates when I baby her, but her illness isn't something she will simply get over. There's no cure for cystic fibrosis. Eventually, it will take her from me, leaving me all alone. Anything I can do to keep that from happening any earlier than it has to, I will do. Even eating reheated broth and pretending it's chicken soup so I can afford to buy the medication she needs to breathe without wheezing. That's how much I love my sister.

"I wasn't going to say anything about the new heating system." I wave my hand in the air like I'm shooing away my overbearing mothering. "I just wanted to wish you luck for your date today." I ensure my voice has an extra hint of sappiness for my last sentence. "It's not every day you have lunch with a world-renowned surgeon."

"Up and coming world-renowned surgeon," Lexi corrects, her dour mood picking up. "And just for clarity: the whole 'gifted hands' thing they refer to when discussing surgeons doesn't always correspond to their title."

Gagging to fake repulsion, I press a quick kiss on her cheek. My mothering instincts kick into overdrive when I feel how cold her face is.

"One time." I hold my index finger into the air to enhance my statement. "Free rein on my entire wardrobe."

I see Lexi's excitement winding up from her stomach to her white cheeks. "Even the dresses Sasha gave you during your internship?"

I twist my lips before nodding. Lexi's squeal is brittle enough I won't need salt to crack the ice sleeting the sidewalk this winter; her girly scream will decimate even the thickest ice.

After returning my gesture of a peck on the cheek, Lexi bolts into our modest clapboard house, slamming the front door behind her. I release a deep breath, grateful my ploy to get her inside worked without a tinge of hesitation. I have no doubt the loss of another dress from my rapidly dwindling designer collection will be worth the sacrifice to keep her warm.

Blowing air onto my blue-tinted fingertips, I trudge to my 1994 baby-poo-brown Buick Century coupe. She was a good car. . . back in 1994 when my parents drove her off the sales lot. Now she has more rust than original paintwork and a big dent in the quarter back panel from Lexi's inability to see our mailbox that's been in the same location the past twenty years of her life.

Snubbing the self-pity party encroaching me, I push my key into the broken lock on my driver's side door and slide inside. With the heater on the blink the last four years, the steering wheel is as frozen as my hands. To say the past four years have been shit would be a major understatement. There aren't enough derogatory words in the dictionary to illustrate how my last four years have been.

My dreary mood picks up when it only takes three cranks of the engine before my old girl's motor finally kicks over.

"I know, Honey; it's been a tough few months," I mumble when she coughs and wheezes as much as Lexi's lungs did over the weekend.

Pretending I didn't call my car a nickname, I reverse out of the driveway and make the short trip to the train station. Even though I only live sixteen miles from work, with tolls and outrageous fuel costs, it's more economical for me to catch the train.

Miguel, my regular station officer and friend, greets me with a broad grin when he notices my car pulling into the parking lot only three short blocks from my home. Returning his smile, I pull into the vacant spot he points out for me.

"How is the darling Cleo today? Did you have the chance to try out that recipe I gave you last week?" Miguel opens my driver's side door and takes my satchel from my grasp.

I curl out of my car and pace toward the booth he will sit in for the next nine hours. "Not yet, but I have the ingredients written down. I'm hoping to cook it for Thanksgiving for Lexi and me." *If I can afford to.*

"That will be lovely, Cleo; my wife will be honored." I don't need to glance into his eyes to know they're relaying the truth. I heard it in his honest words.

I stop pacing and peer up into his glistening eyes. "How is Janice? Is the tumor shrinking?"

Janice and Miguel have been married for nearly thirty years. They live two blocks from my home and were good friends of my parents. Late last year, Miguel's wife was diagnosed with a rare tumor at the base of her skull. Doctors aren't optimistic, but that hasn't stopped Miguel and his youngest son, Jackson, researching possible medical trials for Janice to participate in.

The moisture in Miguel's eyes grows before he shakes his head. "But it isn't growing. So that's something."

"It is," I reply, loving his optimism.

When I spot my train chugging over the tracks on the horizon, I accept my satchel from Miguel, press a kiss on his cheek, then skedaddle to the Montclair Heights platform. Warm air from the train's engine soothes the chill running down my spine from the brisk winds seeping through my thin coat.

Just as I enter the train car, Miguel calls my name. A smile creeps onto my face when he shouts, "I'm still looking for a wife for my eldest son, Preston. A six-year gap is nothing for a girl as smart as you."

"I'll keep that in mind if things don't work out between Jackson and Lexi." Jackson is the gifted up-and-coming surgeon Lexi is going on a date with today. "Besides, most people can only handle one Garcia at a time. I would hate to bombard you."

"Bombard? It would be my pleasure. . ." The remainder of Miguel's sentence is drowned out when the train doors snap shut.

My eyes remain planted on a smiling Miguel as the train car clatters down the track. Once he's nothing but a speck on the horizon, I move along the crammed aisle with the hope of finding an empty seat. My efforts are pointless. The commuter train is bursting at the seams. Suit-clad men and affluent-looking ladies mingle with Montclair University students and retirees going to spend their day gazing at New York's famous landmarks.

Then there are people like me: the lower-class citizen hoping one day to claw her way to middle class. Forget upper class. I don't need any more designer threads or a house worth millions of dollars. All I want is enough money to afford both my sister's medication and food. If I can supply those two things without scrimping and scrounging every week, I'll happily live in the middle-class status.

Fifty minutes—and numerous elbows later—myself and half the population of Montclair merge into Penn Station. A sense of vibrancy hits me the instant I meld into the sea of people clogging the mid-Manhattan sidewalks. I love the vivacity of New York. It doesn't matter if you're poorer than dirt or richer than Donald Trump, this city doesn't judge. My prospects of being mugged are just as high as the lady standing next to me dressed head to toe in Chanel. *She even smells like Chanel.*

Not wanting to look tattered standing next to the nicely scented lady, I undo the buttons on my jacket and run my hands down my white blouse and black pleated skirt. Even though the past two years my bank account has never stepped over double figures unless it's payday, I'm proud of the condition I've kept my Zimmerman ivory lace top and vintage black A-line skirt I was gifted by a work colleague five years ago.

Like all freshly graduated journalism students, I prayed for the pinnacle of internships: Global Ten Media, one of the largest and most profitable media companies in the country. Imagine my surprise when I was not only accepted to intern at Global Ten, but I was also hand-selected to work alongside Sasha Linter, head personal assistant to Viktor Brimmington, Chief Financial Officer of Global Ten Media.

After completing my twelve-month internship, I was offered an extremely lucrative position in the entertainment arm of Global Ten. With my salary nudging toward six figures and mind-boggling perks thrown into the deal, I was set—destined for greatness. . . Until I, along with every other entertainment chief in the state, ran a month-long story on the number one singer in the country doing a stint in rehab when he was actually fighting for his life in the intensive care unit of his hometown hospital.

That blunder saw my position downgraded from chief investigative reporter in the entertainment division of Global Ten Media to the lady who ensures the obituaries have a flair of dignity and respect instilled in every announcement. It was a hard and harrowing fall from grace. I didn't think anything would come close to the knock I took when I discovered my desk was moved to the equivalent of a dark and dingy dungeon.

I was wrong.

That hit was nothing compared to the massive knock my life took four short weeks later when my parents and youngest brother were killed in a traffic accident.

When the chill of 2015 blew into the city a month earlier than usual, Montclair locals were left scrambling to prepare for the icy conditions. While wrangling with the boiler in the basement of our family home, I didn't consider calling my dad to warn him of the conditions. They were returning from a two-week long visit to my mom's hometown in Brazil and were not prepared for the icy conditions they were returning to.

When they hit a section of black ice on the highway, my dad's car veered into oncoming traffic. My parents were killed on impact. Tate held on for ten days. With my dad being laid off, and our family health plan expired, I not only had to submit their obituaries to the local paper, I also had to write them. It was a horrific year I would give anything to forget.

After checking my memories didn't cause sentimental tears to well in my eyes, I step to the edge of the street as I wait for the pedestrian light to illuminate. Although I'll never forget my parents and Tate, I've shed enough tears to last me a lifetime, and I truly believe I don't have any left.

2

"Oh my god! Are you frigging kidding me?" I screech at the top of my lungs when one of the thousand yellow taxis lining the street hits a puddle in front of me, saturating not just me and my designer blouse, but the two people standing beside me as well.

I ball my hands into tight fists, barely suffocating the squeal rumbling up my chest as my eyes drop down to my now ruined blouse. The ivory coloring has been replaced with a mottled mess, similar to the way Lexi's plate looks after eating Grandma G's barbequed skewers covered in rich gravy.

Inwardly cursing at my bad luck today, I hug my coat in tight and cross the road as per the flashing man indicates. Within a few mere feet, I enter my office building. Global Ten Media is a mecca of a building that rises well above the clouds floating in the air. With its crisp steel panels and multihued glass, it's a timeless architectural work of art that adds to the beauty of mid-Manhattan. It's just a pity its insides don't match its outsides. Global Ten Media is a severely depressing place to work.

My day goes from bad to shit when my rummage through my oversized handbag fails to locate my employee swipe card I need to gain access to the secure foyer of my office building. With the owner of Global Ten Media's wealth in the billions, security in this facility is very tight. A security team in the hundreds, a bulletproof glass atrium, and motion cameras scanning every nook and cranny of the space ensure Global Ten Media is one of the most secure locations in the state.

Exhaling my anger in a deep sigh, I pace to the security counter to gain a visitor pass. With my knack for losing things, I have three spare employee ID cards in the top drawer of my desk, but I can't access them without first getting into the bulletproof lobby of my building.

Acting like he doesn't know I've worked here for the past three years, Richard, the head security officer at Global Ten requests to see my photo ID. Gritting my teeth at his leering grin, I hand him my license.

"Your license is expired," His tone is as conceited as his cocky attitude.

"I'm aware of that."

Last month, I had to pick between putting gas in my car or paying my license renewal. I chose gas.

My brow arches high into my hairline when Richard takes his time appraising my license. My annoyance can't be helped. We do this same routine a minimum of once a month. His cockiness never eases, and neither does my bitchiness. I'm not usually a snarky type of person, but when Richard arranged a date with both Mischa from Accounting and me for the same night at the same restaurant, my usually carefree attitude became nonexistent around him. I love a man who holds confidence, but there's a massive difference between commanding respect and just plain being an outright asshole. Richard is an asshole.

"Are we done?" I keep my eyes front and center, refusing to look at Richard's snickering work buddies eyeing our interaction with glee all over their faces.

Richard hands me back my license. I place it into my purse before sauntering to the secondary entrance of my office building, grateful his taunts have been kept to a minimum today.

My brisk strides stop when Richard declares, "I have to frisk you before I can let you enter the foyer, Cleo."

Blood roars to my ears, no doubt accentuating my already tanned cheeks with a vibrant red glow. "You need to frisk me?" I spin on my heels to face the smirking, arrogant, pompous prick. I don't care that he has a face women fantasize about while bringing themselves to climax, he's still an asshole.

Not at all intimidated by my glare, he nods. "We have some very important dignitaries in the building today. With all the cutbacks Human Resources is making, I don't want to give them a reason to fire me."

I cock my brow and glare into his eyes. "And wasting time frisking an *employee* of the company isn't a concern of yours?"

His smug grin enlarges. "Not at all. I'm simply doing my job, Cleo." My skin crawls from the way my name rolls off his tongue in a long, creepy purr. "I'm sure management will commend me for doing my job to the best of my ability."

Acting like I can't feel the eyes of a dozen spectators, I stand still as Richard runs the metal detector gun over my well-worn coat. Although my coat is tattered and faded, it would cost far more to replace than I can afford. So, until it's no longer wearable, it will remain my favorable coat.

I'm not surprised when the metal detector squeals while moving over the midsection of my jacket. "It's the metal buckles on my coat."

Richard bows his brow, rudely ignoring my guarantee. Biting on the inside of my cheek to stop the incessant rant escaping my lips, I undo the buckles of my jacket and sling it over the security desk at my side.

Richard's snickering counterparts' slight chuckle breaks into hearty laughter when they notice my puddle-stained blouse and drenched skirt.

"Assholes," I mutter under my breath.

Straightening his spine, Richard extends to his full height. His tall height and vast frame shadow my five-foot-five stature, but I don't back down. I stand tall and proud, just like the woman my mother taught me to be.

Pride doesn't cost you a damn thing.

Richard scrubs the scruff on his chin as his sullied eyes drink in my skin. Once he has finished his avid and uncalled-for glance, he lifts his hands to my shoulders.

"You touch anywhere inappropriate, being unemployed will be the least of your problems," I warn when his hands glide off my shoulders as he begins frisking me.

I may appear like a little Latin lover with curvy hips and ample breasts, but the knocks of life have hardened my skin so men like Richard may agitate me, but they don't scare me.

After sliding his hand over my midsection, Richard crouches down to search the lower half of my body. My teeth grit when his new position puts him in direct line of my thrusting breasts. Agitation swirls in my stomach when he stares at my chest for several uncomfortable seconds before lifting his heavy-hooded gaze to me.

"You don't need to be worried about me giving you a sneaky touch-up, Cleo. I don't need to put my hands on you. The visual alone is entertaining enough."

Confused by his confession, my brows stitch. I'm utterly clueless as to what his statement refers to. When he fails to ease my curiosity, I follow the direction of his heavy-hooded gaze. My heart twists when my eyes zoom in on my erratically panting chest. With my saturated blouse clinging to my soaked white cotton bra, I look like I've turned up to work minus a few essential pieces of clothing.

Mortified that my light brown nipples are on display for the world to see, my hands snap up to cover my chest. The room feels like it's closing in on me when my inconspicuous sweep of the area registers at least half a dozen pairs of eyes gawking at me.

"Are we done?" I question through clenched teeth as I return my eyes to Richard.

"Yes, we are done. I can't see anything dangerous on you." He tilts in close, ensuring I'm the only one to hear his last words. "Other than your mighty fine tits. They're a danger to any man."

With blood rushing to my cheeks, I snatch my coat off the security desk and race to the bulletproof divider separating the foyer from the public galley. I hear Richard and his arrogant colleagues laughing and spouting lewd comments with every step I take.

When the buzzer of the security bell sounds through my ears, I push open the heavily weighted door. I stop frozen halfway into the foyer when a saying my mom always quoted rings through my ears. "Take a stand for yourself by refusing to let others steal your joy, Cleo. Only those who allow themselves to be ridiculed are ridiculed."

Incapable of ignoring my mother's advice, I spin on my heels and saunter back to Richard standing at the side of the security desk. I lift my chin high, my smile bright and inviting. The gleam in Richard's blue eyes grows with every step I take. He rubs his hands together as his heavy-hooded gaze lowers to take in my bouncing bosoms. When I stop in front of him, he drags his eyes up my body. His gaze is derogatory, and it makes my skin crawl. While licking his lips, he rocks on his heels like he has the world at his feet—like nothing can bring him down.

The arrogance brightening his face is snuffed when I raise my knee and ram it into his groin. His pupils widen to the size of saucers, and the color drains from his face. When he stumbles on his feet, I guide him toward a set of chairs lining the galley. I really shouldn't say "guide." I more shove him into the seat.

The two security officers watching the exchange between Richard and me sit slack-jawed and mute, neither reprimanding or encouraging me. It wouldn't matter even if they did. I'm too far gone serving justice to stop and consider their recommendations anyway.

I patt Richard on the shoulder like a teacher giving a student advice. "Ice may help, but from what I felt, don't leave it on there too long. You don't want any more shrinkage than you already have."

He swallows several times in a row before nodding, his head bobbing up and down like a bobblehead toy. Happy he has accepted my advice, I spin on my heels and pace back to the security partition. I feel numerous sets of eyes on me, but I don't look back. I took a stand, and I'm damn proud of myself.

My high-chin composure cracks the instant I enter the empty elevator. *Holy shit!* I can't believe I did that. I could get fired. Or even worse, sued for workplace harassment. That's the last thing I need. I can barely afford Lexi's medication as it is, let alone living off welfare. I can't believe I acted so foolishly.

Although this was bound to happen eventually, I wish I chose a more appropriate time of the year to teach Richard a lesson. Between wood for the furnace, electricity, and warmer clothing, winter is the most expensive time in my household. We only made it through last year as Lexi got a part-time job that melded with her school schedule. Although she has offered to do the same this year, with her already having a severe bout of pneumonia, I can't risk sending her into the germ-infested world more than she already is.

Pushing my panic to the side, I press the button on the elevator dashboard for the basement. I wasn't joking when I said my desk is now in a dungeon. Just before the elevator doors snap shut, a suit-covered arm stops them. My pulse quickens as the faintest memory of the stranger who offered me comfort four years ago creeps to the surface of my blurry mind. Although my memories of that day are hazy, the man's comforting green eyes have often popped up in my dreams the past four years. They've been my only salvation in a life of torment.

Disappointment slashes me open when a man with inky black hair, a heart-cranking face, and irises as dark as his well-fitting suit enters the elevator car. His well-put-together package makes my disheveled composure even more noticeable.

Smiling at his curious glance at my drenched attire, I take a step back, moving out of his line of sight. In the quietness of our gathering, the sloshing of water in my ankle boots is easily distinguishable.

"Bad morning?" The hairs on my nape prickle from the deep roughness of his voice.

"It could be worse."

It could get a whole heap worse if my fire-breathing supervisor hears of my run-in with Richard this morning. Calling my boss a bitch is putting it nicely. There aren't enough derogatory words in the world to describe her. And with her fondness for Richard—*and every other male employee at Global Ten*—my inability to ignore Richard's daily taunt could be a very costly mistake.

The rest of our ride in the elevator is made in silence. I'm too busy categorizing the life necessities of my budget to hold a conversation. The suit-clad gentleman doesn't appear bothered by my silence. Don't get me wrong; he eyes me with curiosity, but his glare isn't strong enough to push my worry away from working out my expenditures if I find myself standing at the end of the unemployment line.

When the elevator dings, announcing it has arrived in the basement, I adjust my coat to ensure it's hiding my erect nipples from the freezing air-conditioned temperature on my floor before gesturing for the gentleman to exit before me. I want to pretend I'm acting cordially, but, in reality, I just want to use his well-built frame to hide my caught-in-the-rain look from as many people as possible until I can dash into the bathroom halfway down the hallway.

The suit-clad stranger's smile sends blood rushing to the surface of my skin, nearly drying my soaked blouse with its furious heat. "Ah, this isn't my floor."

When he gestures for me to exit, I pace out of the elevator before spinning around to face him. "You do know there aren't any more floors below this one? It's only up from here." My voice relays my shock that a man as astute-looking as him doesn't know the inner workings of an elevator.

The smile on the stranger's face grows. "I'm well aware of that. Thank you."

When he pushes his desired floor on the elevator panel, his suit jacket gapes open. His well-fitting business shirt exposes cut lines of a ridged stomach and stiff pecs. I hold his gaze, confused about why he appears familiar, but I'm confident we've never met. I never forget a face.

Just before the elevator doors close, he locks his dark eyes with me and mutters, "It was a pleasure riding with you, Cleo."

3
---

*S*hock gnaws my stomach as I stand mute in the corridor. Although my normal self-awareness is blinded by worry, I'm certain I didn't offer an introduction to my elevator companion. *Or did I?*

When the shriek of the 10 AM alarm sounds through my ears, my concerns about the mysterious stranger vanish. Just like primary school kids hearing the school bell, hysteria breaks out on my floor. The coffee room goes from a bustling hive of activity to becoming emptier than my wallet after paying Lexi's school fees this semester, and the conversation being held around the water cooler switches from talking about the latest episode of *The Walking Dead* to discussing expenditures and cost-saving strategies. Today's response is nothing out of the ordinary. We all know what the dreaded 10 AM alarm means: the witch is flying her broom into her office.

Wearing my mud-stained shirt with pride, I saunter past Thomas and Kate from Classifieds and slip into my office chair. I scoot down low in my seat so only the top of my head can be seen over the partition separating my "office" from the hallway. With adrenaline still heating my blood from my exchange with Richard, I've lost any trust I had for my logically thinking head.

My heart rate slows to a third of its normal speed as my eyes track my boss making the short fifteen-pace walk from the elevator to her office—yes, I've counted. For every step she takes, the quietness of the room intensifies. I'm not even game to breathe for the fear she will hear my lungs expanding.

I'm not the only one scared of my boss. Even her deputy, Martin, who has twenty-seven years of experience in journalism fears her. That's how terrifying she is.

Only once her office door slams shut does the usual hum of activity awaken in the dead quiet space. I exhale the breath I'm holding in before gasping in another. My lungs wheeze in appreciation, grateful to be filled with fresh air. That's when reality smacks back into me about how foolish my behavior was this morning. Without her medication, Lexi can barely breathe. So as much as I dislike my job and the people surrounding me, I'll do everything in my power to keep it. I'll even side with the devil if I have to.

Setting my guilt to the side, I wiggle up in my seat and swing my eyes around my dingy space. When I'm satisfied the coast is clear of prying eyes, I sneak out of my cubicle and make a beeline for the bathroom. Even if my boss doesn't hear about my confrontation with Richard, my disheveled appearance alone gives her a reason to dismiss me. Only last month, Barbara from Personal Ads was demoted to coffee girl just because her dark gray pea coat didn't match her nearly black slacks.

Any concerns about being fired are left for dust when I spot my appearance in the full-length mirror in the women's restroom. You can't be concerned about something when it's a certainty. Not only are my breasts on display, so are my areolas and capable-of-cutting-diamonds nipples. The thin material I'm wearing as a shirt looks like a sheet of saran wrap. It's completely see-through.

Always being resourceful, I yank my shirt off my head and dig out a laundry bar wrapped in a zip lock bag from my oversized purse. After scrubbing the brown streaks the puddle made to my blouse, I twist the nozzle on the hand dryer fixed to the wall and commence drying it. Thankfully, renovations to the rest of the building haven't reached the basement yet, or I would have been left stranded.

It takes approximately twenty minutes for my blouse to go from ringing wet to slightly damp. When I slip it back over my head, I appraise myself in the mirror. Although my nipples could use an industrial strength Band-Aid to hide their budded appearance, thankfully, the rest of my breasts are concealed by the now murky brown/ivory-colored material.

Happy I've diverted the possibility of being arrested for public indecency, I leave the bathroom with more spring to my step than I entered. My chirpy attitude drains to the soles of my boots when my nearsighted gaze locks in on a flurry of black sitting in my office chair. My pulse rings in my ears when I recognize the jet-black coloring of the woman's hair sitting behind my desk. It's my boss — the devil herself.

"Delilah, umm. . . can I help you?"

Delilah joined our department approximately two years ago. Rumors circulated throughout the mill that she was seconded to her position to whip our department from a money pit to a profitable entity of the Global Ten Media Group. Although we've seen a growth in the number of advertisements placed in our department, that has more to do with the bad flu epidemic that swept through the community than Delilah's placement.

Although nothing concrete has been discovered, numerous long-standing department members argue that she was sent to the dungeon with the same decree as the rest of us. She must serve her sentence in the depths of hell for her treachery to the media mega-giant: Global Ten Media.

Delilah lifts her beady dark eyes to me. "Chloe, so glad you could *finally* join me."

I don't bother correcting her on calling me the wrong name. I've done it numerous times the past two years. Nothing has changed. And there's nothing wrong with being called Chloe anyway. It's better than Delilah's surname. Although, I'll admit, even though her last name is hideous, it suits her. Delilah Anne Winterbottom. Perfect for a cold ass bitc. . .

My inner monologue stops when Delilah suddenly rises from my chair, startling me. Smirking at my skittish response, she runs her hands down the expensive-looking midnight black pantsuit that's tailored to accentuate her fit mid-to-late thirties body. If you could look past the lines on her face from years of scowling, she could be classed as attractive. Her glossy hair is cut in a fierce bob that sits a little longer on the left. She has bright, dark eyes and peachy lips. It's just a pity her insides display she's the spawn of Satan.

"Let's walk." Not waiting for me to reply, she saunters down the narrowed corridor.

It takes approximately ten paces for my inquisitiveness to get the better of me. "If this is about Richard. . ."

My sentence trails off when she interrupts, "Who is Richard?"

I wait for her to press the elevator call button before shrugging my shoulders. "Umm. . . just a client wanting to book bulk obituaries."

I stray my eyes to the ground, ensuring she won't see the deceit in them. I've often been told my eyes are the gateway to my soul, so I'm not willing to risk one sideways glance from her to call me out as a fraud.

When the elevator arrives at our floor, Delilah glides her hand across the front of her body, gesturing for me to enter before her. My knees clang together when I step into the empty space. Politeness is not a strong point for Delilah—hell, I don't even know if she understands the word—so I'm somewhat surprised by her sudden cordial behavior.

My heart drops from my chest when Delilah enters the elevator and hits the button for the very top floor. Clearly, her performance of acting unaware of Richard's identity was an Oscar-worthy act. That's the floor management is located on, specifically Human Resources.

Pleas for clemency sit on the tip of my tongue, but no matter how many times I try to fire them out of my mouth, my lips refuse to relinquish them. Although Delilah scares me more than I'd care to admit, that isn't the reason I'm not falling to my knees and begging for forgiveness. Pride has always been a strong point of mine. Today is no different.

Delilah's fear-provoking demeanor proves solid when we enter the management level of my office building. As we pace through the bright and airy space, the room falls into silence. I've often wondered what it felt like to be a man walking on death row. Now I know.

When we reach an oak door in the bottom right hand corner of the space, Delilah locks her eyes with me. "If you screw this up, don't bother clearing out your desk."

Not giving me the chance to reply, she knocks three times before swinging open the double-width door. The mid-morning sun beaming in the floor-to-ceiling windows causes me to squint my eyes. We're so high in the sky, clouds float past the jaw-dropping New York skyline showcased in all its glory by the gigantic corner office. It's a view that would inspire painters to paint. It's enchanting and breathtaking, and it makes me fall in love with the city even more.

The view changes from breathtaking to soul-stealing when the black leather chair facing the window pivots around. Air traps halfway in my lungs when my eyes run over the gentleman I shared the elevator with earlier.

Upon spotting my shocked expression, his lips crimp in the corners, exposing a tiny set of dimples on his top lip I didn't notice earlier.

"Cleo, Delilah, I'm glad you could join us. Please take a seat."

Noticing he said "us," I shift my eyes in the direction he's gesturing for us to sit. A pretty blonde lady in her late forties is seated in one of the three rolled arm chairs across from the enormous wooden table the unnamed gentleman is sitting behind. With her head angled to the side, she rakes her light green eyes down my body not once, not twice, but three times.

Ignoring the twisting in my stomach, I plunk down in the seat Delilah nudged her head at. My brash movements are missing the grace held by the blonde eyeing me with zeal. Once Delilah takes the last remaining chair left vacant, the unnamed man with pulse-racing good looks shifts his eyes to the blonde. His gaze is wide and edgy. "Thoughts?"

Suspense crackles the air as the blonde scoots to the edge of her chair. "She's perfect. Curvy and innocent-looking but with a hint of vivacity the clients will love."

"Her hostility this morning?"

The blonde appears unfazed by his concern. "Doormats are out. They want a challenge, someone who doesn't follow all the rules." Her voice quickens with each syllable she speaks.

Unease spreads across my chest as I tilt to Delilah's side. "Who are they talking about?"

She shushes me using nothing but an evil glare. I slouch deeper into my chair so I can sneakily watch the situation unfold while fiddling with the chipped polish on my nails. The two unnamed attendees and Delilah continue their conversation as if they didn't request my attendance. They discuss protocols for undertaking such an investigation, monetary values I could only pray to have written on a check in my name, and how it could be the story of the century.

Although I'm interested in their conversation, my ears only prick when Delilah says, "If the sanction you're referring to is Chains, you'll never get in. Rights to invite new members are only bequeathed to members who have been exclusively in the club for a year. Security is tight, but the identities of those who attend is even tighter. I'm not saying I don't understand your interest in breaking this story. If you could get in, the results would be immense. Rumors are that they have judges, DA's, movie stars, and numerous politicians in that *highly* exclusive group, but the likelihood of securing an invitation are zero to none."

For the quickest second, the stern mask Delilah frequents daily slips, exposing a side I've never seen of her when the unnamed suit-clad man says, "We have an invitation. It may have cost me half of my shares in my foreign equity company, but we have an invitation."

The room feels like it's closing in on me when he turns his eyes to me. "And Cleo is our way in."

I straighten my spine when Delilah swings her narrowed gaze to me. The wrinkles on her top lip deepen when she runs her eyes down my half-presentable frame. "Perhaps after a day at the spa and a makeover with Clint." Her words are a hiss, and they're tainted with disdain.

"No." The unnamed man holds his hand in the air like he's stopping traffic. "Leave Cleo exactly how she is. She's perfect just like that. She has a unique look men in that industry crave. Someone they can mold into their ideal mate while bringing her to heel."

An average person may construe his declaration as a compliment. I do not. With an edgy gleam brightening his sable-colored eyes, my first response is alarm, not glee.

Incapable of ignoring the tension thickening the air, I squeak out, "Can someone please explain to me what's going on?"

Seconds feel like hours as I return the imprudent stare of three pairs of unique eyes staring at me. The tension hanging in the air is so thick, it's physically hard for me to breathe.

Just when I think my question will never be answered, the blonde pipes up, "Do you value your position at Global Ten Media, Cleo?"

"Yes, very much so." It's purely for the weekly paycheck and less-than-stellar health coverage, but I keep that snippet of information to myself.

"Well, if you play your cards right, your position here will not only be guaranteed for the remainder of your life, but Mr. Carson has also generously offered for you to join his team as a lead investigative reporter for the New York Daily Express." The blonde gestures her hand to the man seated across from me.

My excitement is too vast for me to register that she called the mysterious dark-haired man Mr. Carson—the owner of Global Ten Media. I'm too shocked to register anything. The man I rode the elevator with while wearing a saran wrap shirt is the owner of the entire company I work for.

Jesus Christ! How am I not getting fired right now?

Snubbing my dropped-jaw expression, the blonde continues, "You'll be given your own office space on the seventy-third floor, an executive assistant, and your salary will be in the six-figure range."

I sit stunned, mute and wide-eyed. I try to force my mouth to say something, but nothing comes out — not even a squeak.

"Chloe," Delilah barks a short time later, her tone clipped.

"Cleo," I correct, loathing that my mouth chooses now to cooperate.

Snarling, Delilah sneers, "So what do you say, *Cleo?* Are you interested in joining the investigative team of the New York Daily Express?"

Unable to speak from the excitement drying my throat, I nod. I've been waiting for this day for years—from the very moment I fell from grace.

Delilah smiles a grin that does nothing to settle the jitters in my stomach. "Wonderful. Then let's get this wrapped up." She bounces her eyes between Mr. Carson and the unnamed blonde. "With Cleo being an integral part of my team, I'm requesting to be brought in on this investigation on a consultation basis. With your strict schedule to get this to print before any other media outlet, I will ensure a satisfactory timeframe is maintained."

They continue negotiating for several minutes. I sit in silence as pieces of paper are passed across the table for Delilah to sign. From the way Delilah is handling all the correspondence, anyone would swear she's my guardian, not the supervisor of my department.

Their excited chatter dulls when, numerous heart-clutching minutes later, I murmur, "What are you wanting me to do when I join this team?"

Although my words are clear, they're crammed with suspicion. My mother always said, "If something is too good to be true, it most likely is." This seems too good to be true.

"I have a bachelor's in media relations with a concentration in investigative journalism. I was the top of my class three out of my four years of college, and I interned with the best journalism department on this side of the country. I have the skills needed for the job, but why the sudden switch in departments? I've been in the dungeon so long, even I'm starting to forget why I was sentenced there."

A stretch of terse silence crosses between us. It's thick and skincrawlingly uncomfortable. After holding a private conversation with Mr. Carson only utilizing her eyes, Delilah turns her gaze to me. As she glances at me, she tries to soften the harsh lines of her face. It's a fruitless effort. Even the world's best collagen can't hide years of scowling.

"We need you to go undercover at an exclusive club in lower Manhattan."

Hearing an "and" hanging in the air, I verbalize it.

"And do anything necessary to uncover the story." Mr. Carson props his elbows onto his desk, then braces his backside on the edge of his chair. "If this story breaks, Cleo, your name will forever be associated with it, thus not only meaning someone as wealthy as me will have a hard time signing your checks, but it will be a struggle keeping you exclusively with the Global Ten entity."

Excitement heats my blood. "Okay. That sounds wonderful. But you still haven't answered my question. You kind of skedaddled around it."

Ignoring Delilah's irate scowl burning a hole in my head, I ask, "What *exactly* do you want me to do in this club, Mr. Carson?"

Several seconds of terse silence stretches between Mr. Carson and me as we undertake an intense stare-down. Although he has pulse-racing good looks that would boil any woman's blood, that isn't the reason I'm sweating. It's the indecisiveness in his eyes causing my biggest concern.

Our teeth-gritting showdown ends when he drops his eyes to the top drawer of his desk and pulls out an embossed envelope. Re-locking his eyes with me, he slides the elegant document across the table. I run my hands down my skirt, not wanting to stain the pristine-looking paper with my grubby fingers. The wild beat of my heart merges into dangerous territory when I grasp the lightweight document in my hand. The article is extremely thin, soft as tissue paper, and scrolled with gold-foiled print. On first impressions alone, I assume it's an invitation to an elaborate wedding more than a party being held in lower Manhattan.

My eyes scan over the document, noticing nothing out of the ordinary to a standard invitation. . . until I hit the disclosure statement at the bottom.

"Since the BD/SM scene includes a wide range of activities involving a negotiation transfer of power between consenting partners, the bottom/submissive will be required to fill in a questionnaire before the commencement of any scenes. All limits and fears will be carefully discussed before the bottom/submissive can perform in any BD/SM scenes. This will ensure a safe, sane and consensual evening for all involved."

My eyes bug, and my jaw muscle slackens. Any words I try to force out my gaped mouth are dust fragments by the time they've been dragged through my bone-dry throat.

Sensing my speechless composure, Mr. Carson assures me, "You're not in any form obligated to attend this party in the matter stated at the bottom of the invitation. All we want is a pair of eyes in the room, Cleo."

"In a room with a group of men who want to beat me for pleasure?"

"Cleo!"

I turn my shocked eyes to Delilah. With my usually calm composure lost, today her evil glare has no effect on me whatsoever.

"You can't seriously expect me to do this?"

Delilah's silence speaks volumes. That's exactly what she expects me to do.

"I'm not being subjected to torture just so you can get a fancier office."

My glaring stare-down with Delilah ends when the unnamed blonde balances on the very edge of her chair and locks her eyes with me. "Your ideas about the BDSM community are vastly different than what it actually is. Anyone in the community knows it's the submissive who truly holds the greatest power."

"Then *you* do it."

I'm not normally so confrontational, but my mind is spiraling so much that my first response is resistance.

"If you have such a *vast* understanding of the BDSM community, why don't you go undercover?"

Not speaking, the blonde stands from her seat. Her movements are so agile and sharp, even Delilah jumps in surprise. Curling her hand around my wrist, she yanks me from my seat. For a lady whose frame is smaller than mine and who is a good two to three inches shorter, she has a lot of guts. The dizziness spiraling in my stomach grows when she drags me across the room to stand in front of a full-length dressing mirror with an expansive wool trench coat hanging off the wrought iron frame.

As we stand side by side, I take in our unique differences: her pale, nearly translucent skin against my sun-kissed tan; her doe-shaped blue eyes compared to my brown oval eyes. How her waif-thin frame looks sickly standing next to my rounded hips and ample breasts. With her hair the color of the sun beaming in the floor-to-ceiling windows, we couldn't be any more opposite if we tried. My hair is as dark as my massively dilated pupils.

"Stop using the personal side of your brain, Cleo, and start thinking with a rational investigative reporter head," the blonde mutters, peering at me in the mirror. "If you were Mr. Carson, and you had the opportunity of breaking the story of the century, who would you choose to send undercover? Me or you?"

Before I can fire a single syllable from my mouth, she continues speaking. "Don't tell me what your gut, intuition or morals are telling you. I only want to hear what the business side of your brain is thinking."

"That's different," I mumble while taking in my glassy eyes and panicked face. "This doesn't feel like business. This feels personal."

She shakes her head, denying my claims. "Nothing in business is personal unless you let it become that way. As Mr. Carson said, we only need eyes in the room. Nothing more."

She takes a step back and slips in to stand behind me. Grasping my chin, she lifts my head high in the air. "Look at that face, Cleo. That is a face that will not only break the story of the century. It's the face that will ensure your sister's final years are lived in comfort."

The air sucks from my lungs, her words physically winding me. From the remorseful gleam in her eyes reflecting in the mirror, I know she felt the direct impact her words had to my heart, but her eyes also expose that our exchange is nothing more than a business transaction to her. There's nothing personal about it.

"That was low."

"Yes, it was," she admits, nodding. "But it was also the truth. Mr. Carson personally selected you for this assignment as he knows there won't be a story without you. So, if I have to occasionally issue a hit below the belt to get our message across, that's what I'll do. That's how imperative a story like this is to our company."

The way she says "our" makes me wonder what her connection with Global Ten Media is.

The room falls into silence as I contemplate a response. As I said earlier, I'll do everything in my power to ensure my sister's every want, need and desire are taken care of. But can I do this? Can I set aside my personal feelings and run purely on the instincts of my astute mind?

Inhaling a nerve-clearing breath, I shift my eyes to Mr. Carson. "I accept the position you're offering."

The tightness in his shoulders clears away as relief washes over his face. His carefree attitude doesn't last long. "On one condition."

Delilah slices her hand through the air, preparing to cut off my attempts at negotiations. Thankfully, Mr. Carson ignores her, his eyes never moving from mine.

"And what's that condition, Cleo?"

My hammering heart echoes through my voice when I negotiate, "Even if this story never breaks, or I'm let go from your company, you agree to pay my sister's medical and school expenses for the remainder of her life."

My pulse is so furious, it drowns out Delilah's incessant rant about my ungratefulness, and how I should feel privileged a man with Mr. Carson's integrity would bestow such an honor upon me. Even catching portions of her belligerent tirade doesn't impact me in the slightest. There's only one person in the world I allow to tilt the axis of my moral compass. She's the person I promised to take care of when she was left in my custody at the tender age of seventeen: my sister, Lexi. For her, nothing is below me—not even accepting an invitation to a seedy BDSM club in lower Manhattan.

I don't know how many seconds pass as Mr. Carson reflects on my statement, but it feels like hours have ticked by before he curtly nods.

"Yes?" I stammer out, wanting to ensure my nearsightedness doesn't have me mistaking a shake as a nod.

"Yes," Mr. Carson acknowledges, filling me with both gratefulness and trepidation.

4

"I don't care if TMZ is reporting that Elvis is eating a cheeseburger at McDonalds, your ass *will* be sitting in the backseat of the limo by 9 PM sharp. Do you understand me?"

Delilah's voice is so loud, she gains the attention of Lexi lying on the two-seater sofa in our cramped living room. She's having a bad day. Her skin is clammy and beaded with sweat, and she has spent the last two hours coughing up more mucus than a normal person would create in a lifetime.

Twisting my body away from Lexi, I whisper, "This isn't a ploy to get out of our agreement, Delilah. Lexi isn't well. Can't we change the invitation so I can attend the next party?"

"No!" I jump from her abrupt response. "It's not brunch at a country club. These events aren't held on a weekly schedule. Who knows when the next one might be," she snarls viciously.

"Does it matter? Without an invitation, the likelihood of another media company breaking the story before us is extremely unlikely. And, besides, what's a few more weeks on an invitation that has taken years to get?"

"Can your sister wait weeks?" Delilah doesn't wait for me to get over the first punch to my stomach before she issues another. "Or are the icy winds blowing into your poorly insulated house knocking more time off her already thin schedule?"

Spotting my worried expression, Lexi lifts herself from the couch. Guilt consumes me when I notice the ratty mess her shirt is in. Moth holes dot the hemline, and the previous vibrant red coloring is now dull from too many wash cycles. With our winter clothing budget going toward a new heating system I had installed in her room and our washing machine on the blink, our cold-weather wardrobes are severely limited.

I pace to the linen closet to yank down a blanket for Lexi. "I only agreed to do this because Mr. Carson said he would pay Lexi's medical bills." I drop my voice to ensure Lexi won't hear the remainder of my sentence. "I've not yet seen a dime of that money. She's sick, Delilah; she needs a nebulizer I can't afford."

Smiling to ease the worry on Lexi's face, I wrap the blanket around her shoulders, then pace out of the living room.

"You won't be able to afford anything if your ass isn't in that limousine at 9 PM sharp!"

Delilah's leather office chair creaks down the line. I'm not at all surprised to discover she's still at the office late on a Saturday afternoon.

"Last warning, Chloe. If you fail to arrive at the party at the designated time on the invitation, don't bother arriving to work Monday morning."

Before I have the chance to respond—or correct her for calling me the wrong name—she disconnects the call. I take a few moments standing frozen in the foyer, racking my tired brain about why I ever agreed to such a ludicrous request. My mother always said, "Never dance with fire unless you plan on getting burned." I haven't even gotten close to the fire yet, and my toes are already charred.

I've spent the last two weeks in my brand-new office researching the world I'm set to enter tonight. Although in-depth research into the BDSM community has eased some of the uncertainty swirling my stomach, it hasn't completely smothered it. From the information I have unearthed, in a properly hosted party, I will not be touched or manhandled in any way unless I give prior consent. It's just my eyes I'm hazy about. Some images you can never wash from your mind, no matter how much you wish you could.

My pity party for one stops when our doorbell jingles in my ears. My eyes instinctively shoot to Lexi. With our tight budget and even tighter sisterly bond, Lexi and I rarely venture out on the weekends or invite guests over, so I'm somewhat surprised by an impromptu visitor.

With a fragile Lexi shadowing me, I pace to my front door. My curiosity is piqued when I peer out the peephole and notice Luke, ex-boyfriend and pharmacist from our local pharmacy, standing on the stoop of the stairs. He has a cardboard box in one hand and his other is gripping his coat in close to his neck, vainly trying to keep the brisk winds seeping into his blazer.

After unlocking the deadbolt, I swing open the door. My nose burns when the below chilly temperatures grace it with their presence.

"Hey, Luke, how are you?" My voice relays my uncertainty. "Are you lost?"

When I notice his lips are a hue of blue, I gesture for him to enter the foyer. It may not be elegant and grand like the house he lives in, but at least it's warm.

Luke scrubs his boots on the bristled mat stationed at the front door before entering. Heat blooms across my chest when his eyes eagerly absorb my modest home. The warmth isn't from shame; it's pride. Nothing but admiration is beaming from Luke's bright gaze.

"Nice place you have here, Cleo."

Heat rises from my chest to my cheeks. "Thank you."

A stretch of silence passes between us. Lexi doesn't help alleviate the situation at all. She just stands to the side of the foyer with her eyes bouncing between Luke and me.

When the silence becomes too great for me to ignore, I mumble, "Is there something. . . did you need. . . Ah, what are you doing here, Luke?"

That's about as gracious as I get — no country club politeness in this household. My abruptness is nothing new for Luke. He dealt with it plenty of times during our two-year relationship in high school.

The rudeness clutching my throat loosens its grip when Luke's smirk becomes a full smile. "Sorry, Cleo, I just realized I've known you for nearly ten years, dated you for two, but have never been inside your house."

The thick stench of awkwardness returns stronger than ever when Lexi mutters, "You've seen inside her panties but not her house?" She locks her shocked eyes with mine. "Nice one, Sis. I knew there was a hussy in there somewhere."

Forget tiptoeing around the edge of the fire. Living with Lexi is the equivalent of dancing in the middle of the raging flames, one scorching moment after another. Unable to stand my furious glare for a moment longer, Lexi excuses herself from our gathering before toddling off to her room.

Once she enters her bedroom at the end of the hall, I swallow down the bitter bile in my throat and return my eyes to Luke. "Well, now you've seen it." Embarrassment dangles off my vocal cords. "And. . . *now you can go?*" The unease in my voice makes what should be a strong declaration sound more like a suggestion.

Nothing against Luke, he was a great boyfriend, wonderful friend, and talented in the bedroom, but my priorities have changed since high school. Unlike him and our numerous combined friends, I grew up—quickly. My life is not about flirty weekends and how many shots I can down in a night. My focus must remain on ensuring my budget and my sister's health are maintained, not my social calendar.

"Ouch." Luke drags my focus back to him. "I'd heard rumors you'd changed, Cleo. Never would have believed it if I hadn't seen it for myself."

I try to think of a comeback, but I'm at a loss for words. I was the epitome of Ms. Popular in high school. I was the head cheerleader, crowned prom queen during our senior year, and voted most likely to succeed. All I achieved the past seven years is two school loans I can't afford, skyrocketing insurance premiums, and a bad attitude. I wouldn't say I'm a negative person, but after enduring knock after knock the past four years, things are starting to creep up on me.

My eyes stray from the ground when a hand runs down my arm. I'm shocked when I lift my eyes and discover only Luke still standing in the foyer. I thought Lexi had rejoined our gathering. I had no clue it was Luke issuing the kind gesture. Although our breakup was amicable, I was the one who started the process, so I'm somewhat surprised by his jovial nature.

My pulse quickens when Luke locks his eyes with mine. "You've got to stop being so damn proud, Cleo. We are a community here in Montclair. We help our own."

His statement causes tears to sting my eyes. "I know," I mutter, nodding.

There's no use denying what he is saying. Montclair is my home-town, and if I weren't so stubborn, I know the locals would help us. But Lexi and I aren't the only ones struggling. Many homes in our area are up for foreclosure, so I can't cry wolf because I'm struggling to make ends meet. We may not have every necessity we need, but we have a roof over our heads. That's more than some people in our community have.

"In saying that," Luke says, stepping closer to me. "If you had told me how much Lexi needed this, I would have delivered it weeks ago." He keeps his deep tone low to ensure Lexi won't hear him. He knows she doesn't need any guilt added to the baggage she's already carrying.

My eyes bounce between Luke's light green gaze when he hands the box he is grasping to me. Incapable of reading the signs his eyes are relaying, I pry open the box. I gasp in a shocked breath when my eyes absorb the state-of-the-art nebulizer and air filter sitting next to a six-month supply of Lexi's medication. Seeing all the essential things she needs to breathe with ease sitting in one little box causes a flood of emotions to slam into me. As a tear rolls down my cheek, I throw my arms around Luke's neck and hug him tightly.

"Hey, easy there," he croons, pulling me in tighter. "I'm just the delivery guy, Cleo. I'm not the one who deserves your thanks."

I pull back and peer into his eyes. "Who?" I want to say more, but the gratefulness sitting on my chest makes it hard for me to breathe let alone talk.

"He didn't leave a card. All he wanted me to say was 'you do know there aren't any more floors below this one? It's only up from here.'" Confusion clouds Luke's bright eyes. It mimics my gaze to a T.

It takes a few moments for the recognition of the quote to dawn on me. When it does, both relief and anxiety overwhelm me. That was the only thing I said to Mr. Carson the day we rode the elevator together. I have to hand it to him: he is smart. Just when I was tempted to back out of our agreement, he dangles a carrot in front of my face and lures me right back in. It displays how he went from a struggling New Jersey boy to billionaire before he reached the age of 30.

After swearing I'll contact him if I require any assistance, I walk Luke to his Jeep parked at the curb.

"I don't know what the first half of his saying referred to, but I do agree with the second part," Luke says, cracking open his car door. Our weekends driving it on the beach caused the rusty hinges to give out a squeak in protest to his firm swing. "When you've hit rock bottom, there's only one way you can go. That way is up."

A grin curls on my lips when he presses a kiss my mouth. I remember when the whiskers on his chin couldn't even cause a shadow in the midday sun. Now, a few hours after shaving his cut jaw is shadowed in darkness.

"I miss you guys," I mumble before I can stop my words.

Luke, Chastity, and Michael were my very best friends in high school. I didn't think anything would shatter our close connection. At eighteen you don't consider how much work goes into maintaining a scholarship at one of the top schools in the country, or how every penny you earn will go toward helping your parents pay the second mortgage they put on their family home to set you up in a private dorm off campus. It wasn't until my parents passed did I realize how much of a burden I had placed on them. Although I knew my apartment was expensive, I thought I'd have years to thank them for the struggles they endured. Their trip to Brazil was supposed to be one gift of many. Little did I know it would be the only one they would receive from me to thank them for being the best parents a child could ask for.

Luke grins a lazy smirk that sets my pulse racing and dampens my somber thoughts. "As we do you, Cleo. There's no rat pack when one is missing."

Ignoring the way his rough and rugged voice prickles the hairs on my nape, I ask, "I'll see you soon?"

Luke tries to hold in his excitement. He fails. The corners of his lips curl, and his eyes flare with excitement.

"I hope so." He places another kiss on the edge of my mouth before climbing into his jeep.

My stomach swirls as I stand on the curb, watching Luke's car disappear into the horizon. You know that giddy feeling you get before you walk down the stairs after spending four hours getting ready for prom? That's how I'm feeling right now. I don't know if it's from being awarded thousands of dollars' worth of medical equipment for Lexi, Luke's two innocent pecks, or that I'm about to go and get glammed up for a night at a BDSM club. But no matter what the reason is behind my sudden new lease on life, I'm going to grasp it with both hands. The past four years have been my lowest, so I'll cherish every giddy feeling I get.

5

---

*C*old winds whip up under my trench coat when I step into the blacked-out sedan idling at the curb of my house. I don't miss the curious glances of Mr. and Mrs. Rachet peering out their lace curtains from the home across the street. Their gaped-mouth reaction isn't surprising. Although our street is positioned in a beautiful tree-lined suburb, it isn't every day you spot an overpriced light gray Bentley parked on the curb.

With my hands shaking with nerves, it takes me several attempts to get the seatbelt to latch into place. Closing my eyes, I calm the mad beat of my heart and repeat the mantra I've cited numerous times this evening: tonight's event is no different than the many other undercover stints I've done for Global Ten Media in the past.

My reassurance doesn't help in the slightest.

Even when camping out with the paparazzi for a sneaky picture of Ben Affleck when the nanny-affair scandal erupted, I didn't feel as scandalous as I do now. It probably has something to do with the fact I'm barely wearing anything under my well-worn coat.

Within twenty minutes of Luke leaving, another impromptu visitor arrived on my doorstep. This time, the caller was unknown to Lexi and me. The unease twisting my stomach into a nasty mess wound all the way up to my throat when I accepted the flimsy white box held together with an elaborate red bow from the unnamed caller. Any chance of keeping my heart away from coronary failure was lost when I ripped off the bow and dug my hand into layers of delicate tissue paper to unveil an outfit I would be wary wearing to bed let alone in public.

The ear-piercing squeal Lexi emitted when I held up the rose-colored I.D. Sarrieri hotel slip dress sent her into a ten-minute coughing fit. Her flabbergasted reaction mimicked mine to a T. From my year of interning under Sasha, I knew the value of the dress clutched in my hand was more than our quarterly electric bill.

From the note scrawled inside a white gift card, Mr. Carson perceived my intentions of sacrificing the pricey garment for the greater good—once it was desecrated at the BDSM club tonight.

One night, then do with it as you please, was all he wrote inside the gilded card the negligée was delivered with.

It isn't just the silky-smooth negligee gracing my sweat-slicked skin that has my heart hammering my ribs. It's the fact Mr. Carson selected the perfect size garment to house my bountiful curves. How could a man who only peered at me for mere minutes divulge enough information to know my rounded hips and busty breasts didn't have a chance in hell of squeezing into a size 2?

Snubbing the unease gurgling in my stomach, I wrangle my seatbelt into place. As the Bentley rolls down my long street, I snag my compact out of my clutch purse, wanting to ensure the sprinkling of rain I dodged while dashing out of my house didn't ruin the bold curls Lexi placed in my hair this afternoon. When she spotted the card from Mr. Carson, she read it more as an invitation than an assignment. Happy for her to read the message how she saw fit, I didn't correct her misguided optimism.

After adding a sheen of lip gloss to the nude palette on my face, I place my compact back into my clutch and turn my eyes to the scenery whizzing by. It doesn't matter how many times I've viewed Montclair's culturally rich landscape, it never fails to amaze me. It's a mesmerizing town full of treasured memories. A place I hope one day to raise my own family.

With the late hour, it doesn't take as long to reach lower Manhattan as I would have liked. As the Bentley glides to a stop behind a phantom Rolls Royce, I slip a sequined mask over my wide eyes. Nerves overpower my efforts to tie the satin straps to the back of my head, but I continue with my mission, not willing to risk having my photo snapped by a group of curious onlookers lurking at the side of the dimly lit club.

Although Mr. Carson is anticipating tonight's gathering will unearth some huge names in the BDSM community, my hopes were dashed the instant I discovered the event was a masked party. I've never believed you need to see someone's face to know their true intentions—even the most guarded people can be stripped bare with the right words—but when your assignment is to unearth their iden-tities, physical masks add another layer to an already complicated mission.

Breathing out my tension, I finish securing my mask over my face before surveying the area. With a bank of affluent cars stretched as far as the eye can see, the normally bland environment has gained a handful of nosey spectators. Although my intuition tells me they're most likely residents shocked by the sudden bombardment of wealth in a less-than-stellar part of Manhattan, my first year at Global Ten Media taught me to never run with a theory before thoroughly evalu-ating it.

When the Bentley pulls onto the curb at the front of a club that looks like its doors closed centuries ago, the driver lowers the privacy partition and gestures with his head for me to exit. One glance into his glassy dark eyes causes a barrage of nerves to hammer into me. I sit frozen, not speaking or moving. I don't even blink.

It feels like my frozen stance lasts hours, but it's mere seconds. It was only long enough for me to remember that exposing a scan-dalous bit of skin is a small price to pay to have Lexi's medical expenses paid in full. There's nothing I wouldn't do for my sister—nothing at all.

Rolling my shoulders, I clutch the Bentley's door handle and swing it open. The cold breeze blowing in from the west does nothing to ease the heat creeping up my neck. I've slid halfway out of the back of the Bentley before reality dawns.

Drifting my massively dilated eyes to the driver, I ask, "What time will you return to collect me?"

"When you're ready to leave, I'll be ready." His voice rough and gritty.

His admission does nothing to ease the panic scorching my veins. "How?" I mutter, my one word displaying I didn't believe a single word he spoke. "How will you know when I'm ready to leave?"

He locks his impressively dark eyes with me. For the first time tonight, my swirling stomach gets a moment of reprieve when he declares, "I'll know, Cleo. I'll be ready."

"Okay. Good."

I continue my mission of exiting the Bentley. Nippy winds blast my face when I step onto the cracked sidewalk. Other attendees waiting to enter the premise eye me with curiosity, but none approach me. The vast range of people is surprising. Clearly, all attendees have wealth I could only dream of achieving, but even with their faces hidden behind masks, the range in age and appearance varies greatly. Some are tall, while others wouldn't reach my chin, and the width of the attendees is also diverse.

When the flash of a camera hinders my vision, I snap my eyes to the side, praying the paparazzi are unaware of tonight's event. The dangerous beat of my heart simmers when I spot the faces hidden behind the lens. Thankfully, the curious onlookers are nothing but a group of teen boys more interested in capturing photos of the cars than the occupants inside.

Shaking off my nerves, I pace into the foyer of the building, acting like I'm about to watch a Broadway show, not an all-out orgy. The inside of the rundown building does not match the outside. Chandeliered ceilings, priceless paintings, and rugs that would only look better positioned in front of a raging fire make the space scream of wealth and importance.

The only thing stopping me from believing I'm in the middle of a bustling Broadway studio is when the patrons in front of me remove their thick wool coats and Burberry leather gloves. Although most the women's bodies are covered with silky sleepwear like I'm wearing under my jacket, it's the shocking sight of a collar and lead curled around one woman's delicate neck that causes my slack-jawed expression.

As the gathering of people grows, the swell of the crowd forces me toward a marble check-in station. For every step I take, the unease in my stomach intensifies. Any chance of settling my nerves is left for dust when the lady standing in front of me hands her invitation to the hostess before lowering onto all fours.

Holy moly, I mumble to myself when she enters a set of thick velvet curtains by crawling at the heels of her male partner. When portions of the scantily dressed people inside the club seep through the gaped curtain, I snap my eyes away, spin on my heels and flee. The only thing that slows my frantic escape is when my panicked gaze locks in on a pair of dark eyes entering the single glass door I'm heading toward. Even with a majority of his face covered with a plain black mask, I know who he is—I never forget a face. It's the driver of my Bentley.

I stand frozen for a beat, unsure if I'm coming or going. When the hostess aims to gather my attention, the sable-haired man in the navy pinstripe suit sneakily gestures his head to the hostess. With my hands fisted at my side, I shake my head. My movements are so frantic it looks like I have a nervous twitch.

Spotting my stubbornness, the demand in the stranger's eyes grows, mimicking every man in the foyer gawking at me with zeal. When he once again nudges his head to the hostess, I grit my teeth and stand my ground. I was wrong earlier; this is way above my paygrade.

When the Bentley driver fails to acknowledge the threat in my silent stance, I head for the door. My brisk steps end when the faintest murmur of "Lexi," rings through my ears. Just hearing her name halts my hasty retreat. Images of the pain her eyes held when she told me about our parents' accident flash before my eyes. It's the same pain her eyes hold every time she gasps for air when she's struggling through a coughing attack.

My back molars grind when I swing my eyes to the suit-clad man. Although he peers straight ahead, seemingly not noticing me, he can't fool me. I can feel his gaze, and I can also see the twitching smirk his conceited lips fail to hide. He knows he has me over a barrel. I didn't just make a deal with the devil two weeks ago; I foolishly gave away my hand. They not only know Lexi is my weakness; they know she's my *only* weakness.

After inhaling and exhaling three deep breaths, I roll my shoulders, swivel around, then saunter to the pretty hostess standing at the counter of the now nearly empty foyer. She accepts my invitation with an inviting smile and twinkling eyes, a complete contradiction to the greeting I issue her. Mine is nowhere near as pleasant as hers.

She raises her pretty blue eyes to me. "Can I take your coat?"

Noticing that she asked, didn't demand, I hug my coat close to my body. "The air is a little chilly. I'd prefer to keep it if I can?"

She seems taken aback, but I hold my ground, pretending I'm not the slightest bit concerned she may deny my request.

When her silence becomes too great to ignore, I sneer, "Is there a problem with me keeping my coat?" I keep my voice firm, remembering that my hours of research uncovered that not only are there male Doms in this lifestyle, there are strong-willed female ones as well.

With my head held high in the air and my nose pointed down at the white-washed young woman's face, I increase my stare.

Relief consumes me when she mumbles, "No ma'am, not at all. The air does have a nip to it."

She places my invitation into a locked box at her side before gesturing with her hand for me to enter the velvet curtains. In an instant, my high-chinned composure slips. My knees wobble with every step I take toward a previously unventured world. The further I move away from the reception desk, the more the faint hum of music replaces the pulse shrilling in my ears. After one final breath to rid my body of nerves, I push through the curtains.

Shock is the first thing that consumes me, closely followed by intrigue. I was expecting to see a mass of naked bodies humping and grinding against each other. Although the outfits the partygoers are wearing would be best described as skimpy, there are more covered torsos than completely naked ones. Multihued lights and soft, ambient music gives the vibe more of a sophisticated club feel than a raging orgy-fest. Booths line the outer walls and soft, sheer curtains shackled to the ceiling lend the space an elegant feel instead of industrial. If there weren't weird fetish attire on over half of the patrons, I wouldn't be able to tell the difference between this club and a standard dance club I frequented back in my college days.

The further I encroach into the club, the more various "scenes" I researched online are unearthed. Heat creeps across my cheeks when a gathering of three in the bottom left-hand corner of the vast space gains my attention. With some type of leather gag in her mouth, the lady who crawled into the club earlier is slouched over her partner's knee while another man wearing a weird leather taped vest pays dedicated attention to a region of her body that shouldn't be displayed in public.

With my eyes planted on the floor, I pretend I didn't witness what I just witnessed as I continue with my mission to find an inconspicuous hiding place. My efforts to remain undetected falter when I crush into a group of men standing at the edge of the room. I can barely see as it is, let alone in a club where dim lighting makes my usually poor eyesight even worse.

The situation goes from curious to downright awkward when the man in the middle of the trio eyes me with more interest than a man of his age should. His being older than my deceased grandfather doesn't stop his degrading ogling of my body. Smiling to mask my disgust, I make a beeline to a topless waitress balancing bottles of water on a silver tray. With stifling temperatures from having so many red-blooded people in the one space added to my coat-covered body, it's the perfect recipe for a sweat-producing disaster.

On the way to the waitress, I catch the impish watch of numerous club spectators. Their gazes make my stomach sick with anxiety. I've never felt so nauseous. Acting like I can't feel my knees clanging together, I straighten my spine and glide across the room while giving myself a stern lecture on being a grown woman who can party with the best of them.

"This is just a college party," I mutter to myself. "And they're wearing the same amount of clothing my girlfriends and I wore at those so-called parties."

Accepting a bottle of water from a smiling blonde waitress with an uncovered chest, I scan my eyes across the room, seeking an ideal research station. As Albert Einstein said, "Condemnation without investigation is the highest form of ignorance." So, until I've had a chance to assess the situation thoroughly, I shouldn't be issuing a judgment.

It takes approximately ten minutes aimlessly wandering around the affluent surroundings for me to find the perfect vantage point in the dimly lit club. There's a bar at the very back of the room that sits higher than the gathering of people mingling below, thus not only keeping me out of the radar of the men who want to mold me into the ideal submissive; but it also gives me a prime view of the entire club.

While pacing toward the bar, I realize my initial assessment about the gleam brightening the eyes of the patrons peering at me is not one hundred percent accurate. Not all their gazes are filled with lust. Some are interested, while others are crammed with suspicion. I can't blame their motives. I've arrived with a poor attitude and a closed mind. My reaction can't be helped, though. I would be acting the same way if you threw me in a clown costume and demand I make animal puppets. When you're thrown into something you're not accustomed to, it often comes with a nasty side dish of apprehension.

"What can I get you?" questions a deep voice the instant I plop my backside onto a polished barstool at the end of a long wooden bar.

Clutching my chest to ensure my heart remains in my chest cavity, I swing my eyes to the bartender wiping the sparkling countertop.

The endeavor to keep my heart in its rightful spot becomes challenging when the bartender locks his unique brownish-black eyes with me.

The rugged grittiness of his voice sends goosebumps racing over my skin when he warns, "Unless you want a group of men charging in your direction, you might want to wipe that doe-eyed look out of your eyes right now."

He stops wiping the glistening countertop and raises his eyes to peer past my shoulder. Following his gaze, I notice the trio of men I bumped into earlier are watching me with a covetous gaze. Women of all ages will tell you that being eyed with zeal is nothing out of the ordinary when attending a function this late on a Saturday night, but there's something different about their avid gazes. It causes my pulse to quicken with an equal amount of excitement and concern. I don't know if my peculiar reaction stems from feeling conflicted sitting amongst people whose lifestyle choices are vastly contradicting from mine, or because I didn't realize how judgmental I was until tonight. I'd say my response is a little bit of column A and a dash of column B.

My moral pendulum swings toward column A when the bartender roughly mutters, "They can smell a newcomer from a mile away."

Swallowing down the bile crawling up my esophagus, I drift my eyes back to him. "That obvious?"

The bartender's smile makes my heart beat a little faster. "If the way you're clasping your coat isn't enough of an indication of your newbie status, then the scent leeching from your pores is a surefire indication."

Even hearing his jesting tone doesn't stop me from sniffing myself. *I certainly don't smell any different.*

Plopping an unopened bottle of chilled water down in front of me, the bartender says, "I'm giving you an hour before you go racing out those doors." He nudges his head to a set of concealed emergency doors on my left, ensuring I'm aware of the closest viable exit.

My fighting spirit emerges as I ask, "What makes you so sure I'm going to flee? I'm not as naïve as half the women in this club."

His smile grows, and it does wicked things to my libido. "That's the majority of your problem. . ." He leaves his sentence open, waiting for me to fill in the gaps.

"Cleopatra," I fill in. *What? I was running on empty. My brain is too busy calculating the distance from the bar to the exit that it doesn't have time to conjure up a believable alias.*

"Cleopatra?" He enunciates my name in a long, throaty purr.

Propping his elbows onto the countertop, he tilts in close to me. "Doms love the brats even more than the naïve virgins romance books told you they like."

"What? Why?" Shock is evident in my voice from seeing the truth in his slanted gaze. "Don't they want pure, untouched women?"

My research may have been a little cliché, but not having anything concrete to work with, I relied on the facts displayed in front of me.

The bartender chuckles. "Not at all." His words are straight to the point. No pussy-footing around for him. "To a true Dom, there's only one thing better than being awarded power in the bedroom." He pauses, soundlessly building the suspense. "It's being handed the power from an equally powerful counterpart. That's the ultimate reward."

I want to act ignorant, like I don't know what he is referring to, but my research into the BDSM community the past two weeks ensures I can't play that card. What he is saying is true. One article noted with an increase in members to the BDSM society the past five years, older participants are seeking newer, more challenging projects.

Noticing my inability to issue a comeback, the bartender sets the timer on his watch, winks cockily, then moves to serve patrons standing at the other end of the bar. Just as his attitude portrays, he walks with a swagger that bolsters his boastful attitude.

Masking the panic on my face with a neutral expression, I swivel in my chair to face the congregation of people mingling in the poorly lit space. For every minute that ticks by on the clock, the room becomes noticeably smaller, and the patrons' clothing becomes optional. As the temperature rises, so do the various "scenes" being played throughout the club. Some skits seem innocent enough. Others. . . they put the late night shows I witnessed Lexi flicking past last Saturday night to shame.

With numerous sexual acts being played out before my eyes, and the unashamed gazes of men and women of all ages, I've been struck with a severe bout of nausea. Don't get me wrong, I've been eyed with ardor before, but this is different. The people eyeballing me aren't watching me with the usual attraction. They're looking at me as if I'm a commodity, not a person.

Hoping to lessen the swishy movements of my stomach, I chug down the bottle of water the bartender set down in front of me twenty minutes ago. It does nothing to settle my flipping stomach. It's beyond suppressing.

When the flashing disco lights add to the wooziness inflicting my head, I slip off my seat and scan the room, seeking a washroom sign amongst the scantily clad group. *Perhaps splashing some cool water onto my face will help calm the panic scorching my veins?*

Like a poorly scripted B grade movie, I tumble off my stool and bump into the gentleman seated next to me. If I wasn't immersed in a debauched world I don't belong in, it would be a perfect time for me to stumble into the man of my dreams. Unfortunately, this is no romance novel.

When the man I bumped into runs his hand down the red hue marring my cheeks, his shoes nearly have a meeting with the bottles of water I guzzled down the past forty minutes.

The dark-haired stranger stares into my eyes with a predatory smirk to ensure I can't misread his intentions. Accepting my apologies for bumping into him with a smile is not on his agenda.

His unambiguous gaze strangles any attempts to investigate this environment thoroughly before passing judgment. It isn't just reading his objective that has me swinging the axe before checking the wood pile. It's the fact he's propositioning me all while ignoring the woman kneeling at his feet, fawning for his attention. His gaze makes me feel sick, and it causes regret to spread through me.

Gritting my teeth to keep my stomach contents in their rightful place, I race toward the exit the bartender gestured to earlier. Splashing water on my face for a situation like this would be nothing but a woeful waste of time. Even with keeping my eyes fixated on the exit door, my vision is bombarded with images no amount of wine will ever replace. A woman hangs from a steel beam like contraption with nothing but rope as clothing, while a man's back is marked with the sting of a leather flogger.

The coolness of the bar lock on the heavily weighted exit door gives relief to my overheated skin when I push down and throw open the door.

"Forty-three minutes and fifteen seconds," the bartender hackles when I charge into the alley. "You lasted longer than I predicted."

6
_____

*R*efreshing winds sneak through my thin coat when I stumble into the alley. While sucking in harsh breaths to ward off a panic attack surfacing, I fiddle with the buttons on my trench coat. My body is so overheated I feel like I'm going to pass out at any moment.

Slinging my coat off my shoulders, I lean against the outer wall of the club and continue with my endeavor to calm the torrent of emotions pumping into me. I've never been more overwhelmed, over-stimulated and overly panicked in my life. That environment was. . . I don't have any words to express it. Wrong. Tantalizing. Intriguingly weird. If my mouth would cooperate with the prompts of my brain, those are some of the words I could use to describe it.

Although flabbergasted, I will say one thing: if this is people's idea of a fun Saturday night, I either need to get out more often or lock myself in my room and never leave. With the crazy beat of my heart, the latter seems the more plausible option.

After giving myself a few moments to settle down, I gather my coat in my arms and push off the brickwork. With a stream of yellow taxis on nearly every street in Manhattan, I'm sure it won't take me long to flag one down. Just before I pass the door I tumbled out of five minutes ago, bright lights beam down the narrow alleyway, hindering my vision. With one hand grasping the steel door to steady my swaying, I lift my other one to shelter my eyes. Relief spreads across my chest when I spot the light gray Bentley I rode in earlier gliding toward me.

When it comes to a stop beside me, I fling open the back door and slide into the backseat.

"Oh my god, thank goodness you're here. This entire. . . *situation* isn't for me."

I freeze like a statue when a deep and highly manly voice says, "I'm sorry to hear that. Perhaps you should reconsider the answers you provided in your questionnaire. Ensuring you're partnered with the correct companion is the most imperative step in this. . . *situation.*"

Only turning my eyes for the fear of snapping my neck from an abrupt movement, I rest them with a man seated in the seat across from me. My loosened jaw muscle drapes even lower when my eyes lock in on one of the most mesmerizing pairs of green eyes I've ever seen. Even behind a silver mask, the effervescence of his dazzling gaze cannot be hidden. His eyes are wondrous, and they soon have me trapped in a trance.

Following my intuition, I angle the top half of my frame to face the mystery companion. My new position awards me with more exquisite features: rich, flawless chocolate skin, straight defined nose, a rigid jawline void of a single hair, and a mouthwatering body encased in a black suit with silver pinstripes. The vision is ravishing, completely smothering the storm brewing in my stomach by replacing it with the potent desire of lust.

Just as eagerly as I absorb him, the mystery stranger angles his head to the side and rakes his eyes down my body. His perusal is long and heart-strangling, and it causes every nerve ending in my body to activate. His avid gaze makes me forget that I'm meeting him wearing nothing but a sheer slip of satin and an even more meager pair of panties. When he returns his eyes to my face, my trancelike state intensifies. His gaze is primal and strong, and it sets my pulse racing.

"Who did your questionnaire partner you with?" The husky roughness of his voice adds to the giddiness clustering in my core.

"Questionnaire?" I squeak out, my voice so high I don't recognize it.

The temperature in the cabin of the Bentley turns roasting when the stranger smirks a devilishly delicious smile. It isn't an inviting or invigorating smile, more of an intriguing grin.

"All subs are issued a questionnaire at the start of proceedings. Were you not given one?"

I sheepishly shake my head. "Umm. . . no."

Sloping his head to the side, he peers at the steel door of the club, attempting to conceal the angry storm growing in his eyes with an impervious look. He miserably fails. My hands twitch, dying to smooth out the wrinkle peeking out of his silver mask. Thankfully, since I'm stuck in a lusty haze, my hands remain fisted at my sides.

"All subs must be issued a questionnaire. It's protocol," the stranger mutters, more to himself than me.

Not giving me the chance to respond to being dismissed as a submissive, he releases the latch on his seatbelt and scoots across the seat, filling the minor portion of space between us. The hairs on my nape prickle when his intoxicating smell graces my senses. Body wash, freshly washed linen, and a spicy aftershave hit a few of my hot buttons, rendering me even more mute than his entrancing green eyes.

As his eyes drink in my flushed neckline, lust rages in my womb. I've met many intriguing men in my life, but the aura beaming from this man, he is just. . . *whoa!* He has a sense of familiarity about him— like I've seen him before—but with his face concealed by a mask, I can't one hundred percent testify to that. His mystery boosts the excitement caking my skin with a fine layer of sweat.

When he tilts in close to me, I pant in a surprised breath when the intensity of his eyes hit me full-force. In the dimly lit Bentley, they appear almost mint green in coloring. They're the most exquisite and unique pair of eyes I've seen. The panic roaring through my body earlier no longer exists as I roam my eyes over the magnificent creature sitting in front of me. My eyes go frantic, wanting to ensure every unique quality of his mask-covered face is absorbed and compartmentalized before they lose the chance.

His perusal of me is just as thorough. His eyes burn into my skin, heating every nerve ending in my body with his powerful gaze. An overwhelming sense of desire scorches through me, forcing my thighs to squeeze together. Acting on the impulses of my lust-driven heart, my tongue darts out to moisten my lips. Although the prompts of my body are absurd, if he is going to kiss me, I refuse for his plump, inviting mouth to brush against a pair of bone-dry lips.

Embarrassment unlike anything I've ever felt swallows me whole when he mutters, "Although tempting, cavorting with a member of Chains is not permitted without the sub first filling in a question-naire." He's sitting so close to me, his liquor-scented breath bounces off my famished lips.

Mortified he read the prompts of my hankering heart so accurately, I sheepishly raise my eyes to his. A parcel of air expelled from his mouth fans my flushed cheeks when he locks his eyes with mine. I hold his gaze as the gleam in his eyes switches from confident to confused. He watches me in silence for several minutes, his eyes bouncing between mine, his breathing low.

The hairs on my nape bristle to attention when he stretches out his arm so the back of his fingers can run down my cheek. His briefest touch sends tingles dancing across my face before zooming to the lower half of my body.

The brutal slap my ego took minutes ago fades when he whispers, "I've never wanted to break the rules as much as I do right now."

I peer into his eyes, returning his covetous gaze while also pleading for him to throw caution to the wind. Sometimes the best things can only be achieved by taking a chance.

Several minutes pass with us sharing the same breath. The silence fills the cabin of the Bentley with enchanting sexual tension.

When he leans in close, I close my eyes and perk my lips. My breathing shallows to a pant and time comes to a standstill. When a buzzing sensation zaps my left shoulder, I pop open my eyes. Mortified realization smacks into me hard and fast when he adjusts the spaghetti strap of my negligée. He wasn't tilting in so our lips could become acquainted; he was leaning across to ensure my heavy bosoms remained in their rightful place.

Even with his briefest touch causing a spark to stimulate every nerve in my body, my humiliation grows tenfold. Not only does he not want to kiss me, he wants to ensure my skin remains covered while in his presence. *Ouch!* That's a second brutal slap my ego never expected to endure tonight.

Burying my pride in a deep pit in my stomach, I stumble out, "I'm sorry for the intrusion. I mistook your vehicle for another. It was a mistake. One of many I've made thus far tonight." Embarrassment hinders my vocal cords, making my words huskier than normal.

Ignoring the tense shake of my body, I reach for the silver door handle and yank it open. Excitement thrums my veins when my rushed movements force his hand to brush my knee.

"I hope you have a pleasant evening." Cringing that he is about to enter a BDSM establishment, I fling open the back passenger door and start to leave the Bentley.

Before I fully exit, the stranger's hand darts out to snag my wrist. His simplest touch surges a rush of desire to my throbbing sex. It's so potent, my thighs squeeze together to lessen its effect. I sit frozen and mute halfway out of his vehicle, shocked his meekest touch could cause such a fervent response out of me, but also intrigued.

"Don't let the unknown frighten you. If you face something you fear head on, you'll realize the unknown isn't frightening. It's the known."

I take a few moments absorbing his statement. Although I do agree with a majority of it, I can't comprehend why he would believe knowledge is frightening. Knowledge is power. It's the one thing that costs nothing to have, but it's worth more than anything.

"Knowledge is power." I twist my neck to peer into his eyes. "It isn't frightening."

"It is when a man doesn't know how to use it." He returns my staggered stare. "Knowledge is useless unless it's attached to an action.

Just because you know something does not mean it can be done. Action is power. Knowledge is a given."

I try to think of a comeback, but I'm left a little stumped. I've never held an intellectual debate with a man while wearing a satin slip and more makeup than I've ever worn, let alone with a man who has turned my normally astute brain to puree by doing nothing more than holding my hand.

"Knowledge may only be a given for you, but it's vital to me. It's what tells me I shouldn't be having this conversation in an alleyway with a man about to enter a BDSM club while wearing an outfit that does nothing to represent the strong and independent woman I am."

I expected my words to rile him up. It has the complete opposite effect. The spark in his eyes grows as does his smirk. "Secondhand knowledge is the reason you've closed your mind to new possibilities. You're allowing others to influence your decisions instead of evaluating them for yourself."

I stare at him, wholly stumped.

Spotting my shocked expression, he says, "Tonight is your first time in a BDSM club."

I attempt to reply, but he continues speaking, making me realize he didn't ask a question, he was stating a fact.

"These events aren't held for people new to the lifestyle. Yes, you can have couples interested in certain aspects of BDSM, but that rarely steps over the line of using a set of fluffy handcuffs or issuing open-hand spankings during sexual exchanges."

My insides tighten when he reaches the last half of his sentence.

"Considering you've been sitting across from me the past ten minutes, and no one has exited the club looking for you, I'm assuming you arrived here alone?"

This time, since his tone alludes to a question, I nod. My sex aches when a relief dashes through his heavy-hooded gaze.

He stares into my eyes. "Can you tell me the last time you saw a solo ballroom dancer perform?"

My brows furrow as I shake my head. "I never have."

"Exactly." The stranger dark brow slant higher than the silver mask on his face. "Chains is a club designed for you to interact with or without a partner, but when you turn up solo, you're to be paired with someone suitable to ensure you experience the club the right way."

My confusion increases tenfold. I'm completely and utterly confused.

"If you were to turn up to a ballroom dancing class without a partner, the instructor would pair you with someone they believe matches your level of skill and experience, would they not?" he questions my confused expression.

Not needing to deliberate on a response, I nod.

"That's what the questionnaire at Chains is for. To make sure you're paired with the right partner."

Although I can see the direction he is attempting to take our conversation, my confusion doesn't ease in the slightest. "But what does that have to do with our conversation?"

"You arrived what..." he stops talking to rake his eyes over my body, "...less than an hour ago. Am I correct?"

Tugging my coat in close to my body to hide its reaction to his quick glance, I nod.

"Did you talk to anyone in that time?" He peers into my eyes. I swear, they have the ability to completely stop my heart. They're so entrancing.

I nearly shake my head before my interaction with the bartender filters into my mind.

"I talked to one man." My voice is louder than I was hoping, startling not just me and the mysterious stranger, but his driver as well. "He was very nice. Pleasant even." *Compared to the many other not-so-pleasant men in the room.*

A new type of excitement scorches my veins when the dark-haired stranger's jaw gains a tick from my confession. From his reaction alone, I surmise he didn't expect me to answer this way. He seems to be able to read me so well; he knew I fled the party without interacting with any of the attendees.

"This man you spoke to, did he request to peruse your questionnaire before approaching you? Or attempt to discuss why you didn't have one?"

The tick in his jaw extends to his hard-lined lips when I shake my head. I've read plenty of romance novels that display dominant man as possessive and jealous, but that cliché doesn't usually extend to Doms. His reaction proves my research may have not been accurate.

"No, but we never really had the chance to talk. It was all *business* for him."

I don't know why I'm goading him. Perhaps it's the fact I love seeing the possessive spark in his eyes flaring brighter with every moment I sit across from him?

"*Business?*"

I nod. "Yeah. He was *very* busy. Quick too." I wait, letting him stew a little before adding on, "The members of Chains are *extremely* demanding. If you know the owner, can you have a word with him or her on my behalf?"

He stares into my eyes, his mesmerizing gaze answering my question without a word seeping past his lips.

"They really need more bar staff. That poor guy was run off his feet."

The conceitedness stretched across my face from making the unnamed stranger jealous turns to panic when he returns to his side of the bench seat, opens the back driver's side door and exits the vehicle. His movements are so quick, he extends his hand to aid me out of the Bentley before I can swallow the hard lump in my throat.

"Why don't we go and have a word with the owner together? I'm sure he will be more than willing to hear your suggestion in person," he mutters.

"Oh... that's not necessary," I stammer out, my words croaky. "He's probably a very busy man."

"I'm sure he isn't as busy as the bar staff." His words are as dangerous as the mouthwatering cut of his jawline.

7

*N*ot giving me a chance to object, the stranger curls his hand around mine and paces to the stainless steel door I stumbled out mere minutes ago. The soft hum of voiceless music overtakes the thump of my pulse when he throws open the door and we step inside the dimly lit club. Just like earlier, numerous eyes swing in my direction.

This time, it's not only male eyes I've gained the attention of. There are just as many female gazes watching every movement the mysterious stranger and I make. Their moods perk up as they glance at him hopefully. From the way they're eyeing us with so much interest, anyone would swear we were the ones performing on stage, not the lady with a giant black ball stuffed in her mouth.

I twist my coat around my wrists before pulling it to my chest. With the mysterious stranger's hand warming my back, the front of my body is noticeably cool. Keeping my head front and center, I sneakily shift my eyes sideways. Shock gnaws at my chest. Although we are surrounded by scantily clad and completely naked bodies, the green-eyed man has his eyes firmly planted on me. His avid gaze heats my skin—from my toes to my sweat-drenched hair.

"I've never been into exhibitionism, but if you keep looking at me like that, I may reconsider," the stranger mumbles, ensuring I'm aware my sneaky glance didn't go unnoticed.

Shockwaves of arousal pump through me like liquid ecstasy. The brittle roughness of his words equally shock and excite me. I'm shocked because of the location we are entering – I assumed exhibitionism would be high on his list of priorities – and excited because his threat means I'm not the only one allowing lust to steer away my inhibitions.

Smirking at my glazed-eyed response, the masked man continues to move through the vast gathering of people. When they see us coming, the crowd parts, giving us a clear path to a long, dark corridor positioned next to the bar I hid at earlier. For every step I take, the sweat misting my skin thickens. I don't know if it originates from the way everyone seems to know the masked man, or because my body failed to shut down its longing. Whatever it is, my body's prompts are shocking and somewhat intimidating, even more so because of the unethical environment.

The distress gnawing my chest drops to my stomach when the bartender notices our approach. "Oh, now I understand why your name is Cleopatra. A queen for the king," he jests, winking playfully. "Maybe next time you can be Bonnie and I'll be Clyde."

Although I can't miss his jeering tone, his banter is lost on the mysterious stranger. His hand stiffens on my back, and for the first time in minutes, his eyes move away from me. The belligerent smile etched on the bartender's mouth is wiped right off his face when the stranger connects his thin-slit eyes with his. Although he doesn't speak a word, his gaze must be threatening enough, because the bartender swallows harshly before curtly nodding. When he paces down the polished bar to serve patrons at the other end, his steps are shaky and lacking the confidence they held earlier.

"He was only playing," I assure him, my words barely heard over the soft hum of music playing from the speakers above our heads.

My eyes rocket to the stranger when he mutters, "Do you like knife play, Cleo?"

My brain didn't register his question. It's too busy prompting my body to breathe through the panic scorching my veins that he knows my name. The color drains from my face as my lungs squeal about the shortage of oxygen.

My panic only recedes when the stranger drops his eyes to mine. Although shrouded by a lifetime of secrets, they have an open honesty to them. He doesn't know me; he just shortened the alias I gave the bartender. *I hope.*

"Knife play?" I question, endeavoring to return our conversation to neutral territory. Well, as neutral as it can be in a BDSM club.

When we reach the end of the corridor, the stranger removes his hand from my back, triggering my body to scream in disgust. Before I have the chance to voice an objection to his lack of contact, my disappointment is replaced with nerves when my eyes take in the word "manager" engraved on the tinted glass door. I was hoping his threat to talk to the manager was just a ploy to get me back inside the club. Apparently, I was mistaken.

"Knife play is often referred to as blood play." He swings open the half-glass door. "Those are scenes that interest a man like Matthew."

I peer into his eyes, ensuring he can spot my confusion. I don't have the faintest clue what he is referring to.

"Matthew is not just a bartender at Chains, Cleo; he's also an invited guest," he explains to my bemused expression before guiding me into the office. "You may have taken your conversation with him as friendly. He did not. He is networking for a new sub."

Even with shock bubbling my veins, my body fails to display its surprise at his admission. My eyes are too busy categorizing every inch of the office we've just entered. Black polished bookshelves line four walls. They're brimming with a broad range of books, from classic first editions worth thousands of dollars to the latest rom-com releases. A thick glass desk with black iron legs sits in the middle of the space, illuminated by the chain-link chandelier shackled to the ceiling.

As I remind my body to breathe, I step further into the space. My lips quirk when I notice the theme of the expansive office is a chain-link design. The furniture is not the type you'd find in any retail store.

This is custom made. With its elegant lines and quality material, it appears more like a piece of art than furniture. If I hadn't noticed the inclusion of painted BDSM scenes adorning the walls, I could have mistaken this place for that of an extremely wealthy businessman, not a seedy BDSM club manager.

"Whose office is this?" I query, spinning around to face the mysterious stranger.

When I neglect to find him standing next to me, my neck snaps to the side. My movements are so abrupt, the muscles in my neck squeal in protest. My pulse surges into unknown waters when my eyes lock in on the mystery stranger sitting in a leather chair behind the only desk in the room. He has removed his suit jacket and rolled up the sleeves of his crisp business shirt, exposing the cut lines of his muscular arm, but, unfortunately, the mask concealing his face remains in place.

Swallowing a brick lodged in my throat, I garble, "This is your office? You're the manager of Chains?"

The corners of his lips tug high; excitement at my flabbergasted response is all over his concealed face. He shouldn't look so pleased. He is the man I'm here to take down. The one person who knows the name of every face mingling outside his office doors. He holds the key I need to unlock the story that could change the course of my career. *He should not be smiling.*

He tilts forward, dragging the cuffs of his shirt even higher on his heavily veined arms. "I don't manage Chains, Cleo; I own it," he informs me. The roughness of his voice sends a chill down my spine. With the vast range of emotions pumping into me, I don't know if it's a good or bad chill.

When he gestures for me to sit in the seat across from him, my first instinct is to shake my head and bolt. But, for some reason unbeknownst to me, I saunter to him. My heart rate turns calamitous the closer I get to him. As if his body and soul-stealing facial features aren't enough to contend with, his eyes, my gosh, they totally squash any shrewdness I hold. They have the ability to render me speechless and turn my brain to mash. *Clearly—as I'm standing in a BDSM club acting as if I'm meeting the President, and I haven't even seen the uncovered version of his eyes yet.*

When I take the seat across from him, the still unnamed man removes a five-page document from a concealed drawer on his left. Like he is aware of the power his eyes have over me, his entrancing gaze never once wavers from mine. While holding his gaze, I catch the rise and fall of my heavy bosoms. The movements of my chest prove I'm breathing, but the tightness spread across my torso says otherwise. I feel like I'm drowning, not in a pool of despair but in a pool of lust.

This man exhibits such animalistic traits I have no doubt he'd be remarkable in bed. He is confident without being overly cocky, like he knows of his sexual prowess, and he doesn't need to shamelessly flaunt it, but there's also an unknown edge to him that's just as intriguing. *A complex man I'd give anything to spend a few hours unraveling.*

A pen scratching on paper gathers my attention from the wicked thoughts of him flaunting his sexual abilities in morally unethical ways.

With his eyes now glancing down at the sheets of paper, the masked man says, "Name, Cleo. Age. . ."

He stops talking and lifts his eyes to me. My spine turns as solid as a rod when he runs his heavy-hooded gaze down my body in a long perusal.

"Twenty-five," he murmurs, returning his gaze to the sheet in front of him.

I can't hide my surprise that he guessed my age from one glance at my body.

"Physical capabilities?" He doesn't wait for me to reply before he mutters, "Physically capable."

I squeeze my thighs together to lessen the manic throb between my legs from the assuredness in his voice.

Any chance to ease the intense tingle flies out the window when he raises his eyes to me and asks, "Submissive's safe word?"

I sit in silence, muted, aroused and confused. From my research online, you only require a safe word if you intend to be involved in a physical activity. Considering I have no intention of doing anything of that nature in this type of establishment, I never took the time to ponder a safe word.

Every muscle in my body tightens when he utters, "We will come back to that one."

Dropping his eyes to the paper, he continues. "Name the Dom/top is to be called during scenes?"

Once again, he doesn't wait for me to answer, he just writes something down.

With my inability to leash my curiosity, I scoot to the edge of my chair so I can peer at the name scribbled across the sheet.

Master Chains, I mumble to myself.

"Who is Master Chains?" My words are surprisingly strong considering the circumstances I find myself in.

Both excitement and fear holds me captive for several heart-clutching seconds when the most devastating smile I've ever experienced spreads across the masked man's face. If his smile didn't answer my question, the truth beaming from his eyes is a surefire indication.

Ignoring the excitement heating my blood, I slouch deeper in my chair and pull my coat into my chest, ensuring *Master Chains* won't notice my budded nipples. Considering the man across from me in a stranger—and enjoys extra-curricular bedroom antics—my body's reaction to his smile is utterly ridiculous. I've never acted so moronic in my entire life.

The situation goes from difficult to downright awkward when he mimics my slouched position before questioning, "Bondage?"

Unsure what he wants for an answer, I shrug my shoulders.

"Have you ever participated in any form of bondage?" he elaborates, the deep rasp of his voice calm, almost soothing.

I briskly shake my head.

"Handcuffs? Rope? Have you had your hands bound behind your back with a tie or some form of restraint?" he queries, his deep voice lowering with each question.

The throb between my legs amplifies with every word he speaks. With a hint of embarrassment, I once again shake my head. Although Luke and I were together for two years, we only had sexual contact the last six months of our relationship. His bedroom abilities were great, and he made it hard for any man following him to steal his limelight, but our adventures never extended beyond altering our position, so it was comfortable in his Jeep. And although I've slept with men since Luke, I was never with them long enough for sexual preferences to be discussed.

The unnamed man's heavy brow arches above his mask. He appears shocked by my response.

His stunned expression morphs onto my face when he asks, "Do you like to be spanked, Cleo?"

Hoping to mask my shock with humor, I reply, "Do you enjoy making strangers squirm in their seats, *Master Chains*?" I drawl out his alias in a long and highly inappropriate purr, my desire to goad him nearly as urgent as my wish to unmask his handsome face.

"Depends," he responds, his voice throaty.

"On what?" I hold his gaze, my interest in discovering his answer unable to be concealed.

He smiles a grin that sets my pulse racing. "On whether or not you enjoy being spanked."

Warm slickness coats my panties. Even hearing a jeering undertone in his timbre doesn't dampen my eagerness the slightest. I'm hot, needy and on the verge of combusting.

"Do you want to spank me?" I try to keep my tone neutral. My attempts are borderline.

His smile grows, as does the lust raging in his eyes. "That. . . amongst many other things."

The coils in my stomach wind so tight, I physically squirm in my seat. My reaction surprises me. I've handled the direct approach some men use numerous times before, but none have caused me to shamelessly writhe in my seat. I'm wiggling around so much, I look like a child busting to use the bathroom.

"You don't even know me," I barely whisper when the entirety of the situation overwhelms me. "How could you possibly know what you want to do to me?"

I suck in a surprised breath when he locks his eyes with mine and says, "I only needed one glance into your eyes, because eye contact is what causes your--"

"Soul to catch on fire," I interrupt, saying a verse my dad quoted many times during his twenty-five-year marriage to my mom. "There's no greater way to see someone's true self than looking at their soul through their eyes."

He nods and smiles, pleased with my response. Until this day, I never understood my dad's favorite quote. Now I do. I fully understand. Because the instant the stranger locked his eyes with mine, a furious blaze raged through my soul, charring it for life. Don't get me wrong, even with half of his face concealed by a mask, the stranger is ridiculously handsome, but there's something about his eyes that tell me not to be fooled by his outer package. His insides are just as temptingly dangerous as his attractive outer layer.

Our fire-sparking stare down ends when he mutters, "So, Cleo, let me ask you again, do you like being spanked?" His voice is deeper and much more rugged this time around.

"Not particularly," I sputter out, shockingly maintaining his gaze.

With how potent the lust is raging in my womb, I'm surprised I haven't thrown my head back, snapped my eyes shut, and gotten lost in the throes of ecstasy. The only reason I haven't is because the nagging voice in the back of my head is warning me to hold my cards close to my chest.

"The only time I've been spanked was when I was naughty. Thankfully, that was not very often in my childhood," I disclose, not the slightest bit embarrassed admitting I was the beloved golden child of my family.

The moisture between my legs grows when Master Chains' lips tug into a wry smirk. "You'll only get spanked when you're naughty here too, Cleo," he mutters, his voice so low I'm certain he didn't expect me to hear him. "Unless you like that type of thing," he continues. This time, there's no doubt he wanted me to hear him.

After glancing into my eyes long enough the satin material of my slip sticks to my skin, he drops his gaze back to the document in his hand. "These next set of questions require you to rate them 1 to 5, one being a definite no, five being a yes, please," he explains.

I lick my dry lips before nodding. I don't know why I'm continuing with this bizarre exchange, but try as I may, I can't tear myself away from our conversation. Some may say it's purely my investigative skills flourishing, but I know that isn't the case. Although this lifestyle is intriguing, and there would be no better way to uncover it than to associate with the man responsible for bringing it to fruition, that isn't what's keeping my backside planted in my seat. It's the intrigue of the man seated across from me. My desire to unmask him is even more voracious than my wish to bring this scandalous story to every news outlet in the country.

My ability to pretend this exchange is nothing but a business transaction is lost when the stranger questions, "Anal sex?"

---

8

*M*y mouth gapes, and my eyes bulge, but remarkably, I squeak out. "Two."

I should be nervous. I should be feeling all types of grievance for continuing a conversation on a world I essentially know nothing about. But my curiosity is encouraging me to trek into a wrong, yet tantalizing discussion with the mysterious masked man.

The stranger marks my response on the sheet of paper before asking, "Asphyxiation?"

In shock, I stare at him, unresponsive and wide-eyed. He revels in my flushed appearance. His eyes flare in excitement, and his lips tug in the corners. This as cliché as they come, but this man's aura screams sex. His eyes are a decoy, the perfect asset to lure unknowing victims out of the shadows, before his deep, cultured voice ensnares the last of their reservations. He's incredibly appealing and undoubtedly dangerous.

A small voice of reason inside me breaks through the lust haze his entrapping eyes created. "What were the numbers again?" I strive to keep my attention on the task at hand, and not the way his eyes have flecks of brown around the cornea.

"One for a definite no, five for a yes, please." His voice doesn't alter the slightest, seemingly unruffled by the current crackling between us.

"Two," I squeak out again, my words not as confident as I hoped.

The anxiety curled around my throat intensifies with every question he asks. "Abrasion? Age Play? Anal plugs? Arm adhesives?"

For the next ten questions, my responses rarely alter from a shaky one or two, but one leaves me utterly flabbergasted.

"Umm. . . can you repeat that? I'm fairly certain I didn't hear you right."

My stomach lurches into my throat when he repeats, "Animal play."

I glare at him, beyond mortified. *He has sex with animals?*

Spotting the repulsion on my face, he mutters, "It's not what you're thinking. Animal play is for people who like to be collared. Or crawl on all fours. Some even occasionally bark."

Flush heats my cheeks as images of the lady lowering herself onto her knees earlier this evening flashes before my eyes.

"Oh. Sorry," I mumble, my words so shaky they're nearly unintelligible.

Although I can tell by his eyes that my inexperience amuses him, they also reveal his hesitation. Clearly, he doesn't deal with BDSM rookies often.

We sit across from each other in silence for several moments. Nothing but my heart thrashing against my ribs is audible. For the first time in my life, I'm at a loss for words. The good manners my mother raised me with are telling me to issue the stranger an apology, but my shocked state due to our peculiar gathering has rendered me speechless.

Since my mouth refuses to cooperate, I issue him my regret by using my eyes. I've always believed apologies are nothing but meaningless words unless you see remorse in the eyes of the person issuing the apology. *I can only hope he sees mine.*

Reading the silent apology brimming from my eyes, the tightness of the stranger's jaw loosens, and the width of his eyes returns to their normal girth. He scoots across his chair, sitting on the very edge before locking his eyes with mine. "This really is your first time at a club like this, isn't it?"

When I nod, he adds on, "And every question you've answered thus far has been the truth?"

I once again nod, my face hot with embarrassment. He throws his pen onto the desk before sinking into his chair. The metal hinges give out a squeak, enhancing the pin-drop silence that has encroached us. He sits, staring at a door on his right. I also remain quiet, unsure what to say in a baffling situation like this. I tried to come here tonight with an open mind, but, obviously, that didn't occur.

After numerous heart-strangling seconds, the stranger returns his eyes to me. "Can I show you something?" For the first time tonight, his voice doesn't hold the same amount of assertiveness it usually wields.

Still mute, I nod.

The sluggish beat of my heart, strangled with remorse, gets a moment of reprieve when he pushes back from his desk, walks around it, then holds his hand out in offering. His chivalry catches me off guard. I fumble like a giddy school girl while placing my coat on his desk and standing from my seat before accepting his kind gesture. A surge of awareness scorches through my veins when he curls his hand around mine. His touch is warm and stimulating, and just like earlier, it causes the hairs on my body to bristle to attention.

Pretending I'm unaffected by the spark of lust firing between us, I allow the stranger to guide me to the door he's been staring at the past five minutes. Glancing into my eyes with a gleam I can't recognize, he slips his empty hand into the pocket of his trousers. My pulse thrums in my neck when he pulls out an antique-looking silver key, the type you'd expect to find hanging out of a treasure chest. The clunking of a heavy lock sounds through my ears when he twists the key into the hole. My lungs take stock of their oxygen levels when he lowers the steel handle and swings open the door.

He flicks on a light switch at his left. It takes several moments for the overhead lighting to illuminate the black room. When it does, I gulp in a shocked breath. When I joke to people that I work in a dungeon, I'm certain this is what they imagine. A chain contraption I've never seen before hangs from the ceiling; sex instruments and apparatuses I'm accustomed with but have never used cause a rush of heat to my cheeks, and the feeling of being in an environment I don't belong in overwhelms me.

Putting on my investigative journalism cap, I pace deeper into the room, appraising it with both the business and personal side of my brain. Even to a BDSM novice like me, it's clear this area is some sort of playroom. It has a manly feel to it, but it's also cold and sterile with the inclusion of black leather and silver chains on nearly every surface.

My eyes rocket to the unnamed man standing in silence outside the door when I spot a flogger draped over a leather studded chaise in the middle of the room. Unlike the flogger the man earlier tonight was being whipped with, this one doesn't have leather tassels attached to the end. It has chain-links, chains that look incredibly painful.

"Chains? Your instrument of choice is chains?" My hammering heart is heard in my words.

He remains quiet, assessing me in great detail. I return his stare, seeking answers to my question in his forthright eyes. My outward demeanor displays both my disgust and arousal. Don't ask me how it's possible to have two vastly contradicting responses, but that's precisely what I'm dealing with right now. His eyes appear just as conflicted as mine.

Sensing my opposing viewpoints, the stranger pushes off the doorjamb and paces toward me. I don't know whether my judgment is impaired by confusion, but even his walk commands more attention in this room. Snubbing my swirling stomach, I hold his gaze as he strides to me. His gaze is primitive and strong, and it enhances the beads of sweat sliding down my back.

The temperature in the room becomes unbearable when he stops in front of me. I stray my eyes to the ground, no longer capable of ignoring the pull his soul-stealing eyes have over me.

"Don't fear the pleasure you can get from pain," he mutters, his tone low and crackling with sexual tension as he lifts my chin back into its original position. "Pain has a reason it was added to pleasure."

"Says the man dishing out the punishment," I mumble before I can stop my words.

Unaffected by my callous snarl, he runs his index finger along my forehead, removing a strand of hair stuck to my sweat-slicked skin. "You fear the unknown."

I shake my head, denying his claim. "No. People only fear the unknown when they're incapable of achieving what they want."

He smiles, pleased by my response. "Exactly. So, what did you want to achieve by coming here tonight, Cleo?"

The hairs on my arms bristle, my body choosing its own response to the way my name rolls off his tongue in a long, seductive purr.

When I remain quiet, he says, "People's views of this lifestyle are often tainted and starkly contradicting to what it is."

I scan my eyes over the room. "Not from what I'm seeing. This is pretty much what I envisioned when I have nightmares about being tortured."

"I acknowledge your concerns, but that does not mean I have to agree with them." His tone is stern, yet understanding. "The people in this club are no different than yourself, Cleo. They just express themselves in a manner you're not accustomed to. That doesn't make them weird or different. It makes them real. And if you sat back and thought about it, you'd realize it also makes them courageous."

Pushing aside the fact he's excluding himself from his assessment, I say, "This is normal to you?" I wave my hand across the room that hasn't relinquished its firm hold on my stomach. "Turning up to your place of employment with your face concealed is normal to you?"

He stares into my eyes, not the slightest bit fazed by the disdain in my voice. "Yes. This is *normal* to me. But despite what you believe, the people in this club do not cover their faces solely to hide themselves. They conceal themselves to ensure they're truly seen. Imagine how different the world would view beauty if it were only seen through the soul of a person's eyes."

I try to compile a response, but I'm at a loss for words. He took beliefs I've been raised with and twisted them in a way that gives them a whole new meaning. I've often said beauty is skin deep. His response replicates my sentiments exactly.

A few minutes pass in silence. I wouldn't say it was any more confronting than the prior thirty minutes we've spent together. It more appears as if he's giving me time to absorb the enormity of his statement.

Once he's happy I've taken in his wisdom, he questions, "What do you want to do, Cleo? Stay and open your mind to the possibility of learning something new? Or leave and continue to wonder if your views are misguided and ill-advised?"

I shrug my shoulders. This is the first time in my life I truly don't know what to do. Intrigue is a potent power that can baffle even the most brilliant minds.

"What do you think I should do?" I sigh, embarrassed I'm leaving an imperative decision in the hands of a stranger.

"You, and only you, can make that decision. Contrary to what you've been told, nothing is *ever* forced in this industry."

The unease twisting my stomach gets a moment of reprieve when I see the honesty in his eyes. Although it doesn't lessen my trepidation, it simmers it enough that I feel comfortable taking my time to deliberate a decision.

While roaming my eyes around the playroom, which doesn't look as stark and uninviting as it did mere minutes ago, I take a few moments contemplating a response to his question. Half of my time is spent returning the stranger's lusty stare, while the other half categorizes all the scary, nerve-surging events that have occurred tonight. The man standing before me intrigues me, more than any man before him, but is that solely based on where I met him? Who can say they've held a conversation with a man who owns a secret BDSM club while standing in his playroom? Perhaps I have done as Delilah and her counterparts requested? Maybe I'm only looking at this from a business standpoint?

Oh, who am I kidding? I'm not standing in this room contemplating my fate to break a story. I'm here solely because the green-eyed man's notable stature refuses to relinquish me from its firm hold. Considering where we met and our interactions thus far, expecting to envision any morally right response is an absolutely ludicrous notion.

With my heart thrashing against my chest, I return my eyes to the still unnamed man. "I want to go home? This lifestyle isn't for me?" I reply. My jittering voice makes my words more questions than demands.

For the quickest second, a flare of disappointment flashes through the stranger's eyes before he shuts it down quicker than it arrived. It was so fast, if I wasn't trapped in his trance, I may have missed it.

Before I have the chance to recant my statement, he says, "Then let's get you home," his tone the lowest I've heard.

In silence, he guides me out of the room, gathers my coat from the table, and leads me out of his office. Just like earlier, my stomach swirls when we reach the main part of the club. Except this time, it isn't just the various scenes playing throughout that have my stomach twisted in knots. It's the feeling I'm making a huge mistake. It's the same unease I got the day my parents and little brother were involved in their car accident.

Before I can gather why I'm having such a peculiar feeling for a stranger, we enter the vacant foyer at the front of the club. The palpable tension between us intensifies in the emptiness of the space. When he moves away from me, regret surges through my veins.

He gathers a white envelope from behind the unmanned check-in station, then paces back toward me. His sweltering green eyes fringed by thick black lashes never once leave mine as he spans the distance between us. His avid gaze makes me feel alive, desired even.

"In case your curiosity gets the better of you," he states, handing the envelope to me.

Never being one to leash my curiosity, I attempt to tear open the envelope. He places his hand over mine, foiling my endeavors. "I said only *if* you are curious. Are you curious, Cleo?"

A small voice inside me screams a resounding, "Yes," but my brain swallows down its absurd response with a brisk shake of my head.

Disappointment flares in his stranger's eyes. He isn't the only one disappointed. The entire evening has my libido at the pinnacle of sexual exhilaration, all to be crashed by the inhibitions cited by my socially acceptable-striving brain.

"Okay. Then it was a pleasure meeting you, Cleo," the stranger bids me farewell, holding out his hand in offering.

Adrenaline ignites the lower half of my body when he presses a kiss to my hand. I yank my hand out of his embrace, startled by the response of my body. I breathe deeply, struggling not to lured into his enticing trap as my eyes check my hand for scorch marks. His touch was so blistering, I was sure there would be a welt.

Smiling at my skittish response, the masked man gestures his head to the door I stumbled in nearly two hours ago. "The doorman will summon a taxi for you."

"Thank you, but that isn't necessary; I have someone available to take me home." I sigh, grateful my voice didn't come out with the shake hampering my curvy frame.

My brows scrunch when a hazy cloud forms over the stranger's bright gaze. It's one I've only seen once so far tonight. It was when I was goading him in the back of the Bentley.

Spotting my confused expression, he mutters, "Envy slays itself with its own arrows."

With that, he runs the back of his hand down my cheek. A little groan involuntarily escapes me before I can shut it down. He pulls his hand away and takes a step backward, as if he too felt the current his touch inspired. Not speaking a word, he spins on his heels and walks into a world where I don't belong without a backward glance.

I stand frozen for a moment. My mind is hazy, my body on high alert. It's only after numerous minutes of silent deliberation does the reason why his eyes seem so familiar smack into me hard and fast. My heart rate surges with unease as my mind drifts back to a moment in time I'll never forget. A moment that both haunts and appeases me. The time a stranger comforted me during my darkest day.

"It can't be him," I mutter under my breath, certain the owner of a BDSM club wouldn't offer a stranger comfort out of the goodness of his heart. *Surely not.* The people in this industry are sick and demented human beings who get off on punishing those beneath them. *Aren't they?*

Certain the debauched environment I'm standing in is weakening my perception, I pivot on my heels and head for the door. The little voice inside me screams for me to stop, but I don't listen. Although intrigued beyond comprehension by the masked man, I plan on pushing one of the most bizarre and unusual nights I've ever had into the background of my mind, where I intend for it to stay for eternity.

I just need my heart to read the memo my brain wrote.

9

The air is sucked from my lungs when I walk into my office Monday morning. It isn't just Delilah sitting in my office chair that has me gasping for air; it's the images of the unnamed man flashing across my screen that have me choked. Since Delilah and Mr. Carson are so engrossed in absorbing each sordid image flicking across the monitor, they fail to notice me sneaking up behind them.

From the images of the masked man alone, I can easily derive that these pictures were taken on Saturday night. What I can't fathom is how they were captured. With the lack of pixelation and graininess to the images, it's clear they were not obtained by a long-range camera. They almost look as if they were snapped by someone sitting intimately close to the unnamed man. Like they were captured without his knowledge.

The bagel slathered in cream cheese I scarfed down on the train to work threatens to resurface when the images flick to a set of pictures taken in the back of a light gray Bentley. Any prospect of keeping my one-night-only appearance at a BDSM club a secret is left for dust when I catch my wide-eyed expression in the reflection of the dark tinted windows. Even with my image not being as clear as the green-eyed stranger, it's clear enough that there's no denying it's me sitting in the back seat of the Bentley.

When the room swirls around me, I reach out to grasp my office chair, wanting to ensure I don't go tumbling to the floor as I fight for my lungs to fill with air. My abrupt movement gains me the attention of Delilah and Mr. Carson.

"Chloe, so glad you could *finally* join us," Delilah snarls, her eyes lifting to the clock that shows I have arrived fifteen minutes before my scheduled start time. "I've been updating Mr. Carson on the progress of your investigation."

Mr. Carson shifts his eyes to me. His dark brows stitch when he takes in my white cheeks and massively dilated eyes. "Are you okay, Cleo?" he questions, his tone revealing his concern.

I shake my head. "Where did you get the images from?"

Mr. Carson braces his hip on my desk, his surprised expression growing the longer I glare into his murky eyes. "There was a pen tip-sized camera installed in one of the beads of your negligée," he informs me, his words as jutted as the hard lines in Delilah's top lip. "You were aware of this, Cleo. Delilah told me you were mindful of our requirement to digitally document your investigation into Chains."

Before a single denial can escape my lips, Delilah stands from her chair. "Yes, Cleo was aware of the camera. She's just a little frazzled by the events of the weekend," she exclaims, her loud voice ricocheting off my office walls.

Glowering at me, Delilah curls her arms around Mr. Carson's shoulders and guides him to my office door. The heavy groove between her manicured brows deepens when Mr. Carson yanks away from her embrace. His stern eyes issue her his reprimand for touching him without a word seeping from his lips. Once Delilah has absorbed every malicious torrent of his silent scold, Mr. Carson swings his eyes to me. The fury in his eyes softens when he takes in my wide eyes and flushed cheeks.

"Were you aware of the hidden camera, Cleo?" he questions, peering into my eyes.

I nearly shake my head. The only thing that stops me is the irate scowl Delilah gives me from behind Mr. Carson's shoulder. Her silent threat is just as effective as the one Mr. Carson issued her. It's heart-clutching and stern, and it renders me speechless.

If her vicious glare isn't enough to render me mute, her mouthed, "Lexi," is as effective as duct tape to my mouth.

Unable to speak through my dry, gaped mouth, I pitifully nod. I know some may construe my reply as cowardice, but that response would only be from people who have not handled the wrath of an angry Delilah Winterbottom. I'd rather have my day with the devil than spar against a woman as evil as her.

Mr. Carson locks his eyes with mine, no doubt trying to gauge my true response. Neither agreeing with or denying my declaration, he says, "You appear to have made some solid contacts in Chains Saturday night. If you keep up this caliber of work, you won't have to rely on any man to supply your sister's medical care."

And there it is: the below-the-belt hit I was waiting for. His remark could be construed as a compliment. I do not see it that way. His comment not only ensures Delilah will continue being my puppeteer, but it also guarantees he maintains the upper hand. He may seem genuinely nice and somewhat intriguing, but like every other man I've met in a high-power position, he didn't get there by playing nice. Just like the gaze of several men at Chains, I'm nothing but a commodity to him.

Once Mr. Carson's broad frame slips into the elevator on my floor, Delilah closes my office door and swivels around to face me. Heat creeps up my neck and curls around my throat from her malicious stare.

"When I spoke to you Sunday morning, you gave me the impression you didn't make any contacts Saturday night." Not giving me a chance to reply, she continues speaking, "You're a silly little girl if you believe you have control over *anything* that happens in this building."

She paces closer to me, nostrils flaring, fists clenched. "You and the lowlifes in the basement may be fine living out your career down there, but I guarantee you, the presidential suite at the Ritz Carlton will feel like the dungeon by the time I'm finished with you if you *ever* lie to me again." Her words come out in a long hiss, vicious and full of threat.

I swallow several times in a row, attempting to cool the fire burning in my throat.

Delilah tugs on the hem of her designer pantsuit before bending her knees so we meet eye to eye. "Do you understand what I'm saying to you, *Chloe?*" She doesn't hide the fact she knows she's calling me the wrong name.

"Loud and clear." I straighten my spine. Each millimeter I gain unleashes more of my Garcia fighting spirit. "But let me get one thing straight." My tone is as vicious as the one she was using earlier. "If you *ever* hide a camera in my clothing again without my knowledge, when I fall from grace, I'll take you to the depths of hell right alongside me."

My threat doesn't deter Delilah's resting bitch face the slightest. If anything, it strengthens it.

"Duly noted." Her words are mocking and full of lies. "Lucky for me, I have a bank account that can sustain the fall from grace. Do you, Cleo?"

Her malice-packed smile tells me she already knows my reply. She has researched me just as much the past two weeks as I have her. From what reports I gathered on her, she doesn't need to work to maintain the elaborate lifestyle she has been living since the day she took her first breath. She's here purely to torture the poor bastards who don't have any other option but to work for the man. *That man being Mr. Carson.*

Happy I have heeded her warning, Delilah saunters to my door. Her head is held high, her steps overly dramatic. Just before she exits, she cranks her neck back and peers at me. "I want the man in the Bentley's name, occupation, marital status and how many digits are in his bank account by the end of the month."

I shake my head. "I can't. That's impossible. There are no scheduled parties for Chains in the near future, and I don't have those types of contacts. My invitation was one-time only," I reply.

I also have an irrepressible desire to protect him from your vindictive claws, but I keep that snippet of information to myself.

"Name. Occupation. Marital status. And how many digits are in his bank account by the end of the month," she repeats, pausing dramatically between each request. "Or find yourself positioned at the end of a very long unemployment line."

I hold in my frustrated squeal until Delilah exits my office. Even with my door shut, I'm certain three floors down heard my malicious tirade on the evil witch. God, I wish I was smart enough to deny their requests weeks ago. Nothing worth having ever comes easily. That should have been a clear indication on how this assignment would unravel.

Slinging off my torn jacket, I hang it on the coat rack in my office, then slump into my chair. Air whizzes out of my nose when I take in the ridiculously large space. My desk alone would be worth more than my annual salary I earned writing obituaries.

While absorbing the freshly cut floral arrangement in the Cartier vase on my desk, I rack my brain about how I can get out of this predicament with an employment status still attached to my name. I don't even care if it's a position based in the dungeon, as long as it pays something, I'll accept it.

No matter how many ways I approach it, the same answer pops up. If I want to remain employed, I must investigate the masked man. Attempting to switch off the personal side of my brain, I click through the pictures of the unnamed man sprawled across my computer monitor. Even through a screen, his pulse-racing good looks and soul-stealing eyes still render me speechless. Although our time together was one of the oddest I've had with the opposite sex, he hasn't steered far from my thoughts the past two days. Not just because of his panty-drenching attractiveness, but because the more my astute brain tried to rationalize with my lust-driven heart that the man in the elevator is not the same man I met at Chains, my heart refuses to listen. It's certain he's the same man.

Even if he isn't the kind stranger from the elevator, I'm still shocked by the impression the masked man made on me Saturday night. I always assumed a dominant man was controlling and manipulative. He showed my representation wasn't entirely accurate. When I said I wanted to go home, he respected my decision. Disappointment may have flared in his eyes, but he never once voiced his concerns. That's a quality not many men hold, let alone a man in a powerful position.

A few minutes tick by on the clock as I recall the events of my weekend with the masked stranger. When the final moments I spent with him surface, my eyes rocket to my tattered coat. I placed the envelope he gave me in my pocket before sliding into the back of the taxi his doorman summoned. Annoyed at the Bentley driver's claim he would be waiting for me being nothing but a pipedream, I completely forgot about the envelope until now.

Pushing back from my desk, I stroll to my coat rack. My heart is thrashing against my chest, my eyes wide. Ignoring the shake of my hand, I delve it into the coat pocket. Panic scorches my veins when my hand comes out empty not even two seconds later. Harshly grabbing my jacket, I dig my hand into the opposite pocket. It's just as empty as the first. A fine layer of sweat slicks my skin when I search every nook and cranny of my coat, vainly trying to secure a document that could guarantee my employment status.

I stand still, muted and confused when my avid search fails to find the envelope. I was sure I put it in there. My frozen state only ends when my cell phone vibrates on my desk. Since my sister is the only one who has my number, I rush to my desk and snag my phone off the top. The terror thickening my blood thins when I drop my eyes to the phone screen and read.

Lexi: *If I log into this website, is there a possibility I'll see your snatch? Even if the possibility is slight, I still want a warning.*

Laughing to ward off my confusion, I sit in my office chair and type my reply.

Me: *What website? And for future reference, my snatch has rarely seen daylight, let alone a camera lens. P.S – Snatch is a nasty word; I much prefer something like lady garden or beaverville.*

Any worries about being unemployed by this afternoon are

pushed to the background of my mind when an image flashes up onto my phone screen. It's the envelope I've spent the last thirty minutes searching for. It's attached to another message from my deviant sister.

Lexi: Unless your S.N.A.T.C.H is hairy with two buck teeth at the front, you can't call it a beaver. P.S – This is the envelope I was referring to. P.P.S – I already peeked inside. P.P.P.S - If you ever visit a place like that again without me, you won't need to worry about a stranger spanking you. I'm sure I can find a wooden paddle here somewhere.

My eyes bulge at the last half of her message. With how strict the security was at Chains, I assumed the envelope wouldn't have any identifiable marks on it, so how does she know where it came from?

Me: Angry?

It feels like hours pass before a reply finally pops up on my screen.

Lexi: Ah, no. Jealous. I want a Christian Grey.

My dainty laugh quickly fills my expansive office.

Me: I hate to tell you this, but the closest you'll get to finding Christian at that establishment would be dating a man the age of his grandfather.

Ignoring the deceit darkening my blood, I lift my cold canister of hot chocolate to my mouth as I wait her reply. Although none of the men inside the club sparked an interest out of me, the owner most certainly did. If the caliber of men at Chains matched its owner, I'm sure it would be inundated with attendees willing to pay any price to enter its tightly shut doors.

Brown spit covers my computer monitor when my cell phone suddenly rings, startling me. While dabbing up the stains of hot chocolate from my cream skirt with a tissue, I swipe my finger across the screen of my phone.

"I'll take whatever I can get," Lexi says down the line, not bothering to offer a greeting. "If you date Christian's grandfather, you're bound to meet Christian at some point."

"Then you'll just steal him from Anastasia with a few bats of your eyelashes and a cunning smirk?" I ask, my voice doused in laughter.

Lexi laughs. It's husky and exposes the rough weekend she had. "No. I'll just borrow him for a few years; then Ana can have him back."

Although Lexi's tone is joking, it causes a stabbing pain to hit my chest. I know as well as anyone that Lexi is living on borrowed time, but it doesn't make it any easier to acknowledge.

Pretending she can't feel the sentiment pouring out of me, Lexi asks, "So how long have you been leading this double life? Journalist by day, BDSM madam at night."

I sink deeper into my chair. "It's an undercover assignment I'm supposed to be working on," I confess, no longer capable of keeping secrets from the woman who is more like a best friend than a sister.

Lexi gasps, seemingly surprised.

"I was hand selected by Mr. Carson himself," I continue, my voice pompous and showy.

"Oh la la," Lexi croons, "is that who sent you the slip?"

I nod, even knowing she can't see me. "Yep," I reply, the one word drawn out dramatically. "He wouldn't want the lead investigator of the New York Daily Express turning up to an assignment looking shabby."

Lexi sighs heavily down the line. "*Please.* You could wear a paper bag, and it would look like you were draped in diamonds."

"Only because their scan wouldn't drop any lower than my bosoms." My voice cracks with laughter.

Minutes pass with nothing but Lexi's laugh shrilling down the line. God, it's a beautiful thing to hear. I cherish every single one as I know one day I'll never hear it again.

When her laughter starts playing havoc with her overworked lungs, Lexi says, "I love you and your impossible big rack, Cleo the Creep."

"Not as much as I love you and your monstrous tatters, Lexi the Leech," I reply as a broad grin stretches across my face.

After issuing our farewell in a more cordial manner, I lower the phone from my ear. Just before I switch it off, I hear Lexi calling my name.

"Yeah." I push the phone back to my ear.

"If it was a person at this club that caused you to come home with more life in your eyes than you've had since Tate passed away, don't treat it like an assignment. Treat it as if it's an adventure."

Guilt hangs heavy on my heart. "It's not that simple, Lexi. For one, I don't belong in that lifestyle. And two, I could lose my job if I don't hand in this assignment by the end of the month."

"So?" Lexi replies, her tone abrupt and clipped.

That's fine for her to say; she wasn't the one counting measly pennies from our childhood piggy bank last month to pay the electric bill.

Lexi sighs heavily. "I'm the one living on borrowed time, Cleo. Not you. Stop worrying about everyone else and for once put yourself first."

Stealing my chance to reply, she disconnects the call.

10

While placing freshly laundered clothes into my drawers, the quickest flash of white gathers my attention. Although there's only the smallest portion of the document sticking out from a pile of bills, I know what it is. It's the envelope the masked man handed me two weeks ago. He told me to only open it if I was curious. Although he has rarely left my thoughts the past two weeks, my curiosity has never reached the level it is now.

With the most scandalous of all political scandals unearthed earlier this week, Mr. Carson has seconded all investigative journalists at Global Ten Media onto the story dividing the nation. I won't lie, relief consumed me the instant he relieved me of my investigation into Chains.

Although I turned up to work and did my job to the best of my ability every day the past two weeks, my heart wasn't in the investigation. Not just because the digital security at Chains is the tightest I've ever seen, but because I knew the instant the story broke, I was not just exposing the men and women who value Chains' exclusivity clause, but the man behind the helm as well. The person who opened my eyes to the possibility not everyone who attends BDSM parties are evil and sadistic; they're humans as well. And quite possibly they could hold the traits of a man who would give a stranger comfort in her moment of need.

Granted, my research into the BDSM community has never gone as far as it did two weeks ago, but I've been broadening my horizons. Don't get me wrong, I haven't spent my weekends tied to someone's bedposts or had my backside spanked until it's red raw; I've just been interacting with members of the community in a non-physical element—via online chat forums.

Although I've had to take down a handful of creeps, I've also met some lovely people. Surprisingly, the careers of those involved in the BDSM lifestyle differ greatly. I've spoken to a school teacher, a single dad, an emergency room doctor, and even a handful of stay at home moms.

I kept my career title out of our conversations, but for the most part, I was forthright on why I was talking to them. I explained that their lifestyle was something placed on my radar, and that I was researching to see if it was a fit for me. Other than the three unsolicited dick pics that popped up, the information I've been given has been beneficial in my investigation.

Did it ease my curiosity on the identity of the unknown man? Not at all. But I feel like I understand him a little more now than I did during our exchange two weeks ago. Does that mean our gathering would have ended differently if I'd done more thorough research before we met? I doubt it. Although my curiosity remains piqued, I don't believe the BDSM lifestyle is for me. *If only I could say the same thing about the masked stranger.*

I change into a pair of fluffy pajamas and refill my glass of wine before snuggling under my thin feather down quilt. While sipping on the fruity wine in my glass, I log into my Kindle account. With Lexi's date spilling into the early hours of the morning, I'll continue my motherly stalk from the comfort of my bed. What better way to do that than with a bottle of aromatic wine and the latest new release from my all-time favorite author?

Thirty minutes and numerous missed lines later, I rest my kindle on my knees and swing my eyes to the envelope. Even with the engrossing words of a romance novel sucking me into a fictional world, my attention remains focused on the envelope. It's been glaring at me from across the room the past half an hour, begging for curiosity to eat me alive. *Clearly, the late hour has made me a little batty.*

Unable to harness my inquisitiveness for a second longer, I peel back my pink ruffled-edge quilt and pad toward my desk. A last-minute change of heart sees me logging into my outdated computer and firing up my email account. I gasp in a surprised breath when my computer dings, announcing I have one new email. In haste, I click on the attachment. My eyes skim the screen at a rate too quick for my brain to register. After exhaling the nerves jangling in my throat, I re-read the email. A dash of excitement thickens my blood when I spot the invitation from Luke, inviting Lexi and me to his twenty-seventh birthday party in a few weeks' time.

I return Luke's email, accepting his invitation before slumping into my chair and flicking my eyes to my bedside table. I sigh when I notice the time. It's a little after one AM. I'm glad Lexi's date is going well, but I'm beyond exhausted. Endeavoring to keep my eyelids from drooping, I play a few games of solitaire on my computer. The entire time I'm playing, the envelope from Chains calls my name on repeat.

When its efforts become too great for me to ignore—or for me to pretend I'm sane—I yank the envelope from its inconspicuous hiding place and rip it open. Just like the invitation I handed the hostess two weeks ago, this paper is super thin and elaborately gilded. Unlike the invitation, it's void of a lengthy disclosure statement. All it has is a website address and a pin code.

Adopting a nonchalant approach, I type the web address into the search engine and hit enter. I swear, I've never seen my internet provider work so fast before. The website pops up before a single qualm can filter through my overworked brain. The website format-ting is basic: nothing but a plain black screen with a silver chain filling the edges.

Snubbing my shaking hands, I click my mouse cursor into the

security access box and type the 24-digit code listed on the paper. Following the prompts on the screen, I pretend I'm downloading the latest movie on Passionflix. The only time I stop to think of what I'm doing is when an arrow pops up on the screen.

Following the direction of the arrow, my confused gaze locks in on a flashing red dot at the top of my monitor. I jump out of my skin when a computerized voice says, "Smile," before a clicking noise booms out of my ancient speakers. I sit slack-jawed and muted, shocked my computer snapped my picture without my consent.

My panic dulls from an out-of-control boil to a feeble simmer when a message flashes across the monitor, disclosing that the image was taken for security purposes and that all files are stored on a secure server even the world's best hacker couldn't infiltrate. *Like that helps the panic scorching my veins.*

Setting aside my churning stomach, I navigate through the website, seeking any clues that may assist in my investigation if the case into Chains is reopened.

"Yeah, keep telling yourself that, Cleo," I mumble under my breath.

There's only one man's identity I'm here to seek out. It isn't the gentleman with a creepy porn star mustache and slicked back hair that pops up on video chat within seconds of me joining the private chat room of Chains. It's the unnamed man with the mesmerizing green eyes.

Thirty minutes later, I haven't unearthed anything more compelling than the information I obtained in the private chat rooms I've been mingling in the past two weeks. Although Chains members' names are displayed in alphabetical order, just like the username I chose, all clients are utilizing an alias of some kind. And the handful of members who have photos attached to their accounts either have their faces covered by a mask, or they're concealed by a shadow.

I don't know whether to be disappointed or happy my scan of the members' faces failed to find a man with piercing green eyes and an alluring smile. I should run with happy, appreciative he isn't out trolling BDSM websites for a new submissive. *Unless he already has one?*

Unwarranted jealousy crackles through me, spurring an epidemic of emotions to consume me—confusion being the most potent of them all. I have no reason to be jealous of a man I don't know, but there's no doubt it's anger bristling my blood pressure. It's so strong, it's almost blinding.

Shutting down my unwarranted jealousy as nothing more than a bout of idiocy, I conclude that Chains' website was a waste of thirty minutes. With a twisted heart, I drag my mouse cursor to the logout button in the bottom right hand corner of my monitor. While hovering my mouse over the button, a new messenger window pops up. My heart lurches into my throat when it displays who is in the process of typing a message: *Master Chains.*

Although I'm two seconds away from logging out, no matter how much my rational brain encourages me to push the logout button, my hand refuses to comply with its demands. Before I have the chance to register my disgust that I'm having a heart versus mind battle over a man I have no right to be conversing with, a message pops up on my monitor.

Master Chains: *Curious?*

I consider not typing a response. The only reason I do is when I notice "seen at 1:43 AM" displayed at the bottom of the message screen. I may be treading into shark-infested waters, but the polite manners handed down from my parents make my decision less difficult.

For how many objections are running through my mind, I waste no time responding.

Cleopatra: *More like bored.*

The tightness clutching my heart loosens when I read his reply.

Master Chains: *If this is where you end up when you are bored, I wish I weren't so intriguing two weeks ago.*

Smiling that he remembers me, I type my response.

Cleopatra: Don't go out in the wind, your tickets might blow off.

Time stands still as I await his message.

Master Chains: If I'm going to be classed as weird, I may as well do it with confidence.

My girlish laugh bounces around the room as my fingers fly over my keyboard.

Cleopatra: So you're admitting you are weird?

Even with my tone aiming for playful, anticipation for his response still hangs thickly in the air.

Master Chains: I said "classed as weird," not "I'm weird." There's a difference.

Any concerns lingering in the back of my mind that I'm inter-acting with an owner of a BDSM clubs vanish as I type a response to his witty remark. There's nothing but silly giddiness fluttering in my stomach.

Cleopatra: That sounds like something only a weirdo would say.

His reply returns in an instant.

Master Chains: Precisely. . .

An inane grin stretches across my face as butterflies take flight in my stomach.

Cleopatra: You're so weird.

Master Chains: Says the expert on what is and isn't weird.

For the first time in weeks, I throw my head back and laugh.

When a set of headlights flash into my room, my eyes rocket to the alarm clock on my bedside table. The muscles in my jaw loosen when I notice the time displayed. Quicker than a blink of an eye, an entire hour has passed. I have no clue how to describe what Master Chains and I have talked about the past sixty minutes. It was an odd interac-tion of witty banter, corny jokes, and a handful of flirty messages between two people who should have nothing in common, but just gobbled up an hour of precious time via an internet chat.

Just like our impromptu get together two weeks ago, it has been an eye-opening experience. For the past hour, I truly forgot the stigma attached to Master Chains' lifestyle. I interacted with him as if he's a man, not a Dom attached to a paradoxical universe I know nothing about.

My attention shifts to my bedroom window when a car door closing booms through my ears. *Lexi must be home from her date.*

Setting aside the feeling of regret curtailing my regular breathing pattern, my fingers tap my keyboard.

Cleopatra: My sister has just returned home from a date. I should probably go.

I won't lie, I'm hoping he begs me to stay. The past hour has been unlike anything I've ever experienced. I enjoyed it so much, I'm not willing to let it end just yet.

Disappointment consumes me when he replies.

Master Chains: *Okay. It was nice talking to you, Cleo.*

Cleopatra: *You too. This was fun. . . although slightly weird.*

Master Chains: *I thought we already established this? Weird is my specialty.*

The heavy sentiment of regret on my chest weakens from his reply. Even though he's technically a stranger, I can hear the playful tone of his words. Perhaps that's why the past hour flew by so quickly? Within a matter of minutes, we both had an understanding of our personalities. I'm forthright, cheeky and have a bizarre desire to goad him. He has an edge of mysteriousness, accepts my attempts at inciting him with a sense of maturity, and he makes me forgot the heavy slate of worry I've been carrying the past four years. For the past hour, I was merely Cleo, a twenty-five-year-old New Jersey native talking to a man who can make her heart beat faster with nothing more than black words typed on a white screen.

Smiling, I type the perfect response to his message.

Cleopatra: *A wise man once told me being yourself doesn't make you weird or different; it makes you courageous. So, wear your weirdness with pride, Master Chains.*

A raging fire combusts in my core when I read his reply.

Master Chains: *Considering it's the only thing I'm wearing, I guess it must do.*

Like he can sense my frozen-in-lust stance his message instigated, another message closely follows his womb-combusting one.

Master Chains: *Goodnight, Cleo.*

I scrape my teeth over my bottom lip as I reply. It takes all my strength to type my three word response.

Cleopatra: *Goodnight, Master Chains.*

I stare at the monitor for several moments, hoping it will announce he's typing another message. Unfortunately, all I see is a blank message box. Swallowing down my uncalled-for disappointment, I push away from my desk and go hunt for Lexi.

After consuming two glasses of the wine Lexi brought home from her date and gorging on the orange poppy seed pudding she picked up at an all-night diner, I head back to my room, beyond exhausted. Even though it's a bitterly cold fall night, warmth is blooming across my chest. Not just because Lexi's date with Jackson went even better than the first five they've had, but because of my communication with Master Chains.

While relaying our exchange to Lexi, I realized how beautiful it was for him to spend an hour of his time with me just to kill my boredom. The last time we spoke, I was close-minded and unable to see the man behind the industry he worked in. Tonight strengthened my belief about evaluating a person before judging them. Although I'll never fully understand the metaphor, I didn't truly see Master Chains until I didn't see him.

The heat spreading across my chest inflames when my scan of my computer monitor has me stumbling upon a message that was not there earlier. I scramble across the room, tripping over a pair of jeans sprawled on the floor on my way. Excitement slicks my skin with sweat when I read his message.

Master Chains: *This may be pretentious of me, or perhaps even weird,* *but would you care to do what we did tonight all over again? Say 10 PM tomorrow?*

A childish smile etches onto my mouth as my fingers work the keyboard like a pro. My message is delivered before a single gripe is cited by my astute brain.

Cleopatra: *I'll bring the boredom; you bring the weirdness. See you tomorrow at 10 PM sharp.*

"I'm coming!" I shout from the hallway before entering my room. "Between work and a train derailing, I've only just walked in the door," I continue notifying my computer, like it will magically type what I'm saying and send it to Master Chains waiting on the other end.

Just as it has been every night the past two weeks, the message box on my computer monitor displays the same greeting.

Master Chains: I brought the weirdness. Did you bring the boredom?

Wanting to ensure he doesn't disappear before I've changed into some comfortable clothing, I drag my hand across the keyboard and hit send. My reply is gibberish, but it sends a clear message to Master Chains that I'm here. I could sit down and type a proper response, but considering our conversations extend into the wee hours of the morning, I would prefer to get comfortable before commencing our one-on-one chat.

"Have you eaten tonight?" Lexi startles me from her protective post in the hallway between our rooms.

While sliding down the zipper of my A-line business skirt, my spare hand digs into my oversized purse. A groan tears from Lexi's hard-lined lips when I produce a protein bar I purchased on my dash from my office building to Penn Station.

"Really?" Lexi's brows arch high into her hairline. "A protein bar? That's your idea of a nutritious meal?"

Grateful the overbearing mother baton I've been wielding the past four years has been passed to Lexi, I nod. Lexi laughs, shakes her head dismissively, then leaves my room. We've had similar interactions the past two weeks. She always responds in the same manner. I guess this is her way of showing she's here if I need her, but she's choosing not to meddle in my private affairs.

I want to say I've done the same for her in regards to her prospering relationship with Jackson. Unfortunately, that isn't true. For years, I've lived vicariously through my sister's love life, so even a heart-stopping kinship with Master Chains hasn't dampened my eagerness in her relationship in the slightest.

With Lexi needing to cram many years of living into her shortened lifespan, I want to ensure she cherishes every moment. If that can only be achieved with a bit of sisterly meddling, I'm willing to get my hands a little dirty. Because if anyone deserves to be swept off their feet by a prince on a white horse, it's Lexi.

Striving to ignore the sentimental tears looming in my eyes, I throw my hair into a messy bun, crack open my protein bar, and sink into my office chair. When I catch my reflection in the duchess mirror on my left, I'm not surprised to see excitement has heated my blood, enhancing my already tanned cheeks with a vibrant hue, and my eyes are wide and bright.

Although our conversations have stepped over a level acceptable for pen pals, nothing Master Chains and I have discussed the past two weeks has made me feel uncomfortable. Giddy. Intrigued. Horny. Those are words I would happily use to describe our hours together online. Me and the mysterious dark-haired man only known as Master Chains talk about everything: the news, my dragon boss, our plans for the upcoming festive season. The only thing we haven't discussed is what led to our nightly chats.

If I push aside that one small point, the budding relationship we are building is one of the closest I've had since my high school days. I don't know if it's because I'm hiding behind a computer monitor, but I'm myself around Master Chains. His appreciation for my witty banter has me exposing sides of my personality I haven't seen since my tragic loss four years ago. Somehow, he gets me, which is ludicrous considering I don't even know his real name.

Heat spreads across my cheeks when I read Master Chains' latest message.

Master Chains: *If that's a code you want me to decipher, I hate to tell you, I don't have the patience for riddles.*

My fingers glide over the keyboard at a record pace.

Cleopatra: *For some reason, I highly doubt that. You seem to have a lot of patience. It's nearly saint-like.*

My message isn't a total lie. Although we've only communicated via the internet, I've witnessed many sides to Master Chains the past two weeks. He's a little bossy, extremely forthright, kind and understanding, and he has a slight dash of patience. My theory is mainly based on the patience he has shown me the past two weeks. He can hold a flirty conversation without pushing for it to go to the next level. He's the only guy I've spoken to exclusively online who didn't demand a more tangible form of communication at the end of our first conversation.

Although I would love to hear his deep, manly voice again, it's guaranteed I won't make the move to push our relationship in that direction. I'm not just protecting my heart; I'm protecting my employment status. To me, our relationship doesn't cross any of the invisible lines I drew in the sand regarding my investigation into Chains last month. It may slightly blur them—or even fill them in a little—but it certainly doesn't cross them.

My eyes drop to my screen when I notice a new message flag flashing on the screen.

Master Chains: *Saint is a word not in my vocabulary.*

Cleopatra: *Then maybe you should add it? Master Saint has a nice ring to it—even my blasted eardrums agree.*

His reply is almost instant.

Master Chains: Blasted eardrums?

I exhale a deep breath.

Cleopatra: L.O.N.G story. . . One I'd rather tackle after a steamy shower. Desecration is best discussed with a clean slate.

My challenging week had one final hurdle I had to leap over before I was granted escape to the wonderment of a weekend. I had a two-hour sit down with Delilah. Pleasant is not a word I'll ever use to describe that lady. Even with Mr. Carson requesting for our department's focus to remain on the political scandal covering every front page in the country, Delilah demanded an update on my investigation into Chains—and she wanted it last week.

Guilt made itself comfy with my chest during our meeting, but no information I handed Delilah had me double-guessing my friendship with Master Chains. As requested during our initial meeting in Mr. Carson's office, I keep my personal and business lives separate. Nothing I mentioned during our longwinded meeting included the private conversations I've held with Master Chains.

Although Master Chains works in an industry that leaves a bitter taste in my mouth when people mention it, the past two weeks taught me that doesn't mean he's a horrid person. What he said the night in his playroom is true. He's just a regular person. . . but in a weirder, kinkier type of way.

As I throw my arms into the air to stretch out a tiresome week, another message pops up on my computer screen.

Master Chains: Where were you tonight, Cleo? You're over an hour late.

Even through a typed message, I can't miss the concern in his voice.

Cleopatra: Slaying a fire-breathing dragon one witty line at a time.

His reply arrives in an instant.

Master Chains: Was it a female or male dragon?

My lips quirk as keys tapping sounds through my ears.

Cleopatra: Does it matter either way? As long as the dragon was slayed, and the princess was saved, the gender of the dragon shouldn't be of any concern.

My breathing shallows as I await his reply. I stated earlier I've witnessed many sides of him the past two weeks, but this is a side I have yet to witness. Rarely do our conversations mention an outside party. Usually, the focus remains solely on us.

Master Chains: Maybe not to mere mortals, but for weirdos like me, the gender, orientation, and intention of the fire-breathing dragon you were wrestling late on a Friday night is something I want to know. Desperately.

My heart rate climbs to a never-before-reached level as I type a reply.

Cleopatra: How desperate?

For how quickly he responds, I swear he intuited my reply.

Master Chains: Desperate enough my hands are twitching.

My brows stitch as confusion etches onto my face.

Cleopatra: What does desperation and twitching hands have in common?

The instant I hit the enter button, the reasoning behind his message smacks into me. It excites me more than I'd care to admit. Leaving my hang-ups about whom I am conversing with, my fingers fly over the keyboard.

Cleopatra: I'm sorry, spanking or any other sexual activities must first be discussed between the Dom and submissive in lengthy detail before such tasks can be undertaken. It's protocol.

Even knowing I shouldn't be riling him up, I can't help it. What the bartender said is right. I truly am a brat.

I brace my elbows on my desk when his reply flashes up on the screen. His message is short—six small words, but I have to read it three times in a row, certain my tired brain isn't understanding it correctly.

Master Chains: What's your cell phone number?

This time, my reply takes me a little longer to type.

Cleopatra: I don't think that's a good idea. Have we reached the talking on the phone stage of our friendship yet?

Panic, mixed with a strong sense of excitement makes my stomach a horrid mess as I await his response.

Master Chains: You can either give it to me, or I'll have someone in my IT department find it for me.

I should be appalled by his response, but for some reason unbeknownst to me, I'm not. Nothing but unbridled excitement is blazing through my veins, clouding my perception. Clearly, since I reply:

Cleopatra: Please disregard every derogatory name I've called you the past two weeks. You are not at all weird. You're a creepy stalker. I can't believe I got them mixed up. They're two entirely different entities.

I push send before I lose the nerve.

Master Chains: You're approximately five seconds away from finding out exactly how creepy I am.

Adrenaline pumps through my heart so fast I fear it will burst out of my chest.

Cleopatra: Is that a threat, Master Chains?

All noise surrounding me ceases to exist as I glare at the monitor, eagerly anticipating his reply.

Master Chains: A threat is something issued when it isn't a guarantee. So, no, Cleo, that was not a threat.

I graze my teeth over my bottom lip as I contemplate a response. I'm genuinely at a loss on how to reply. Numerous times the past week I've typed out a similar request, only to delete it before I hit send. Courage has never been a weak point for me, but there's something about this man that has me acting differently than I usually would. I don't know if it's because every conversation we've had makes me giddy or because I truly know nothing can come from our bizarre connection. Not just because I was assigned to investigate his club, but because we live entirely different lifestyles. Although I've always believed opposites attract, that logic can only stretch so far before it would eventually snap. Wouldn't it?

In an apparent response to my internal battle, another message from Master Chains pops up on my monitor.

Master Chains: You stood in my playroom with your face as white as a ghost, and your eyes panicked, yet that hasn't stopped us talking the past two weeks. Don't you think we're past sexting?

My throaty laugh bounces off the stark walls of my room.

Cleopatra: Sexting? If the past two weeks have been your idea of sexting, you need to up your game, Mister.

My lips form into an O when I hit send. I really should stop and consider my responses before hitting the enter button. The logical side of my brain knows our conversations have hit a point of being unacceptable for friends, but my lust-driven heart is too focused on its goals to listen to its morally right counterpart. It's beyond saving when it comes to this man.

Master Chains: Master. And hence the point in me asking for your number. . . I'm trying to "up my game."

My fingers fly over the keyboard so fast, I'm certain I've just broken the Guinness Book of World Records for the fastest typing speed.

Cleopatra: Up your game or whisper wicked thoughts into my ear, Master Chains?

Jesus, where did that naughty vixen emerge from?

The angry scold of my astute mind blurs into the background when I read Master Chains' next message.

Master Chains: Grrrr <<< That's me growling. If we were talking, I wouldn't have to type it out.

I punch my cellphone number into the message box so fast, my fingers threaten to go on strike. What? I'm not a complete idiot. Who wouldn't want to hear a man with pulse-racing good looks growling over the phone? Furthermore, I'm an adult who can shut down our friendship the instant it steps over a level no longer acceptable.

I roll my eyes skywards. "Yeah, sure you can, Cleo," I reprimand myself.

My eyes rocket to the side when my cellphone vibrates on my bedside table not even ten seconds later. Pushing back from my desk, I stand from my chair and pace to my phone. My heart is thrashing against my chest, and a crazy throb has clustered low in my stomach.

After wiping the sweat coating my palms on my stretchy yoga pants, I swipe my finger across the screen of my phone advising I have a private number calling me.

"Hello," I greet, my voice husky with both arousal and excitement.

"Cleo."

His deep and rugged voice sends a shiver of excitement down my spine. I don't know why, but for the past two weeks, I didn't hear his voice with the same amount of authority it commands in real life. I shouldn't be surprised, though. You can't express anything via a computer program, let alone the raspy roughness of an alluring male voice.

The first question fired off Master Chains' tongue sets alarm bells ringing in my ethical brain, "Are you seeing anyone, Cleo?"

Three long heartbeats pass before I stammer out, "Not right now."

"Does that mean you're seeking a relationship?" he queries, his words low and thigh-shakingly dangerous.

Even hearing a range of emotions in his voice doesn't help gauge his true feelings. I can't tell if he's angry right now? Curious? Jealous? Is he just being nosy? Or is he genuinely interested in my reply?

I guess there's only one way to find out.

"Maybe. . ." I breathe out slowly, my voice high in uncertainty.

Five minutes pass without a syllable escaping his lips. I'm so convinced our call has disconnected, I pull my phone away from my ear every twenty seconds to check the timer is still counting down. It is.

I lick my dry lips before asking, "Is me wanting to date a problem for you?"

Disappointment slashes me open when he replies not even two seconds later. "No."

My freshly cut wounds stop gushing blood when he adds on, "Yes. No. I don't know." His words are as ruffled as my composure.

My jittering hands make it hard for me to keep my phone pressed to my ear. "If it makes you feel any better, between work and talking to you every night, I barely have time to shower, let alone date."

"There's a difference between not having the time and not wanting to make the time. Saying you're 'too busy' is just an excuse. If dating is something you truly want to do, you'll make the time for it," Master Chains responds, his deep voice teeming with antagonism.

I stand frozen in my room, replaying his words over and over again in my head. No matter how many times I hear it, I come to the same conclusion: he sounds jealous.

"Maybe at this stage of my life, I don't want to date."

My high voice exposes my excitement to his unwarranted jealousy. There has only been one man on my mind the past month. Him. It's nice to know I'm not the only one harboring confusion regarding our bizarre kinship.

The swiftness of Master Chains' reply shocks me. "You just said you want to date. Now you're saying you don't want to. It's either one of the other, Cleo; which one is it?"

"Jesus, did someone wake up on the wrong side of the bed? Why are you so moody? You asked me a question; I answered as honest as I could. Do I want to date? Yes, I do. Does that mean I'll drag myself around Manhattan like a floozy desperate to get a ring on her finger? No, it doesn't. Unlike you and your lifestyle, normal people don't have a pre-drawn questionnaire to fill out to make sure they're partnered with the right person. Thus, not only making dating hard, it also means it sucks!"

Clearly, Master Chains isn't the only one having a bad day. My mood is just as woeful as his.

"Maybe if those normal people you mention in every conversation had a questionnaire like the one at Chains, you wouldn't have such a hard time finding a suitable man to date." .

I gasp in a shocked breath, stunned at the bluntness of his reply.

"Oh, believe me, Master Chains, if I truly want to date, I'll have no troubles finding a fitting suitor. Actually, this conversation is enticing me to jump back onto the dating bandwagon. As riveting as our conversations have been, there are some key elements missing only face-to-face contact can achieve."

Apparently, my desire to goad him over the phone is just as potent as it is in person.

My breathing turns labored when he mutters, "You should count your lucky stars we are talking over the phone, Cleo. My hands have never twitched so much."

I try to fire a smart-ass remark off my tongue, but no matter how much my mouth moves, not a single noise seeps from my lips — not even a grunt. My body is too engrossed in calming the fiery rage burning in my stomach to hold a conversation, let alone one with a man whose voice hits every one of my hot buttons.

Reading the silent prompts of my body like he intimately knows me, Master Chains drops his deep voice to a seductive purr while muttering, "From the breath you just took, I'm going to mark down a five in the spanking column of your questionnaire."

"You still have that?" The arousal curled around my throat makes me sound like I'm in the throes of an earth-shattering climax.

My ears prick when I hear the ruffling of paper. Although embarrassed he can hear my rapid pants, I like this new element of our kinship, the one that includes background noises. I've often wondered what he was doing in the process of our messaging. Was he at Chains, or surrounded by family and friends? With nothing but the soft exhalations of his breath sounding down the line, I can imagine he's in a similar environment to me—a quiet spot in the comfort of his home.

Master Chains' deep timbre drags me back to the present when he says, "I carry your questionnaire with me everywhere I go."

A rustle of air parts my lips. "You do?"

He waits a beat before replying. "No, I don't. But I heard flattery gets you everywhere."

My cheeks groan in protest from the sudden incline of my smile. "You better watch out, Master Chains. My corny metaphors are rubbing off on you."

"That isn't what I want you to rub against me," he growls down the line, causing every fine hair on my body to stand to attention.

His playful banter forces me to ask, "Is this the way it will be every time we talk? You whispering wicked thoughts into my ear?"

God, I hope he says yes.

"Depends." He draws out the one word as if it's an entire sentence.

The swiftness of my reply displays my eagerness. "On what exactly?"

He waits until the suspense thickening the air becomes murderous before saying, "On how long it takes us to finish your questionnaire."

I've barely caught my breath from the raw huskiness of his voice when he asks, "Blindfolds? Beatings? Being bitten?"

It takes a lot of effort, but I push out, "Are we really going down the questionnaire road again?"

"Yes," he replies, his stern voice unwavering. "You said it yourself, Cleo. Spanking or any other sexual preferences must first be discussed between the Dom and his sub in lengthy detail before such tasks can be undertaken. It's protocol. I would hate to break protocol."

"If protocol is truly a concern of yours, shouldn't you be the one answering the questionnaire?" My voice is back to its usual self, friendly with a hint of cheekiness. "How come I've been designated as the submissive? Because I can sure as hell tell you, if anyone is going to be flogged with the chain flogger you have in your playroom, it won't be me."

Blood surges to my pussy when the manly growl I wanted to hear earlier tears through my eardrums. It's rugged and drawn out, and it sends my libido into unchartered waters.

"Does that mean you've been thinking about my playroom, Cleo?"

Even knowing I should shut down this conversation before it ventures into a situation not acceptable for a budding friendship, I brazenly whisper, "Maybe."

"And?" he growls in a low, raspy tone.

Although we are talking on the phone, I swear I can feel his breath on my neck.

"And what?" I fill in when he fails to expand on his question.

He waits four heartbeats before asking, "Does that mean you're curious about this. . . lifestyle, Cleo?"

I swear, I nearly fall into orgasmic bliss from the way he growls "lifestyle." I take a few moments considering a reply before stammering out, "No."

He releases a sharp, disappointed breath, forcing me to say, "Yes. No. I don't know."

My response mimics the reply he gave when I asked if me dating bothered him. Obviously, I'm not the only baffled by our peculiar friendship.

"Well since we are both harboring confusion in regards to what we want to achieve from our acquaintance, why don't we get the formalities out of the way first, then we can work on the confusion," Master Chains suggests.

"I'm not confused," I argue, my tone strong. "I know *exactly* what you want from this acquaintance."

I hear him adjust his position, but he doesn't utter a word. Wanting to coerce a reaction out of him, I declare, "You want to fuck me, Master Chains." I stun myself with the crudeness of my statement.

My brain doesn't have the chance to register its disgust before he replies, "Fuck is not a word I'd use to describe what I want to do to you, Cleo." His words are unaffected by my lack of dignity. "Devour. Worship. Possess. Those are more suitable words for what I want to do to you."

Just like the night we met, his words make me hot and needy. But, thankfully, this time he's unable to see my reaction to the frankness of his reply. Although, I'm sure my quick breaths give away my excitement, he can't see the childish squirming I'm doing to lessen the throb between my legs.

I don't know how much time passes before Master Chains asks, "So, Cleo, let me ask you again. Blindfolds? Beatings? Being bitten?"

Enough time passes that the insane pulse between my legs simmers to a dull ache, but it isn't long enough for me to regain my shrewdness. Obviously, since I ask, "What was the number scale again?"

12

_____

"Happy Birthday, Cleo."

The rough huskiness of Master Chains' voice drawing out my name causes every nerve in my body to activate. My breathing turns labored as a feverous wildfire takes hold in my sex. Just like we did the weeks following our first internet conversation, for the past two weeks, Master Chains and I have continued with our nightly discussions. But now, instead of interacting via a computer, we talk on the phone—every day.

I should be embarrassed admitting this out loud, but I'm not. My conversations with Master Chains have led to many self-induced, mind-blowing orgasms the past two weeks. I thought our chat messages were risqué; they're _nothing_ compared to our phone conversations. They're just. . . _whoa!_ They blow my mind. His voice alone quickens my pulse, let alone the vast range of libido-bolstering words coming out of his sinfully wicked mouth.

Don't get me wrong, we don't just discuss sex when we talk. We talk about anything and everything that crosses our minds, but his voice is so deliciously seductive even the most mundane conversation is ten times better when spoken by him.

Sauntering deeper into my room, I reply, "Thank you."

My short reply is unable to conceal my slurred words. After drinking half a bottle of the decadent wine he gifted me for my birthday, I may be slightly tipsy—if not drunk. I've always been a cheap drunk, rarely getting past two glasses before the welcoming alcoholic buzz warms my veins. *Obviously, tonight is no different.*

It feels like an eternity passes before Master Chains asks, "Did you drink the entire bottle by yourself, Cleo?"

"No." The childish hiccup parting my lips weakens my statement. "Although, the half a bottle I drank has me slightly adrift from tipsy and well on my way to being drunk."

If I've learned anything the past two weeks, it's that I can't lie to Master Chains. No matter how many times a little white lie sat on the tip of my tongue, begging to be released, my mouth refused to relinquish it. I don't know why, but I have a feeling even if I were to lie to him, he'd tell, so why bother?

"Do you have a glass of water beside your bed as stated on the gift tag?"

I nod. "Check!"

"Headache tablets?"

"Sure do." I pull back the covers of my bed.

"Did you eat before drinking?"

"Uh huh," I answer, nodding.

"Would you care to be my sub?" he groans in a low, pussy-shaking growl.

Standing frozen next to my bed, I demand for my lungs take in air as I strive to ignore the little voice inside of me screaming "yes" on repeat. My lungs follow the commands of my body, but no matter how much air they gulp in, it doesn't feel like enough. The room is strangled of oxygen since the heady aroma of lust is thick in the air. Giddiness clusters in my mind just as rampantly as a tingling sensation gathers in my stomach. I'm breathless, panicked, and incredibly turned on.

I only start breathing again when Master Chains says, "I'm being facetious, Cleo. You were overly obliging, so I thought I'd test the waters. I would have hated to miss the opportunity to have you shackled to the St. Andrews Cross in my playroom if you had had a change of heart."

The pulse in my soaked sex goes from a leisured canter to a brisk gallop when the image of me bound and at his complete mercy flashes before my eyes.

Blaming my body's disturbing response to his tease on the alcohol, I say, "The instant I have a change of heart, you'll be the first to know." My words are strangled from the arousal curled around my throat.

"That sounds like a challenge, Cleo. Are you challenging me?" His voice is gritty and spine-tinglingly delicious.

It's the fight of my life to say, "No. That was merely a fact; not a challenge."

My frozen stance resumes when his wicked growl sounds down the line. It's panty-wetting good and sets my pulse racing. Softly sighing at my lack of dignity around him, I slip into my bed and nuzzle into my comforter. It isn't as warm and inviting as Master Chains' flirtatious invitation, but it's better than nothing.

After rolling on to my side to lessen my woozy head, I ask, "Can I ask you something, Master Chains?"

I hear him adjusting his position before he replies, "Anything."

His simplistic response doesn't surprise me. He's been nothing but forthright with me since the first night we spoke. He expressed his desires for me in a confidence most men lack, but he did it in a way that didn't make my skin crawl. If I'm being honest, his approach made me wish I could step outside the lines I deem acceptable for our friendship. Every minute I talk to him adds another minute of doubt to my muddled brain. He has me thinking dangerous thoughts —*reckless thoughts*. But no matter how many times I try to shut down the friendship I know has branched into hazardous territory, I can't do it. Talking to him is the highlight of my day, so how can I be expected to give that up?

Hearing my name breathed heavily down the line returns my focus to the present.

"Sorry, I kind of spaced out there for a minute," I say, explaining the reason behind my absence.

"Spacing out I can handle. You falling asleep. . . not so much. With you trekking across New York today, we've barely had a chance to talk as it is."

His reply strengthens the giddiness the half a bottle of wine caused to my head. It also proves I'm not the only one cherishing our daily talks. I'm glad I have a similar effect on him. It may be a bizarre and weird sensation, but it's still there nonetheless.

"Ask your question, Cleo, before the alcohol takes hold." The smooth command of his voice enhances the knowledge of his statement.

I scraping my teeth over my bottom lip. "Have you ever hurt anyone? In your playroom?"

My eyes bulge. The alcohol lacing my veins must be making me more brazen than normal. Although we've discussed many topics the past four weeks, I usually strive to keep our conversation away from the BDSM lifestyle. But after enduring a day that can only be described as perfect, my interest in unveiling the man with the molten lava voice is becoming as desperate as my lungs' desire to breathe.

Master Chains waits a beat before answering, "Yes."

Air whooshes out of my mouth in a brutal grunt, amplifying my dizzy state.

"But only because my sub wanted me to." His words are as fast as my pants of breath. "I'm not a sadist, Cleo. I would never hurt a sub unless she indicated an interest in that type of play. I don't instill pain for my own pleasure; I issue it to entice it."

"Pain for pleasure? That doesn't make any sense." My words slur with an equal amount of alcohol and confusion.

"It doesn't have to make sense to you, Cleo. Just like your sexual preferences may not suit every native New Jersey girl, the preferences of a sub vary greatly. It's the compatibility of the Dom and his sub that should be your greatest concern, not what they do behind closed doors. Contrary to what society tells you, what happens between them is no one's business but theirs."

I take a moment to consider his reply before saying, "But what if a Dom shows an interest in someone who doesn't want to be hurt? Would he just coerce her or him to change their mindset?"

Although my questions allude to Doms in general, the uncertainty in my words reveals who my questions are really directed at: us.

"A BDSM relationship isn't molding someone to be whom you want them to be." His quicken voice displays he knows whom my questions are referring to. "It's about understanding someone's differences and appreciating them."

"Appreciating them? Or power tripping them? Isn't a BDSM lifestyle just a ruse for a modern man cave? A place where men can bang their chests and be the king of their castle without giving two hoots about the poor defenseless slaves entrenched under them?"

"A slave is a person with no power or rights," Master Chains retaliates, his voice void of the snarkiness mine is holding.

"A slave is a person who must legally obey his master, *Master Chains*." My voice cracks with emotion, hating that he doesn't crave a normal relationship like me. "Slaves don't have any power, as it's taken away from them, just like it's taken away from submissives."

"No, Cleo, that's where you're wrong." Although I can't see him, I can imagine him shaking his head. "A sub does *not* have their power taken away from them. They give it, fully, willing and able. When they entrust their rights, their desires, and themselves to another, it's given as a gift, not taken."

"Why would they do that? Why would anyone in the 21st century give up their power?"

"Because they understand the importance of power to a man who had none." The pain in his voice startles me. "The transfer of power between a Dom and his sub is a gift, Cleo. A treasured gift. It's not something ever stolen."

Regret curls around my throat, tightening more and more as his reply plays on repeat in my hazy mind. Even with the buzz only alcohol can create hindering my perception, I couldn't miss the pain in his words. They sliced through me like brittle shards of glass, cutting and disfiguring my heart so it's as ugly as my callous and baseless words. I called him to thank him for his kind generosity today, and all I ended up doing is arguing about a world I know nothing about using fictitious information obtained by others. I thought I was a broad-minded person. Clearly, I'm not.

"I'm sorry," I force out through a sob. "I shouldn't have pushed. . ." *I'm just scared to death of how you make me feel.* "It's been a long day, and I'm letting my tiredness speak on my behalf--"

"Cleo, stop," Master Chains demands, interrupting my apology.

My body jumps to his command. I smack my lips together and level out my breathing. For several seconds, nothing but my pants of breath sound down the line as I struggle to keep my conflicting emotions at bay. Our conversation was heated, but full of intrigue, and it has my emotions sitting on edge.

"It's your birthday; please don't cry," he pleads softly, proving his uncanny ability to read my emotions by hearing nothing but my breaths. Considering most of our interactions have only been over the phone, I find that astounding.

"Why don't we save our discussion of the complex neuroses of a Dom and his sub for a day you're not celebrating?"

The gentleness of his words make my endeavor not to cry nearly unwinnable, but I give it my best shot. I bite hard on the inside of my cheek as my eyes drift to the bouquet of red roses sitting on my bedside table—one of many birthday gifts from Master Chains to me.

"Tell me what you did today?" His soft purr drags my focus away from a complex issue too complicated for my tipsy brain.

My teeth scrape over my bottom lip before I answer, "I had an adventure. One of the best days of my life."

"Until we meet again."

Even the demand in his voice can't stop a huge smile spreading across my face.

The alcohol warming my veins speaks on behalf of my heart. "Until we meet again."

I hear his cheeks rising over the phone, pleased at my agreeing response. He has dropped several hints the past month about us meeting. I've never taken his bait until now. Just interacting with him is a careless move on my part, but he makes me so reckless, I refuse to consider the repercussions our friendship could cause to our lives.

"In my playroom?"

Giggling, I offer him the same response I've given every day the past two weeks. "Keep dreaming."

He chuckles a pussy-tingling laugh. "Lucky I'm an optimist determined to make my dreams come true."

I roll my eyes while adjusting my position. My annoyed response is a complete lie. I'm far from annoyed, more like grateful we've steered our conversation back in the direction it usually follows: flirty and friendly.

"That's the problem with optimists; they think they changed the world. Little do they know it was the realist who did all the work."

"Spoken like a true pessimist."

I screw up my nose and stick out my tongue.

His rough groan causes the hairs on my neck to prickle. "There are much better things you could be doing with your tongue than immaturely sticking it out."

"Yeah. . . but it wouldn't be as much fun." My words are tainted with laughter.

"Oh, baby, I assure you it would be ten times better."

"Is that a challenge, Master Chains?" I mimic the deep tone he used earlier.

"No, Cleo, that wasn't a challenge. It was a guarantee," he breathes out heavily, forcing my thighs to squeeze together. "And unless you're determined to discover I'm a man of my word, you better tell me about this adventurous day you had before I jump on the first flight to New Jersey to prove it to you firsthand," he continues, pretending he's unaware of what my day entailed.

His response is an utter lie. He knows exactly what I did today, as he planned the entire thing. Although the diamond pendant dangling around my neck is one of the most dazzling I've seen, that isn't the reason I love it. It was the journey I undertook to discover it that was the most awarding. A simple text message started a day unlike anything Lexi and I have ever experienced. We went on a treasure hunt across New York using nothing but the clues Master Chains sent me.

It all started with a riddle.

Master Chains: *New York City is being terrorized by monkeys who escaped the zoo. Hurry Cleo, the people of Manhattan are counting on you.*

It took Lexi and me approximately ten minutes to discover what the riddle was referring to: the Manhattan Mayhem Room. With nothing but time on our hands—and Master Chains not replying to my calls—we drove to the location stated in the riddle. We were greeted by the hostess of Manhattan Mayhem Room with a single red rose and an hour-long experience of their reality escape game. It was a thrilling and addictive morning.

Upon exiting, the hostess handed me a printed card. From the impressive cursive and the elegant gilded paper, it didn't take a genius to realize the message was written by Master Chains. It read:

Since the monkeys have returned to the zoo,
why don't you go watch one scratch his head too?

I didn't need to ask Lexi if she wanted to continue with the game Master Chains instigated. The inane grin etched on her face gave her reply. She was just as eager as me. And thus, our day continued. For every location we visited, we received a single red rose and another clue. We stopped by classic New York landmarks we've seen many times, and ones we've always wanted to visit but never had the chance.

Our final location was Steven Kirsch's jewelry store on W 46th street. That was the first time doubt entered my mind the entire day. What Master Chains did for me today was beautiful and heartfelt, but I had already taken advantage of his generosity, so I wasn't willing to accept something of great monetary value as well.

When I informed Lexi of my reservation, she dragged me through the single glass door like a woman on a mission. My god, for a little petite Latin lady, she has the strength of ten gladiators.

My plan to leave without the gift Master Chains purchased for me was left for dust when the shopping assistant showed me what Steven Kirsch had personally designed for me. It was a white gold pendant shaped into a chain link. The half carat perfectly cut brilliant diamond suspended in the middle of the link gave the manly design a feminine touch. It was simply striking and so unique I couldn't resist picking it up and slipping it around my neck, where it has stayed the past four hours.

"Then I drank half a bottle of wine and gorged on cake like it was calorie free." I finish the story Master Chains already knows. "It was sugary and delicious, and it made me wonder if your lips would taste just as sweet."

I snap my mouth shut, mortified I said my private statement out loud. I've had many reckless thoughts about Master Chains the past six weeks, but I've never once carelessly blurted them out.

The panic roaring through my veins dulls when Master Chains' virile laugh barrels down the line. It's a beautiful noise that pushes aside every reservation lingering in the back of my mind. Not just the ones that popped up today, but every one I've had since the day we met.

"Note to self, a tipsy Cleo is the most honest of them all," he snickers down the line, his commanding voice choked with laughter.

With my hand hovering over the budded nipples his laughter incited, I say, "I don't know how to lie to you. You seem to have this magic hold over me that ensures I speak nothing but the truth when it comes to you."

"Hmmm," he murmurs down the line. "If that was the case, Cleo, you wouldn't have denied my advances weeks ago in my playroom. Instead of listening to your wants, you allowed the philosophies of others to guide your decision."

"That's not true." I shake my head. "I'm not a sheep. I make my own decisions."

Master Chains coughs to clear his throat before saying, "The first thing members of this lifestyle overcome are people's misguided mindsets. They learn that at one stage, every relationship has a stigma attached to it, whether it's religion, age, gender or because their sexual desires don't follow the line deemed acceptable by society. Even Adam and Eve were frowned upon at one stage."

"Preaches the man who conceals his face in the one place he should feel the most comfortable," I blurt out, my words muffled by a soft moan rippling through my lips.

"Throwing a man into the unknown ensures he will come out more determined than ever." Before I can demand clarification on his statement, he continues speaking, "You wanted me that night in Chains, but you were too blinded by the public's concept of normal to act on it."

I remain quiet, unable to negate his accurate statement. What he's saying is true. Even being immersed in an environment unlike anything I've ever imagined, I wanted him—*badly*—but I refused to act on the prompts of my body, believing my moral compass was pushed off-kilter from the demoralizing acts I witnessed the hour prior.

My inability to deny his account of the night we met commences the first stretch of silence our conversations have had the past two weeks. Normally, we only pause for bathroom breaks or when Lexi snatches my cell out of my grasp before tearing through our house like a three-year-old with me snapping at her heels, demanding the return of my phone.

Although a gap of silence is a rare occurrence for us, it doesn't feel awkward. It enhances our bizarre connection and allows my body to begin shutting down from a thrilling, yet exhausting day.

A short time later, I hear sheets ruffling before Master Chains breathes out, "You know that would feel better if I were doing it."

I freeze for a minute, confused by his comment. It's only during another period of silence does the reasoning behind his statement become clear. Without realizing what I'm doing, I'm rolling my erect nipple between my thumb and finger. I assumed the zapping of ecstasy tingling down my spine was from Master Chains' sultry laugh; I had no clue it was because I was stimulating myself while listening to his rugged pants of breath rustling down the line.

I snap my hands away from my chest, appalled at my deplorable behavior. My panic soars when the entirety of the situation dawns on me.

How did he know what I was doing?

My tired eyes bounce around my room. Shock and panic are smeared over my face. Ever since I had the surveillance camera placed in the bead of my negligée, I've been mindful of my personal security. I've never felt as violated as I did that morning in my office. Not even when being propositioned at an exclusive BDSM club.

Failing to find anything suspicious in my room, I return my focus to my cell. "How did you know what I was doing?" I cringe, loathing that I just admitted I was touching myself. "Not that I was doing *that*."

A tiger-like yawn breaking free from my mouth nearly drowns out Master Chains' reply, "Your breathing gives away your excitement, Cleo. You were panting heavier than normal."

"Maybe I fell asleep? "I reason, saying anything to lessen the embarrassment heating my cheeks. "I'm extremely tired."

"Because it's your birthday, I'll let your lie slide." Master Chains' deep voice lowers to a husky purr entices my breathless state. "It would be wise not to test my patience tomorrow, Cleo."

Another tense stretch of silence descends upon us, once again void of any awkwardness. It enhances our undeniable sexual connection while also adding to the tiredness drooping my eyelids.

The fatigued expression marring my face switches to anticipation when Master Chains mutters, "Don't stop what you were doing on my behalf, Cleo." His voice sounds labored, as if he too is struggling with conflicting viewpoints. "Sometimes the best way to learn how you can please someone is by pleasing yourself."

"I'm fairly sure that's something only a desperate person would say." My words are strangled with need. They're breathless and evidently display my heightened state of arousal. "Are you desperate, Master Chains?"

"Desperate to touch you." I hear the quickening of his pulse in his words. "To lick, caress, and bite you. To see your skin turn pink under the hand."

My back arches from the sheer hunger displayed in his deep tone. I try to think of a witty comeback to switch our conversation to a more respectable territory, but my attempts come up short. My senses are too heightened by his confession to form a rational thought, and the alcohol warming my blood is encouraging my recklessness.

"Do you want to come, Cleo?" His voice sends a shiver of excitement down my spine. "To end your birthday reveling on the high of an orgasm?"

I take a second to consider a response before moaning, "Yes."

I've tiptoed too far into the haze of orgasm to register the aftermath my confession may have. Nothing but the chase of climax is on my mind.

"Do you want me to help you come?" The animalistic roughness of his voice tightens every muscle in my body.

"Yes, please, Master Chains," I beg as my eyes flick to my bedroom door to ensure it's closed.

I don't know why I'm being so modest. I just asked a stranger to help me orgasm. I don't think modesty has a place in my personality anymore.

My legs scissor together when Master Chains' throaty groan sounds down the line. I've never heard anything as provocative in my life.

A chair being dragged across a wooden floor booms into my ears before he says, "If you follow every command I give, I'll let you come."

My lungs saw in and out as I nod. "Okay."

"Every command, Cleo. No hesitation."

"I understand," I advise, panting.

"Good girl." He sounds pleased.

With my eyes snapped shut, I follow the instructions he recites down the line. I slither my hand over my quivering stomach, stopping just above the rim of my daisy-printed panties. My heart rate kicks up a notch when I dip my fingers inside the waistband of the cotton material. I'm still inches away from the area aching for release, but

I'm panting, hot, and on the verge of ecstasy. Master Chains' voice alone is enough to have me sitting on the edge of a very steep cliff, let alone the wicked things he's whispering in my ear.

"You're not to touch your clit, Cleo. You're too sensitive, and I don't want this to be over yet," Master Chains instructs, his voice stern and tempting.

Nodding, I slip two fingers between the folds of my pussy to coat them with wetness. I'm shocked by my brazenness. I didn't even flinch when my arousal graced my fingertips.

What's this man doing to me?

At the request of Master Chains, I open my eyes before sliding my fingers inside my clenching core. We moan in sync, a rough, thunderous groan that strengthens my excitement when my fingers push in deeper.

"Tell me what it feels like, Cleo. Are you wet? Tight?" His voice strained with arousal.

"Uh huh." My two short words are drowned by a breathless grunt. "It's snug and warm." *And would feel ten times better if it were your fingers.*

Master Chains' rough groans force my fingers to pump into me faster. I raise my backside off my bed and rock my hips in a rhythm matching the thrusts of my fingers. My mind is shut down; my body overwhelmed by the chase of climax.

With my other hand, I press my cell closer to my ear, loving the fast pants of his breaths coming down the line. He sounds as if his own orgasm is building as rapidly as mine, and it adds to my excitement.

In an embarrassingly short period of time, the familiar tightening of an impending climax spreads across my core. My vagina clamps around my fingers, and it grows wetter.

"I'm close," I warn, my entire body quaking.

The scent of my arousal mingles with the air when I kick the duvet off my legs, my body too overheated with desire to need a blanket. My knees shake when I use my palm to add pressure to my throbbing clit. It sends a jolt of ecstasy all the way to my drenched core.

"Oh god," I grunt over and over again, too stuck in the trance of climax to garble more coherent words.

"Not yet," Master Chains shouts down the line. "Do not come, Cleo. Do you understand me?"

"Oh. . . please. . . I'm so close." My words are separated by desperate moans, my need to come blinding me.

"Control the desire, Cleo. Enjoy the sensation of being in the current without being swept away by it." His clipped tone ensures my body jumps to his command.

I lick my dry lips while slowing the grind of my fingers. The tingle spreading from my core to my budded nipples remains strong, but the haze of climax isn't as powerful.

"Good girl," Master Chains praises, noticing my breaths have decreased. "Enjoy the feeling—the sensation. Take your time exploring your beautiful body without racing to the finish line."

While listening to him whisper in my ear, I take in the way my vagina massages my fingers with every plunge I do. How there's a little nub at the end of my cervix that spasms when my fingertips brush past it, and how there isn't a drug in the world that could replicate the high I get during sexual activities. I also close my eyes and think about the man with the entrancing green gaze and more-than-tempting body.

I don't know how much time passes before Master Chains finally says, "Use your shoulder to hold your cell to your ear so your other hand can play with your clit."

Eagerly, I nod before doing as instructed. The slickness coating my sex dampens when my thumb rolls over my clit. I release a throaty moan, expressing everything my body is feeling without a word seeping from my lips.

"Start slow, Cleo. Gentle rolls and soft flicks. Work your body until you feel like you're about to combust, then stop."

I groan as disappointment sears through me.

"Soon, Cleo. Very soon," Master Chains promises.

As my fingers pump in and out of my soaked sex, I roll, tweak and flick my clit with my thumb. I build up my excitement to the point of snapping three times before he finally gives me permission to come.

"Prepare yourself, Cleo. It will be unlike anything you've ever felt."

He wasn't lying.

I scream a glass-shattering squeal when the most life-altering orgasm I've ever experienced shreds through me. I thrust and buck against the mattress, my mind hazed with lust, my body heightened beyond belief. Dizziness clusters in my mind as my entire body quakes. My orgasm is powerful, strong, and so blinding, I fail to notice my phone has slipped away from my ear.

It takes several long and tedious minutes for the shakes of climax to dissipate. My orgasm is welcomed and long, but utterly draining. It's the strongest I've ever had, not just self-induced.

After running my hand across my sweat-beaded forehead, I secure my cell off my pillow and push it against my ear.

The tingles still causing havoc with my libido intensify when Master Chains whispers, "Happy Birthday, Cleo."

It's the struggle of my life to reply, "Thank you, Master Chains."

eeling my cell phone vibrating in my pocket, I attempt to interrupt Mrs. Collard, Miguel's ninety-six-year-old legally deaf grandmother. When she fails to acknowledge my attempts to interrupt her reciting the pumpkin biscuit recipe she used to make the rock-hard brick sitting untouched on my plate for the fifth time, I inconspicuously slip my phone out of my dress pocket and peer down at the screen.

The girly giggle rippling through my lips gains me the attention of Miguel and his oldest son, Preston, who are refilling their drinks at a bar in Miguel's living room. With Lexi and Jackson's relationship blossoming nicely, Miguel's wish for us to have a combined Thanksgiving like our family did years ago was granted. It not only gave me the chance to cook the secret family recipe Miguel's wife Janice shared with me months ago, but it also gave Miguel the opportunity to set me up with his eldest son, Preston.

Preston is a wonderful man. Just like his youngest brother, he works in the medical field. His conversations are intelligent, and his looks are top shelf, but he's missing one element I seem to be craving the past eight weeks: the intrigue of mystery. Now, if I were being fair I would admit it isn't Preston's fault he has failed to secure my attention. That blame solely lies with the gentleman who just sent me a GIF of Tinker Bell being spanked.

Snubbing Lexi's curious glance peering at me over her wine glass, I reply to Master Chains' text.

Cleo: *She doesn't look very impressed.*

Agitated excitement makes me restless as I await his reply.

Master Chains: *That's because she hasn't reached the good part yet.*

Cleo: *Good part?*

Time slows to a snail's pace as I wait for my phone to buzz, indicating it has received a new message.

Master Chains: *Sweet sex is nice, Cleo, but being taken hard and fast after being spanked is even nicer.*

I adjust my position, ensuring no one sees the heat creeping up my neck from his reply. Even receiving numerous messages like this one the past two weeks hasn't dampened their effect in the slightest. They're still as core-tingling as ever.

Just as we did the weeks following our first conversation, Master Chains and I have continued with our nightly discussion. Although we now text numerous times throughout the day as well. I like to pretend my little slip-up the night of my birthday didn't alter my relationship with him, but that would be a lie. Although our conversations are still fun and flirty, the sexual vibe cracking between us has most certainly ramped up a notch.

Our relationship has always been bizarre, but we've now reached the fevered pitch of oddly compelling. I shouldn't be surprised, though. What he planned for my birthday was out of this world—it was the most kindhearted thing anyone has done for me—so I shouldn't have expected the day to end on anything but an awe-inspiring high.

A smile cracks my lips when an ideal response to Master Chains' text pops into my head. My fingers fly over the screen of my phone, drowning out the silence encroaching me.

Cleo: *I guess that's something I'll have to take your word on. I have no experience being fucked after a spanking.*

Like he has done several times the past six weeks, Master Chains intuits my reply. His message arrives at the same time mine was received.

Master Chains: *If I have it my way, that won't be a concern of yours much longer, Cleo.*

A shudder runs down my spine when I recall the seductive way my name rolled off his tongue after our exchange two weeks ago. If I'm being honest, not all my spine-tingling response is from remembering the way he says my name. Some of it's from his assumption we'll be meeting soon. Although the subject of us meeting has been discussed many times the prior six weeks, his efforts have been bolstered since my birthday. I don't know if his eagerness stems from our heated exchange or because he has stated numerous times he's returning home this week after an extended stint on the west coast of the country.

My focus shifts back to the present when my phone vibrates in my hand.

Master Chains: *Was that a pause of contemplation or commiseration?*
Cleo: *More like condemnation!*

His reply pops up in an instant.

Master Chains: *Don't be too hard on your heart. It's the sensible one. It's the only one not denying its desires.*

My mouth gapes, shocked he read the hidden statement in my text. I wasn't condemning him or his suggestion; I was condemning my body's reaction to his playful text. You'd think the effect his wicked words create would dampen since we've been talking for weeks. They haven't. Not the slightest. I don't think months or years will ever change the outcome his words create on my body. And don't get me started on his sultry could-melt-chocolate voice. My apprehensions are at my weakest when we talk. Thank god today we've reverted to texting each other. It may be the only chance I have left to maintain my shrewdness when it comes to him and my woozy-with-wine brain.

The only reason we've relapsed to messaging each other today is because we are in the attendance of Thanksgiving functions and didn't want to be rude to those who invited us. I'll be honest, I miss hearing his voice. I've spent the last three hours glancing at the clock, calculating how much time I need to wait once dessert is served before I can excuse myself without being rude.

Is that bad of me to say? Should I be ashamed to admit I'm missing a man whose real name is still a mystery to me? The little voice inside me says no, it doesn't believe you need to see someone in the flesh to have a connection with them, but my rational head knows I'm wading into muddy waters. I only met Master Chains as I was investigating a BDSM club he owns, so believing I have any type of connection with him should be utterly absurd. *Shouldn't it?*

Swallowing down the overcooked glazed duck creeping up my esophagus from my silent thoughts, I shut down my cell and slide it into my oversized purse. With my heart the heaviest it's been the past eight weeks, I accept the glass of chardonnay Preston is holding out for me.

"Boyfriend troubles?" Preston nudges his head to my purse.

My heart squeezes in my chest. "Umm. . . no." I shake my head. "Just an acquaintance checking in."

Preston's lips quirk. He seems genuinely surprised by my response. "That wasn't the same person you've been texting all afternoon?"

I lift my eyes to his, taking in the crispness of his buttoned-up shirt, the five o'clock shadow on his rigid jaw, and his straight and defined nose on the way. A sense of familiarity overcomes me when I lock my eyes with his glistening baby blues.

"Yeah, it was," I answer honestly, sick of the constant lies spilling from my lips the past six weeks.

The shock on Preston's handsome face intensifies. "So is the pained look in your eyes because your stomach is having a disagreement with Grandma's biscuits, or is it twisted up over the man your mind hasn't wandered from the entire night?"

Shock gnaws at my chest. I've never had someone read me so easily before. Well, excluding Master Chains. He doesn't even need to see my face to know what I'm thinking. He can read my emotions by hearing nothing but the sounds of my breath over a cell phone.

"I'm guessing it's the guy you've been secretly texting all night," Preston continues when he spots the chaotic range of emotions expressed by my forthright eyes.

"Am I that readable?"

The remorse in my words defeats my effort to be playful. I'm not remorseful over my confusing relationship with Master Chains; I'm regretful at my lack of politeness. Miguel and his family invited me into their home for Thanksgiving, and I've shown my gratefulness by spending the entire time on my phone. My mother would be rolling in her grave at my appalling behavior.

Preston's laugh eases the heaviness sitting on my chest. "Your distraction was just a wee bit obvious." He expands his index finger and thumb to emphasize his response.

"Sorry," I apologize, beyond revolted by my lack of manners. "I swear I'm not normally so rude."

"You have nothing to be sorry about, Cleo. Your distraction means no one has noticed my own disinterest in grandma's burnt turkey," he jests with a waggle of his brows.

Heat spreads across my chest. This is the Preston I remember from my childhood years. Although he isn't as vocal as his younger brother, he has a welcoming and forthcoming side.

My brow cocks into my hairline. "Is your *distraction* anyone I know?" I drawl out dramatically, more than happy to steer our conversation away from my rude behavior. "Because you know as well as I do, if your father discovers you're not dating a Montclair local, you're *not* dating."

For the first time in the years I've known him, Preston's cheeks get a hue of pink. My heart rate kicks into overdrive. I've never met a man who blushes before.

———

By the time Preston shares details of his newly flourishing relationship, hours have ticked by on the clock. I'm glad I reined in my rudeness long enough to appreciate the kind gesture Miguel and Janice instilled by inviting us for Thanksgiving dinner. Tonight proved why they were such close friends of my parents': they're wonderful people who have raised two very smart and well-mannered men.

"Thank you so much for inviting us; I had a wonderful time." I press a kiss to Miguel's cheek, the sentiment of my words unable to be missed.

"The pleasure was mine, dear Cleo; let's hope another four years doesn't go by before we do it all again," he responds, returning my gesture.

"It won't; I promise," I vow before issuing the same farewell to Janice.

After bidding farewell to Preston and Jackson with a brisk wave, I slide into the driver's seat of my baby-poo brown Buick. With Lexi's goodbye to Jackson taking a little longer than I anticipated, I pull my phone out of my purse and fire it up. The lazy beat of my heart kicks up a gear when the screen illuminates I've missed six text messages from Master Chains and even more unanswered calls.

Through a trembling heart, I decide to read his messages before tackling my full voicemail. His first two messages follow a similar path as the ones we've been exchanging a majority of the day. They're playful and flirty, and clearly show we've stepped over the line acceptable for friends. The middle two texts allude to his annoyance at my failure to reply to his messages. They're crammed with palpable tension and send my heart rate rocketing. The last two messages. . . they abundantly prove his creepy stalking skills have flourished the past few weeks. They're somewhat concerning, to say the least.

I'd like to say I'm surprised by his reaction, but that would be a lie. It doesn't take a genius to assume a man with a commanding aura like Master Chains has a possessive vibe attached to his personality. I've used it numerous times the past few weeks when taunting him. Even knowing I shouldn't goad a man like Master Chains, I can't help it. There's something about him that makes me act young and reckless, and unfortunately, along with that recklessness comes the desire to make him jealous. I won't lie, my confidence skyrocketed every time he reacted to one of my teases. It's a dangerous game I shouldn't be participating in but can't help but love. It's kind of like candy. You know it isn't good for you, but you don't stop eating it until every delicious piece is devoured.

Acting purely on the instincts of my guilt-riddled heart, I scroll down my list of my contacts, hit Master Chains' name, and lift my phone to my ear.

He answers not even two seconds later, "One of my drivers will collect you tomorrow afternoon," he says, not bothering to issue a greeting.

"It's Cleo," I reply, assuming he has mistaken my number as another caller.

"I'm well aware of that," he informs me, his deep tone clipped and brimming with tension.

A sense of unease washes over me. Although I anticipated his cold response to my lack of contact the past four hours, something still seems off-kilter with his abrupt replies. Not once has he exerted anger toward me the past six weeks—not even when we tackled controversial issues like his need to have control in the bedroom, or how he hasn't had a relationship outside of the usual Dom/sub liaison affiliated with the BDSM lifestyle. So, to say I'm somewhat shocked by the invisible anger radiating down the line would be an understatement—a major one.

"What are you doing?" I ask when the pants of his breath increase. He sounds like he's running a marathon.

"Packing," Master Chains snaps.

A tense stretch of silence passes between us, crammed with palpable friction. My mind is too scrambled trying to work out where he is going to uphold an intellectual conversation. He has only just returned home yesterday, so I'm shocked—and perhaps a little devastated—he's packing again so soon.

I push my phone in close to my ear when a male voice I don't recognize breaks through feet stomping down a set of stairs.

"Tell Cameron I want to be in the air in an hour; I want to touch down in New York no later than dawn," I hear Master Chains instruct his male caller.

"Yes, Sir. Your car is waiting out front as per your request," responds a mature male voice.

When the silence makes my shrilling pulse noticeable, I mumble, "You're coming to New York?" I'm sure he can hear my hammering heart in my voice.

"Yes, Cleo, I'm coming to New York." His voice is gruff and loaded with annoyance I haven't dealt with the prior eight weeks.

When a vehicle door slamming shut sounds down the line, closely followed by tires rolling over asphalt, reality smacks into me.

"You're coming to New York now?!" I squeal in surprise.

My eyes rocket to the clock in the dashboard of my car. It displays it's a little after 2 AM.

I hear muffled static like a cell being connected to Bluetooth before Master Chains tersely replies, "Yes."

"Why?" I practically scream while striving to overlook the way his clipped replies aren't just sending my heart rate into overdrive. My libido has also gone into meltdown mode.

"You wanted me to react, Cleo. I'm reacting." The serene calmness of his low tone doesn't match his response.

I balk as my mouth gapes open and closed, but not a peep escapes my lips, my mouth refusing to relinquish another lie from my indecisive brain. Although I'd like to plead innocence, I can't. After hearing Preston talk about the dates he and his new flame have been on, I was struck with a severe case of envy, which in turn, pushed me into idiocy territory. I want to have a picnic in Central Park before taking a ride in the back of a horse-drawn carriage.

I try to tell myself I don't want my relationship with Master Chains to go any further than pen pals using modern technology to our benefit, but that isn't true. I ignored his calls as I wanted to force a reaction out of him, because if he didn't react, I'd know the bizarre feeling that twists in my stomach every time I think of him is nothing but foolish hope—*hope that I'm not completely insane.*

My lips quiver as I begin to speak, "I'm sorry for not returning your calls. What I did was immature and uncalled for, but it doesn't require you to fly to New York at 2 AM. Why don't we take tonight to calm down, then we will talk about this like adults tomorrow?" I suggest, my words as weak as my apology.

The heavy regret on my chest lightens when Master Chains replies, "Talking is one of the many things we will do this weekend." My heart hangs halfway between my chest and my stomach when he continues, "Because I very much look forward to hearing your reasoning for taunting me in person."

"In person?" I strangle out, my words choking past the lump his declaration rammed in my throat.

"Yes, Cleo, in person." He sounds calm and put together—a stark contrast to the hyperventilating composure his response caused me.

"You're going to need to fill me in; I'm a little lost," I declare, my voice a hushed whisper.

Pretending he can't hear the deceit in my comment, Master Chains explains, "You're spending the weekend with me at my property in New York."

"Ah. . . no, I'm not," I reply, briskly shaking my head. "I have commitments, work, plans with. . ."

My voice trails off when I fail to find another excuse to issue him. The only plans I have this long weekend is catching up on the episodes of *The Walking Dead* I missed the past six weeks talking to him, striving not to fall into a food-induced coma from eating the truckload of carbs Janice sent us home with tonight, and if I'm brave, Lexi and I may tackle the Black Friday sales. My plans are no different than any other single American girl.

Master Chains' thigh-quivering growl returns my focus to him. "Just a word of warning, Cleo: if you lie to me in person, some form of punishment will be issued."

Blood surges to the lower region of my body from his threat. I writhe in my seat as a range of ways he could punish me filter through my dirty mind. They all involve the leather studded chaise in his playroom and his big manly hand.

Hearing my quickening breaths, Master Chains asks, "Curious,

Cleo?" His voice is not as calm as it was earlier. It's more gruff and tainted with sexual tension.

It takes a mammoth effort, but I force out, "No."

The pulse in my soaked sex reaches never-before-achieved levels when Master Chains grinds out, "Strike one. You don't want to know what the repercussions will be when you reach three."

The air is forced from my lungs in one painfully long grunt. *What the hell is wrong with me?* I'm being coerced into spending my weekend with a man I don't know, all because I didn't answer his messages in a timeframe he finds suitable, yet, my body gets turned on by his malicious threats. I'm stronger than this, and I'm sure as hell no one's submissive.

I stop squirming in my seat at the same time the passenger side door opens and Lexi slides inside my car. Snubbing her curious glance taking in my wide-eyed expression, I whisper down the phone. "I didn't ignore your messages to force you to react. I simply wanted a few hours to bask in the glory of solitude."

I grow more winded when Master Chains growls, "Strike two. If you wanted solitude, you should have done it without a man gazing in your eyes like you were a present sitting under his Christmas tree waiting to be unwrapped."

My eyes bulge. "What the hell are you talking about?" My words are laced with an equal amount of sexual exhilaration and utter shock.

I jump out of my skin when my cell buzzes, announcing I've received a new text. When I pull my phone down from my ear, air traps in the back of my throat, choking me with anxiety. My lungs strain for breath as my eyes drink in two of the three pictures Master Chains forwarded to me. From the red long-sleeve jersey dress I purchased specifically for Miguel's Thanksgiving function, I can easily deduce that these images were taken of me tonight, but the inclusion of Preston in every picture is another foolproof indication.

The reasoning behind Master Chains' switch in composure becomes apparent when I flick to the last picture. With Preston's head angled away from the prying photographer snapping our picture unaware, and my chin tucked into his neck to ensure I could hear him over the music playing, we appear as if we were in an intimate tryst.

"It isn't as it seems," I mutter down the line, pushing aside the fact someone has grossly invaded my privacy. "Preston is a friend. Nothing more."

Several moments pass in uncomfortable silence before Master Chains mutters, "I very much look forward to hearing you tell me that in person tomorrow, Cleo."

14

$\mathcal{A}$fter making the short four-block trip home, I pace into my room and sit on my bed, where I remain in silence for several moments, dumbfounded. I'm at a complete loss about what has occurred tonight. Yes, I taunted Master Chains, hoping he would react, but I didn't expect it to go to this level. Furthermore, I never expected to have my privacy invaded. Who in the world would take secret pictures of me with Preston, then forward them to Master Chains? It truly doesn't make any sense. What benefit would they get out of making Master Chains jealous?

Like a truck crashing into a brick wall, reality crashes into me. *I'm going to kill her.*

Pushing off my bed, I charge out of my room, my speed unchecked as I search our modest three-bedroom home for any signs of my meddling sister. I find her sitting in the den talking on her cell phone five minutes later. Spotting the fury beaming from my eyes, she advises her caller she needs to go and promises to call them later. I don't wait for her to disconnect her call before I snatch her cell out of her hand and scroll to her messages. The air in my lungs is brutally removed when I discover three identical pictures matching the ones Master Chains forwarded me sitting in the sent box of her messages.

"Are you kidding me?!" I scream, twisting her cell phone around so she can see the pictures of Preston and me sprawled across the screen. "Do you have any idea what you've done? He isn't just jealous about your ridiculous messages; he's coming here—tonight!"

The fear in Lexi's eyes is masked by exhilaration when she processes my declaration. "Chains is coming here?" Her high tone abundantly proves she has no qualms about meddling in my private affairs. "To see you?"

"Yes!" I reply, throwing my arms up in the air. "When I called to apologize for my childish behavior, I discovered he was in the midst of packing. If that wasn't already shocking enough, imagine discovering he was packing because he assumed I was ignoring his messages due to my getting cozy with another man!"

I feel my anger growing from my toes to my face when the excitement blazing in Lexi's eyes turns blinding. "Come on, Sis, you have to admit, his reaction is hot. He's coming here because he wants to stop you playing tongue wars with anyone but him. That's fucking hot."

"That's *not* hot; it's childish!" I sneer, my low voice successfully hiding the deceit in my reply. Even though I'm beyond ropeable, excitement is still quickening my pulse.

Lexi glares at me like I've grown a second head. "What woman doesn't love a brooding, temperamental, jealous man?"

"The woman investigating him!" I shout, my face reddening with anger.

"*Was* investigating," Lexi corrects. "Your assignment regarding Chains ended *weeks* ago—the instant you started talking to him."

"And if they decide to reopen it?" I cock my hip and spread my hands across my waist. "What happens then?"

Lexi shrugs. "We'll cross that bridge when it comes."

"It isn't that simple," I shout, throwing my hands into the air.

"Yeah, it is. If the case gets reopen, you cite bias," she suggests, like she has taken some time considering my predicament.

"The job of a journalist is *not* to stamp out bias. We're supposed to *manage* it."

"Then manage it!" Lexi's scratchy voice relays she's close to having a coughing fit. "You knew from the moment you returned Chains' first message you were creating a conflict of interest between your personal life and work life, yet, you still sent it, and thousands of messages since."

"That doesn't change the facts, Lexi. You had no right to do what you did! No right at all."

My anger isn't as high strung as it was when I first walked into the den. It's been strangled by the truth in Lexi's replies. I knew my relationship with Master Chains was tiptoeing in a dangerous minefield, but no matter how many times I tried to shut it down, I couldn't.

"I did what I did as I knew you would never work up the courage to do it," Lexi enlightens me as she stands from the couch. "It's time for your relationship with Chains to move forward. I helped you do that."

I hold her gaze, my lips twitching, my fists clenched at my side. "The pace of our relationship wasn't your decision to make. And even if for some insane reason it was, who's to say this is what I wanted?"

"Your six-hour-long conversations you've had with him every night the past month," Lexi fires back, her voice rising in anger. "The combined hours of your conversations are triple the amount of time I've spoken to Jackson in our entire relationship. We've been together for over two months; I've studied every groove of his body, and I've slept with him more times than I can count, but do you see us burning the candle at both ends talking for six hours every night?"

Not waiting for me to reply, she continues speaking, "No, you don't, as most people realize when they've reached the next step in their relationship." She locks her determined eyes with mine. "You've reached the next step."

"Did you ever stop to think we only communicate over the phone as the ability to hold an intellectual conversation is the only thing we have in common?" My brows become lost in my hairline. "Compatibility is much more than just holding a conversation, Lexi."

While crossing her arms over her chest, Lexi glares at me. Her narrowed gaze calls out my deceit without a single word escaping her hard-lined lips. She knows me well enough to know every vicious word fired off my tongue is a complete lie.

"This isn't what I wanted, Lexi. Not like this," I continue to argue, my Garcia stubbornness not allowing me to back down from our disagreement. "I wanted us to take the next step when we were ready, not because we were forced to."

Needing to leave the room before she spots the indecisiveness in my eyes, I spin on my heels and enter the hallway.

My brisk strides down the corridor stop when Lexi yells, "It isn't nice having your whole life planned out for you, is it?!"

I take three calming breaths before pivoting around to face her. The fury turning my blood black dissipates when I see the pain etched on her beautiful face. Her eyes are red and brimming with tears, and her lips are quivering.

"I've had that my whole life, Cleo. What I can do. What I can eat. What I can wear. I even get told how to breathe," she whispers, her voice relaying she's on the verge of tears. "First by Mom, then by you."

"That's because we love you, Lexi; we only want the best for you." The heavy sentiment in my voice bolsters my statement.

Lexi nods in agreeance. "As I do for you too, Cleo. That's why I did what I did. Just as you've done every day of my life, I'm pushing you to live your life to the fullest."

The angry tension firing between us becomes a distant memory when she moves to stand in front of me. "If only you could see the way your face lights up when you talk about him, Cleo, then you'd understand why I'm begging you not to run away from this like every other relationship you've had. You want this—*you need this*—you're just too scared to admit it."

"It's not that," I reply, running my index finger across my cheek to ensure no tears have fallen from my eyes. "Even if I wasn't scared about how crazy he makes me feel, we are from two different worlds. I don't even know his real name, Lexi. He's practically a stranger."

Lexi shakes her head. "I don't believe that, not for a single minute. Our walls are paper thin. I've heard you talking to him many times the past month. You know him, and he knows you—the real Cleo, not the one you think is socially acceptable."

Even with a surge of blood gushing to my heart from her declaration, I continue to argue. "You don't understand. What we have isn't normal. He isn't. . . *normal.*"

Guilt overwhelms me, making it hard for me to breathe when the last sentence is forced out of my mouth. I've spent weeks debating with Master Chains my ability to make my own informed decision, yet I'm still judging him because he owns a BDSM club, instead of the man presented to me every night.

Lexi runs her hand down my arm before locking her glistening eyes with mine. "Thank god for that, as the last thing you need is someone normal. Normal is predictable. Normal is boring. Normal is living your life without a single adventure. Nobody wants normal, Cleo. I sure as hell don't, and neither should you."

"I'm no expert, but I'm fairly certain it isn't normal to get incredibly turned on at the idea of being spanked," I spit out before I can stop my words.

"It isn't?" Lexi recants, her voice high and void of its earlier emotions. After looping her arm around mine, she walks down the corridor, dragging me with her. "I sure as hell hope Jackson doesn't catch on to your ideas of what is and isn't normal, because spankings are one of my favorite things."

I gasp in a shocked breath as my wide eyes rocket to Lexi. She glares at me with her manicured brows waggling. I bump her with my hip, which sends her beautiful laugh into the night air. I shouldn't be surprised by her admission. She has always been the wild child of our family. I'm not. I'm the safe, guarded sister who dreams of long walks on the beach and soft, gentle lovemaking.

The little voice inside me roars to life, vehemently denying every statement I just made. It stomps its feet like a five-year-old and crosses its arms over its chest. I'm so goddamn confused. Logically, I know just talking to a man in the BDSM lifestyle is frowned upon. But Master Chains' logic of not caring about the opinions of others is rubbing off on me. Nothing but silly giddiness consumes me when I think about him. Shouldn't something like that be explored instead of ignored?

Wanting to change the tempo of our conversation before I hear reason to my reckless thoughts, I keep my voice friendly while saying, "You know how there are certain things you can never erase from your mind?"

Lexi nods, a little overeagerly.

"The vision of Jackson spanking you is one of those things," I mutter, faking a gag. "The next time you want to share details of your sex life, can you issue a warning first? I'm having a hard enough time keeping down the charcoaled turkey as it is."

Lexi's infectious laugh fills the space, instantly erasing any left-over anger harbored in the back of my mind.

"Okay, I promise to issue a warning about all future sex discussions. . . on one condition," she barters, spinning around to face me.

A smile cracks onto my mouth when I see the cheekiness beaming from her eyes. She truly is the most annoying, opinionated and beautiful young lady I've ever met.

My smile sags the instant she mumbles, "Give Chains a chance. If you meet him and hate him, we'll never mention his name again."

"And what if I have the opposite reaction? What if he's everything I've wished for and more?" I ask, expressing my true concerns for the first time this evening.

Lexi grasps my hands in hers and squeezes them tightly. "Then you grab ahold of him and never let go."

"And my job?" I barely whisper. "What happens to that?"

Lexi peers at me with a set of eyes much wiser than her twenty-one years. "You go back to writing about people who lost their lives instead of living yours as if it has already ended."

15

"*C*leo Garcia?"

Hugging my dressing gown tightly to my body, I nod to the male caller standing on the stoop of my stairs. With the clock only just hitting 8 AM and it being Black Friday, I'm somewhat ill-prepared for guests.

"Sign here please," he instructs, twisting a steel clipboard around to face me.

After scribbling my name across the courier delivery strip, the blond-haired man tears out the receiver's copy of the delivery confirmation form and hands it to me with a plain white envelope.

"Thank you," I stutter out, confusion in my tone as I shut the door.

With the early winter chill left outside, I loosen my grip on my dressing gown and rip open the thin envelope. Before my eyes can skim the six-page document, I spot Lexi staggering out of her room. Her eyes are puffy, and she has a drool stain on her left cheek.

"Did I hear a male voice?" she queries, her voice groggy from just waking up.

I nod. "Yeah, it was a courier driver delivering this document," I reply, nudging my head to my hands.

Shock morphs onto Lexi's face, mimicking mine to a T. As she trudges toward me, I drop my eyes to the document. The longer my eyes scan the official-looking paperwork, the more my empty stomach rumbles. It isn't grumbling due to lack of nutrients; it's protesting about the blank non-disclosure agreement the courier just delivered.

Upon spotting the contempt on my face, Lexi's pace quickens. "What is it?" She stops beside me. Her Roxy perfume filters into my nostrils when she leans across my body so she can peruse the document.

"This is your idea of normal." My raging heart is relayed in my voice. "Master Chains requires me to sign a non-disclosure agreement before we can meet today."

"No shit," Lexi squeals, her eyes bugging out of her head. "I told you he was *loaded*." She emphasizes the last word of her sentence with a shameful flair money-hungry trophy wives use.

"More like insane if he thinks I'll sign this," I interrupt, my tone lowering as anger boils my veins. "Not only can I not legally sign this form, I morally refuse to."

"You have to sign it," Lexi debates, removing the document from my hand. "If you don't sign it, you can't spend the weekend with Chains."

I shrug my shoulders. "Exactly. No skin off my nose," I lie.

I barely catch Lexi's dropped-jaw expression as I spin on my heels and stride to my bedroom.

"Cleo, we discussed this last night. I thought we came to an agreement?" Lexi bickers, shadowing me into my room.

"That was before he slapped me with an NDA," I interject, padding to my bed. "If you think I'll spend a weekend with a man who requires me to sign a contract before we can officially meet, you don't know me very well. That document is not just rude, pretentious and arrogant, it undermines every conversation we've had the past six weeks."

"How?" Lexi disputes, her eyes watching me like a hawk as I hunt for my cell phone in the overnight bag I packed in haste this morning.

Failing to find my cell amongst the mountain load of clothes I packed, I twist my body to face Lexi. "Because it represents that every word he spoke was a lie."

Lexi stares at me, her confusion growing tenfold.

"If he was being honest, don't you think it's a little too late for a non-disclosure agreement?" I implore, my voice cracking with emotion.

"No." Lexi shakes her head. "He's protecting his identity, Cleo, not himself. In his industry, it's a smart thing for him to do."

The way she defends him makes me wonder if last night was the first time she's had contact with Master Chains.

"And who's protecting me?" I retaliate, my angry voice lowering to a whisper.

"Me," Lexi replies without pause for consideration. "Do you truly think I'd encourage you to meet him if I thought he was dangerous? I might be desperate for you to start living, but I'd never put you in danger."

She uncrosses her arms and pushes off her feet. "Stop looking for an excuse to get out of this meeting. You want this; you're just frightened by what that means."

I scoff, feigning innocence. Lexi arches her brow, silently calling out my deceit. She knows exactly what I'm feeling. I barely slept a wink last night as my stomach was a horrid mess of excitement and unease. I do want this; I just don't want the messiness associated with it. If I had met Master Chains under different circumstances, I wouldn't hesitate to meet him. But considering I only met him as I was investigating his club makes the unease gurgling in my stomach wind all the way up my throat.

Pulling her cellphone out of the pocket of her fluffy robe, Lexi hands it to me. "Instead of getting yourself all worked up, call him and explain your concerns about the NDA. If he doesn't understand your hesitation, don't go and see him. Simple."

Ignoring the feeling of disappointment pumping into me, I accept the cell from Lexi, dial Master Chains' number I know by heart, and push her phone to my ear. My brows scrunch when I get an automated response saying the number is no longer in service. Acting like I'm unaware of the workings of cell phone service, I scroll to the messages Lexi sent him last night and type a short message requesting for him to call me. The same automated response about his number no longer being in service is received via text not even two seconds later.

Lexi's confused eyes track me as I cross the room and log into the Chains website. The already dangerous beat of my heart kicks up a gear when I discover a big red cross next to Master Chains' online account. His profile has been stripped of any information, and his shadowed profile picture has been replaced with the standard inactive account one you find on all social media sites.

"What the hell?" I mumble, my confusion boosting by the second. "His account has been revoked."

A blinding smile stretches across Lexi's tired face. "I guess he doesn't need an online persona when the real Master Chains is about to be unveiled."

Panicked excitement engulfs me. Spotting my flabbergasted appearance, the smug look on Lexi's face grows. "Does that mean you have to tell him in person you have no intention of signing his NDA?" she asks, her girly voice tainted with glee.

Barely holding in my flipping stomach, I reply, "Yeah, I guess that's what I must do."

Lexi's eyes flare, and exhilaration beams out of her. Fighting not to let her excitement rub off on me, I force a fake snarl onto my face. Lexi doesn't buy my attempts at acting unaffected. She knows as well as I do, I don't have a chance in hell of listening to my astute brain when I'm in Master Chains' presence. The odds of me backing out of our agreement in person is just as unlikely as me not meddling in Lexi's love life. They're slim to none.

Approximately six hours later, I'm sitting in the back of a silver Jaguar as it rolls toward the Brooklyn Bridge. Nervous butterflies flutter in my stomach and a misting of sweat coats my forehead. Snubbing the handkerchief hanging out of a pocket of the overnight bag Lexi placed on the seat next to me, I secure one of the tissues from the middle console of the Jaguar to dab the sweat off my face.

"Just in case you change your mind," Lexi jested while placing my bag next to me.

My eyes open wide in shock when the Jaguar veers off the road just before we hit the Brooklyn Bridge. It comes to a stop at an underpass a few streets back. The rise and fall of my chest intensifies when a high-class BMW pulls in next to us not even ten seconds later. I exhale a deep breath to calm the nerves running rampant through my body. It does nothing to ease the panic scorching me alive. I'm a quivering bag of nerves.

The skittish tension making my skin a clammy mess gets a moment of reprieve when a fierce looking middle-aged gentleman clambers out of the BMW and paces toward my stationary vehicle. Not speaking, he opens the back passenger door and slides into the seat next to me. Wanting to ensure his wide frame has enough room, I remove my overnight bag from the seat and place it on my lap. My nerves have me jittering so much, my bag physically shakes.

After wiping a thick layer of sweat from the top of his brow, the man mutters, "NDA," his voice demanding.

"Excuse me?" I'm unsure if he's talking to me or the driver. Considering he hasn't looked at either of us—let alone issued a greeting—I can't be sure whom he's speaking to. "Are you talking to me?"

The buttons on his dark blue business suit struggle to conceal the rigid bumps of his stomach when he adjusts his position to face me. My heart smashes against my ribs when his desolate eyes glare into mine. If this man is setting out to intimidate me, he's doing a mighty fine job.

"The NDA that was delivered to you this morning, Cleo; where is it?"

Shocked by his rudeness, my lips thin in grimness, but not a syllable expels from my stunned mouth. When my eyes unwittingly drop to the white envelope sitting between us, he follows my gaze. I balk when his hand delves out to snatch the envelope off the dark gray leather bench.

After placing the document under the crook of his arm, he hands a single yellow post-it note to the Jaguar driver before exiting the vehicle.

"Oh... I didn't sign it," I stammer out.

My words are too late. The Jaguar door is brutally thrown closed, and it commences rolling off the curb before the first word escapes my lips.

With my heart in my throat, I scoot to the edge of my seat and lock my shocked gaze with the pair of blue eyes peering at me in the rearview mirror. "Excuse me, I need to speak to the gentleman at the bridge. Can you please take me back to him?" I point to the brute of a man talking into his cellphone at the side of the BMW to emphasize my request.

"No," the driver replies, his voice slurred with a heavy accent I don't recognize. "We go to this address." He taps his finger onto the post-it note stuck to his steering wheel.

"I don't want to go to that address. I need you to either take me back to the gentleman in the BMW or take me home," I request, my voice sterner than the jittering one I was using earlier.

"No," he repeats, "we go to this address." He taps on the post-it note so hard, the Jaguar's horn sounds into the late afternoon air.

"Sir, please, you need to understand what I'm saying. If you don't take me back to that man so I can explain I didn't sign the forms he just took, your position could be compromised." My next sentence comes out in a flurry when the driver commences rolling up the privacy partition between us. "I'll pay you double the rate they're paying if you take me back to the man at the bridge."

I plead to my reflection in the tinted glass window for twenty minutes before I give in to the fact I'm not going anywhere other than the address listed on the post-it note. Slouching in defeat, I yank my cellphone out of my pocket to send Lexi a message on my kidnapped status.

Me: Thanks to you, I've been kidnapped. Send help. I'm trapped in the back of a Jaguar as it weaves through the streets of Tribeca.

Lexi: Your GPS has been tracked, and a SWAT team is on high alert. At first signs of an orgasm, a group of tall, dark, and drool-worthy armed men will arrive to rescue you from such treachery! Do not fear, Cleo, your virtue will not be sacrificed for the greater good.

Even with nervous butterflies fluttering in my stomach, a giggle topples from my lips when I read her reply. I don't know why I'm shocked by her response. There has only been one time I've seen Lexi serious: the months following our parents' and little brother's death. I lost a lot of sleep those months wondering if she would ever recover from our loss. It was a challenging time for everyone involved, but it seemed to hit Lexi harder than anyone.

It was only after enduring one of the hardest discussions we ever had did I realize what her worries pertained to. Lexi wasn't just grieving our devastating loss; she was suffering the effects of guilt. Unlike me, her guilt wasn't attached to her grief. It was because the morning after Tate's wake she realized, one day, I was going to be left all alone. I've never loved my sister more than I did that day. She wasn't worried about CF taking her away in the prime of her life; all she cared about was leaving me alone. That selflessness was what made me pledge to do everything in my power to ensure her final years are her best. I've strived for that goal every day since.

After wiping under my eyes to ensure no sneaky tears spilled, I respond to Lexi's message.

Me: I'm not sure dark, drool-worthy men will help save my virtue, but thanks for the offer.

Lexi: You're so hard to please, Cleo. First, you're fighting off a man whose voice sounds like it could melt chocolate, now you're denying the help of a group of core-clenching SWAT members. What's wrong with you?

My mouth gapes as suspicion runs wild through my veins.

Me: How do you know what Master Chains' voice sounds like?

Traffic, beeping horns, and the angry slurs of road-raging motorists fade into the background as I await Lexi's reply.

With how much time passes, I'm certain she isn't going to respond.

Just as I'm about to hit the call button at the top of my message screen, another text from Lexi finally pops up.

Lexi: *We may have spoken previously. But I don't have time to discuss that now, Jackson is about to drive under a bridge. . . I may lose you. . . C..l..e..o, are you there? You're. . .breaking up. . .*

My fingers punch into my phone so hard I'm shocked I don't break the screen.

Me: *You can't fake static interruptions via a message, Lexi!*

Lexi: *Like hell I can't. My big sister taught me I can do anything I set my mind to.*

I grit my teeth.

Me: *Lexi. . .*

Lexi: *Bye Cleo. I'm switching off my phone now. . .*

I stare at my cell for several moments, struggling to find an appropriate response. Although my suspicions ran high this morning that she'd been in contact with Master Chains, I pushed it to the background of my mind. Not because I wasn't curious what they talked about, but because I didn't want to run the risk of Lexi finding out about my conversation with Jackson.

I wasn't joking when I disclosed my meddling in Lexi's love life. As her guardian, it's my job to ensure her dates are given the same lecture Luke got from my dad when we first began dating. Although my sermon on the rules of dating a Garcia woman was minus the sweat-producing panic my dad's instilled in Luke, it still had Jackson trembling in his boots.

My heart leaps out of my chest when my phone vibrates in my hand.

Lexi: *I'm not switching off my phone. If an emergency does occur, call me. Until then, let down your hair, push out your monstrous rack and go and have some fun! P.S: I want all the juicy details. P.P.S: opening your* *heart doesn't mean you have to open your legs, but it's a lot more fun if you do!*

My anger dampens slightly.

Me: I'm restricting your cable access the instant I get home.

Lexi: Meh! Like that's going to help.

The uncertainty curled around my heart loosens its firm grip when Lexi's next message comes through.

Lexi: I love you, Cleo the Creep, and if you'd just give people the chance to see the Cleo I see, the entire world would love you too. Stop listening to everyone around you. Just breathe and be yourself, then everything will turn out fine!

My heart bursts when I read her last sentence. That's a quote our mother always said to us. She was such a beautiful woman. She never judged, yelled at, or ridiculed us. She just encouraged us to be who we wanted to be, not what society classed as acceptable. *God, I miss her.*

For how long it takes for me to type my reply, anyone would swear I was writing an essay instead of a simple three-word text.

Me: Okay. I'll try.

16

orty minutes and numerous messages later, the Jaguar pulls into an isolated driveway at the end of a narrow road. The crazy beat of my heart surges to a new level when a black wrought iron gate chugs open, exposing an architectural wonder of steel and glass. The curved design of the stainless steel roof softens the hard lines of the white brick pillars holding up the monstrous dwelling, and the floor-to-ceiling windows bounce a multihued beam of light onto the in-ground pool positioned in front of the spectacular residence.

Dragging my eyes from the wonderment in front of me, I send a final message to Lexi.

Me: *I'm here. Wish me luck.*

Her message returns in an instant.

Lexi: *You don't need it, but I'll give it to you anyway. Good luck! Bye xx*

Me: *Bye xx*

After placing my cell into my overnight bag, I peer out the tinted window. The view switches from magnificent to awe-inspiring when my eyes lock in on a blur of black standing at the front of two double doors. Disdain for my nearsightedness twists in my chest when my poor vision hinders my endeavor to unveil the face of the person standing in wait. I don't need 20/20 vision to know who is waiting for me, though. From his build alone, I can easily distinguish it's a man, but it's the energetic spark surging through my body that reveals his true identity: it's Master Chains.

After taking a few deep breaths to clear the panic smeared across my face, I curl out of the door the driver is holding open for me. I issue my disdain for his earlier ignorance with a nasty stink eye before I commence walking up the platform-like stairs. My shaking knees becomes more apparent with every step I take to the blotch of black standing in front of me.

The further I encroach, the more my vision improves—as does the crackling of energy.

"Holy shit," I mumble under my breath when three long blinks clear my vision enough I can see the face of the man waiting to greet me.

"Holy fucking shit," I murmur, louder this time when it dawns on me why his face is so recognizable. He isn't just the ridiculously handsome owner of an exclusive BDSM club in lower Manhattan, nor the man who hasn't strayed from my thoughts the past eight weeks. He's a member of one of the most successful bands in the world. A man worth millions and millions of dollars. He's Marcus Everett, bassist of Rise Up.

"Cleo," Marcus greets in his deep timbre when I stop in front of him, sending goosebumps to the surface of my skin.

"Hi," I squeak out, my voice so high it sounds like I haven't hit adulthood yet.

I'm not just shocked to discover Master Chains is a very well-known man; I'm stunned at our bizarre connection. It was the story I ran on the lead singer of Marcus's band being in rehab when he was fighting for his life in ICU that caused my fall from grace four years ago. For months, I blamed Rise Up for being the catalyst of events that destroyed my life. It was only after discovering their publicist was fired for issuing false reports to the media on Noah's where-abouts did I realize the demise of my career wasn't Rise Up's fault. It was the lady behind the helm of their publicity, a woman whose identity I'm still striving to uncover to this date.

My focus reverts back to the present when Marcus places his hand under my chin and lifts my downcast face. I gasp in greedy breaths when the intensity of his eyes hits me full-force. My god, they're truly mesmerizing. I thought they were impressive on the numerous front page spreads he has been on the past four years of his success, but nothing compares to seeing them in real life.

His eyes scan my face as if he's memorizing each individual pore on my skin. "You're just as I remembered," he murmurs more to himself than me. "I'm glad you came, Cleo. I was concerned the NDA would scare you away."

"Oh. . .umm . . .I. . ." I roll my eyes at my inability to form a sentence. I'm a grown woman for crying out loud, not some teenage girl crushing over a sexy rock star. He's still a man, for goodness sake. *A very handsome, panty-melting man, but still a man nonetheless.*

I wave my hands across my body, physically pushing away my nerves. "In regards to the NDA," I start to say before a stunning middle-aged Latina lady appears at his side.

"Do you require anything else, Mr. Everett?" she questions, her beautiful accent on full display.

The heat on my cheeks cools when Marcus removes his scorching eyes from my face to lock them with the lady standing at his side. "No, thank you, Aubrey. Everything is perfect. You are free to go."

The smile on Aubrey's face expands when she's awarded with Marcus's breathtakingly beautiful smile. "Yes, Sir, thank you." She bows her head and steps backward.

The quickest flash of agitation blazes through Marcus's eyes from Aubrey's response before he shuts it down quicker than it arrived. Once Aubrey climbs into the passenger seat of the Jaguar I just exited, it pulls out of the driveway and disappears into the rapidly setting sun, leaving only two living souls in the entire property: Marcus and me.

Oh, shit, this isn't good.

"They're coming back, aren't they?" My voice quivers with nerves.

The heat spreading through my body intensifies when Marcus places his hand on my back and guides me into his residence without a peep from his deliciously plump lips. While my eyes bug in awe at the wonderment of his property, he undoes the three buttons on my coat.

Although the foyer is decorated in a neutral palette of white veined tiles and sleek furnishings, it still thrusts his wealth in my face. If I weren't already skeptical, this space undoubtedly proves we're on opposing ends of the financial scale. I'm standing in a foyer that screams wealth wearing a tatty coat, while he melds into the opulent surroundings in a dark suit tailored to showcase every spectacular ridge of his panty-drenching body.

After guiding my jacket off my shoulders, Marcus places it and his suit jacket in a concealed coatroom on his right. While pacing back to me, his eyes lower to drink in my whimsical Adrianna Papell dress. This was the very first dress Sasha awarded me with during my internship. It has remained my favorite since that day. With its rounded neckline and free-flowing skirt, it gives a hint of my voluptuous curves without being inundated by them, and the white satin printed material adds an edge of sexiness to the plain design. I've always felt like royalty any time I've worn this dress. Even more so when I'm eyed with the zeal Marcus is awarding me with right now.

Stopping in front of me, he rakes his eyes down my body before locking them with me. He's standing so close, my budded nipples connect with his light blue dress shirt with every inhalation I take. No thoughts pass through my mind as I return his lusty stare. My brain has once again become mush in his presence.

Just as the tension in the air becomes so dense storm clouds form on the horizon, Marcus asks, "Are you hungry?"

From the way his voice is laced with sexual innuendo, I can't tell if his question is truly about food. I don't know if my confusion stems from being stuck in the haze of lust, or because I'm literally brain-dead from staring into his entrancing eyes too long.

My horrified eyes snap down to my stomach when a loud grumble sounds from it, my body choosing its own response to his question. The embarrassment slicking my skin with a fine layer of sweat gets a pardon when the corners of Marcus's lips tug high before the most dazzling smile graces me with its presence.

"I'll take that as a yes," he mutters, his deep tone unable to hide the laughter in his voice.

Biting on the inside of my cheek, I nod. I'm famished, but not all my desires are associated with food. Attraction is too tame of a word to describe what I'm feeling standing across from Master Chains in the flesh. The extreme sexual connection we've been building the past eight weeks is nothing compared to the palpable tension bouncing between us now. It's so explosive it crackles in the air.

The pleas of my hungry stomach are pushed to the background of my mind when Marcus runs his index finger down the sliver of silk draped over my shoulder. He straightens the strap of my dress. His meekest touch sends a scorching pulse to my soaked sex, urging me to squeeze my thighs together. I'm equally appalled and excited by my body's response to his touch and incredibly turned on.

After ensuring the strap is in its rightful spot, Marcus locks his eyes back with me. "While we eat, we have a few matters we need to attend to," he informs me, his voice having an edge of antagonism to it.

"I thought we covered everything with the questionnaire?" I jest with a weak waggle of my brows.

I sigh, grateful my moronic trance is lifting. There's no bigger turn-off than a grown woman shamefully fawning over a man. Yes, Marcus is an attractive man who makes my mouth salivate, but if I want any chance of keeping our bizarre kinship on an even playing field, I need to rein in the childish prompts of my body by occasionally using its more astute counterpart: my brain.

"We did, but there were a few things the questionnaire didn't elaborate on," Marcus responds as his beautiful eyes dance between mine, holding me captive with both intrigue and wonderment.

"Then why don't we get the formalities out of the way now, then we can enjoy our meal in peace? Tension and food don't mix well," I suggest. "Furthermore, with how much my stomach is twisting, I don't think putting food in there would be a wise idea."

My gaze stops mimicking the movements of Marcus's eyes when he questions, "Did you kiss Preston, Cleo?"

I step backward and gasp in an exasperated breath. With my mind a blurred mess of confusion the past twelve hours, I completely forgot what lead to our impromptu meeting.

"No," I answer with a brief shake of my head. Trying to work out how Marcus knows Preston's name makes what should be a confident statement come out sounding unsure.

I release the breath I'm holding in when Marcus continues with his interrogation, verifying he perceived the honesty in my eyes. "Did you want to?" He peers straight into my shocked gaze, his demeanor calm.

Not trusting my voice to relay the honesty of my reply, I shake my head. Either not seeing my response, or choosing to ignore it, Marcus continues staring into my eyes, silently demanding a response.

"No," I eventually mutter when the tension thickening the air becomes too great to ignore.

The tightness in his shoulders physically relaxes as a spark of relief filters through his ageless eyes. Every second we stand across from each other in silence lures me deeper into what's certain to be dangerous territory. *Womb-clenching, will-never-view-sex-in-the-same-light-again, but still dangerous nevertheless.*

Shaking my head to release myself from the invisible pull his eyes stimulated, I say, "Since we are sharing, I have a question for you." My words sound forced due to the exhilarating unease wrapped around my throat.

Marcus watches me for a long moment, studying me in-depth before he curtly nods, agreeing to my cross-examination.

Ignoring the hunger for friction against my skin, I ask, "Was last night the only time you've had contact with my sister?"

Bile creeps up my esophagus when Marcus abruptly responds, "No."

He gives me a few moments to absorb his statement before he

adds on, "Lexi contacted me the morning following our first phone conversation, then again this morning."

"And?" I question when he fails to elaborate on his response.

I prick my ears, wanting to ensure I can hear him over the mad beat of my heart when he says, "Both conversations contained the same warning: if I didn't treat you right, there would be repercussions for my actions."

My brows stitch. "That doesn't sound like Lexi," I mumble, my voice tainted with suspicion.

Marcus's lips curl into a wry smirk. "Well, she said it more along the lines of, 'If you fuck with my sister, I'll fuck you over,'" he quotes, his expression deadpan.

I burrow my head into the deep groove in his chest, praying he won't see the humiliation smearing my face. *That sounds exactly like something Lexi would say.*

Embarrassment is the last thing on my mind when Marcus's manly smell engulfs my senses. Just like the quick whiff I caught in the back of the Bentley, he smells freshly showered, spicy, and intoxicating. I nuzzle my cheek in harder against his firm chest, hoping to get enough of his scrumptious scent imbedded onto my skin to last me a lifetime. A scent is often the strongest tie to a memory. I love the way the faintest aroma of my mom's perfume causes a flurry of memories to bombard me. Now I've just added another spicy scent to my sensory palette—one I'm certain I've smelled before.

I suck in a sharp breath as recollection dawns in my blurry mind. That's the same scent I smelled that day in the elevator. I'm certain of it. Unashamed, I take another long sniff of Marcus's invigorating smell. The crazy current zapping through my body stills as muted shock registers its intention. It's indisputably the same smell—there's no doubt in my mind.

Before my brain can catalog the commands of my heart, Marcus places his hand under my chin and lifts my head. Time comes to a standstill as his movements mimic those made on that eventful night four years ago. His touch calms the torment twisting in my stomach and clears my mind of any thoughts. This time, instead of bouncing my eyes away when he releases a deep sigh, I connect my disarrayed eyes with his. Even with his eyes veiled by lust and his lips tugged at the corners, I can confidently say he's the same man from that night in the elevator.

While dancing his truth-exposing eyes between mine, Marcus mutters, "I should have kissed you that night." Every word spoken is done with a brush of his thumb over my exposed collarbone. "Would have saved me weeks of torture."

"By handing it to me," I mumble before smacking my lips together, mortified at my inability to think before I speak.

I've dreamt of this exact day many times. My response to discovering the identity of the mysterious stranger in the elevator was more cordial and graceful in my dreams. Heck, even my thoughts about how I was going to interact with Master Chains were more refined than the tactless behavior I just displayed.

A dash of euphoria runs through me, shoving my embarrassment to the side, when Marcus growls before leaning intimately toward me. As if his tempting growl was already spiking my libido, his impressive stature sends a knee-clanging chill of excitement down my spine.

Endeavoring to keep the miniscule snippet of dignity I have left, I take a retreating step. Marcus angles his head to the side, cocks his brow, then takes a step forward. Pretending I can't feel the zapping of energy between us growing instead of decreasing as I'm aiming for, I take another step back. Seeing my defiance as a challenge, Marcus stares straight into my eyes as he steps forward. He has the gaze of a man on the hunt, and it sets my pulse racing.

In silence, we continue our routine until my back splays on a polished concrete pillar in the foyer. Marcus stands so close to me I can't tell where my body ends and his begins. My breathing pattern alters as excited panic heats my blood. I'm barely holding it together as it is, but having him standing so near is squashing every reservation I've ever had about our incompatibility.

When he curls his hand around my jaw, my traitorous tongue darts out to moisten my lips. His eyes drop to track the path my tongue takes, the hunger growing in them with every second that passes.

His breath bounces off my newly slicked lips when he mutters, "What would you prefer, Cleo, me hand it to you, or you continuing to handle it yourself?"

Ignoring the way his manly voice causes the hairs on my nape to prickle, I ask, "Whatever do you mean?"

His smugness grows, right alongside my horniness. Giddiness clusters in my head, making me dizzy and whimsical. I should have realized our flirty banter would be just as powerful in person as it is over the phone. The tenseness surging between us is fire-sparking.

"How many times did you touch yourself after we've talked?" Marcus queries, his words strong and determined, a complete contradiction to my body's reaction to his highly insensitive question. My knees are wobbling so badly, if he didn't have me pinned to the pillar, I would have buckled to the floor by now.

"I don't have the faintest clue what you're referring to," I stammer out, my voice relaying my hammering heart. "I don't do *that.*"

I draw in a lung-filling gulp of air when he places his leg between my quaking thighs. The fire raging in my belly grows. Our conversation already has me forgetting what planet I live on, so having part of his body near an area begging for his attention is pushing me into full-blown moronic mode.

The breath I've just gulped in is fiercely forced back out when Marcus tugs my bottom lip away from my menacing teeth. The taste of copper fills my tongue when I run it along the seam of my stinging mouth. Shockwaves jolt through me. I was having such an out-of-body experience I didn't realize I was chewing on my lip so harshly.

After guiding his thumb along the path my tongue just took, Marcus connects his eyes with me. "If I didn't believe you're around five seconds from fleeing, I would call strike three. But since I'm feeling generous, I'll let your little lie slide."

After he drinks in my flushed cheeks and wide eyes, he says, "I don't just know you touched yourself after we talked, Cleo; I also know you screamed my name every time you came."

Jesus, who is this man? How the hell can he read me so easily?

Not willing to back down without a fight, I mumble, "Who said I was thinking about you? Maybe I was--"

My words stop when Marcus pushes his index finger against my lips. "Think before you speak, Cleo. You only have one strike left; use it wisely. The repercussions of your lies could be endless."

I ignore the way his finger causes my lips to tingle. "And what repercussions will you serve for your lies?"

Confusion spreads across his face like a tidal wave of misunderstanding. "I haven't lied, so I have no concerns of ramification."

"Then why ask me to sign an NDA?"

His entrancing eyes bounce between mine. "It's a commitment of confidentiality. Not just for me, but for you as well. NDAs are not uncommon in my lifestyle." His words are as confident as the agreement we're discussing. "If you had concerns regarding the NDA, why did you sign it?"

"I didn't." My voice is crammed with worry about how he will respond to me not signing the NDA.

His brows slant in confusion. "My lawyer called me an hour ago. He has your signed NDA locked in the safe in his office."

His last sentence comes out slower than his first when he notices me shaking my head. "If your lawyer is the man I met under the Brooklyn Bridge, he never gave me the chance to speak, let alone advise I had some reservations I needed cleared up before I would sign the agreement."

"Reservations? What possible reservations could you have about an NDA? They're pretty straightforward." His voice has a nip of irritation to it.

"The fact they're pretentious, arrogant, and intimidating." My snarl bounces off the stark white walls before shrilling into my ears. "If you truly want to know someone, it can be done without slapping a legal document in their face. Real men don't hide behind legal propaganda. They know what they want and go for it without getting lawyers involved."

Marcus balks as if my words physically slapped him. "*Real men?*

You think me asking you to sign an NDA doesn't make me a real man?"

The arrogance pumping from his eyes sends my libido rocketing to the next galaxy, but it doesn't stop me from nodding.

"If I wasn't a *real man*, Cleo—" My breaths increase from the seductive way my name rolls off his tongue "—that night at Chains, I would have taken you over the chaise in my playroom like your eyes were begging me to do."

"A *real man* would have said 'fucked over the chaise in my play-room,'" I mock, hating that my ability to goad him hasn't diminished in person.

"I don't fuck, baby; I decimate," He growls in a low and highly intimidating tone. "By the time I'm done with you, you won't even recognize yourself."

My pupils widen as a furious wildfire combusts in my heavy stomach. I've never been more turned on or intimidated in my life. How can six simple words snarled in arrogance cause such a vehement response from me? *I don't fuck, baby; I decimate.* Jesus, they're just as effective the second time around, even hearing them in my own voice.

"Flattery may get your everywhere, but intimidation gets you nowhere."

My weak tone relays the uncertainty of my reply. I'm truly at a loss about which way to take this conversation. Half of me wants to kiss the arrogance right off his face, where the other half wants to teach him a lesson like I did to Richard months ago—with a hard knee to his balls. I'm so baffled by the opposing set of emotions hammering into me. I truly feel like I'm two different people when I'm with him.

The egotism in Marcus's eyes grows. "Lucky for me, intimidation intrigues you enough your feet refuse to move."

"I'm here because you intrigue me, not because you intimidate me."

My pulse quickens when he steps even closer, not leaving an ounce of air between us. His new position ensures I can feel every rock-hard inch of his six-foot height and muscular frame. "Intimidation scares girls, but intrigues women."

"You think intimidation intrigues me?"

I release a shameful moan when he rocks his hips forward, dragging his thick rod along my heated core. "No, Cleo, I think intimidation turns you on and that's what intrigues you."

"You've only known me for a matter of weeks; you can't possibly believe that gives you enough insight into who I am."

"I know you well enough to confidently say your mouth speaks on behalf of your brain; your eyes express the pleas of your heart, and your body is the most revealing of them all. It not only expresses the sentiments of both your mind and your heart; it discloses your desires. The ones you're intimidated by."

I maintain his gaze. "It isn't intimidation that turns me on." My breathless words expose my aroused state. "It's you, *Master Chains*. Your eyes, your sinful mouth, your voice. Those are the things that brought me to climax when I touched myself after our conversations, not intimidation."

He stares at me, chest thrusting, eyes blazing. I maintain his heart-stuttering gaze, allowing my heart to win this round in the tormented heart versus mind battle I've been struggling through the past two months.

We stand as one for several moments. Even if I couldn't feel every inch of his delicious body pressed against mine, my body's awareness of his closeness would still be paramount. It can seek out its mate in a crowd of millions.

Only now do I realize it wouldn't matter how many objections my brain cited, this was never going to be a fair fight. Logic and common sense don't stand a chance against a man who holds the commanding appeal Master Chains has, because lust is truly the most potent poison to an ethical mind.

My eyes rocket to Marcus when he mutters, "I don't know whether I want to kiss the indecisiveness out of your eyes, Cleo, or spank it out." The deep manliness of his voice tracks through my veins like liquid ecstasy.

I lick my lips, giving my brain time to conjure an appropriate response. It's a pointless endeavor since I disclose, "If you play your cards right, I might let you do both."

Before the entire sentence can escape my lips, Marcus seals his mouth over mine.

17

*M*arcus growls a long, menacing groan when my mouth cracks open at the request of his tongue. Feeding off weeks of torturous foreplay, I scrape my fingernails over his clipped afro before sliding my tongue along his. The dizziness wreaking havoc with my stability earlier turns calamitous when the intoxicating flavors of his mouth overwhelm my taste buds. He tastes manly and sweet with a hint of expensive whiskey.

When I drag my tongue along the roof of his mouth, the intensity of our kiss switches pace. Marcus weaves his fingers through my wavy locks before tugging my head back roughly. I gasp, incredibly turned on by his dominant hold. Giving in to the command of his skilled kiss, I relinquish my mouth to his. He awards my submissiveness by rocking his hips forward, allowing me to discover I'm not the only one aroused by our tantalizing kiss. His cock is firm, hard, and struggling to be contained in his dark blue trousers.

As our tongues duel in a core-clenching showdown, I run my hands down the ridges of his back. I don't need to see him naked to confidently declare he has an amazing body. He's tall, but not gigantic, slender with a smattering of muscles in all the right places, and from what I feel braced against my heated core, well-equipped.

The more our kiss evolves, the louder the purrs rumbling up my throat become. If his kisses are anything to go by, his abilities in the bedroom will be out of this world. His kiss is strong, dominant and as captivating as his personality. It's above and beyond what I dreamed the past eight weeks. It's truly breathtaking.

Listening to the pleas of my heaving lungs, I throw my head back and gasp in some quick breaths. Taking advantage of my new position, Marcus drags his lips away from my tingling mouth to place a succession of bites and sucks on my exposed neckline. After sinking his teeth into my collarbone, his tongue soothes his bite. My breaths are greedy and rampant, shamefully displaying my enhanced state of arousal.

Marcus's fingers roll my budded nipple, making it impossible to catch my breath. Even through my satin dress and a padded bra, the twists and turns of his fingers cause me to writhe and buck against him. Shameful pleas for "more" roll off my tongue with every tweak. I thrash against him, willing him to go further, pushing him to give me more.

A whimpered moan simpers from my lips when his painful twist of my nipple sends a raging current to my soaked sex. My eyes snap open, and my breathing turns ragged as I fight through the frantic flow of desire scorching my veins. I'm both shocked and turned on by my body's response to his aggressiveness.

"Your nipples are extremely responsive," Marcus growls against my neckline. "Nipple clamps will increase their sensitivity even more."

Ignoring the pleas of my brain to seek clarification on nipple clamping, I thrust my chest out, urging him to repeat the action. A stronger, more potent current rockets to my sex when he twists my nipple again, a little harder than the first time. I writhe against him, my mind shut down, my body heightened beyond reproach. Nothing but the race to climax is on my mind.

Lost in the throes of ecstasy, I curl my legs around Marcus's waist and reacquaint our lips. I kiss him with all my might, striving to make him forget the callousness of my earlier words. He returns my kiss with just as much passion, a mind-stimulating blur of nibs, sucks and lashes of his delectable tongue.

I'm so entranced by his kiss, I don't register him moving us until the hardness of the pillar is replaced with the soft comfort of a deluxe couch. While matching the movements of Marcus's tongue stroke for stroke, I work on the buttons standing between me and his rock-hard body.

When the last button of his shirt is undone, I tear my mouth away from his. The dampness in my panties grows when my eyes drink in every delicious inch of his uncovered torso. Just as I had expected, his body is mind-spiraling: rippled abs, smooth, lickable pecs, and two bulges of muscles sitting on his shoulders all women love to sink their nails into when in the haze of climax. He's *P.E.R.F.E.C.T.*

The core-clenching visual of a shirtless Marcus is stripped from my vision when he flips me over. Modesty encroaches me when my skirt glides up my thighs to gather around my waistline. My doubt doesn't linger for long when Marcus runs his hand along my satin panties clinging to my soaked sex.

"You're drenched," he growls in a raspy groan.

With my head buried in the couch and my ass thrust in the air, his gifted hands work me into a frenzy. He plays my body as well as he plays the bass guitar in his chart-topping group, with a dominant confidence not many men embrace. Indescribable moans trickle from my O-formed mouth when his long strokes trigger more wetness to pool between my legs. I wriggle and buck uncontrollably, my body silently pleading for more.

My knees scrape across the expensive-looking couch when an unexpected slap stings my left butt cheek. "Stop wiggling so much," Marcus demands.

His commanding and stern voice bolsters my excitement, which in turn increases my wriggling. When a second slap hits the area still tingling from its first punishment, I cry out. It isn't a painful cry, more a cross between turned on and confused. The sting rocketing through my body is oddly arousing, but painful enough I follow his command and stop wriggling.

"Good girl," Marcus praises, his tone strangled by lust.

Panting to lessen my desire to climax, I twist my neck to the side when a strange scraping noise sounds through my ears. My pulse quickens when my eyes zoom in on Marcus's thick leather belt being dragged through the loops of his suit pants. Panic overtakes some of my unbridled horniness when images of what he may be planning to do with that belt bombard me.

I suck in nerve-calming breaths as my body pleads with my brain not to pass judgment before evaluating the situation. *Perhaps he's just removing his belt to ease his trousers down his thighs?*

Any possibility of my brain listening to the pleas of my body are left for dust when Marcus mutters, "Safe word, Cleo? I need to know your safe word."

Paralyzed by an equal amount of fear and arousal, I shake my head. Not noticing my silent rejection, Marcus adjusts my position. He alters the angle of my hips so I'm erotically exposed to him before tethering my hands behind my back with his leather belt. The coolness of the material is refreshing to my overheated skin, and the tightness of the restraint is constricting but not painful.

"You need less clothes," Marcus mutters while running his hand up my thigh, his touch warm and inciting. "But that will have to wait. I've grown impatient."

My breathing quickens when his hand reaches my aching-with-desire core. He pinches my throbbing clit before rolling the bud between his talented fingers and thumb. My grunts turn wild as confusion clouds me. I'm so conflicted. I shouldn't be enjoying this. I should be demanding for him to untie me this very instant. But I'm so aroused, even my astute brain has shut down. It can't focus on anything but the sheer brilliance that Marcus has me precariously dangling on the edge of orgasmic bliss by doing nothing more than spanking my ass and stroking my pussy through my panties. *God—if it didn't feel so good, I'd be calling myself a hussy.*

When Marcus slides my panties away and slips his finger inside me, all coherent thoughts vanish. "I knew we put a five down on spankings for a reason. You're saturated. Did you enjoy being spanked, Cleo?"

My muscles pull taut as every nerve in my body begs for release. "Yes," I breathe out heavily, unashamed and on the brink of combusting.

"Yes, what?" Marcus questions, increasing the tempo of his thrusts.

My shaking thighs echoes in my voice when I stammer, "Yes, Master Chains."

Pleasure ripples through me when Marcus growls a pleasing moan at my submissive response. When the lunges of his finger increase, so does the rock of my hips. I moan and rock, moan and rock over and over again until every fine hair on my body bristles with awareness of a lingering climax. A beading of sweat dots my forehead, and every muscle in my body is aching, but I don't slow my pace; I meet Marcus thrust for thrust.

My sways turn frantic when Marcus switches from one finger to two. I buck against him so uncontrollably the sofa feet jump along the thick wool carpet. I purr long, husky moans, loving the way his fingers are stretching me wide as he grinds them in and out of my drenched sex.

"Safe word, Cleo," Marcus demands again, his voice raising to ensure I can hear him over the frantic moans ripping from my mouth.

As one of his hands works me into an incoherent, blubbering mess, the other one slithers up the planes of my stomach before curling around my throat. His mouth swallows my throaty moans when he forces my head back and seals his lips over mine. His tongue assaults my mouth at the same frenzied pace his fingers fuck me.

I must be mad. I'm fully clothed, bent over a couch in an unknown location with a man I only officially met thirty minutes ago straddled over me, defiling me like no man has ever done before, and I'm the most turned on I've ever been. *Stuff mad, I'm a genius.*

"Oh god," I purr, when Marcus moves his lips away from my mouth to nibble on my earlobe.

"Safe word," he demands again before sinking his teeth into my ear.

My legs shake as my stomach muscles firm. I'm sweating, panting, and on the verge of combusting. My mind is in lockdown mode, my body fully relinquished to the man commanding every inch of it.

"Safe word," Marcus growls again, his stern tone snapping me out of the trance his talented fingers have me trapped in.

Sweat trickles down my inflamed cheeks when I shake my head. "No," I push out breathlessly. "No safe word. We don't need one."

"Without a safe word, I won't let you come," Marcus warns, his words gravelly and spine-tinglingly delicious.

His threat doesn't faze me in the slightest. My vagina clenches around his fingers as the shimmers of an earth-shattering orgasm come to life. By the time I give him a safe word, my orgasm will have already reached fruition.

My body screams blue murder when Marcus withdraws his fingers in one fell swoop. Before I have the chance to announce a protest, he exerts another slap to my left butt cheek. This one is even harder than the first two. I throw my head back and call out, appreciating the sting of warmth spreading across my backside.

"Safe word?" Marcus commands again while rubbing his palm over the blistering burn on my bottom.

"Pineapple," I mumble, my perception garbled by arousal. "My safe word is pineapple."

"Pineapple?" Marcus confirms, his voice relaying his uncertainty.

When I nod, he slips his fingers back into my throbbing core and increases his thrusts. He plunges into me so deep, he hits the sweet spot inside. He works my body like he knows every inch of me intimately, like he has studied every depth of me inside and out. I'm so wet, my thighs are glistening with my arousal, and his fingers slide into me without any hindrance.

I rock back and forth, forcing his fingers to plunge into me faster —harder. My mind is spiraling; I'm out of control. Nothing but incoherent grunts part my parched lips.

"Now, Cleo!" Marcus roars, his loud voice reverberating off the pristine walls of his sunken living room.

Aroused by his command, satisfied screams shrill into the cool night air as a blistering of fireworks detonate before my eyes. I quiver and shake, and my entire body pulls taut as a feverish orgasm overtakes me. The rough grunts tearing from Marcus's mouth increase my climax, pushing it from fire-sparking to earth-shattering.

When the manic throbs controlling my body become overwhelming, I back off my thrusts against Marcus's hand. I feel like I'm spiraling out of control, like I'm nearly on the verge of collapse. My muscles have never ached so much in my life.

Sensing my desire to slow down the lust running rampant through my veins, Marcus removes his fingers from my quivering core. With one of his hands gripping my hip, he glides his slick fingers through the swollen lips of my pussy and occasionally toys with my clit. His gentle touch tethers me down enough I can enjoy the revitalizing shimmer sparking through my body without feeling the disordered rebellion of my morals twisting my stomach.

Several minutes pass before every mind-hazing tremor of my orgasm has been exhausted. My climax was long and welcomed, completely shredding me of any energy I had left.

I'm so drained, I don't realize we have company until it's too late.

---

18

*I*t takes me stumbling backward and landing on my ass with a sickening thud before I realize the deep voice sounding through my eardrums is coming from an intercom attached to the wall of Marcus's sunken living room. We are still alone.

"Jesus, Cleo, don't hurt yourself," Marcus pleads, like he isn't the man who just spanked my backside until it's red and burning.

After adjusting my position to conceal my dripping core, I shift my eyes to Marcus standing at the side of the room. I watch him for several moments, absorbing all his silent prompts. His brows are beaded with sweat; his hands are fisted at his side, and his pants are well-extended at the crotch. He looks angry, confused and incredibly aroused. His expression mimics mine to a T. Well, except the angry part.

The dampness making my panties a sticky mess grows when he scrubs his hand over his hairless jaw. Evidence of my arousal glistens on his fingers. It's a rapid reminder of what we were in the process of doing before we were interrupted.

After taking in the grainy image of a man's face on the security monitor, Marcus turns his eyes to me. My heart falls from my chest when I see the apprehensive on his face. The only thing that stops disappointment from consuming me is my inability to register if his indecisiveness stems from wanting to ignore his impromptu caller or not wanting to mix business with pleasure.

Even if I weren't trapped in the haze of lust, I'd still recognize the face beaming out of the security panel. It doesn't take a genius to identify who a set of heart-thumping dimples on a soul-stealing face belong to. It's the lead singer of Marcus's band: Noah Taylor.

"Come on, Marcus, open up; we know you're home," Noah grins into the monitor, pushing the intercom buzzer a few times for good measure. "Hawke had Hunter trace your cell."

Marcus murmurs something under his breath. He's so quiet, I miss what he said. After pushing a button on his security panel, he paces back to me still sprawled on the floor. His commanding walk complements the demand emitting from his heavy-hooded gaze. He walks with a sense of importance, but not in an arrogant, pompous way you'd expect a man of his stature to hold.

After tugging my dress down to a respectable level, he connects his eyes with mine while uncoiling my bound wrists. His silent stare deepens the intense connection between us, making it feel more personal than just a physical attraction. It's raw and real, and it causes my heart to shudder.

I plead with my lungs to breathe when the veracity of our exchange filters into my spent brain. For that short instance on the couch, I truly let go. I was so caught up in the moment, I never once stopped to assess the barriers I've been placing between us the past eight weeks. Nothing was on my mind. Not a single darn thing.

Dropping his thick leather belt to the side with a clunk, Marcus carefully inspects the red welts circling my wrists. "Does it hurt?"

I shake my head. "Not in a bad way."

It feels nice wearing his marks.

He runs his thumbs over the indentations before lifting and locking his eyes with me. Unease spreads through me like a wildfire when I see a dark cloud of concern dimming his entrancing eyes. The thrumming of my veins slows as my worried eyes bounce between his. I hate that he's harboring uncertainty about our encounter when I'm feeling nothing but elation.

Noticing I've spotted his distress, the uncertainty in Marcus's eyes softens before a smirk forms on his kiss-swollen lips. His attempts at acting impassive curtail some of the regret slicing through me, but it doesn't completely vanish.

Remaining silent, he stands from his crouched position before brushing the wrinkles from his clothing. Once all the creases our tryst on the couch caused have been cleared, he drops his eyes to me. They don't look as barren as they did mere seconds ago. My lips crimp when he extends his hand in offering to assist me off the floor. The instant his hand curls around mine, my heart rate turns tempestuous, and it makes me wish I didn't see the quickest glimpse of a black stretch limousine rolling to a stop at the front of Marcus's property.

Instinctively, my hand darts up to flatten my disheveled hair. I'm not prepared for guests, let alone integral ones in Marcus's life such as his bandmates. My hair is a knotted mess from his firm hold, my lips are swollen from our kisses, and evidence of my climax is glistening on the inside of my thighs.

Heat extends across my lower back when Marcus spreads his hand on my spine and guides me out of his living room. Priceless paintings and smooth, crisp lines lead the way to a long hallway on our right. My legs are wobbling with the aftereffects of climax, making my steps down the elegant hall rickety. Have you ever tried to walk after an energy-draining orgasm? It's nearly impossible.

Gratefulness replaces some of the anxiety plaguing me when Marcus opens a door halfway down the corridor. "You can clean up in here while I get rid of my guests," he mutters, nudging his head to the pristine guest bathroom.

Sick gloom spreads across my chest, making it hard for me to breathe. Discovering the reason for the apprehension in his eyes hits me harder than I'm expecting, knocking me off-balance. Marcus grips my arms, thankfully halting my ungraceful topple to the floor. Even mad that I'm good enough to fondle on his couch, but not good enough to meet his bandmates doesn't stop an electric current surging up my arm from his firm hold.

Gritting my teeth at the opposing set of viewpoints pumping into me, I pull out of Marcus's grasp and take a step away from him. I feel dirty, ashamed—and quite frankly—used.

"I can go if you want me to," I suggest, loathing that my voice comes out shaky.

Marcus's eyes rocket to mine as his jaw muscle tightens so firmly it nearly snaps. "You want to leave?" he questions in a deep, hair-bristling tone.

I shake my head. "No. I just don't want to interrupt your normal flow," I reply, grateful my voice comes out sounding as it normally does, friendly, but composed. "I understand our meeting was unplanned, so I'm not expecting you to have a clear schedule." *Or hide me in a bathroom like a dirty secret*, but I keep that snarky comment to myself.

The confusion on Marcus's face intensifies with every word I utter, as does the anger in his frank eyes. When he stares down at me, nostrils flaring, eyes blazing, I begin to wonder if I said my silent thoughts out loud. A car door closing booms into the uncomfortable silence surrounding us, breaking our tense stare down.

"Look, forget I said anything. I'll just hide out in here until your guests leave," I mumble.

My brisk pace into the washroom halts when Marcus's arm darts up to brace against the doorframe. I inhale a sharp breath when his abrupt movement causes his intoxicating scent to invade my nostrils. As his panty-melting eyes bore into mine, he presses the palm of his opposite hand to the other side of my head, once again trapping me between him and an unmovable object.

I close my eyes and count to three before reopening, hoping to calm my nerves screaming in excitement. Any composure my deep breaths awarded me with vanishes the instant I lock my eyes with Marcus's narrowed gaze.

"Do you think I'm embarrassed of you?"

God—why does it hurt just hearing him suggest he's embarrassed of me?

"Answer me, Cleo," he demands, his voice crammed with palpable anger.

I shrug my shoulders. "Why else would you want to get rid of your guests?"

My body fails to breathe when he leans in intimately close to my side and mutters, "Because I want to finish what I started," into my ear. "I want to *possess* every inch of your body, then I want to do it again with you bound and gagged in my playroom."

Aftershocks of my orgasm quiver through my weary body. *Or is it a new climax?* I can't tell. I'm fairly sure it's a new one when a shameful moan topples from my O-formed mouth from Marcus sinking his teeth into my earlobe. My thighs meet when his tongue exonerates his bite with a pain-erasing lick.

Once the sting of his teeth is a distant memory, Marcus's mouth drops to pay dedicated attention to my exposed neck. His nips on my neck aren't as painful as the one to my ear, but they're strong enough to add to the wetness slicking my panties. They have me sucking in air like I've just ran a marathon, and I can't help but feel I'm being lured into a trap by his skillful mouth.

I'm so immersed in the chase of climax, I don't notice the ringing of Marcus's doorbell until he pulls away from my neck. I try to hold in my annoyance from the loss of his contact, my attempts fall short. An annoyed whimper parts my lips before my brain has the chance to register its arrival.

Satisfied with my shameful response, a sinful smirk etches onto Marcus's kiss-swollen mouth. "There will be plenty of time for that," he mutters, running his fingers along my neckline like he's erasing the marks his mouth made to my skin.

Once he's happy he has soothed the love bites on my neck, he locks his eyes with mine. My god, his eyes are beautiful. . . and so very familiar. How could I have ever doubted he was the same man in the elevator? I know I've seen his face splashed across the front pages of gossip magazines for years, but the feeling of familiarity I got when we first met was much deeper than the bizarre connection a fan gets with their idols. I know he's famous; I know he has more money than I could ever wish for, and I know he has a fascination with kink, but there's something more—much, much greater—that draws me to him. I just hope I can work out what it is before his overbearing aura swallows me whole.

Marcus runs his index finger down the crinkles in my nose from my confused expression, dragging my attention back to him. When I lock my eyes with his, he says, "Five minutes, Cleo. If you aren't out of this washroom in five minutes, I'll come find you."

"And?" I say when his sentence sounds unfinished.

His commanding gaze holds me captive as he mutters, "And I'll show you how disobedience requires discipline."

The threat in his words sends a shiver down my spine. Before I can ask exactly what discipline he's referring to, the doorbell ringing is replaced with fists banging on glass. Their knocks are so hard, I can imagine the glass warping from the undiluted pounding.

"Five minutes," Marcus warns again.

When I nod, he places a kiss on my mouth before spinning on his heels and ambling to the door. Even watching him walk away from me is a riveting experience. His steps are gracious, yet full of command, and it showcases his spectacular backside in the brightest light.

19

I wait until Marcus's retreating frame is no longer in view before stepping into the bathroom. As I pace toward the double sink and full-length mirror on the far wall, I absorb my flushed face, wide eyes, and kiss-swollen lips. The heavy swell of my breasts, still engorged with desire, bounce against my chest with every step I take. I've never seen myself like this before. Don't get me wrong, I've seen my aroused face in the mirror before, but not like this. I don't just look aroused. I look happy. Taken. *Claimed.*

My pupils grows when I spin around and peer over my shoulder. Shockwaves jolt through my body when I raise my dress and notice a red handprint marking nearly my entire left butt cheek. I should be appalled Marcus marked my skin. I should be marching out of this bathroom and demanding an apology for being handled so roughly. But the only thought passing through my lust-crazed head is how can I get a matching mark on the opposite side of my bottom.

What the hell is wrong with me? I'm not a submissive. I'm a strong-willed and determined young lady. I don't have a submissive bone in my entire body. *Do I?*

After taking a few moments to store away my concerns for a more appropriate time, I use a washcloth stored under the double vanity to clear away evidence of my arousal glistening on my thighs. As the warm material scratches my delectable skin, the events of the last forty-five minutes run through my mind. Although shocked at discovering Master Chains' true identity, that wasn't the most shocking part of my evening. And no, it isn't what you're expecting.

I'm not surprised by Marcus's dominance. If I hadn't met him entering a BDSM club, the dominating personality he displayed the past eight weeks was all the indication I needed to know he would be controlling in the bedroom.

My biggest surprise—the one that leaves me utterly flabbergasted —is my body's response to his aggressiveness. I'm not submissive, but that didn't stop my body from enjoying every spank, painful grip and twist he inflicted upon it. It relished it. *It loved it.* That's why I'm so damn confused.

Is it possible a feminist can be turned on by being controlled in the bedroom? If you had asked me before my interaction with Marcus tonight, I would have said no. Now, I'm not so sure.

A deep chuckle barreling down the hallway draws my focus away from my conflicting internal quarrel. Not willing to discover Marcus's idea of punishment, I finish clearing the smears of climax off my leg before running my fingers through my ratted hair. After dabbing the sweat off my face with an extremely soft hand towel, I hang it on the vanity and pace to the door. I inhale courage-building breaths before pulling open the door.

Chatter filters through my ears the instant I step into the hallway. Clearly, Marcus's endeavor to "get rid of his guests" was ineffective. Following the noise, I pace down the hall and round the corner. The first person I notice as I approach the sunken living room is Marcus standing near an attached bar at the side. The sleeves of his dress shirt have been rolled up to his elbows, and the crinkles our tumble on the couch created are barely seen with his shirt tucked back into his well-fitting trousers. The buttons are realigned and appear untouched. With his hair clipped close to his scalp and his lips already plump and inviting, he appears unaffected by the intermission to our heart-cranking gathering.

The only thing that gives it away is his leather belt sprawled on the floor next to the couch we were making out on. It's slithered between the legs of two extremely attractive brunettes who are eyeing me with suspicion. I'm not surprised by their reaction. I probably look a little weird frozen at the side of the living room, not moving or speaking.

Oh god—I hope they don't think I'm a deranged stalker.

Following their shocked gaze, Marcus's grip firms on the decanter of whiskey in his hand. After having a quiet word with the blond man standing at his side, he sets down the decanter and paces toward me. My pulse quickens with every prowling step he takes. It isn't just the spark of lust firing in his eyes sending my heart rate skyrocketing, it's the pin-drop silence surrounding us. It appears I'm not the only one stunned into silence. My reaction can be expected; I'm standing mere feet from one of the world's most prolific bands, but what's their excuse for their muted composure?

"Breathe, Cleo," Marcus demands when he stops to stand in front of me.

My body jumps at the clipped command in his voice by inhaling a lung-filling gulp of air. The endeavors of my struggling lungs double when he weaves his fingers through mine and guides me toward the beautiful group of specimens staring at me. Their faces are washed with confusion, their mouths gaped and hanging.

"Cleo, these are my band members, Slater, Noah, and Nick." Marcus points to a set of faces I've seen many times the past four years splashed across entertainment magazines. "And this is Emily, Jenni, and Kylie," he continues introducing. "Everyone, this is Cleo. My . . ."

His bandmates fail to notice he doesn't finish his sentence. They're too stunned to do anything but stare. I noticed, but I'm still reveling in the high of climax, and so speechless at the caliber of beauty in front of me, my brain hasn't had the chance to convey its thoughts.

When the silence shifts from unsettling to downright uncomfortable, I run my hands down my dress before lifting them to my face.

There must be a massive blemish on me somewhere the floor-length mirror in the restroom failed to point out.

I jump out of my skin when a deep voice on my left yells, "Marcus, you dog! Now your disappearing act last night makes sense." The voice is coming from Slater, the handsome blond man Marcus was speaking with earlier. He's the drummer of Rise Up.

With a grin that exposes his cheeky personality, Slater struts toward us. "So you're the one who's had Marcus's panties in a twist the past month," he says, peering into my eyes.

While accepting the hand he's holding out in offering, I shrug my shoulders. "Whatever do you mean?" I force out, my words not as strong as I'm hoping. "He'd have to be wearing panties before I could twist them up." I sigh when my voice comes out with the edge of playfulness I was aiming for.

My spirited response loosens Marcus's tight grip on my hand and causes Slater to throw his head back and laugh.

And just like that, the awkwardness plaguing our gathering is lost.

After accepting greetings from Nick and Noah in the form of a handshake, I am welcomed into the Rise Up family by Jenni and Emily with kisses to my cheek and tight hugs. Kylie's greeting still warms my heart, but it's a little more reserved than her predecessors. *Thank god.*

"You'll eventually get used to them," Kylie mumbles in my ear while giving me a brief hug. "They're a little heavy on the PDA, but they're wonderful people."

"Thanks," I reply, returning her gesture. Pulling back from her embrace, I drop my eyes to the tiny curve in her belly. "How long until you're due?"

"Twenty torturous weeks," Slater mumbles, his words muffled by the slice of pizza he's shoving into his mouth—pizza my grumbling stomach didn't know we had until now. "This baby isn't as willing to submit to the jam donut negotiation I made with Penelope."

Heat blooms across my chest from the glimmer Slater's eyes got when referring to his daughter. Although I've heard rumors Slater and Kylie want to keep their three-year-old daughter, Penelope, out of the spotlight, I've seen numerous paparazzi snaps of her. That's the one part I don't like about my job: the sleazy underhanded tactics some reporters will stoop to for a story. To me, the band members of Rise Up are fair game. They knew when they chose their career path that they were going to be targeted by the paparazzi, but I don't believe that logic should extend to their children.

"Speaking of children, where are they?" My brow archs into my hairline. With Marcus being the only member of Rise Up not in the family way, it's rare to see the band minus their mini counterparts.

"With the band just returning from a six-week press tour, the grandparents were chomping at the bits to get their mitts on them," Emily explains before her light brown eyes drift across the room to Noah, who playfully winks at her. "So we decided to take advantage of their eagerness with a weekend visit to New York."

"In other words, Slater was so desperate to know who Marcus was sneaking off to talk to every night, we used our naughty weekend privileges to find out," Kylie adds on.

My hands itch to cover my inflamed cheeks, but they remarkably remain in place. Mainly because of Marcus's firm grip.

"Hey, don't go putting this all on me. You guys were just as interested in discovering why Marcus up and left town in the middle of Thanksgiving as I was." Slater hooks his thumb to his bandmates, who don't attempt to deny his claims. "We only just got home, and Marcus was flying out the following morning at 2 AM. We all smelled a rat. I was the only one brave enough to go after it."

My heart thrashes against my chest when he locks his dark eyes with me. "Now we know where the smell is coming from."

Before he can spot my flaming cheeks his admission instigated, he connects his gaze with Kylie and mutters, "And don't worry, baby, I've got your naughty weekend covered. Didn't you see the big pool Marcus has out front?"

My confusion grows when Noah utters, "It's nearly winter."

"Pftt, do you think that will stop me?" Slater replies, his tone dead serious.

When everyone in the room laughs, I stand out of place, either not privileged to understand their private joke, or completely missing the punchline. Either way, their laughter is so contagious, I can't help the smile that curls on my lips.

My confusion increases tenfold when Marcus pulls me to his side before muttering, "Remind me tomorrow to get my pool drained."

By the time the three pizzas the band brought have been demolished, four hours have ticked by on the clock. Just from spending the last few hours with the integral members of Rise Up, I can confidently say any rumors circulating about the band dismantling are complete and utter lies. Within minutes of being introduced to them, I stopped seeing them as multi-platinum-selling artists. They're nothing more than a group of friends from a little unknown town in the state of Florida. Their bond is as strong as their unique personalities.

I place my empty wineglass onto the coffee table in the living room when Slater takes the empty seat next to me. Sensing my need of a refill, Marcus's pulse-racing eyes lock with mine. He silently questions if I'd like another without a word spilling from his lips. A flurry of giddiness inundates me. He has done the same thing numerous times this evening. He intuited my desires without a syllable needing to leave my mouth.

Not wanting to interrupt his conversation with Noah and Nick, I shake my head to his silent question. His attentiveness combined with my earlier orgasm is already making me lightheaded, let alone adding more alcohol into the mix.

"So," Slater drawls out, over-enunciating the short word in a long and rugged drawl. "What's the deal with you and Marcus?"

I pop my feet under my bottom and swivel my torso to face Slater. "I think you have our roles confused," I jest while taking in the way the lightness of his clipped hair makes his brown eyes pop off his face. Slater is a ruggedly handsome man, slightly larger in build than Marcus but of a similar height.

When he peers at me, confused, I add on, "Shouldn't I be probing you for information? You've known Marcus a lot longer than me."

"Yeah, but the shit I'd be sharing would be no different than his Wikipedia profile. You've got the good *stuff*. The secret *stuff*." He waggles his brows in a suggestive manner. "The *stuff* only someone who has his panties in a twist would know."

Masking my surprise that Marcus's enigmatic personality is just as strong with men who have known him for years, I say, "Oh, I didn't realize you swung *that* way."

Slater's brow cocks, and his face goes deadpan. "What way?"

"*That* way," I jest, peering into his eyes with a jeering expression stretched across my face.

It takes Slater a few moments to get the hidden innuendo in my cheeky response. When he does, his cheeks whiten and pupils dilate. "What the fuck?!" His roar gains the attention of everyone surrounding us. "I do *not* swing *that* way thank you very much."

"Why else would you want to know Marcus's sexual prowess unless you were planning on using it?"

When Slater gags, five sets of eyes gawking at us return to their earlier conversation. Clearly, his childish reaction is nothing out of the ordinary for them. The only pair of eyes that remain steadfast on us is Marcus. I don't need to take my eyes off Slater's repulsed face to know he's watching us. I can feel his gaze burning into me, searing me from the inside out as it has numerous times the past four hours.

Before tonight I never understood the saying, "Eye contact is more intimate than words could ever be." Now I do. I fully under-stand. I've heard more words expressed by Marcus's eyes the past four hours than I've heard from his mouth the last six weeks. Every glance he has directed at me has felt like a silent promise, a guarantee that he too is counting down the seconds until it's just him and I in his sprawling mansion once again.

Doing anything to stop me squirming in my chair, I return my focus to Slater. "Well if *that* isn't your thing, why do you want to know about Marcus's *secret* business?"

"Do you want me to be honest? Or sugarcoat it in a way Jenni and Emily appreciate?" Slater is the most serious I've seen tonight.

"I'd prefer honesty over sweetness any day." *Perhaps that's why I loved Marcus's dominance so much?*

"Alright, but don't say I didn't warn you," Slater warns, his voice a unique mix of humor and caution. "For years, I thought Marcus was either a virgin or into some fucked-up kinky shit."

Wow—the virgin part I wasn't expecting. But the fucked-up kinky shit pretty much hits the nail on the head when it comes to Marcus and his sexual proclivities.

Slater slouches deeper into the luxurious couch before drifting his eyes to Marcus. "In the beginning, I was certain my virgin theory was solid, but a saint wouldn't resist the temptations thrown at him every week the past four years. Being the only single guy in the band, Marcus could have pussy on a platter. . ."

Slater keeps talking, but I don't hear his words over the unwarranted jealousy ringing in my ears. I know I have no right to be jealous—Marcus isn't mine—but I can't stop the wave of possessiveness smashing into me. It grows and winds and twists in my tummy until the pizza I consumed at dinner is sitting in the back of my throat, begging to be released.

It's so strong, I dart my hand up to clutch my throat, trying to keep the contents of my stomach from seeing daylight. The instant my fingertips brush my neck, a flurry of memories bombard me. Images of Marcus kissing and caressing my neckline outside the bathroom come rushing to the forefront of my mind, overtaking the horrid images of him and scandalously clad groupies making out in the wings of the many stages he has graced in his illustrious career.

Fighting not to let him see my suspicion, I connect my fearful eyes with Marcus. Just as he has done every time I've sought his gaze across the room, he twists his head to the side and returns my ardent stare. Not speaking a word, my truth-seeking eyes silently interrogate him, asking a set of questions I'd never be game to articulate out loud. *Is this something you do every time you return home? Do you have a different woman waiting for you in every city you visit? Am I the only one who feels the ridiculous connection between us?*

Marcus's gaze is so commanding, his silent response never alters. "No. No. No."

My attention diverts from Marcus when a hand encloses over mine. "Hey, you alright?" Slater's voice is low and brimming with concern. "You look a little unwell."

Mine and Slater's necks crank to the side in sync when a low and simmering growl sounds over the gleeful hum of chatter filling the space. Marcus's jaw is tense, and his eyes are transfixed on mine and Slater's connected hands. His gaze remains stagnant until I tear my hand away from Slater's tight clutch. After bouncing his narrowed gaze between Slater and me for numerous terrifying seconds, Marcus returns to his conversation with Noah and Nick.

"Holy fucking shit," Slater murmurs under his breath, his voice low and overdramatized. "That noise did *not* just come out of Marcus's mouth."

Unaware if he's asking a question or stating a fact, I remain quiet. I don't think I'd be able to talk even if I wanted to. Marcus's manly growl has me frozen in place with desire. I can't speak nor move.

Slater stares at Marcus for several minutes, his face amused, his eyes bright. After scrubbing the scruff of his chin, he shifts his focus to me. The longer he studies me, the closer his brows join.

His perusal is so long and terrifying, I'm expecting something much more unsettling to come out of his mouth than, "Do you have any plans on the fifteen of December?"

20

The bristling of energy firing between Marcus and me is so dense, the air is infused with the pungent aroma of lust. From the moment he curled his hand around mine and commenced guiding me through his vast residence, an electric current has been surging up my arm nonstop. After bidding farewell to Marcus's bandmates, we've spent the last two hours like an ordinary couple on a date. The only difference between us and any other first-date couple is that our time was void of the usual awkwardness you'd expect. Because we've been communicating the last six weeks, we sidestepped the standard first date discomfort. Favorite foods, pet peeves and minutes of uncomfortable silence have already been achieved, leaving nothing but a clean slate.

Although the sexual connection between us is abundant, it isn't the only connection we have. Marcus is an extremely intelligent man. Conversing with him on any level is an inspired event, but doing it in person is truly mesmerizing. His bossy, kind-hearted, and opinionated personality displayed to me the past six weeks was replicated tonight, just in a more compelling, earth-shattering way. Visually seeing him express himself enhances his commanding voice. It was an invigorating, spine-tingling, and if I'm being honest, arousing experience.

Marcus has all the attributes you want in a man. He's devilishly good-looking; has charisma, charm and wit; and he portrays a sense of confidence that not only assures you'll be thoroughly taken care of in the bedroom, but that you'll also never forget the experience. His only downfall is every conversation we've held includes the words submissive, discipline, and last, but not at all least, safe word.

I don't know about you, but the fact Marcus needs to hear any other word than "stop" to know I've reached my limit sends warning alarms off in my head. Don't get me wrong, I knew from the instant I met him in the alley of Chains he was never going to be a man to sprinkle rose petals over a four-poster bed while Chopin played softly in the background. I didn't arrive here expecting hearts and flowers, but I also didn't envision a cold and sterile feeling during our interactions either.

How can a man who exudes so much raw sexual energy not exert that same feeling while discussing his sexual ambitions? Why does he treat sex like it's a business transaction instead of an act of pleasure?

My thoughts stray from analyzing the inner workings of a complex man when Marcus's deep timbre sounds through my ears. Shifting my eyes to him, my breath traps in my throat. From the way his jaw is ticking and the thinness of his eyes, anyone would swear he heard my inner monologue.

I swallow down the unease twisting my stomach. "Sorry, I kind of spaced out for a minute."

He nods, accepting my pitiful excuse, but my assurance does nothing to lessen the twitch in his razor-sharp jawline.

While walking the elegant hallway in the top level of his house, he gives me a rundown on the layout of his property. "Powder room, gym, media room and spare guest bedroom." He points to a door corresponding to each location.

He places my overnight bag on the floor just outside a set of double doors before delving his hand into his pocket. My heart rate climbs when he produces a silver key similar to the one he used to unlock the door of his playroom in Chains. I stand frozen in lust when he slides the key into the lock and twists the handle.

Shock—and a dash of disappointment—consume me when he swings open the door, revealing a bright, airy room with a white four-poster bed covered by a rose-printed bedspread. A highly inappropriate giggle seeps from my lips before I have the chance to shut it down. My response can't be helped. Although it isn't exactly what I was envisioning earlier, it's pretty darn close.

Hearing my quiet laughter, Marcus drops his gaze to me. He takes a few seconds absorbing my raised cheeks and glistening eyes before asking, "Is there something you find amusing?"

"No." I shake my head. "It just isn't what I was expecting for your bedroom."

"This isn't my bedroom." His response is direct and straight to the point.

"It isn't?" The disappointment in my tone can't be missed.

Marcus shakes his head. "My room is down the hall and to the left."

I twist my neck in the direction he's pointing. "What's on the right?" I ask when I notice the hallway splits in two at the end.

Remaining quiet, he gathers my bag and paces deeper into my room. Just when I think he isn't going to answer my question, he mutters. "It's my playroom."

My eyes bug. "You have a playroom in your house?"

"Yes."

"Why?"

My heart falls from my chest when he says, "Because I need. . . *more*, Cleo."

"More than we did on the couch?"

I silently pray he says no.

My prayers go unanswered when he answers, "Yes. What I did earlier was wrong. I shouldn't have done it."

His words physically impact me, pushing my confidence to a level I've never experienced before. *It's a dark and very lonely place.* Fighting against my wobbly legs, I pace deeper into the room and sit on the bed. I feel sick. Actually, I feel disgusting. How could I have misread things between us so badly? I was certain his eyes were revealing just as much excitement as mine. I've never read someone so poorly before.

I'm so immersed in keeping in the contents of my stomach, I don't notice Marcus crossing the room until he's crouched down in front of me. He places his fingers under my chin and lifts my head. He peers into my eyes, his face washed with confusion. I can tell the exact moment he reads the prompts in my eyes. He intakes a sharp breath, and his pupils dilate.

"It was nothing you did, Cleo." His voice is smeared with uncertainty. "It was me. I lost control. I did things I've never done before. Things I'm ashamed of."

The confusion in my eyes grows tenfold. I'm completely and utterly gobsmacked.

Marcus scrubs his tired eyes before admitting, "I've never *interacted* with a sub outside of a playroom."

"I'm not your submissive, Marcus," I interrupt, my words garbled by the nausea swishing in my stomach.

He nods, agreeing with my admission. "That's another mistake I made."

The regret in his eyes doesn't match his statement. If he's trying to ease the conflict tearing my heart in two, he's doing a terrible job.

"Maybe I should go." I stand from the bed. "Maybe the only mistake you made was bringing me here."

"No!" Marcus pleads, his voice growing louder. "Give me a chance to work out a way to explain this to you in a manner a *normal* person would understand."

Grief makes itself comfortable with my chest from the pained way he said "normal." I had no idea he was taking my taunts on his weirdness the past eight weeks literally. If I did, I would have stopped being so narrow-minded and expressed my confusion on his sexual preferences with more diligence. He has been open and upfront with me for weeks, and I returned his candidness with hurtful jokes I'm sure he's heard many times before.

Breathing out my guilt, I wrap my hand around his and sit back on the bed. "Give it to me straight, Marcus. Don't worry about hurting my feelings or sugarcoating it, just hit me with honesty."

He takes a few moments glancing into my eyes, gauging the truth in my request before saying, "Because I've only had Dom/sub relationships the past four years, all sexual contact was done in a playroom situation, the one place I have complete control. Tonight, I struggled because I wanted to exert that same level of control over you, but I couldn't."

His confession surprises me. He was already displaying command I've never experienced, so it has me wondering how much dominance does he instill in his playroom?

"I've blatantly defended the transfer of power in a BDSM lifestyle as a choice. Tonight, I took away your choice."

I glare at him, shocked and confused. "You didn't take anything away from me. Not anything I didn't want to give."

"Yes, I did. I should have never interacted with you without first knowing your safe word, and I most definitely shouldn't have forced you to give me one. That's not the way things in this lifestyle work. The transfer of power is a gift, not a rule. There's just something about you, Cleo. You make me reckless, and quite frankly, I don't like it."

An inappropriate smile stretches across my face before I have the chance to stop it. My response can't be helped. I've had many heedless thoughts about Master Chains the past two months. It's nice knowing I'm not the only one harboring confusion about our bizarre connection.

I lift and lock my eyes with his. "Doesn't your recklessness make you wonder if there's something more between us than just a Dom/sub relationship?"

"Yes." He curtly nods, "But that isn't something I want."

Although I can appreciate his honesty, my smile is wiped straight off my face. "Why?"

"Because I need the power, Cleo. I need the control. Tonight proved that. You have no idea how hard it was for me to hold back. Dominance is who I am; I can't just switch it off."

"So you need to hurt me to get pleasure?" I ask with my brows scrunched together, confusion in my tone.

"No." He shakes his head, "I'm not a sadist, Cleo. I just need the control and the trust that comes along with a Dom/sub relationship. There, I know the boundaries and the rules. I can't offer the same amount of assurance outside of that."

I sit muted for several minutes, unsure how to respond to his affirmation. I'm glad he has continued being truthful, but it doesn't make it any easier to swallow. He isn't the only one who needs more. I want the affection that comes from a partnership—the cuddling after sex, the dates that lead to a night of lovemaking. I want someone who doesn't look at me as if I'm lesser than he is. I get that enough in my everyday life. I don't need it in my personal life.

Marcus catches my eye for the briefest second, pushing my doubts to the very background of my mind. Clearly, since I ask, "Theoretically, what would a Dom/sub relationship involve?"

Over the next ten minutes, he gives me a general rundown on how his previous D/s agreements worked. For the most part, I listened attentively, but occasionally, I interrupted him to get an explanation on BDSM jargon I was not familiar with. It was an informative and eye-opening discussion that eased some of my curiosity while also increasing it.

It wasn't just the vast range of information I was bequeathed that added to my confusion, it was my reaction to his admissions. I was expecting uncertainty to be the greatest emotion I'd be handling during our discussion, but it wasn't. It was jealousy. Even with Marcus not interacting with his previous subs in any form until they signed a legally binding contract didn't diminish the vehement jealousy consuming me. I hated the idea of him being with anyone—*hated it*!

The only thing that eased the furious rage blackening my blood was when Marcus advised why the band acted so shocked this evening. Not once in the thirteen years they've known each other have they met anyone associated with Marcus's personal life. Until tonight, he kept his business and personal life at opposing ends of the field. I'm the very first person to meld them together.

My focus shifts from staring into space when Marcus stands from the bed. "I've given you a lot to consider, Cleo, so why don't I give you some time to actually deliberate?"

Not waiting for me to reply, he strides to the door. Just before he exits, I call his name. He pauses halfway through the door for four long heartbeats before swinging his eyes to me. His expression mimics mine perfectly. He's just as confused, aroused, and conflicted as I am.

"Have you ever considered the possibility of having the best of both worlds?"

His throat struggles to swallow before he replies, "If you'd asked me two months ago, I would have said no."

Not elaborating on his response, he spins on his heels and exits my room.

---

21

*B*y the time I wake the following morning, the sun isn't even hanging in the sky yet. With most of my night spent tossing and turning, my temples are throbbing, and my eyes are presenting the effects of a restless night. I'm so incredibly confused as to what happened last night. I can smell Marcus's cologne in my hair, feel where he has been inside me, but the area that races every time I think about him hasn't beaten the same since he stalked out of this room.

For weeks, I tried to convince myself that my attraction to Master Chains was nothing more than craving something I couldn't have. But that isn't true. Yesterday proved that. The more I battled my desires, the stronger my feelings grew. Have you ever tried to deny the pleas of your heart? It's harder than refusing to let your eye blink. It's impossible. That should mean something, shouldn't it?

That's why I stopped fighting my attraction yesterday. I gave in to the desires of my body and heart. Our steam-filled tryst on the couch was perfect; even my astute brain has a hard time finding a flaw, so why can't Marcus look past his need to dominate me? Why can't he see our encounter for what it was? An intense connection between two red-blooded humans.

Realizing I'll never get the answers I need here, I throw off the rose-printed bedspread and trudge to the attached bathroom of my suite. Even with my mind scrambled with confusion, it can't miss the invigorating tightness only an ego-bolstering orgasm can cause to weary muscles. It's a blissful reminder of the cruel and tormented night I had.

When I reach the pristine bathroom, I undo my dress I slept in and let it drop to the floor. In silence, my desecrated panties closely follow it. As I step into the double-sized shower, the quickest glimpse of my marked bottom in the vanity mirror freezes both my feet and my heart. Just like the past six weeks, the pleas of my heart and brain are on disparate sides, neither willing to back down on their stern beliefs. My body... that's an entirely different story. It doesn't give two hoots about the pleas of my brain nor my heart. It just wants Marcus.

My heart rate quickens when I recall what Marcus said to me yesterday, "*I know you well enough to confidently say, your mouth speaks on behalf of your brain; your eyes express the pleas of your heart, and your body is the most revealing of them all. It not only expresses the sentiments of both your mind and your heart; it discloses your desires, the ones you're intimidated by.*"

He truly can read me like no man before him.

My love of a long, steaming shower is forgotten when I'm bathed and dressed in less than three minutes. With my desire to find Marcus more compelling than my urge to wrangle my hair into a presentable state, I throw it into a messy bun before exiting my room.

The cuff on my ripped jeans drags along the polished wooden floor as I search each of the rooms located on the lower level of Marcus's residence. When I fail to locate him, I gallop back up the curved stairwell. While gliding through the impressive gym and twelve-seater media room, I roll up the sleeves of my paisley-print long-sleeve shirt. With the heating in the house set to a sweltering temperature, my body is slicked with sweat.

My tornado speed through Marcus's residence slows when I walk past a cracked open door that was closed last night. It's the door opposite his bedroom, the room that had me tossing and turning until the wee hours of this morning: his playroom.

With my teeth grazing my bottom lip, I knock on the door with a silver key dangling out the lock. "Marcus? Are you in there?"

I prick my ears, seeking any signs of life. When I neglect to find any, I push open the door. Nerves spread across my chest as my eyes roam uncontrollably around the room. Although it's void of the same dark, dingy feeling Marcus's playroom at Chains has, there's no doubt this is his playroom. It isn't just the variety of floggers on the wall that gives it away; it's the studded leather chaise that featured in my fantasies the past eight weeks, and a weird cage-like contraption in the middle of the space.

Allowing my inquisitiveness to get the better of me, I pace deeper into the room. As my eyes drink in a wood cross contraption bolted to a wall on my right, I run my fingers over the leather chaise. Flashes of Marcus spanking me yesterday rush to the forefront of my mind when the coolness of the leather graces my fingertips. I could image how tantalizing heated skin from being spanked would feel when placed onto the cool smoothness of his chaise.

My aimless wandering around Marcus's playroom ends when a shimmering of white captures my attention. After checking I'm still alone, I move toward the wooden chest tucked under a matching set of drawers. The closer I get, the more my heart rate climbs. I don't need a PhD in BDSM to know what the pearl-like balls the size of marbles are. I'm just grateful they look unused.

My desire to open the wooden chest slips from my grasp when I notice a pile of paperwork sitting on top of the only drawers in the room.

Angling my head to the side, I scan the document. My heart lurches into my throat when I read the first line under 1.0.0 of the contract. "Submissive agrees to give power to Dom/Master for the agreed period of time as stated in this contract."

That's one of the biggest dilemmas a night of contemplation was unable to erase. What happens to me once Marcus has had his fill?

Will I be disregarded and forgotten as easily as his last submissives were? Will he just move on and find another sub the following week? Those thoughts are more sickening to me than the idea of being whipped with the metal flogger I saw in his playroom at Chains. I hate the thought he could lose interest in me as quickly as he gained it. I guess that's why he so adamantly declared last night that a relationship between a Dom and his sub is not about love. It's purely about a sexual connection.

My heart rate steps toward coronary territory when a deep voice sounds into the room. "What are you doing in here, Cleo?"

Clutching my chest to ensure my heart remains in its rightful spot, I swing my eyes to the left. With an impressive frame filling the doorway, the sheen of light illuminating the room fades, aiding my nearsightedness. I don't need a light to identify the man standing by the door, though. My quickening pulse and the bristling of the hairs on my nape is the only indication I need to distinguish the shadowed stranger.

"You scared me, Marcus." I saunter closer to him.

With his frame no longer blocking the light beaming into the room, my poor eyesight has no troubles spotting him. My steps stop as rampant horniness clusters in my womb. I demand my lungs to breathe as I watch a rivulet of sweat roll off Marcus's firm pec before weaving through the bumps of his abs. Once the bead of sweat has been absorbed by the dark blue coveralls he's wearing unclipped, I raise my eyes to his, taking in every cut muscle on his glistening torso on the way.

The throb of my pussy switches from barely controlled to manic when I notice a length of chain around his neck. The links are loosely coiled around the impressive muscles sitting on top of his shoulders before draping down the deep groove in his chest. *I've never seen such an erotic visual in my life.*

My hand darts up to clutch my chain link pendant when I notice one of his chain links is positioned in the exact spot my pendant sits. They're nearly identical in size and coloring. When I lock my eyes with Marcus, the shift in the air between us is so great, my knees buckle.

My inquisitiveness soon gets the better of me."What are you doing?"

"You shouldn't be in here."

"Why?" Disappointment rings in my tone. "You want to show me the real you. Why not do it in a place you feel most comfortable?"

Gratefulness spreads through me that my tone didn't come out with the usual snarkiness it holds when I taunt him.

"This isn't a game, Cleo. This isn't a place you enter to ease your curiosity. This is a place you come once it no longer exists."

"It's a little hard to ease my curiosity about a world I know nothing of if I can't first enter it." My voice is stern yet pleading. "You say you need more. Well, so do I. More information. How can you expect me to understand your desires if you're not willing to explain them in a way I can understand them?"

His stares at me with blazing eyes. His jaw muscle is tense, his fists balled. After what feels like an eternity, he pushes off his feet and saunters deeper into the room. With his entrancing eyes locked on me, he unravels the chains draped around his neck. I watch him with eagerness when he unscrews a U bolt at the top of the cage-like contraption in the middle of the room and attaches the chain he was wearing to the end. The muscles in his cut arms flex when he yanks down hard on the chain, ensuring it stays in place. Happy it didn't budge an inch under his rough pull, he paces to an oak wardrobe on his right.

My barely-put-together composure is placed under pressure when Marcus removes a padded leather chair from the top shelf of the cupboard. I'll be the first to admit I'm a novice when it comes to sexual apparatuses, but I can still recognize what he's clasping. It's a sex swing. It isn't your typical-looking sex swing, though. It's much sturdier than the ones my internet research into the BDSM community unearthed. This one has chains weaved throughout the padded design and looks like it could hold the weight of twenty people.

After attaching the seat to the steel cage, Marcus turns his eyes to me. "I made this for you. I drew up its design the night you left Chains with the intention of claiming you in it."

"You made it for me?"

My words are ditzy and make me want to cringe, but my flabbergasted response can't be helped. He not only made a sex swing for me, he wanted to claim me as his from the night we met.

Marcus stares into my eyes before nodding. He doesn't need to speak for me to know the words he really wants to say. *This is me, Cleo. The real Marcus. The one you're intimidated by. The one you're too scared to admit you're turned on by. The one you want to dominate and control you.* Okay, maybe the last sentence was my inner monologue, not Marcus's.

Following the demands of my body, I push off my feet and head toward Marcus. The warning growl simpering through his hard-lined lips nearly halts my steps, but I push on, determined to prove there's something greater between us than just a Dom/sub relationship. Not just to him, but to me as well. And if I'm being honest, I'll also admit I'm incredibly aroused at the idea he made a sex swing for me. From its technical design and the pure sturdiness of it, this isn't something he just whipped up overnight. This took time. Time a busy man like him doesn't have.

For every step I take, the sexual tension between us thickens. The pungent aroma of lust filtering through my nose strengthens my strides while also increasing the wetness between my legs. He holds my gaze, his eyes warning me that I'm skating on thin ice. His whole composure screams of dominance, and it has me the most aroused I've ever been.

By the time I stop in front of him, the reasoning behind my original endeavor has been lost. Nothing but the desires of my body are at the forefront of my mind.

"Show me how it works," I request, my voice displaying the plea associated with it. I'll be beyond devastated if he walks away from me now.

Marcus eyes me for several moments, appraising the true response from my forthright eyes. *I want you to claim me—badly!* I can see his ambiguity winding up from his stomach to his entrancing eyes. For the first time, the confident shield he wears like armor doesn't appear as shiny as usual.

Just when I think he's going to deny my request, he commands, "Remove your jeans."

22

I comply with Marcus's request, removing my jeans at a rate quicker than their skintight design is accustomed to. I peel them off my quaking thighs before kicking them to the side.

With his eyes connected with mine, he gathers my jeans, folds them, then places them on top of the set of drawers housing his Dom/sub contracts. I swallow several times in a row when he pivots back around to face me. The indecisive he was dealing with mere minutes ago has vanished, replaced by a man whose aura demands respect.

My shoulders roll when his eyes drop to take in my thrusting chest. He assesses every inch of me in a long, dedicated sweep, like he's categorizing each individual piece of me as if they are prized treasures.

The unease burning my veins simmers when Marcus mutters, "You can keep your shirt. . . for now."

When he strides toward me, I close my eyes and draw in some deep breaths. My heart is racing, and my knees are curved inwards. I'm both nervous and excited.

My eyes pop back open when the sweetness of his breath hits my lips. The air from my lungs rushes out in urgency when I find myself glancing into a set of determined eyes. It comes charging back in when Marcus reaches between my legs and snaps my panties off my body.

He stares at me, studying my reaction to his aggression. I feel nothing but dizziness, my head woozy with the potent desire of lust. His lips tug in the corner, no doubt pleased at my submissive response. His lewd smirk boosts the wetness puddling between my thighs, and it forces me to squirm on the spot. My hands twitch to touch him, but I keep them fisted at my side, remembering I'm not the one calling the shots.

Like he can sense my desire, Marcus reaches out and secures my hands in his. He runs them over his sweat-glistening torso and down the bumps of his abs before stopping at the bulge in the crotch of his overalls. My breathing kicks up a notch when I feel how hard and thick he is. He wants me to know how aroused he is. He wants to assure me I'm not the only one being ruled by my libido, and that he's just as attracted to me as I am him.

After running my hand down his rod, Marcus shoots his other hand out to clutch my shirt. He waits until I've secured an entire breath before he raises the hem and pulls it over my head. My nipples bud as the scent of my arousal lingers in the air.

He holds my gaze for several terrifying moments before he drops his eyes to my exposed breasts. I snubbed the tight restraints of a proper bra as my shirt has a built-in one. After giving both of my breasts an equal amount of attention by using nothing but his soul-captivating eyes, he lowers his gaze to my glistening sex.

I swear, I nearly combust into ecstasy when his tongue delves out to replenish his dry lips. I should be ashamed by how wet I am. I'm so drenched, I can feel dampness on my thighs. But I'm not embarrassed or ashamed. From the way Marcus is looking at me, I feel nothing but desired.

He truly is a Master. He has me sitting on the edge of ecstasy, and he hasn't even touched me yet. That's remarkable. . . and slightly concerning. If he has so much power over my body using nothing but his eyes, imagine how intense it will be when he actually touches me?

I guess I'm about to find out since he's reaching toward me.

Goosebumps prickle my skin when he curls his arms around me and dips me backward.

"Oh god," pants from my mouth when the coolness of leather graces my backside.

Maintaining a quiet approach, Marcus adjusts my position so I'm nestled deep into the padded seat of the swing. Soft leather hugs my curves while the double-stitched edge digs into my nape. My new position exposes my throbbing core to Marcus's more-than-avid eyes. I'm poised in front of his half-dressed form as naked as the day I was born, but not a skerrick of indignity encroaches me. I squeeze my legs together to lessen the scandalous throb. My efforts are fruitless when Marcus slides his hand up my thighs to pry them apart.

"If you move them again, I'll spank you," he warns, his tone low and bristling.

When my knees join to ease the excitement his threat instigated, he adds on, "With the cane."

That instantly halts my childish squirms. *I can't imagine how that could ever be pleasant?* After peering at me beneath a set of incredibly long lashes, Marcus moves around the cagelike contraption, adjusting the thick chains shackled inside the pen before untethering the leather cuffs at the side of my head.

Agitated excitement sears through me when I realize what the cuffs are for. They will bind me to this chair—willingly! They ensure I'm not just going to be unable to move; I'll be at the complete mercy of Marcus. That's why he designed this swing, so I'd be under his complete control. I won't be able to move without his assistance, let alone steer the direction of our exchange. *Why do I find the idea of that incredibly arousing?*

Within minutes, my legs are suspended midair, and my wrists bound above my head. The chains woven through the leather seat are draped across my breasts and positioned in a crisscross pattern down my stomach. The urge to squeeze my legs together grows when Marcus adjusts the chains so they form an X above my glistening sex.

The coolness of the material gives relief to my overheated skin, while also adding a naughty edge to an already wicked exchange.

Keeping his eyes on the task at hand, Marcus asks, "What's your safe word, Cleo?" His voice as smooth as melted chocolate.

I lick my dry lips before answering, "Pineapple."

"Say it again," he demands. The command in his voice gains the attention of my slicked sex.

"Pineapple," I breathe out heavily.

After shackling the chains draped between my legs to the seat of the swing, Marcus lifts his eyes to me. My pulse quickens when I see the command beaming from them. He's in full control and loving every minute of it.

"If at any stage you feel uncomfortable, say your safe word, Cleo. It will immediately stop what we are doing."

I nod, acknowledging I understand. I may be a BDSM novice, but I've researched a lot on this lifestyle, and I believe I now have a broad understanding of why a safe word is needed during exchanges of power like this.

"But don't use your safe word haphazardly. Because the instant you say it, our play session immediately ends, and it will not start back up," Marcus warns, his voice direct and firm.

While grazing my teeth over my bottom lip, I nod. "I understand."

My skin inflames with heat when Marcus runs his index finger across my collarbone before trailing it down my thrusting chest. He tweaks right nipple, twisting and rolling it until it's stiff and puckered. He plays with my nipple for mere seconds, but it feels like hours. His skills are impressive. He's barely touched me, and I'm panting, wet, and dying for release.

Once he has my nipple painfully sitting on edge, he switches his devotion to my left breast. "You're very responsive to touch. I like that," he declares with a wicked gleam in his eyes.

When my left nipple is as hard as my right, his finger traces the chain pattern crisscrossing my stomach. My muscles tighten with every millimeter he gains toward my aching-with-desire sex. My head flops back, and my eyes shut when he runs his hand down my glistening mound.

"You're drenched," he growls out, his voice raspy. "And you haven't even gotten to the good part yet."

Before I can request an explanation, I'm suddenly flipped over. A frightened squeal emits from my lips when I freefall toward the hardwood floor of the playroom. I thrust out my arms to soften the blow, forgetting that they're restrained at the side of my head.

Suddenly, my panic switches to excitement when the coolness of metal hits areas of my body inflamed and throbbing. I gasp in a quick breath before releasing it in a low throaty moan. The chains weaved in the leather swing aren't just stopping me from plummeting to the rigid floor; they're rubbing against erogenous zones of my body, predominately, my pounding clit and tweaked nipples.

My concerns of falling to my death are pushed aside as I writhe in my seat, trying to increase the pressure of the chain link on my aching clit. My frantic breaths level, and my body prepares for climax when my thrusts against the chain spur a surge of anticipation to cluster through me. The odds of me descending into orgasmic bliss matures when a firm slap hits my right butt cheek. Marcus's hit is so hard, even the thick padding in the chair can't take away from its fiery sting.

"Do not come, Cleo," Marcus demands, his voice stern and commanding. "Until I say the word, you're not to come. Do you understand me?"

It takes a mammoth effort, but I squeak out, "Yes."

"Yes, what?" he asks while adjusting the chains provocatively draped around my sex so they produce the perfect pressure to my throbbing clit.

"Yes, Master Chains," I reply, my voice quivering with arousal.

Marcus cups my pussy. His movements increase the pressure on my clit, while his hand expands my excitement. My chin quivers as I fight with all my might not to let the throes of ecstasy overwhelm me. My attempts nearly become unwinnable when he slips two fingers inside my quivering core.

With the chain links painfully pinching my nipples and clit, and his fingers grinding into me at a frantic pace, I grunt incoherently and lose all cognition. My breathing pans out as my body prickles with awareness of a pending orgasm. The rush of desire is frantic, over-whelming me.

"Please," I beg shamefully, no longer capable of holding in the silent screams of my body. "Please, Master Chains. I want to come. I need to come."

"Need and want are two very different things, Cleo. Which one is it?" He quickens the thrusts of his fingers, driving me to the edge even more.

I call out as the signs of an earth-shattering orgasm surface. Goosebumps prickle my skin as my body shakes uncontrollably.

"I *want* to come," I grunt, my words barely recognizable. "But I *need* you to make me come."

"Good girl," Marcus mutters, his voice temptingly pleased.

With his other hand, Marcus grabs the edge of the swing and yanks it toward him. My thighs quake when his fingers plunge into me even deeper. He's so deep, I can feel the tips of his fingers brushing my cervix. Sweat gathers between my breasts before rolling down my torso and dripping on the floor near Marcus's bare feet. As his fingers grind in and out of me on repeat, I feel the storm of climax rolling in. It's angry and full of torment, and dying to break free.

"Now, Cleo!" Marcus roars, his loud voice enhancing the shakes hampering my body. "Come now!"

I pop my eyes open as pure, unbridled wildness scorches through me. I grunt and moan, my muscles pulling taut as an intense orgasm inflicts every inch of me. Marcus continues stimulating me, taking me to the very brink of sanity by using nothing but his talented fingers.

"Stop. Oh, god, please stop. It's too much. Too strong. I can't handle it," I beg when the most awe-inspiring orgasm I've ever endured continues to pummel into me.

"If you truly want me to stop, say your safe word, Cleo," Marcus replies. His voice sounds exerted, like he's enduring the throes of orgasm right alongside me.

The roughness of his tone intensifies the strength of my climax. My ankles push against the cuffs curled around them before my body gives in to the upwelling of desire striving to overtake it. I stop thrashing against the restraints holding me firm, shut my eyes, and let the bliss of orgasm sweep me away.

My core tightens as waves of pleasure roll over me. Tingles race from my budded nipples to my quivering thighs. My orgasm is powerful, long, and utterly exhausting.

"Good girl," Marcus praises, his words barely heard over my long, winded grunts.

I've barely emerged from the clouds of climax when Marcus flips the sex swing back over. I inhale my first full breath in over twenty minutes when the pressure of the chains is alleviated from my chest. My eyes flutter open and closed as an extreme bout of tiredness over-whelms me. I'm panting and hot, both from arousal and the shock of our intense exchange. Blinking to ward off sleep, I take in numerous lung-filling gulps of air to calm the mad beat of my heart.

The heat burning me from the inside out grows when my eyes stumble upon a breathtaking visual. I was so immersed in the paroxysm of climax, I didn't notice Marcus had removed his overalls. Mesmerized by the deliriously handsome specimen standing in front of me, I run my tongue along my parched lips as my eyes scan-dalously drink him in. He has such an amazing body. Firm and hard, and so very masculine. It's like God designed him only using the best parts: slender hips; banging guns; tight, firm pecks; and rippled abs that hit every one of my hot buttons.

The struggles of my heaving lungs double when my eyes drop to Marcus's thick, jutted penis. I suck in deep breaths as I stare at his naked package unashamed. I knew from what I felt earlier his cock was going to be impressive; I just didn't realize it would be *that* impressive. It's long and mouthwateringly thick. If I wasn't bound to a sex swing like an out-of-control nymph, I'd be tempted to measure its sheer girth with my tongue. I'm certain one long lick would never be enough.

A low moan escapes me when I return my gaze to Marcus. The

corners of his plump lips are tugged high, and his eyes are dark and commanding. I thought the standing ovation orgasm he awarded me with would be the end of our encounter. It isn't. His forthright eyes reveal it wasn't the conclusion of our event. It was just the beginning.

He isn't even halfway done with me yet.

23

Swallowing to relieve my parched throat, I lower my thrilled eyes to Marcus's cock inching toward me. While gripping the base of his impressively thick shaft, he glides it through my shimmering sex, coating himself with the residue of my climax. The position of the sex swing is the perfect height, allowing our pelvises to connect without any hindrance. Nothing at all is between us. Not a single thing.

I moan a low, simpering groan when the head of his cock flicks swollen clit. "You make me reckless, Cleo," Marcus grinds out through clenched teeth. "You make me irresponsible and careless," he continues before dipping the tip of his engorged shaft into my drenched sex.

My vagina clenches around him, urging him in deeper, silently pleading for more. My wishes are left unanswered when he pulls his cock out until it's bracing against my heated core.

"I don't know whether I should punish you for making me reckless or punish myself?" Marcus breathes heavily, his words strained and husky.

"As long as that punishment doesn't involve sexual deprivation, I can handle anything you want to dish," I reply, shocked I can articulate anything with how tightly arousal is curled around my throat.

"Be careful what you wish for, Cleo," Marcus warns before gripping the edge of the sex chair and dragging it forward with an ardent thrust.

I snap my eyes shut and erotically scream when his wide cock impales me in one fluid thrust. Tears prick my eyes as my body fights through the pain of taking a man as well-endowed as Marcus. I can feel all of him. Every glorious inch. Although I love being filled by him, I'm glad he awarded me with a pussy-soaking climax before we reached this stage of our exchange or my pussy may have never recovered.

My sex grows wetter when a muffled growl tears from Marcus's lips. "You feel so good," he hisses through clenched teeth. He closes his eyes for a second, like he's rejoicing the moment. I can understand his response. I too am beyond excited.

After cracking his eyes back open, Marcus tilts his head to the side and watches me, reading the prompts of my body like a true master. He waits until my nostrils stop flaring and my pupils have returned to their normal width before he glides his cock back out of my weeping pussy. Even with a stinging burn hampering me, my vagina hugs his cock, coercing him to stay. My silent pleas fall on deaf ears when he drags his cock all the way out until his glistening knob is resting against my swollen cleft.

Before disappointment has the chance to rear its ugly head, Marcus jerks his hips forward, once again filling me to the brim. A crackling of energy zaps up my spine when the head of his cock slams into my cervix. It's painful enough to enhance the sexual responses of my body, but not painful enough to be intolerable. *I don't think anything he could do to me would ever be intolerable.*

"Remember the rules, Cleo," Marcus grunts when he registers the signal of pain crossing my face. "If you need me to stop, say your safe word."

I shake my head. "I don't want you to stop," I confess quickly, panicked he will stop. "It's painful, but it's not a normal type of pain. It's. . .It's--"

"The feeling of being thoroughly *claimed*," Marcus fills in when I fail to find a word to describe what I'm feeling.

"Yes," I agree, nodding. A whimpered moan spills from my lips when his cock flexes at my confession, stretching me more.

Since the discomfort shooting through my uterus has eased to a dull ache, Marcus withdraws his cock while muttering, "Yes, what?"

"Yes, Master Chains," I splatter out in a breathless grunt, my brain too busy trying to work out how to keep him inside of me to articulate a more confident response.

For the next ten minutes, Marcus continues with the same routine of entering me quickly before stilling his movements. With every thrust he does, the tingle of an approaching orgasm overtakes the tenderness stinging my core, but no matter how many times I plead with him for more, he doesn't increase the speed of his pumps. He just watches me carefully, studying every expression crossing my face.

Only once he's happy the pain rocketing through me has been replaced with pleasure does he speed up his pace. He grinds in and out of me with controlled precision, like a man who knows how to drive a woman wild. *Like a man who knows how to fuck.* The muscles in his cut body flex and contract with every pump he does. Just watching the way he moves so fluidly is a riveting experience, one I could happily watch for hours.

Over time, the familiar tingle of ecstasy races down my spine as my skin flushes with arousal. My pants shift from soft moans to incoherent grunts. When sex strums in a rhythm matching Marcus's perfect thrusts, I close my eyes and pray for the bliss of orgasm to carry me away.

"Keep your eyes open," Marcus demands, increasing the pace of his pumps.

As skin slapping skin filters through my ears, I weakly pry my eyes back open.

"Good girl," Marcus commends as droplets of sweat glide down his temples. "This time, we will come together. Do you understand, Cleo? You're not to come before me."

Unable to speak through my dry, parched throat, I shake my head.

Marcus throws his hips forward, grinding into me harder, almost uncontrollably. "If you come before me, you'll be punished, Cleo," he warns, his low tone threatening.

"It's not that," I force out, my voice husky and exhausted. "I can't come during sex. I've never been able to come during sex." Embarrassment dangles on my vocal cords.

Confusion registers on Marcus's face for the quickest second before he shuts it down faster than it arrived. I curl my hands around the chains attached to the cuffs on my wrist when he moves his hand off my hip to toy with my clit. He rolls and pinches the firm bud until my womb tightens so firmly, it nearly snaps.

But, unfortunately, it still isn't enough.

There must be something seriously wrong with me if I can come from being stimulated by fingers, but not by a man with a mouthwatering cock. I don't know if it's a mental issue or not, but I've always been this way. Not once in my entire adult life have I come during sexual intercourse.

"You need more," Marcus mutters, his voice strained with arousal.

I feel hollow when he suddenly withdraws and stalks to the corner of the room. My pupils widen to the size of dinner plates when he stops in front of the wall housing enough whips and floggers to make any Dom proud. While keeping his eyes locked on my exhausted face, he clasps a long bamboo cane in his hand. I exhale a deep breath as panic envelops me. The idea of being beaten with a cane scares me.

Reading the silent prompts of my body, Marcus moves his hand to the cat o' nine tails sitting next to the cane. My body registers the same amount of concern, but it isn't as strong as its response to the cane. When he clutches the black leather riding crop, I inhale a deep breath as my knees curve inward. It doesn't look anywhere near as frightening as the cane and the cat o' nine tails.

"Riding crop it is," Marcus mutters to himself, pacing toward me.

My safe word sits on the tip of my tongue when I see the dominant command radiating from his beautiful eyes. But no matter how many times I try to fire it off my tongue, my mouth refuses to relinquish it. That probably has something to do with the fact it's too busy hanging open from witnessing the glorious visual of Marcus completely naked from head to toe. *My god—I've never seen a man scream sex as much as he does.*

"What's your safe word, Cleo?" Marcus questions again, easing the uncertainty thumping in my chest.

Swallowing harshly, I confirm, "Pineapple."

While running the end of the riding crop across my sweat-misted chest, Marcus asks, "Do you trust me?"

Before I can answer, he flicks the riding crop on my right nipple, his tap a direct hit.

"Yes," I cry out as excitement takes hold of every nerve ending in my body.

"Yes, what?" he growls before inflicting another perfectly placed flick to my left nipple.

"Yes, Master Chains," I pant out, my nostrils flaring, my entire body on high alert.

Every fine hair on my body bristles to attention when he trails the riding crop down my sweat-soaked stomach in a long slithering pattern like a snake weaving its way through the desert sand. I throw my head back and moan a long, hungry grunt when the riding crop sends a spasm of painful pleasure rocketing through my sex from his precise hit on my clit.

Before I've come down from the high his strike instigated, Marcus slams his cock back into me. "Grip the chains and don't let go until I say so." He nudges his head to the chains above my bound wrists, his voice labored. "When I give you permission to let go, you can come."

Nodding, I do as instructed, appreciating his confidence in his ability to make me wild enough with desire that I'll come during sexual intercourse. When I grip the chains, my heaving bosoms thrust into Marcus's face, and he takes me even deeper. He drives into me so hard, he bottoms out at my cervix before he draws his cock back out. He fucks me so hard and fast, nothing but frantic grunts and breathy moans are heard for the next several minutes.

My entire body quivers as the signs of an orgasm shimmer to life. "Oh god," I grunt, my words barely audible.

I grip onto the chains so hard, it's painful, but my body doesn't cite an objection. It's blinded by lust, unable to concentrate on anything but the man pounding into me at a breakneck pace. Sweat beads at Marcus's temples before rolling down his rich chocolate skin. He gives it his all, taking me to the very edge of orgasmic bliss; I can taste it on the tip of my tongue.

As he increases his thrusts, Marcus says, "Let go of the chains, Cleo."

Following his command, I let go of the chains. I fall back into the leather chair at the exact moment the riding crop flicks my clit three times. His strikes are skilled and precise, hitting the exact spot he intended without a smidge of hesitation.

"*Ohh...I'm...*"

I throw my head back and yell as a wave of pleasure spreads through me, starting at the center of my core and sweeping through my entire body. Marcus's cock jolts inside me, throbbing and pulsing with every squeeze of my pussy as ecstasy awakens in my body. I shudder and shake, my body loving the ability to milk his cock. My pussy squeezes around his densely veined shaft, begging to feel his cum mixed with mine.

Marcus pumps into me four more times, thrusting harder and faster with every plunge until my name leaves his mouth in a painful groan and the hotness of his cum coats the walls of my clenching sex.

24

*G*roaning a long, tedious grunt, I flutter my eyes open. I jackknife into a half-seated position when the unfamiliarity of a room greets me. Unlike the room I awoke in this morning, this one is manly and stark with pristine white walls and black-trimmed edges. The bed I'm lying in stands in the middle of the vast space, and artistic black and white retro paintings line the walls. The thick black drapes block out a majority of the sun, but not enough I can't tell it's hanging well into the sky.

After inhaling a deep breath to settle the dizziness clustering in my head, I swing my legs off the bed. My face grimaces when my weary muscles scream in protest from my sudden movements. If my entire body wasn't rejoicing in the revitalizing shimmer of the two earth-shattering orgasms Marcus awarded me with, I may have listened to the objections of my muscles with more diligence. But since it's more a pleasurable pain than a hurtful one, I'm going to push its complaints to the side and enjoy it for what it is. *Bliss.*

I throw my arms above my head and have a stretch as my eyes turn to look at the rumpled bed. If waking up alone wasn't already enough of an indication that I slept alone, the fact the left side of the bed is smooth and unwrinkled is a surefire sign Marcus placed me in the bed before leaving the room. I'll be honest, I don't recall exactly what happened after our exchange. I remember climaxing harder than I've ever climaxed, and Marcus unbuckling the restraints tied around my wrists and ankles, but everything after that is a little fuzzy.

I didn't realize sex could be so exhausting. I swear, I used every muscle in my body when I came. I probably collapsed from exhaustion before Marcus even lifted me out of the swing.

My body shudders just thinking about our time together. That entire experience was just. . .*whoa!* Like. . .*wow!* With the stigma attached to playrooms, I thought any time spent in one would be torturous and fear-provoking. It wasn't. Not even close. Don't get me wrong, I'm sure not every Dom is like Marcus. If they were, the BDSM lifestyle would be inundated with novices wanting to join the fun.

Ignoring the niggle in the back of my head warning me that Marcus went easy on me because it was my first time in the playroom, I pace toward a stack of shelves concealed behind the wall the bed is pushed up against in the hope of finding some clothes to cover my naked frame. With how pristinely clean the rest of Marcus's property is, I'm not surprised by the sparkling condition of his expansive walk-in closet. Expensive dress shirts, designer trousers, and custom-made suits line the entire back wall. They're color coordinated, going from light gray to midnight black. Even the polished shoes sitting beneath them are sorted by shading.

While running my hand across the high threadcount material used in Marcus's dress shirts, I move to a stack of white undershirts in the middle of the space. Images of the exchanges between Marcus and me flash before my eyes when his freshly laundered scent emits from the stack of shirts into my nostrils. After plucking one shirt out from the pile, I lift it to my nose and inhale deeply.

"Oh. My. God. I don't think I've ever smelled anything as delicious."

My heart leaps into my chest when a deep voice says, "I have."

I swing my eyes to the side in just enough time to watch Marcus prowl across the room. There are mere feet between us, but it seems to take him forever to reach me since everything has slowed to a snail's pace. When he stops in front of me, he inhales a deep and unashamed whiff of air through his nostrils before releasing it in a low groan. My thighs squeeze together, alerting me to my nakedness.

After quickly throwing Marcus's shirt over my head, I shift on my feet to face him. "My perfume is--"

"It isn't your perfume I'm smelling," he interrupts, his voice husky and rough. "It's you."

If I were wearing any panties, the rough ruggedness of his voice would have decimated them.

He cups my jaw before locking his eyes with mine. "Your scent matches your beauty to perfection—as sweet as your angelic face and as sinful as your tempting body."

If I didn't see the truth in his eyes, I would have denied his claims. But even seeing the honesty in his panty-melting gaze doesn't stop heat from creeping across my cheeks. Who wouldn't be flustered receiving a compliment like that from a deliriously handsome man who screams sex and sensuality? Flattery may be its own form of evil, but I have no qualms accepting it in small doses.

Marcus watches me for several moments, absorbing me in silence, assessing every inch of my soul. "How are you feeling?" he questions, like he hasn't already read the truth from my eyes.

I smile. "Good. A little sore, but good."

"That can be expected," he explains while removing a strand of hair stuck to my forehead. "Even though the swing is designed to take your weight, your muscles naturally pull taut to aid in the suspension. It's not as trusting as your mind."

I want to ask him how he knows that, but I won't, because I don't want to think about him doing anything like what we did with anyone but me.

Marcus bounces his eyes between mine before dropping them to the lower half of my body. "And down there? Any pain, redness or swelling?"

"Nope," I reply, briskly shaking my head, praying it will ward off any embarrassment associated with his question. "It's perfectly A-Okay."

He connects his eyes back with me. "Did you check?"

No. "Yes," I lie as the redness of his compliment blazes into embarrassment.

Marcus sees straight through my lie. "Oh, Cleo, that was strike three. Now you must be punished."

I swallow as alarmed excitement burns through me. I'd be lying if I said I wasn't interested in what his punishments will entail.

While rolling up the cuffs on his light gray business shirt, Marcus strides to a white ottoman in his dressing room. My pulse quickens when he sits on the ottoman before locking his eyes with mine.

With a nudge of his head, he summons me. "What do you say, Cleo? Three spanks for three lies?" he questions with his dark brow slanted high. "I would say that's a fair agreement, wouldn't you?"

I don't answer him. I can't. I'm frozen in place with desire.

Smirking, Marcus once again summons me with a gesture of his head. "Defiance will only make matters worse, Cleo." His voice slithers through me like liquid ecstasy, adding to the heat between my legs. "Once a punishment has been issued, it must be delivered. There's no cause for delay."

Pretending it isn't utterly absurd for a grown woman to be punished like a child, I pad toward him. The hankering in his eyes forces me to roll my shoulders back and swing my hips. The seductive movements of my body switch my regular walk to a provocative prance, intensifying the strength of the electric current zapping between us. It also makes me feel desired and sexy.

Once I'm within reaching distance, Marcus seizes my wrists and yanks me down until I'm sprawled across his splayed thighs. When the breeze of the inducted air-conditioning cools my heated core, I become more aware of my exposed state. A rough groan tears from Marcus's mouth when he lifts the hem of his shirt. I draw in deep breaths, attempting to calm the cluster of lust tingling in my core as he caresses and gropes the globes of my ass with gentle squeezes and rubs.

When he moves his hand away from my backside, I grit my teeth and prepare for a hard blow. The first one barely registers; it's nothing more than a playful tap. He puts a little more grunt behind the second one, but it still only entices excitement out of me. The third one. . . that one is the firmest of them all, but it still isn't strong enough to erase my eagerness.

The reasoning behind Marcus's gentle approach becomes apparent when he mutters, "Goddamn it, Cleo, why didn't you tell me I'd marked your skin yesterday?"

He doesn't give me a chance to respond before he stands from the ottoman and strides into the bathroom, taking me with him. After placing me onto my feet near the long marble counter, he rummages through his vanity. While he seeks god-knows-what, I drift my eyes around the opulent space. This bathroom is gigantic, nearly the size of most living areas. An egg-shaped bath sits in the middle of the space, and a double rainforest shower is nestled in the far righthand corner. The glass medicine cabinet Marcus is rummaging through spreads across nearly the entire wall, and there are four sinks instead of the usual two.

Shrugging off my confusion on why anyone would need four sinks, I return my eyes to Marcus, who is pacing toward me with a bottle of aloe vera in his hand.

"This will ease the burn," he advises, passing the lotion to me. "If you had told me last night, I would have given it to you then. I can't take care of you if you don't tell me you're in pain, Cleo."

I hate the unease in his words. "Sorry. Everything was a little frantic, so a sting to my backside wasn't my utmost priority."

I assumed my confession would ease the torrent of pain pumping through his eyes. It didn't. If anything, it made it grow.

"I promise to tell you from now on," I stammer out, saying anything to lessen the uncomfortable friction between us, while also praying there will be another time.

Thankfully, this time, my confession has the effect I'm aiming for. The hurt in Marcus's eyes dissipates, revealing more of the commanding allure they generally hold.

"Okay. Good," he mutters while walking to the door. "Shower, then meet me downstairs for breakfast."

My body tightens in exhilaration, loving the clipped command of his voice.

His brisk strides stop when I ask, "Do you want to join me for a shower?"

The dampness slicking my skin moves to the lower half of my body as I await his reply. I'm shocked by the boldness of my suggestion, but incredibly proud I listened to the pleas of my body without first stopping to evaluate them.

Marcus doesn't turn around to acknowledge me. He simply utters, "No. I can't trust myself around you. Particularly when you're naked."

With that, he exits the bathroom, closing the door behind him.

orty-five minutes later, I bounce down the stairwell of Marcus's elaborate home wearing a burgundy one-shoulder dress. Although not as pricey as the dress I wore last night, this is still one of my favorite dresses. The impeccable threadcount of the wool material aids the aloe vera lotion soothing the sting in my backside, and the elegant cut showcases my voluptuous curves in a pleasing light.

When I round the corner of the airy kitchen, the first person I notice is Marcus. He's seated on one of the four stools tucked under the granite island counter of the well-equipped space. I prop my shoulder on the doorjamb of the kitchen, not wanting to interrupt his call, while also giving my eyes the opportunity to drink in his delicious suit-covered body. I still can't believe the stranger in the elevator four years ago and the man I met at a BDSM club two months ago is the man sitting before me now.

I guess I shouldn't be surprised. Marcus has two very opposing personalities depending on what situation he's in. Around his bandmates and in public, he's Marcus: the quiet, reserved bassist of Rise Up. With me, he's Master Chains: a dominant, sexy lover who seems to know my body better than I do. It truly is the best of both worlds. I'm tempted to pinch myself just to ensure I'm not dreaming.

Excitement stirs my blood when a heated gaze gathers my attention. I was so occupied thanking my lucky stars for Marcus, I didn't realize he had finalized his call. After he finishes absorbing every inch of my body with as much detail as I bestowed upon him, he locks his panty-wetting gaze with mine.

"Hi," I mumble, glancing into his hypnotizing eyes.

I should be embarrassed he busted me ogling him, but I'm not. Mere hours ago he had me strapped in a sex swing in the middle of his playroom. I don't even understand the meaning of the word embarrassed anymore.

"Hi," he greets back, his lips curving into a sultry smirk. "Come and eat breakfast."

I skip into the room, my mood as playful as the cheeky gleam in Marcus's gaze from me rolling my eyes at his commanding tone.

"No reprimand for eye rolling?" I ask, exposing my love of erotic romance novels may have misguided my beliefs on the BDSM lifestyle.

The lusty smile on Marcus's face grows as he pulls out a stool for me. "An occasional eye roll outside of the playroom I can handle. But I'd be cautious doing it inside that domain." He breathes into my ear, "Unless you want to be spanked."

My body tightens, beyond aroused by his frisky tease, but I ignore its prompts, deciding the pleas of my stomach are more important than the desires of my heart. Once I take my seat, Marcus hands me a coffee cup full to the brim with steamy hot chocolate. My mouth salivates when I spot two white marshmallows floating in the rich goodness.

"How did you know I like marshmallows in my hot chocolate?"

I blow on the steamy liquid, then take a sip. It's the perfect temperature, but at the exact moment it hits my taste buds, it reminds my stomach it hasn't been fed in over sixteen hours.

He pushes a plate of cream cheese-coated bagels to me. "It's my job to know your every want, need and desire, Cleo."

"I thought that was only in the bedroom?" I pluck a bagel off the plate and popping a piece into my mouth, hoping it will hide my smile.

I moan, loving the savory flavor engulfing my taste buds. I've always had a healthy appetite, but it's even more rampant after my session in the playroom with Marcus this morning. I take another bite of the bagel. It tastes just as delicious the second time around.

While taming my hunger pains, I scan my eyes over the eat-in kitchen we are seated in. Just like the rest of Marcus's house, it's extremely modern with crisp lines and smooth surfaces. The latest appliances grace every surface, and not a dust bunny can be seen. The elegance of the room still thrusts his wealth into my face, but the more time I spend with him, the less concerned I am about our vastly contradicting bank balances. I'm not here for financial gain.

A chunk of bagel traps halfway down my throat when my inquisitiveness has me stumbling onto something even more scandalous than the number of calories I'm consuming at a record-setting pace.

After swallowing the trapped bagel, I ask, "What's that?" pretending I haven't recognized the set of papers sprawled across the countertop.

Marcus places his half-empty mug of coffee onto the glistening kitchen counter before gathering the documents into a neat stack. His Adam's apple bobs up and down as his attention diverts to the Dom/sub contract he's grasping. "I thought we should settle some formalities before we continue with our weekend."

I stop chewing since the once delicious bagel now tastes like it's been laced with arsenic. It's as poisonous as the sick gloom spreading through my chest.

I force the remainder of the bagel past the solid lump in my throat before mumbling, "What type of formalities?"

"I want you to be my sub, Cleo." Missing my slack-jawed expression, he adds on, "With our sexual compatibility being so strong, I adjusted the terms on your contract to a six-month agreement, instead of the usual three I've stipulated on previous contracts." He sounds confident, like I should be pleased he's awarding me double the amount of time his previous subs received. I'm not pleased. I'm disgusted.

Since he isn't looking at me, he fails to read the fury reddening my face as he continues explaining the terms of the pre-drawn contract. "Rise Up leaves on a world tour in three months' time, so I added an appendix to your contract to include the provisions of international travel."

"You want me to go on tour with you?" When Marcus nods, I sneer, "I work, Marcus. You know this."

Nodding, he flicks over the document to a hand-written appendix added to the bottom of page six. "That's why I added this amendment to the contract this morning. As well as a clothing and living allowance, your income will be supplemented by me for the period of time stated on the contract," he explains, his calm composure not matching the life-altering conversation we are undertaking.

"During the first half of the contract, we will be based either here or at my residence in Florida, but the final three months will be at hotels chosen by my record company. If you don't find the accommodation suitable for your needs, we can move to a new location or discuss a monetary value for compensation."

The bagel I've only just forced down creeps back up my esophagus as his words ring on repeat in my ears. It doesn't matter how many times I hear it, I reach the same conclusion every time: he thinks I'm a prostitute.

"You want to pay me to sleep with you?" I ask, my brow cocked, my jaw hanging.

He keeps his gaze on the contract. "No. I'm compensating you for being my sub, not paying for services."

Black fury rages through my veins when my silent demands for him to make eye contact with me fall on deaf ears. During my research into the BDSM community, I heard it's not uncommon for Doms to request no eye contact from their subs, but this is ridiculous. If he had no qualms glancing into my eyes during our exchange in his playroom this morning, why can't he look at me now?

"And what happens once the contract ends, Marcus? What

happens then?" My shouted words are unable to conceal my anger at being disrespected like this.

He takes his time configuring a response before muttering, "What do you mean?"

"What happens to me? You just simply move on to another sub, but what happens to me?" I bang my open palm on my thumping chest. "Perhaps I might get lucky and find another money-foolish Dom to take care of me once you've had your fill? Or maybe I should jump from Dom to Dom now until I find one willing to extend my contract from the 6-month one you're offering to a full year."

Marcus's furious growl doesn't have half the effect on me it normally does. My body is too boiling with anger to listen to any absurd prompts of my lust-driven heart.

No longer hungry, I place my half-eaten bagel onto the plate and shift my eyes to the side. With a range of emotions pumping into me, I need to look at anything but the man who is the catalyst of my problems, even more so since he's refusing to make eye contact with me. It seriously feels like this weekend has been one giant step forward, two mammoth steps back with him. Every time I think I'm making headway in our odd connection, he's quick to remind me this is nothing more than a Dom/sub relationship to him.

No longer capable of ignoring my swirling stomach, I push back from the granite countertop and slip off my seat. Before I have the opportunity to move away, Marcus's hand darts out to seize my wrist. "You haven't eaten nearly enough to sustain your appetite until lunch."

He can't be serious, can he? How can he expect me to sit down and eat with a man who refuses to look at me, let alone one who wants to sign over my God-given rights to him for a stipulated amount of time?

"You need to eat, Cleo," he demands, his voice as commanding as ever.

I lick my dry lips before snapping, "I'm not hungry."

I keep my gaze front and center, refusing to let him see he has me on the verge of tears.

"Even if you're not hungry, you need to refuel your muscles that were exhausted in the swing," he argues, his composure calm and unaware of the emotional wreck standing beside him.

Gritting my teeth, I drift my eyes to his, too hurt to conceal my devastation for a moment longer. When Marcus notices the glossy sheen in my wide gaze, he murmurs under his breath before abruptly standing from his chair. His movements are so quick he sends his barstool toppling over. Its brutal crash to the tiled floor is barely audible when he curls his arms around my back and draws me into his chest.

When his familiar smell lingers in my nostrils, my fight not to cry is virtually unachievable, but I give it my best shot. Tears are something I reserve for my darkest days, and although the range of emotions I've been dealing with the past eight weeks has seen my moods swing from inspiring highs to devastating lows, it isn't even a tenth of the pain I felt four years ago when my parents and Tate passed away—not in the slightest.

After inhaling a deep breath to calm my nerves, I take a step back, pulling out of his embrace. When I connect my eyes back with his beautiful green irises, it makes what I'm about to say ten times harder.

"I want to go home."

26

———

The worry Marcus's eyes held when he discovered he'd marked my skin is nothing compared to the anxiety they're holding now.

"I'll never be who you need me to be," I mumble before I chicken out. "I like you, Marcus; I like you a lot, but I can't help but feel you only want me to be your sub. You're treating me like a disposable plaything instead of a real woman."

It feels like a big ugly knife is stabbed into my chest when he doesn't deny my claims. I stand frozen for a moment, debating with myself about what I was hoping my confession would achieve. I pick at the lint on my dress, then fiddle with the cuff before I realize I'm just delaying the inevitable. I'll never fully submit, and he'll never want anything more from me than to be his sub.

I count to ten before locking my eyes with his. Now, I wish I didn't. His eyes will forever be my weakness. They cause my doubts to waiver without a word needing to spill from his lips. Not able to ignore the pull of his alluring eyes, I drop my disarrayed gaze to his chest and try to force some sort of goodbye out of my mouth. My lips twitch, but not a syllable escapes them.

Disturbed by my lack of self-esteem in his presence, I pivot on my heels and pace out of the kitchen. Just before I enter the hall, Marcus wraps his broad arms around my waist. I can feel his heart smashing against his ribs when he draws me to his heated torso. My body is aroused, stimulated by his closeness. It truly doesn't care how angry he makes me; all it cares about is how good he makes it feel.

"I know this is new to you. I know it's daunting and scary," Marcus murmurs into my hairline, his voice barely a whisper. "But you're letting your fears lead your desires, instead of dancing with them."

When I spin around to face him, he tightens his grip on my wrist, refusing my request. I grit my teeth, hating that he won't let me see his forthright eyes. If he has nothing to hide, why won't he make eye contact with me?

"Would you listen to yourself? You tell me to dance with my fear, but you won't even face yours head on. If you were being honest with yourself, you'd admit I'm not the only one scared. You're just as frightened as me."

A rustle of air parts Marcus's lips, fanning the misting of sweat on my neck his firm hold caused. Silence engulfs us, amplifying the tick of his jaw. It's a torturous and teasing time. My body relishes him being curved around me, but my heart is locked down and confused. My brain... don't even ask.

It feels like eternity passes before he mutters, "You make me reckless." The calm neutrality of his voice sets my nerves on edge, but it doesn't lessen the vehement anger pumping through my blood.

I smack my back molars together. "Yeah, well, you make me mad."

He tightens his grip around my waist, foiling my attempt to pull away from him. Awareness of his nearness sizzles through my veins and stills my movements, my body too exhausted to fight the man who took it to the brink hours ago.

Happy he has subdued my attempts to flee, he asks, "Mad enough you want to leave?"

"Yes!" When he expels a harsh breath like my confession suckerpunched him, it forces me to say, "No. I don't know. You confuse me, Marcus!"

"Self-judgment can confuse you, but emotions never lie. What's your heart telling you, Cleo?"

"That I need more than a stipulated amount of time on a contract." My tone is low, equally panicked and angry at what his response may be. "What we did yesterday and today was beautiful, but I don't want to feel worthless the instant it's over."

His fingers flex against my hip. "I made you feel worthless?" The pain in his voice somewhat dampens my anger.

My hair clings to the five o'clock shadow on his chin when I shake my head. "No."

His relieved breath rustles the hairs clinging to my sweat-soaked neck. "Then tell me what's wrong, Cleo. I can't fix your concerns if I don't understand them."

My heart melts a little from his confession. He could have just brushed off my worries without a second thought, but he didn't. That alone lessens some of the unease twisting in my stomach.

I take a minute to contemplate how I can explain my concerns in a way it won't sound clingy. It's an extremely long minute.

"I don't believe love is a necessity for a sexual relationship; but I don't think it should be cold and lacking of any emotion either."

"So you believe our exchange lacked warmth?" he probes, eager to understand my concerns.

"Not necessarily." My words shake with nerves. "During sexual contact, I feel desired. It's how I felt after it that's my greatest concern."

"So you enjoyed our time in the playroom?"

My heart rate kicks up a notch. "Yes." *Very much so.*

His tight hold around my waist loosens. "So what happened between now and then that changed your mind?"

I try to spin in his arms. He once again denies my attempts.

"You asked me weeks ago to open my mind to the possibility of seeing things from a different prospective," I say, pretending I can't feel his heart hammering my back. "I did that this morning in your playroom. I pushed aside the opinions of others and tried to see your world in a new light. It was beautiful—truly it was. But the moment I wanted to cherish for eternity will be forever tainted now."

"Why, Cleo?" He sounds confused.

"Because you took something beautiful and made it hideously ugly by judging our exchange for our sexual compatibility." My words crack off my tongue like a whip.

"It was not about that at all." The strength of his words ensure I hear the truth in his reply. "It was about opening your mind to the possibility not everything you believe is true. You have needs and desires you're too afraid to admit you have, Cleo. The playroom let you voice who you truly are."

I try to defend his false claims, but I'm left a little stumped. I loved our time together in the playroom. It went above and beyond anything I could have wished for. But I can't stand the to and fro feeling associated with it. Why can't that experience extend beyond those doors without the need to sign a contract?

"You went to Chains seeking something, Cleo. Until you stop allowing the opinions of others to consume you, you'll never find what you went there looking for." His tone softens with under-standing.

I desperately want to tell him I was only at Chains on assignment, but I can't. Something deep inside me won't let my mouth relinquish the truth. I don't know if my hesitation stems from being afraid he will no longer be a part of my life, or because for some stupid reason, I believe my assignment was the universe's way of bringing us together. Some may say the connection we have was built on a lie, but that isn't true. The buzzing sensation that consumes me when he's close was just as strong in the elevator four years ago as it was in the backseat of the Bentley. *Clearly, I'm the only one harboring unexplainable feelings regarding our incontestable connection.*

"Don't be afraid of the unknown, Cleo. Conquer it," Marcus mutters into my hairline, taking my silence as deliberation on his request.

"I'm not afraid, Marcus." My voice reveals the pain shredding my heart in two. "And I'm also not your submissive. I would have never agreed to come here if I knew it was on the premise of you signing me on as your sub."

He coughs to clear his throat. "A D/s contract is nothing more than a way of laying down a set of boundaries both parties agree to. It's a smart thing to do at the beginning of any relationship, as it means there will be less chance of disappointment when it ends."

My heart clenches. Our relationship hasn't even started yet, and he's already preparing for it to end. That hurts.

"By laying boundaries at the start of our relationship, there will be *no* relationship." My anger returns stronger than ever. "A sexual relationship may just be an emotionless transaction to you, Marcus, but it means more than that to me. I can't just switch off my emotions like you; I have a heart."

"As do I, Cleo." His voice sounds angst-ridden, like he doesn't even believe his declaration.

"Clearly not. All you want is a sub to play silly games with." Hurt overtakes the anger in my voice. "That's one thing I'll never be, so why don't we just cut our losses and pretend we never met?"

Using his loosened grip to my advantage, I pull away from him and charge for the hallway. My brisk movements cause the first tear to roll down my cheek. Before I can brush it away, my wrists are snatched. In less than the time it takes for me to blink, I'm trapped between the hallway wall and a hot, brooding hunk of a man.

Marcus stands so close to me I can feel every vein in his body working hard to contain the anger pumping out of him in invisible waves. His hot breath hits my flushed cheeks as his furious green eyes bore into mine.

"Let me go, Marcus." The bagel I was eating earlier bounces off his lips and filters into my nose.

He leans in deeper, stealing my ability to breathe and think. "No."

I thrash against him, fighting with all my might to break free. All I end up achieving is more wetness between my legs, my body choosing its own ridiculous response to his closeness. I've never felt more ashamed of my lust-driven heart than I do now. Yes, Marcus is gorgeous and seems to know me and my body better than any man before him, but the responses of my body are absurd. I'm angry, goddammit! I'm not supposed to get aroused while angry.

"What do you want from me, Marcus?!" My words are forced through a sob in the back of my throat. "Tell me what you want or let me go!" .

"I want you!" His short reply is unable to conceal his anger. "In my playroom. In my bed. Over my knee so I can spank the sass right out of you. You think you're confused, Cleo? Try being me. I've never wanted this. I've never carried a sub out of my playroom and put her in *my* bed. I've never introduced her to *my* bandmates. I've never wanted to mark every inch of her skin so everyone knows she's *mine*. I want that with you. I want *you!*"

My wailing stops, closely followed by my heart. Although I had hoped he'd reply this way, I truly didn't expect him to. Perhaps I'm not the only one jolted by the breakneck speed of our connection? Maybe he's just as confused as me?

I bounce my eyes between his. "Then do that."

"I can't," he snarls through clenched teeth, his words barely a whisper.

"Why?" Shock is evident in my tone. "Why can't you?"

Three long breaths rattle through his chest before he replies, "I need the control. I need the power. I don't know how to give that up."

The raw edginess in his voice cuts through me like brittle glass. He sounds both angry and confused. The urge to forget our entire argument consumes me when I see the chaotic cloud brewing in his beautiful eyes. Although his alluring irises are obscured with palpable tension, they're still his biggest ally, because they show him as the man he's: both Master Chains and Marcus.

The chaos in his eyes dulls from a raging tornado to a summer storm when I say, "You don't have to give up your power or control. You said dominance is a part of who you are. I don't want you to change, Marcus; I just want you to understand how it feels for the person on the other end of that contract."

He peers at me, his confusion growing by the minute. "How can I do that?"

A ghost of a smile cracks onto my lips, grateful he's opening up to the possibility of changing the stringent set of rules he's been following the past four years.

"You just have to open your eyes to the prospect not everything is as it seems," I quote, referring to something he has said to me many times the past six weeks. "Sometimes you have to take people at face value, Marcus, not by a set of rules they're forced to follow."

His eyes flare with an array of emotions I can't decipher. "My dad has always said 'rules stop idiotic people making heedless mistakes."

"Do you want to know one of my dad's favorite quotes?"

Marcus's brows join. He appears more fretful now than he did earlier when he noticed my tears. After his chest rises and falls, he nods.

"There's an exception to every rule." I fist his dress shirt nervously in my hand. "Maybe I'm your exception?"

"Exception? I don't think you could ever be classed as an exception, Cleo." His voice is stern but calm at the same time. "You're too disobedient to be classed as anything more than a brat."

Just like every minute I've spent with him, I act before I consider the repercussions of my actions. A heady grunt parts his lips when I jab my fingers into his ribs. He jerks, surprised by my fierce response. He isn't the only one shocked. My mouth is gaped, and my eyes are wide. *I really need to think before I act.* He has me sprawled against a wall in his residence at his complete mercy, and I just struck him. *I'm a complete idiot.*

Before panic can make itself known, a hearty chuckle parts from Marcus's plump lips. His rapturous laugh slides through my veins like molten lava, activating every one of my hot buttons. It's such a beautiful thing to hear in the middle of the strangling situation we've faced the past twenty minutes. In no time at all, it switches the energy zapping between us from a heated debate to a heightened conversation between two people who know each other well—*intimately well.*

After regaining his composure, Marcus drops his amused eyes to me. In an instant, the tension in the air shifts from tense to tantalizing. The humor in his gaze fades as his eyes darken with desire. The crackle of attraction firing between us bristles the hairs on my arms, making me needy and hot. How can he not see the unique bond we have is greater than a D/s relationship? He must be blind. It's so bright, I'm sure they could see it from space.

My concern about him not noticing the sparks firing between us fades when he mutters, "Tell me what I need to do to make this happen, Cleo. I can't guarantee I can cross off every item on your list, but that doesn't mean I'm not willing to try."

My lips curl upwards, pleased with his response. "You want to compromise with me?"

He shakes his head. "A compromise is an agreement where neither party gets what they want. This is a negotiation."

"I'm pretty sure negotiating and compromising are the same thing."

"Not in my industry, it isn't," he argues, shaking his head.

I assume he's referring to his BDSM lifestyle, until he continues talking. "By compromising, Rise Up would have taken the first contract extension offered to ensure our label was managed by Cormack. By negotiating, we not only kept Cormack as our manager, we also secured a larger cut of royalties and a bigger percentage of any advertising campaigns we undertook the past two years. Compromise and negotiation are two very different things."

"Okay, so how does this work?"

I quirk my brows, my earlier bad mood a distant memory. Even though tension still hangs thick in the air, it also has a hint of understanding mingling throughout it.

"We lay our cards on the table until we reach an amicable decision we are both happy with."

I don't know why, but I get the feeling this isn't going to be a fair fight. It probably has something to do with the fact my defenses have already weakened from peering into his gorgeous eyes the past ten minutes.

Shaking off my unease, I say, "Alright, let's negotiate. What's your first offer, Master Chains? What's the one thing you want the most out of this negotiation?"

"You," he answers without pause for consideration.

Now I have no doubt this isn't going to be a fair fight.

Smirking at my flushed expression, Marcus asks, "What's your counterbid, Cleo?"

I quirk my lips, pretending I'm considering a reply. I don't need time to deliberate, though. I already know what I require for our relationship to move forward. I'm just worried about what his response will be once he discovers my terms.

Deciding there's only one way to unearth his reaction, I say, "I'm happy to fulfil your request with one stipulation."

His smirk enlarges to a full smile, no doubt satisfied with my response. "And what is that stipulation, Cleo?" The cultured smoothness of his voice makes my stomach quiver.

Pushing aside my heart's desire to sign the D/s contract mere feet from us, I negotiate, "I want the contract taken off the table."

When a flare of panic blazes through his eyes, I add on, "For now. I'm not asking for it to be removed indefinitely; I just don't want it thrusted in my face every two seconds this weekend. We barely know each other, Marcus. For all you know, you may be chomping at the bits to get rid of me by tomorrow afternoon. Forty-eight hours straight with a Garcia woman is a hard limit for any man."

The heaviness on my chest lightens when he mutters, "Maybe for a foolish man."

It feels like the sun circles the earth five times before he says, "I agree with your stipulation, but only with adding one of my own."

My teeth graze over my bottom lip as I wait for him to continue. "I need control, Cleo. This is something I cannot negotiate on. If this condition is not agreed upon, I will not continue with our negotiations."

Panic squeezes me, stealing my ability to breathe even more than Marcus's well-formed body pushed up against me. Just the thought of our relationship ending makes me feel sick. Although I was threatening the exact same thing mere minutes ago, a little voice in the back of my head was praying he would come after me. If he hadn't, who knows what I would have ended up doing.

With my jaw tight with worry, I ask, "How much control are we talking?"

He remains quiet, which fuels my worry more. The only thing that eases the swishing movements of my stomach is his eyes. Although they still have the same command they've always held, there's a smidge of confusion dampening their appeal.

Just when I think he's never going to answer me, he says, "I need full control in the playroom."

His response doesn't shock me whatsoever. Any man with a dominant command like Marcus would have a hard time giving that up, so I never considered requesting for that term to be revoked during our negotiations.

Although not shocked by Marcus's first statement, his follow-up sentence surprises me. "But I'm willing to try and rein in my need for control outside of that domain."

I don't have a chance in hell of stopping the smile dying to stretch across my face, so I set it free. This is a huge step for him to take. It feels like he just leaped us over all the barriers standing between us. *Well, nearly all of them.*

Spotting my glaring grin, he mutters, "I said I would try, Cleo. That's not a guarantee it will happen."

Shrugging my shoulders, I say, "Just the fact you offered is already a step in the right direction."

I fist his shirt more firmly before pulling him closer to me. When the thickness of his cock braces against my heated core, my playful statement comes out sounding more needy than I'm aiming for. "Besides, I've never had a problem with your need for control. I like your domineering personality, just as much as you like my goading one."

A whizz of air parts his lips, silently denying my interpretation of our odd connection. "Your desire to tease me is one of your many quirks I plan on straightening out in my playroom."

Hearing the playfulness in his tone stops panic from engulfing me. I'd like to say my body also had a neutral response to his tease. It didn't. Just the thought of entering his playroom again has my pulse quickening, and don't get me started on the response from the lower extremities of my body.

Marcus places his hand on my jaw, shifting my focus from my wicked thoughts to him. His hand strips away the icy barrier that's been dividing us the past thirty minutes, and the hunger in his eyes makes my stomach knot with thrilled anticipation. I've never had my morals severely waver like they do when I take in his beautiful features. His plump, delicious lips; straight, defined nose; and eyes so powerful their heat and hunger spur on my reckless desires. They provoke me to be daring—*to be me.* The real Cleo, not the socially acceptable one I've been hiding behind the past four years.

Locking my eyes with his, I say, "I accept the terms you're requesting, Master Chains."

"No counterbid, Ms. Garcia?" he replies as his morally corrupt eyes drift between mine, his pleasure at me agreeing to his terms beaming out of him in invisible waves.

My teeth catch my bottom lip as I consider his question. My mind is completely blank. The only thing I hope to gain from our agreement is the man standing in front of me. Considering that was crossed off at the very beginning of our negotiations, I can't think of a single thing to counterbid.

Warm dampness forms between my legs when Marcus saves my lower lip from my menacing teeth before his thumb tracks my top lip. His touch is brief, but strong enough to annihilate any lingering doubt in the back of my mind that I'm treading into dangerous waters.

"I have one final request," I breathe out, my voice crammed with lust.

He cocks his brow as his eyes demand further explanation without a word leaving his plump lips.

"That we seal our deal in a more *pleasant* way then the usual handshake most deals are agreed upon," I elaborate, shocking myself with my brazen request.

My breathing lengthens when his deliriously sinful-looking lips incline closer to mine. "I accept the terms of your agreement without the need for an added stipulation."

"Do we have an agreement, Cleo?"

I drift my eyes between his while nodding. "Yes."

"Yes, what?" he growls in a way that makes my knees shake.

Lost in a lust haze, I reply, "Yes, Master Chains."

His smiling eyes are the last thing I see before the skill of his kiss clears away the mess our heated conversation caused to my muddled brain.

27

"Are you ready, Cleo?" Marcus firms his grip on my hip. Snubbing the way his fingers digging into my skin forced my heart to skip a beat, I nod.

"Keep your chin low and your eyes on your feet," he warns again before lowering a New York Yankee's cap down low on my brow.

Noticing the nervous sweat beaded there, he says, "Remember, you asked for this."

"I know." My words are jittery and low. "Doesn't make it any less nerve-racking though."

He chuckles softly, easing the uncertainty burrowing a hole in my stomach. "You want to know the real Marcus. This is my life."

I exhale a nerve-clearing breath before nodding. Although what he says is true, I had no clue a simple request over breakfast would have me entering a second previously un-ventured world in less than twelve hours.

Before I got fully caught up kissing a man who makes me feel like life didn't exist before him, my stomach announced its rampant hunger.

Not wanting to relinquish Marcus's delicious lips from mine, I continued to nibble and suck on his coffee-flavored mouth. My ploy was working. . . until the grumbles of my stomach grew louder. Incapable of pretending he didn't hear the pleas of the starving hole in my stomach, he pulled his lips away from mine, guided me back into the kitchen, and forced me to eat.

While devouring the plate of bagels under his watchful eye, we continued with our negotiations—although it was a little more risqué than our first and void of the earlier tenseness. His stipulations followed a similar path to his earlier ones: he needed control, power, and me. Mine were a little less demanding than his. I just wanted him —the real Marcus.

It was that confession that saw us driving an hour into the city and standing in the alley we are at now. He believes this location will show him as the real man he is. I guess I'm about to find out.

After another nerve-clearing breath, I say, "Alright. Let's do this."

I gag, loathing that my words are shaky. I've been in the media industry for a little over five years. If I can't handle the press by now, I'll never get the hang of it.

Smiling, Marcus pulls me in to his side, then steps out of the alleyway and onto the sidewalk. In a matter of seconds, a swarm of paparazzi bombards us. The oversized Hollywood glasses covering my eyes do nothing to diminish the bright flashes of camera bulbs coming from all directions. With Marcus's highly recognizable face, I knew it wouldn't take long for the paparazzi to track him down. Pictures of any Rise Up members are still highly lucrative even years into their success.

Tugging my cap down low, I lean tighter in to his side as he weaves us through the gauntlet of paparazzi.

"Marcus, this way!" screams one paparazzi.

"Do you wish to comment on recent rumors of a Rise Up rift?"

"Where's the rest of the band? Will they be joining you at the grand opening?"

The questions continue coming hard and fast as Marcus guides me toward a black steel door at the side of a converted warehouse. He doesn't speak a word. Not even when e'ss rudely probed about his sexual orientation or whether he and last year's Grammy winner,

Wesley Heart, had a bisexual relationship with the bassist of Big Halo.

I'd like to say I'm shocked by the aggressiveness of the paparazzi, but unfortunately, I'm not. I witnessed their tactics firsthand my inaugural year at Global Ten Media. Although the laws have changed, the drive to give the public what they crave hasn't dampened the slightest. I'm not defending the paparazzi; I'm simply stating they use any tactics available to them to give the public what they crave: their much-loved celebrities.

I'll say one thing, though, it was a whole lot less unsettling on the other side of the lens. By the time Marcus cracks open the steel door, I've been elbowed, had my ear drum nearly burst, and asked my own set of derogatory questions pertaining to Marcus and his sexual proclivities.

The only good thing about being bombarded by the media is that it prompted me at some stage this weekend to inform Marcus of my career title. Even though I'm concerned about what his reaction will be—as he and his bandmates have a clear love/hate relationship with the media—it isn't something I can keep hidden from him.

I just hope Marcus understands legally and ethically, I can't disclose any information pertaining to my actual position. Although I want to be honest, the confidentiality clause included in my employment contract has me weary on what information I can share. If I were to disclose restricted information to the wrong person, I could be fired. Or even worse—sued! Considering that's something I can't afford, I need to be diligent in how I approach this prickly situation.

Once we scurry through the thick steel door, it slams shut, blocking out the paparazzi and their endless questions. While Marcus assists me in removing my coat, my eyes drift around the space. Exposed brick and thick black beams feature predominately in the open space. A commercial-sized stainless kitchen sits in the far lefthand corner and several long corridors weave off the vast area.

Not noticing our presence, a group of builders sitting at a makeshift table continue consuming the cut sandwiches and steaming cups of coffee served to them by a pretty African American lady.

After hanging our coats on a rack in the foyer, Marcus pulls open a glass door with "Links" etched into it and gestures for me to enter.

"Links? As in chain links?" Curiosity highlights my tone.

When I glide past him to enter the main room of the warehouse, fresh paint lingers into my nose, only just overtaking Marcus's delicious aroma I caught on my way past his suit-clad body.

Marcus smiles a grin that sets my pulse racing. "Links is a conglomerate of Chains. Kind of like its sister company."

I tack my brows in close while my disarrayed eyes bounce around the area. I'm utterly confused. Why would he conceal his face while entering Chains, but turn up to Links without a disguise? Although he ensured my eyes and face were concealed from the press, he didn't even wear a cap. That truly doesn't make any sense.

Clasping the chain link given to me on my birthday between my thumb and finger, I slant into Marcus's side. "Is this another BDSM club?" I keep my voice low, ensuring the pretty sable-haired lady eyeballing us from afar won't hear me.

Marcus laughs a muscle-clenching chuckle. "No, Cleo." He shakes his head. "This is not a BDSM club. It's a shelter for victims of domestic violence. The profits from Chains' first year of trading allowed me to purchase this old recreation center from the county. With the help of three anonymous donors, I had the building remodeled so it can sleep one hundred occupants comfortably."

He doesn't need to elaborate on who the three anonymous donors where. His sparkling eyes tell the entire story. They are his bandmates: Noah, Nick and Slater.

"This will be the rec/dining room." He points to a hall on our right. "Down the end of the hallway is the sleeping quarters and washroom facilities. The configurations range from single rooms to ones that hold up to eight guests."

Tears prick in my eyes from the pride radiating in his voice. This is clearly a project very close and dear to his heart.

I spin on my heels to face him, my movements a little wobbly in my stiletto heels. "So how is this a sister company of Chains?" Although I understand the capital to start this project came from Chains, it doesn't explain their correlation.

Marcus takes a moment to consider his reply before saying, "People often mistake the BDSM lifestyle with violence. They don't see the transfer of power between a Dom and a sub as a choice; they think it's something taken from them."

I nod. I had similar misguided assumptions, so I'm not surprised by his response.

"Although Chains practices the sane, safe, and consensual rules many BDSM members follow, the same can't be said for all members of our community." His jaw muscle tightens as his eyes darken with anger.

"Just like every community, the BDSM lifestyle has a handful of bad seeds ruining the image of the entire community," I fill in, reading the response from his eyes.

"Yes," he answers, the fury in his eyes softening. "Chains was a part of a pledge I made to a friend three years ago. She wanted a place people could go play in safety. Links is part of our combined pledge. It's a place where people who have had their safety compromised can seek shelter."

"So Links is only for members of the BDSM society?"

He shakes his head. "No. Links is for anyone affected by domestic violence. Just some of their care will be handled by associates of the BDSM community. The stigma attached to this lifestyle extends further than being ridiculed by people not understanding someone having different sexual preferences than them. It's seen members fired from their workplace, or their children ridiculed at school. Our vision is to use Links as a way to break the taboo in this lifestyle. Most of the people who contributed to bringing Links to life and ensuring its success are part of the BDSM community."

My first response to his admission is shock, but it only lasts as long as it takes for me to recall the many professionals I spoke to during my two-week investigation into the BDSM lifestyle. The caliber of expertise was astounding. One was a world-renowned heart surgeon who preferred to leave the tough decisions he makes every day in his industry at work, which is why he's a submissive. Every decision about his sexual pleasure was left in the capable hands of his Domme. All he had to do was sit back and relax, and entrust that his Domme would take care of him.

An intrusive question sits on the tip of my tongue, but I'm unsure of how I can ask it without it coming out sounding judgmental, so I keep my mouth shut.

"You won't learn about the real me if you don't ask questions, Cleo," Marcus says, once again intuiting my needs by hearing nothing but my breaths.

I chew nervously on my bottom lip before blurting out, "You defend the lifestyle choices of your members so vehemently, but I've never once read a report linking you to the lifestyle."

"That isn't a question," he snaps, his clipped tone sending a shiver down my spine.

After licking my dry lips, I ask, "You defend the lifestyle choices of your members so vehemently, but I've never once read a report linking you to the lifestyle. Why?"

He locks his forthright eyes with mine. "Although I believe people shouldn't be judged on their sexual preferences or orientation, my beliefs don't extend to members of my family," he answers, his face expressionless.

"Oh." His honesty blindsides me, and I can't think of a more appropriate response. "That's sad."

He scoffs. "More like ill-advised, arrogant, and narrow-minded," he murmurs more to himself than me.

"That too," I agree, nodding. "It's unfortunate they can't see you for who you really are." I arch my brow. "It's quite an intriguing visual."

His lips curve sardonically. "Listen to you defending the BDSM lifestyle. There may be hope for me yet."

I roll my eyes before playfully slapping him on the chest. He bands his arms around my back and draws me in so he can nibble on my lips. I melt into his embrace, loving every playful nib and suck he makes. You would swear our argument this morning was months ago. It was swept to the side as quickly as our kiss heats up.

Before I can get carried away in the sensuality of Marcus's kiss, an ear-piercing scream roars through my eardrums. The squeal is so loud my heart leaves my chest, and Marcus pulls away from our embrace to crank his neck to the side. Following his gaze, I spot the lady who was earlier serving sandwiches glaring at us. With one hand spread across her hip and the other clasping a coffee pot, her massively dilated eyes bounce between Marcus and me. Her stunned reaction deepens dramatically the longer she takes in our huddled embrace. She looks shocked, distressed, and confused.

Oh, god—I hope she isn't one of Marcus's previous subs.

The likelihood of the bagels I scarfed down an hour ago resurfacing grows when Marcus intertwines our hands before pacing toward the dark-haired beauty. His tug on my arm ensures I fall in step behind him, even though my feet want to stay planted. While battling to settle my swishing stomach, I take in the approaching stranger.

The smile she directs at Marcus is bright and confident, but her stance portrays more intimacy than a general business associate would hold when greeting a fellow colleague. She has beautiful rich African American skin, a button nose, and plump lips. Her makeup palette is so natural I wouldn't be surprised if she was wearing nothing more than a neutral lip-gloss. Her eyes are hazel in color and stand out against her sable-colored hair, which is trimmed close at the edges but is long enough on the top to give it a sexy mussed appearance. She's young and gorgeous, with beauty that makes me green with envy.

Her gaze narrows as she assesses me, studying every inch of me as avidly as I did her. She starts at my panicked face, taking in the slight shimmer of powder I dusted on my nose on the car trip over and my rosy-colored lips. After absorbing my unruly hair twisted into a French braid, she lowers her eyes down my body. Her perusal is long and heart-strangling, and it coats my skin with nervous perspiration.

The insecurity plaguing me gets a moment of reprieve when she returns her glistening eyes to me, and I spot the gleam of approval in them. My nerves tingle. I shouldn't be pleased I've secured her seal of approval, but for some reason I am.

The logic behind my relieved response is made apparent when Marcus stops in front of the unnamed lady and says, "Cleo, this is my baby sister, Serenity."

My heart warms from the pride glowing out of Serenity's eyes from Marcus's introduction.

"Serenity, this is Cleo, my. . . " His words trail off into silence.

If Serenity didn't throw her arms around my neck and hug me tightly, I may have been tempted to kick him in the shins for his failure to give me a title for the second time in less than twenty-four hours. I guess I should be grateful he didn't introduce me as his submissive. *I'd rather have no title than that one.*

"It's so wonderful to meet you, Cleo," Serenity says, pulling back from our embrace. Her gleeful eyes bounce between mine for several moments before she mutters, "Wow, you're as gorgeous as Marcus described."

I balk, stunned Marcus told her about me. He mentioned previously his family isn't welcoming of his BDSM lifestyle, so I'm shocked I came up during his conversations with his sister. I wonder how he introduced me to her then?

Not registering the shock on my face, Serenity weaves her arm around my elbow and gives me a guided tour of Links. Although Marcus follows closely behind us, he remains quiet, allowing his sister to express his sentiments on the charity he established from the ground up with his bare hands. The pride in Serenity's voice is easily distinguishable. She's just as proud of her brother as I am.

This is an extremely early call, but if the little thud I get in my chest every time I think about Marcus is love, it's been thudding a little faster since we arrived at Links. Coming here had the exact effect Marcus was aiming for. I got to know him—the real Marcus Everett—not the millionaire recording artist or BDSM club owner— him! The man who has no qualms spending millions of dollars to give victims of domestic violence shelter during their roughest days.

The man whose briefest touch sends a flurry of excitement to both my core and my heart.

"We have last minute touch-ups happening on the murals today, then the furniture arrives on Wednesday, all ready for the grand opening next Saturday," Serenity explains when our tour returns to the rec room it started in.

"Wow, that sounds like a lot of work." Although the space has been perfectly remodeled, it is void of a single item of furniture. How can she possibly have enough hands on deck to assemble one hundred beds in that short amount of time, let alone all the other mammoth tasks she has been explaining the past thirty minutes?

Serenity's head bobs up and down as her eyes take in the space. "It is, but it will be worth it. There are men, women and children sleeping in the alleyway waiting for this facility to open." She places her hand onto my arm and tilts toward my side. "Between me and you, if regulations weren't so strict, I wouldn't have to hide them in the alleyway every time an inspector arrived unannounced."

Oh, my god, she's a sweetheart. Although now I can recognize the similarities between her and Marcus, the past thirty minutes have exposed that their personalities are on opposing ends of the spectrum. Serenity is bubbly and full of life. He seems reserved and somewhat shy in the presence of others. Don't get me wrong, his aura still demands respect, but he doesn't need to express it with words.

The one way Marcus and Serenity are identical in every way is their hearts. By combining Marcus's vision and bank balance with Serenity's go-get-'em personality and determined work ethic, victims of domestic violence will have a place to call home until they can get back onto their feet. That's a beautiful thing to do—celebrity or not.

"Well, if there's anything I can do to help, please don't hesitate to ask." My tone exposes the honesty of my statement.

Serenity's eyes bug, "Really?" When I nod, she asks, "Can you handle a ladle?"

I smile before once again nodding.

"Great! Because we could really use some help serving food in the kitchen next Saturday. If you're free, I wouldn't turn down a volunteer." Her girly voice echoes in the pin drop silence surrounding us.

I shift my eyes to Marcus to gain his approval. This project is his baby, and I don't want to step on his toes by attaching myself to it without his permission. That could just make this incredibly awkward if things don't work out between us this weekend.

While his eyes give me permission to accept Serenity's request, he walks over and joins our conversation. Ignoring the way his fingers interlocking with mine causes my breathing to shallow, I return my eyes to Serenity and say, "Sure. I'd love to help. I could bring my little sister as well?"

Serenity dances on the spot, revealing she's closer in age to Lexi than me and Marcus. "Do you have a younger brother too?" she questions, waggling her brows in a suggestive manner. "If he looks anything like you, I sure could put him to good use."

Although I can hear the playful mirth in her question, it doesn't stop a jab of pain hitting my chest. Tate was a wonderful young man whose life got cut way too short. He was a senior in high school and the much-loved quarterback for the Montclair Mounties. His loss didn't just impact my family; it impacted the entire community.

"Umm... I did. He and my parents were killed in a traffic accident four years ago," I enlighten her, my voice cracking with emotions.

Marcus's grip on my hand tightens as the smile on Serenity's face sags. "I'm so sorry," she apologizes, her eyes full of regret. "Oh my goodness, Cleo. I feel so bad being disrespectful like that."

"Please don't apologize. It's fine. You didn't know." I wave off her concerns with a sweep of my empty hand.

My attempts at defusing the situation are woeful. Serenity is stunned into silence, and Marcus is peering at me with concern. The uncomfortable silence continues as I search for something to say to ease the discomfort depriving the air of oxygen. Before a single thing is discovered, a man in a crisp black suit at the side of the room requests Serenity's assistance. I take a relieved breath, grateful for the interruption.

While squeezing mine and Marcus's conjoined hands, Serenity

locks her eyes with me. "Let me take you to lunch next week as a form of apology."

"It's not needed, truly, Serenity," I reply, hating that I've made her feel remorseful.

"Please, Cleo." She peers at me with big hazel eyes. "You'll be doing me a favor. With all my girlfriends being back home, I don't have anyone to hang with in New York. It's getting lonely eating by myself every day."

I highly doubt her reply. She has an aura that instantly makes you want to befriend her. But since I dislike the spark of remorse in her eyes, I nod.

"But I'm paying," I say, wanting to ensure she knows I'm only agreeing to dine with her under the presumption we are eating as friends, not because she owes me an apology.

"A free lunch! Yay!" Serenity claps her hands together before pressing a quick kiss to my cheek.

"You take good care of this one, Marcus. I really like her," she says to Marcus before mimicking our farewell with a peck to his cheek.

After giving our hands one final squeeze, Serenity saunters to the man requesting her attention. The seductive sway of her petite hips doesn't go unnoticed by the men devouring homemade sandwiches like they've never been fed.

The smile their sneaky glances caused grows when Marcus moves to stand in front of me. After tucking a felonious hair behind my ear, he locks his striking eyes with mine. "Why didn't you tell me about your parents and brother?"

My left shoulder lifts into a wee shrug. "There was never an appropriate time."

We've talked about many things the past six weeks, but siblings, careers, and our vastly contradicting bank balances never came up. It also isn't the best starting point for a blossoming relationship. Usually all it achieves is hours of awkward uncomfortableness and a string of sympathies I've heard many times the past four years.

"I still wish you would have told me, Cleo. I don't like secrets."

Although you could construe his words as a scold, the softness in his eyes doesn't relay that. He isn't angry; he's compassionate.

His eyes stop dancing between mine when a man in his mid-twenties wearing a paint-splattered shirt stands beside him. "Hi...ah... Marcus. I'm a huge fan of yours. When Jimbo said we were working on one of your projects I thought he was pulling my leg." His deep voice is accentuated with an Australian accent. "Would it be too much if I snapped a quick photo with you to show my sisters back home?" He drifts his eyes between Marcus and me as if he's requesting my permission as well.

When Marcus nods, I accept the cell phone from the unnamed man and take multiple shots of him and Marcus together. After handing the stranger back his phone, he requests to introduce Marcus to the remaining four men seated around the table. I move to the side of the room, happy to watch Marcus interact with his fans without invading their space. It's not often you get a chance to meet an idol one-on-one, so I don't want to take anything away from their experience.

The happiness beaming out of the men when Marcus offers them his hand to shake forces a huge smile on my face. They clumsily stumble out of their chairs before accepting his offer. I bet my starstruck face yesterday was similar to the expressions their faces are holding now.

The heat sluicing my veins from seeing him in his element doubles when I secure his utmost devotion from across the room. Even though he converses with the unnamed men for the next ten minutes, his eyes rarely leave mine. His gaze is primitive and strong, and it forces my eyes to stray to the ground on numerous occasions. Giddy nervousness envelops me as heat rises to my cheeks. I'm shocked by my body's response to his avid stare. My personality could never be described as shy or timid, but I'm certain that's the foreign feeling pumping through me right now. *Or maybe it is the feeling of being desired?*

When Marcus finishes autographing an old electric bill found dumped on the floor by one of the tradesman, he heads in my direction. His steps are predatory and full of command, adding to the dampness pooling between my legs. I force my lungs to secure a deep breath, feeling the need to replenish them before they lose the ability to secure an entire breath.

The prompts of my body are spot on when he drapes his arm around my waist and pulls me to stand in front of him. He's just as aroused as I am, his cock hard and thick against my lower back.

"That could have ended disastrously," he mutters, his hot breath fanning my sweat-slicked neck. "Imagine the influx of questions about my sexuality if the paparazzi discovered I got hard while talking to male fans."

Before I can ask what caused his aroused state, he says, "I didn't think anything could top the visual of your face in ecstasy, Cleo, but your smile. . . Jesus. It made me instantly stiff. I know you make me reckless, but I didn't know you had that type of power over me."

I grind my backside along his rod, thanking him for his compliment with a touch of the friskiness it awarded me with. His rough groan sends the aroma of lust into the air. It's heavy and thick, a seductive mix of our combined scents. I can't hold back my excitement. I grind against him again, more firmly this time around.

His lips brush my earlobe when he mutters, "Naughty girls get punished, Cleo. Do you want to be punished?"

I pant in anticipation, my mind spiraling with endless possibilities when his hand flattens on my stomach so he can draw me in closer to him. My new position allows me to feel how excited he's about the prospect of punishing me as well.

"The idea of being punished turns you on." He isn't asking a question; he's stating a fact. "I can feel the heat of your pussy through layers of clothes."

I don't respond to his admission. I just grind against him once more. Sexual tension bursts through me when his manly scent invades my senses. He smells fresh and clean, but intoxicatingly virile at the same time. My nostrils flare as I fight the desire to grind against him again since our closeness has gained us the inquisitive stares of the tradesman. It's a tough fight. I'm desperate for him, my hunger blatantly displayed by my flushed face and wide eyes.

"Why did you have to buy a house an hour out of the city?" I whine, my rickety voice revealing my heightened state.

My knees crash together when Marcus sinks his teeth into my shoulder blade. My moan is only just concealed by chairs scraping across the hardwood floor, signaling the end of the workers' lunch break. I weakly wave to the tradesmen bidding us farewell with a dip of their chins and friendly smiles.

"Can we leave too?" I request, my voice husky with lust.

"Are you growing impatient, Cleo?" Marcus's commanding tone is unable to conceal that I'm not the only one eager.

"Yes," I respond, my one word needy. "I've waited eight weeks to taste your cock. I don't think I can wait a moment longer."

"Jesus, Cleo." His grip tightens around my waist so firmly it is almost painful. "When you say things like that, I want to take you hard and fast until nothing but pleas for forgiveness spill out of your filthy little mouth."

"That's the point. I want you to *fuck* me—hard and fast." I nearly do a jig on the spot, I'm so stoked I articulated my body's desires without a smidge of hesitation.

Marcus's cock scorches my back when he rocks his hips forward, dragging his thickened shaft along the ridges of my spine. "I'm not above clearing the room, Cleo," he warns, his voice strained. "If that's what it will take to ensure your every desire is met."

His admission dampens my excitement somewhat. Serenity has been working nonstop on this project the past month. I can't let my inability to harness my unbridled horniness set her schedule back for even a minute.

Snubbing the screaming protests of my body, I spin on my heels and face Marcus. His eyes are wide with lust, and he's breathing harder than normal. It makes what I'm about to say ten times harder.

"I can't let you do that." The uncertainty of my words weakens what should be a confident statement. "But I can let you do me. . . *in around an hour.*"

Marcus's lust-filled eyes bounce between mine for several minutes. It's the first time I've ever noticed a tinge of hesitation in them. The more he takes in my flushed expression, the darker his eyes become with desire.

My pulse thrums when he mutters, "Get your coat. I have a hotel room two blocks from here."

28

*E*ven being bombarded by paparazzi on our way to the hotel can't dampen my excitement. Perspiration is misting my skin, and stupid butterflies are fluttering in my stomach. I keep my cap-covered head down low and follow Marcus as he weaves through the nosy reporters and wide-eyed New Yorkers crammed on the bustling sidewalks. I'm not the only one eager. I can feel Marcus's excitement thrumming through his hand curled around mine. I'm not going to lie; it makes me giddy knowing he has the same uninhibited attraction to me as I do him.

The nerves twisting my stomach switch to excitement when we enter the revolving glass door of an elegant hotel in lower Manhattan. With the door manned by a group of beefy security personnel, the two-block paparazzi chase comes to an end the instant we slip inside. As Marcus guides me through the expansive foyer, my eyes shoot in all directions, eager to absorb each beautiful feature.

A gorgeous silk-pleated panel covers the entire back wall of the foyer; dark-veined wood panels line the walls in a checked design, and the floor is done with gray tile in an asymmetrical pattern. The three round chandeliers dangling from the ceiling bounce multihued beams of light onto the dark coloring, softening the starkness of its design. It's a beautiful space that screams of modernity and wealth.

Shock registers on my face when Marcus forgoes the usual check-in process most guests must endure when first arriving at a hotel. He heads straight for the bank of silver elevators tucked behind the concierge desk. Upon entering, he dips his chin in greeting to the elderly elevator attendant before moving to the back of the crowded car. I'm tempted to ask why he neither checked in or advised the elevator attendant of his floor number. But then I realize, we are from two very contrasting worlds. This type of process is probably nothing out of the ordinary for a man as wealthy as Marcus.

A thrill of excitement courses through me when Marcus tugs me to his side. His firm grip on my hip adds to the throb between my legs. The temperature in the elevator car becomes roasting as lust permeates the air.

I can barely contain my excitement when he murmurs into my ear, "Remove your panties. I want nothing in my way when we arrive at my room."

My knees crash together as my eyes rocket to his. I'm practically panting to control the excitement thickening my blood. Although I'm incredibly aroused by his request, I shake my head. The elevator is brimming with hotel guests. I'm not talking one or two; I'm talking over a dozen.

Marcus's alluring eyes burn into mine as he mutters, "It was not a request, Cleo. Remove your panties or be punished." His commanding eyes strengthen his statement, but they don't faze me in the slightest. For some inane reason, the idea of being punished by him sounds more like a treat than a penance. Even more so since he doesn't have access to the scary torturous instruments in his playroom.

Spotting the defiance brightening my dark eyes, Marcus whispers, "Do you want to come, Cleo?"

The hotness of his breath on my ear spurs on a new type of excitement, the one only he can muster: the anticipation of orgasming during sex.

I nod, unashamed.

"Then remove your panties," he requests again, his voice smooth and silky. "Or I'll withhold your ability to climax indefinitely."

The command in his voice causes my thighs to tremble. Fighting past my shaking legs, I sink into the corner of the elevator, slither my hands under my skirt and grasp my satin panties. Using Marcus's frame as a shield, I slide the damp material down my quaking thighs before kicking them to my side. The wetness between my legs grows, loving the edge of naughtiness in our exchange. Just the thought of being caught has the veins in my neck strumming.

The scent of my arousal filters through my nose when Marcus gathers my panties from the ground by pretending he's tying the laces on his shoe. My thighs push together as I feel his breath on my right kneecap. He's mere inches from my dripping core.

Keeping his eyes front and center, he slips my panties into his pocket before extending to his full height. Even with his crotch mostly covered by his suit jacket, I know he's hard. The pleats of his trousers are fully extended, and the zipper is jutted out as it struggles to contain his impressive manhood. I lick my lips, hoping to God my brazen request in Links is about to be fulfilled. When I squirm on the spot, fighting hard to ease the throb between my legs, evidence of my excitement extends to my upper thighs. I've never felt more scandalous or desired in my life.

My squirming comes to a stop when an unexpected smack hits my right butt cheek. I bite on my bottom lip to hold in my excited moan before drifting my eyes to Marcus. He faces the front of the cart, unaware of the blaze his smack caused to my thumping sex. Although he concealed his slap with an impromptu cough, the unexpected noise still gains us the attention of numerous sets of eyes.

Ignoring the inquisitive stare from the lady standing next to Marcus, I murmur, "What was that for?"

He doesn't answer me. He simply smiles a wickedly delicious smirk that sets my pulse racing. Squeezing my knees together, I divert my eyes to the elevator dashboard, silently praying it will arrive at our floor before I combust into ecstasy without being touched. For every floor the elevator takes, the excitement vexing my libido grows and the number of occupants in the car decreases. In no time at all, it is just Marcus, me and the elevator attendant left.

Before my lust-hazed brain can register the elevator's arrival at the very top floor, Marcus grips my hand and steps into the empty corridor. The elevator doors have only just snapped shut when he curls his arms around my back, dips me, and seals his lips over mine. His tongue plunges into my mouth with a sense of urgency, like he couldn't wait a moment longer to kiss me.

Clearly, that's the case when he pulls his lips away from mine and murmurs, "I couldn't wait a second longer."

He guides me toward a set of doors at the end of the long corridor, his steps urgent. The instant we enter a massive room, I pounce. My hands go frantic, trying to figure out a way to remove his jacket and trousers at the same time. I need his flesh against mine, and I need it now.

My endeavor to remove Marcus's clothes is left for dust when he throws his arm across the entranceway table, sending all the contents on top scattering onto the floor with a clatter. Placing his hands under my arms, he lifts me to sit on the solid wooden table. Before I can comprehend what's happening, the flare of my skirt is bunched around my waist, and he burrows his head between my legs.

I call out when his tongue runs along the cleft of my pussy before it plunges inside. I clench my thighs around his head; I'm so close to climax I can taste it. He devours my pussy with a set of greedy licks and playful nibs until the tension in my sex coils so tightly, I can no longer hold back.

"Oh god, I'm going to come," I grunt, my words barely coherent. "Can I please come, Master Chains?" I ask, knowing the desires of my body are no longer controlled by me. Their sole rights belong to the man who can have me teetering on the edge of orgasmic bliss by simply speaking.

Gratitude scorches through me when Marcus murmurs, "You can come."

The vibration of his deep voice against my soaked sex is the final push I need to freefall over the edge. With his teeth grazing my clit, Marcus's name tears from my throat in a grunted moan as I get lost in the throes of ecstasy. My nails bend harshly into the muscles on his shoulders as every nerve in my body fights through a blinding orgasm. I quiver and shake against his tongue, my mind shut down, my body overwhelmed by the shimmers of climax.

Once every climatic shudder has been exhausted, Marcus places one last lash of his tongue onto my clit before he raises his head. His mouth is glistening with evidence of my arousal, and his eyes are wide and bright.

"Ever since the day you fell onto your knees in the elevator, I've been dying to taste you," he discloses; his voice has a hint of possessiveness attached to it.

My heart squeezes in my chest, beyond exalted he remembered our very first meeting. "You remember that day?"

Marcus toys with my clit before slipping two fingers into my wet core. "You thought I forgot?"

My breaths quicken to match the pace of his fingers pumping into me. With my pussy still throbbing with the aftermath of a toe-curling orgasm, it doesn't take long for his talented fingers to work me into a frenzy.

"Answer me, Cleo."

My muscles tense in anticipation from the clipped command of his voice. "No." I briskly shake my head, sending droplets of sweat flinging off my inflamed cheeks. "I just didn't realize I was so memorable."

I tighten my grip around his neck when his fingers flick the little nub inside me that drives me wild. The familiar tingle of ecstasy grows with every dedicated thrust of his fingers. My body coils tightly, preparing for another release. I snap my eyes shut when the fiery warmth spreading through my womb becomes too much to bear. I personally know Marcus's skill level in the bedroom, but I'm still shocked by how quickly he has my next orgasm building.

"Open your eyes." Marcus's voice is stiff. "I want you to see what your ecstasy-riddled face does to me."

I flutter my eyes open and am awarded with the glorious visual of him removing his cock from the tight restraint of his trousers. His suit pants drop to the floor with a flutter before his other hand works his boxers down his splayed thighs. His cock is so thick, the veins weaving up his long shaft are throbbing with need, and the tip is glistening with pre-cum. His balls are pulled in close to his body, preparing for imminent release. Just the sight of him finger fucking me with his trousers gathered around his ankles shifts my race to climax from a frantic pace to a desperate dash. I need to climax even more than I need to breathe.

I reach out to touch Marcus's thick cock, only to have my hands snapped away. I pout. I'm dying to feel his flesh in my hand and to taste him in my mouth.

My disappointment doesn't last long when he grinds his fingers into me deeper, ensuring his fingertips brush the sensitive nub inside me with every pump he does. I rock my hips forward, meeting his rhythm thrust for thrust. All thoughts vanish as a blistering of stars form before my eyes. My body quakes as a second orgasm shimmers to life.

"Now, Cleo!" Marcus demands, plunging his fingers into me at a frantic speed. "Come now!"

The desire to snap my eyes shut overwhelms me when the intensity of my orgasm hits full fruition. I grunt and moan, battling the sensation roaring through every inch of my spent body.

"Eyes on me, Cleo," Marcus demands. "Watch what you do to me. Watch how reckless you make me."

A guttural moan tears through my lips when my eyes snap to him in just enough time to see the first jet of cum rocket out of his engorged knob. The hotness of his seed pumps out of him in raring spurts, coating my throbbing pussy and landing halfway up my stomach. I moan even louder, loving the possessive vibe sparking the air. I did that. Me. My face in ecstasy was the only thing needed to make him cum. That's a highly thrilling and addictive experience, and it hurtles my orgasm to a never-before-reached level.

It feels like hours pass before my body stops shaking with the effects of climax. My muscles are weary, and my body is slicked with sweat. After removing my coat from my shoulders, Marcus locks his lust-crazed eyes with me.

"You were the first woman to fall to her knees in front of me," he admits, his alluring eyes bouncing between mine. "I always had the desire for power in the bedroom, but it was that day that catapulted my needs to the next level."

"What?" I ask, certain my sexually satiated brain isn't registering what he's saying accurately. "What are you saying? I'm the reason you became—"

"Master Chains," he fills in.

He waits a moment, giving me a chance to fully absorb his confession. I honestly don't know what to think. I'm flattered. Obviously. But I'm also a little unsure. His lifestyle choice is my biggest cause of concern, so to discover I'm the reason he entered into that lifestyle is a little unsettling.

"Should I be flattered or upset?" I ask Marcus, my brain too exhausted to decipher the whirlwind of emotions pumping into me.

He bounces his captivating eyes between mine for several heart-stuttering seconds before saying, "No matter which journey life takes, you always end up where you're supposed to be. This is my life, Cleo, so even if you didn't fall in the elevator all those years ago, I truly believe this is who I would have eventually become."

My heartbeat slows when he cups my jaw. "Just like I truly believed I would eventually find you again. Whether it was ten years or four, I knew one day I would find you."

My eyes burn from the sudden influx of tears in them. He's been looking for me this entire time? That's crazily beautiful. I'll be the first to admit the speed of our relationship is crazy, but that doesn't lessen the intensity of it. Marcus knows me. Master Chains knows me. And I know him—both sides of him.

"Will you please kiss me, Master Chains?" I request, dying for any part of his body to be on mine.

Smiling, he seals his mouth over mine. I can taste myself on his lips. It's a tangy and sharp flavor I've never experienced before. I lap it up, loving all the firsts I've been experiencing this weekend. My first time in a playroom. My first time climaxing during sex. And my first time falling in love. I thought I loved Luke, but only now do I realize it isn't the same feeling I get when I'm with Marcus. At the time, my relationship with Luke was heartwarming, but it didn't utterly consume me like Marcus does. He's on my mind all the time. Even before I knew his real name.

After banding his arms around my waist, Marcus pulls me off the entranceway table and moves deeper into the suite. I grind my pussy against his crotch, loving that every grind increases his cock's thickness. The softness of high threadcount bedding graces my back when he lays me on the kingsize bed in the middle of the suite. His mouth captures my breathy moan when he pins me to the bed, my body relishing the weight of him pressed against me.

We kiss for several minutes until nothing is on my mind but cherishing every delicious inch of the man in front of me.

With his knee keeping my shuddering thighs apart, he undoes the buttons of his business shirt. The warm wetness between my legs grows when his delicious body is seductively freed from the tight restrictions of his clothing. He takes his time, building the sexual tension firing between us until it reaches a fevered pitch. My pussy clenches when his crisp blue business shirt gapes open, exposing inches of his rigid stomach.

While pulling off his blue striped tie, Marcus asks, "What's your safe word, Cleo?"

"Pineapple," I murmur, my body heightened beyond approach.

A girly squeal emits from my lips when he steps back from the bed and flips me over. Anticipation follows the path my zipper takes when he unlatches my dress and slides down the fastener until it is sitting in the small of my back. His breathing hitches when my dress falls off my shoulders to crinkle around my knees pressed into the mattress. My heavy breasts fall forward when his talented fingers make quick work of my satin bra. He dumps it on the floor next to his removed trousers before cupping my soaked sex.

"You're drenched, Cleo," Marcus grinds out, his voice deep and tempting. "Have you been a bad girl?"

Unashamedly, I nod. "Yes."

Fiery heat spreads across my naked backside when he exacts a painful spank to my right butt cheek. "Yes, what?"

"Yes, Master Chains," I stammer out, my words unable to conceal my pleasure.

My mind spirals with possibilities when the softness of silk lowers over my eyes. After fastening his tie to the back of my head, Marcus runs his hand down my back. My knees scrape across the bedding when he adjusts my hips, erotically staging me for his visual pleasure.

A violent shudder courses through me when I feel his breath against the puckered hole of my rear. "What's your safe word, Cleo?"

It's the fight of my life to murmur, "Pineapple."

29

*T*he buzz of a cell phone distracts the enticing visual of Marcus shaving in front of the vanity mirror of his hotel suite. It's fascinating watching the man who drove me to the brink of ecstasy more times than I can count doing something so domesticated. I don't know what I was expecting, but I'm certain a man as wealthy as Marcus wouldn't need to shave his face if he didn't want to. He could just summon someone to do it for him. That's why I find it so refreshing to discover he maintains a lot of power in regards to his personal life. Not just in his playroom, but in every walk of his life. I guess it is all part and parcel of him needing to be in control.

Ignoring the pleas of my tired muscles, I roll out of the bed I'm sprawled on and pace to my handbag left dumped on the floor. I've spent the last twenty minutes struggling to regain the use of my sexually satiated muscles so I can join Marcus for a shower before we make the hour trip back to his residence. I swear, muscles I didn't know existed are hurting.

After yanking open the zipper of my handbag, I pull out my cellphone. A faint smile cracks onto my lips when I read the message displayed on the screen.

Lexi: Just checking in to ensure you haven't died of sexual exhaustion.

After checking Marcus's location, I return Lexi's text.

Me: *Before today, I would have never believed there was such a thing as death by sexual gratification.*

Lexi's reply is almost immediate.

Lexi: *Do share!*

My laugh fills the space, gaining me the attention of Marcus, who's wiping shaving cream from his cut jawline. From the hungry gleam in his eyes, no one would know he came four times already today. He looks as hungry for sexual relief as ever.

When his eyes drop to my phone, I jingle it in my hand. "Just Lexi checking in," I inform him, my tone breathy from his compelling stare.

Marcus's plump lips curl into a smirk. "When you're done, join me in the shower." He nudges his head to the double shower my nearsightedness displays as nothing but a blur of white. Although his voice is as commanding as ever, it couldn't hide the plea in his words. He wants me as badly as I want him.

Once I nod, agreeing with his request, he enters the bathroom, closing the door behind him. I drop my eyes to my phone to begin typing a reply to Lexi. Halfway through my false vow of saintly virtue, my cell buzzes, announcing my battery is low.

"Oh, bugger," I mumble to myself. I delete my original long-winded reply to Lexi and send a much simpler one.

Me: *My phone is about to go dead. I'll update when I get home.*

I send thanks to God for Lexi when I read her reply.

Lexi: *I placed a charger in your purse yesterday morning. Now you have no excuse for keeping me on tender hooks.*

I laugh while typing.

Me: *Can't talk, just about to have a shower with a handsome, drool-worthy man whose rich chocolatey voice is one of his lesser attributes.*

I attach a cheeky winking emoji to my message. Lexi's reply is instant.

Lexi: *Cleo!!*

Before I can reply, my phone shuts down. My rummage through my handbag only awards me with a USB charger. While racking my brain for a solution to my situation, my eyes scan the room. Like the stars are aligning in my favor, my examination of the vast space has me stumbling onto a MacBook Air sitting beneath a stack of papers on a dressing table in the corner of the room.

I pace toward the Mac, silently praying it will have enough power to give my battery some type of charge until I can fully charge it at Marcus's property. With Lexi's medical condition, I've never allowed my battery to run flat. More times than not, a cellphone is the most valuable asset in an emergency situation.

After plugging my phone into the Mac, I hit the power button. Gratefulness pumps into me when the screen on the Mac instantly fires up. Happy it has adequate power to charge my cell, I place it on the dressing table and move toward the bathroom, more than eager to join Marcus in the shower. My brisk strides stop, closely followed by my heart, when the screen on the Mac fully illuminates.

"What the hell?" I mumble under my breath while pacing back to the Mac, my steps shaky.

My rickety stride has nothing to do with the effect of multiple muscle-weary orgasms, and everything to do with the live image being streamed on the monitor of the Mac. My eyes frantically scan the screen, wanting to ensure my exhausted brain isn't misreading the visual displayed before me. This can't possibly be what my eyes are relaying. There must be some type of mistake.

My heart falls from my chest when my avid assessment reaches the same conclusion time and time again: a live feed from my bedroom is being streamed on the laptop monitor. I may have believed it was an old video if it wasn't for the I.D Sarrieri hotel slip Mr. Carson purchased for me sitting packaged on my bed. After removing the felonious hidden camera, I placed the slip up for Auction on eBay last week. It sold the day of Thanksgiving. I only packaged it for delivery yesterday morning, moments before the NDA from Marcus was delivered.

My hand darts up to my mouth. I feel sick—incredibly sick. Not trusting my legs to keep me upright, I sit on the chair in front of the dressing mirror. This can't be true. What benefit would someone get from putting a camera in my bedroom? And why would they plant a laptop in Marcus's hotel room?

My blank stare at the monitor has me stumbling onto more evidence of my gross invasion of privacy. A document sitting in the bottom lefthand side of the screen has been saved under my name. It looks like an email saved to the desktop. Snubbing my shaking hands, I glide my finger over the touchpad on the MacBook Air and click on the file.

It's lucky my stomach is empty. If it weren't, the violent heaves racking through my body would have seen the Mac's keyboard covered with vomit by now. After taking a moment to settle my squishy stomach, I scan my eyes over the email document.

"Dear Mr. Everett, Please find attached the background search you requested for Cleo Garcia of 160 Valley Road, Montclair, NJ 07042. I hope this search is to your satisfaction. Harry Closter."

I feel sick—horribly sick. My stomach twists as violently as my heart when reality dawns. This Mac wasn't planted in Marcus's room. This is *his* computer. I don't give my heart the chance to plead with my brain to stop and consider the facts. I just click on the attachment at the bottom of the email without a single thought passing my mind.

Just as my brain suspected, the form places the final nail in Marcus's coffin. My name, date of birth, address, negative bank balance, and employee status are displayed in a neat bullet point format. Its plain and stark presentation is vastly contradictory to the blatant fury raging through my blood right now.

As I scroll down, the situation gets worse. Pages and pages of the online journal I kept as part of my grieving process filters onto the screen. Lexi's therapist suggested for her to write down her thoughts she didn't want to voice out loud. I thought it was a brilliant idea, so I did exactly that the past four years. I wrote down my fears, my pain, and my desire to meet the man who offered me comfort in my hour of need. These words were not meant to be seen by anyone but me— they are sacred.

I guess one good thing has come from my privacy being so horribly invaded. It proves Marcus doesn't know me at all. He couldn't tell I was on the brink of climax by hearing the pants of my breath or know I was on the verge of crying because of one spoken word. He only knew because he's been spying on me this entire time! The date on the email ensures there's no misconception. It's dated the morning following our first communication on the Chains website.

No longer capable of holding in my fury, I grit my teeth, slam the Mac screen closed, and send it hurling across the room. It crashes into the wardrobe before grumbling to the floor. Its deformed and mangled appearance matches the sentiments of my heart to a T. How could I have been so stupid?! Why was I so blinded with lust, I couldn't see what this weekend was really about? A stupid game between a power-craving Dom and the belittled sub beneath him.

Hot, salty tears burn my eyes, but I refuse to let them fall. He does *not* deserve my tears. *He does not deserve me!* My entire body shakes with anger as I stand from my seat and snag my dress off the floor. I angrily yank it over my head before pulling my arms through the long sleeves. I don't bother securing the latch at the back; I'm too angry to care about the opinions of others. I just want to get out of here. I just want to go home.

While running my fingers through my hair to settle the disheveled mess, my eyes scan the room for Marcus's trousers. *I'm not leaving this room without my panties.* My privacy may have been grossly invaded, but I still have my pride. I also refuse to let him have a single piece of me—even if it's something as measly as a scrap of satin.

I race to the other side of the bed when a portion of Marcus's dark slacks peeks out from the other side of the bed. The view of the twisted bedsheets intensify the swishy movements of my stomach. I shift my eyes away, refusing to look at a place I felt worshipped mere minutes ago. *How stupid was I?*

The pocket in Marcus's trousers rip when I roughly yank them open, seeking my panties. For the first time in five minutes, I secure an entire breath when a silky smoothness graces my fingers. I wipe under my eyes to ensure no rogue tears have fallen before sliding my panties up my thighs and slipping into my stilettos.

The instant my dress hits my knee, my body's awareness of Marcus activates. I take in a nerve-calming breath before lifting my eyes from the ground. Just as my body intuited, Marcus is standing in the doorway of the bathroom. He has a white towel wrapped around his drenched hips, and his brow is arched high. Time slows to a snail's pace when he rakes his eyes down my body, absorbing my clothed form.

When he shifts his eyes to the MacBook Air sprawled halfway across the floor, my eyes follow his movements. A dash of panic mingles with the anger lacing my veins when I notice my cellphone is still tethered to the Mac. Although my bank balance has slightly improved the past eight weeks, I can't afford to replace my phone if it's as broken as the Mac. I have four years of catching up bills before my money can go toward luxury expenses.

Swallowing away my worry, I return my eyes to Marcus. Fury blackens my blood and flushes my face when I see the truth beaming from his eyes. He knows what I saw on his Mac. His eyes tell me the entire story. Snarling, I issue him a wrathful stare. I've never been so angry in my life. It feels like it's burning me alive.

"*Cleo. . .*" His voice comes out in a warning, like I'm the one who invaded his privacy. "I can explain."

Angrily shaking my head at his failure to refute my silent accusation, I bob down to grab my cellphone off the floor. My yank is so rough it snaps the USB charging cord in half. After gathering my handbag off the bed where I dumped it, I make a beeline for the door.

Marcus beats me to it.

He dives over the bed and flattens his back against the hotel suite door before I even get one foot into the entranceway. His ninja-like moves forced the towel around his hips to slip, leaving him as naked and exposed as I feel. I'm so angry, my body doesn't even request for me to look down.

"Move," I sneer through clenched teeth, my tears threatening to fall at any moment.

Marcus stares straight into my eyes before shaking his head. His stance is as determined as the strong gleam beaming from his eyes.

"Move!" I scream again as the first tears topple from my eyes.

I angrily brush them away, loathing that they're making me look weak. I'm not weak. I can't say the same about the so-called man in front of me.

Marcus moves with such agility, he has me wrapped up in a firm hold before I can comprehend what's happening. I thrash against him, hating that my body's first response was to melt into his embrace. The instant his familiar scent was detected my body forgot the rage scorching my veins. *He's the reason my heart is being torn in two, so why is my body craving his touch?*

"Let me go!" I yell, hoping my startled cries will alert another hotel guest on our floor to my distress.

Marcus firms his grip. "Not until you give me the chance to explain," he responds, his words pleading.

"What's there to explain? You spied on me! No further explanation needed!"

I continue fighting, not willing to give this man another second of my time. He has already had more than he deserves. My heart smashes against my ribs as my lungs fight to secure an entire breath. My mind is shut down, my heart beyond repair.

"I told you you make me reckless, Cleo. I warned you that I can't control myself around you," Marcus says, his tone confused.

Even hearing the pain in his words doesn't stop my wailing. I kick my arms and legs out wildly, ensuring the heels on my stilettos connect with his shins. He doesn't deserve my sympathy. I showed him a side of me no one has ever seen. I gave him pieces of me I'll never get back, and this is how he repays me.

When his fingers cause a sting of pain to rocket to my core, our time together in his playroom comes rushing to the forefront of my mind. It's a cruel and twisted reminder of the rollercoaster of emotions I've been dealing with the past twenty-four hours. I thought the longest day I'd ever endured was the day my parents were killed. It wasn't. Today has felt like an eternity. A horridly beautiful day that saw my heart expand so much, it had no other choice but to shatter.

The only good thing that comes from being bombarded with

memories of Marcus's playroom is that it reminds me of the one word that will instantly halt his campaign. The one word he promised would ensure our exchange would end the instant I said it.

"Pineapple," I murmur, hiccupping through the stream of tears rolling down my face. "Pineapple," I repeat, ensuring there's no way he couldn't hear my request.

Marcus's grip around my waist firms before he finally lets go and takes a step back. I keep my gaze locked on the tiled floor for several moments, gasping in breaths like it's my last chance to breathe. After brushing the tears off my cheeks, I lift my disarrayed gaze to Marcus. The torment in his eyes replicates mine to a T. They're full of despair and regret.

But even knowing he's hurting doesn't stop me from saying, "Goodbye, Marcus."

When he steps toward me, I hold out my hand and shake my head. "Please don't make me say my safe word again. You said once it's used, there's no going back; the scene is ended. Show me you are a tenth of the man I thought you were by being a man who keeps his word."

Marcus's nostrils flare as his eyes bounce between mine. I can see he wants to say something, but thankfully, not a sound seeps from his lips. It takes my brain screaming at my body for me to push off my feet and walk past him. The tears welling in my eyes grow when his familiar freshly showered smell hits my senses, but I keep my gaze forward, refusing to look at the man who so grossly broke my trust.

"*Cleo. . .*please," Marcus murmurs when I lower the door handle and swing open the door.

I don't stop. I continue with my endeavor to reach the bank of elevators at the end of the hall. If I don't leave now, I may say something I can never take back. Marcus's heated gaze warms my back the entire way. It never once wavers until I step into the elevator car several minutes later. After dipping my head in greeting to the elevator attendant, I move to the far corner of the empty car.

The instant the doors snap shut, I crumble to the ground and howl.

------

30

*T*hrowing my keys into the glass bowl on the entranceway table of my home, I pace deeper into the foyer. I honestly don't recall how I got here. I'm fairly certain I caught the train, but I can't one hundred percent testify to that. My body has gone into autopilot mode. I'm exhausted, hurt and heartbroken.

Lexi's perfume engulfs my nasal cavities when I'm wrapped up in a pair of strong arms. "Oh my god, Cleo. Are you okay? Did he hurt you?"

When she pulls back from our embrace, her eyes go wild, scanning my face and body for any physical signs of injury. She won't find any. All my damage is internal—it can't be seen by the naked eye.

Lexi's warm hand takes the chill out of my cheek when she cups my jaw and glances into my eyes. "I've been calling you the past two hours." Her calm words don't hold the same panic her forthright eyes have.

Her admission shocks me. *Maybe I didn't take the train straight home?*

Lexi licks her dry lips before saying, "Chains called hours ago to tell me you were coming home. I've been trying to reach you ever since."

Just hearing his name amplifies the stabbing pain hitting my chest. "My phone is dead." My voice is so flat I don't even recognize it.

I suddenly stiffen. "I need a shower."

Cold sweat clings to my skin as I close my eyes. I can smell Marcus on me. In my hair, on my skin, inside of me. I shiver as my lips thin in grimness.

"I *really* need to take a shower," I murmur, my words relaying my utter desire. I've never felt more dirty.

"Okay." Lexi nods. "You go and grab a shower while I make you a glass of tea. You look exhausted."

She runs the back of her hand down my cheek, her eyes growing more concerned by the minute. I want to tell her what happened, but I can't right now. I'm having such a hard time processing it all that I can't be expected to relay the information to a third party.

I press a kiss to Lexi's temple, silently thanking her for the sympathies her dark eyes are transmitting before trudging to our shared bathroom. I take my time in the shower, ensuring my skin is free of Marcus's scent. I wash my hair, shave my legs and scrub my skin until it's red and raw.

By the time I walk out of the bathroom, we are out of hot water and my dour mood isn't as rampant as it was earlier. Don't construe my statement the wrong way. I am still fiercely angry. I'm just not wallowing in self-pity anymore. Marcus might have played me for a fool, but that charade is now over.

My switch in mood has a lot to do with a saying my mom always quoted to Lexi and me at the beginning of our teen years, "Instead of wiping away your tears, wipe away the people who created them."

That's exactly what I'm going to do.

And I know the very first place to start.

After wrangling my hair into a messy bun, I pace into my bedroom. From the determination of my strides, no one would be the wiser to the pain shredding my heart. I stand in my room for several seconds, wanting to ensure Marcus can see his betrayal has had no effect on me whatsoever. From the angle of the livestream on the Mac, it doesn't take a genius to realize the webcam in my computer was the source of the bug. I wouldn't be shocked to discover it's been streaming since the day I logged into the chains website weeks ago.

Once I'm satisfied Marcus has spotted my determination, I saunter to my desk, yank my computer out of the wall and dump it into the waste receptacle at the side of our house, removing the trash from my life as if it's nothing but rubbish.

I feel invigorated and free, like nothing can bring me down. . . until I spot the chain link pendant dangling around my neck in the full-length mirror of my room. That's all it takes for a flood of tears to bombard my eyes. *How could such an awe-inspiring day turn into a clusterfuck in a matter of minutes?*

While battling to keep my tears at bay, horrid shudders wreak havoc with my body. When they become too great for me to bear, I crash onto my bed and burrow my head into my pillow. He will not break me. I'm stronger than this. Tears are reserved for my darkest days.

Lexi finds me five minutes later huddled in a ball in the middle of my bed. Not speaking, she places a glass of chamomile tea onto my bedside table and crawls into my bed. She curls her body around mine and whispers reassurances in my ear on repeat. Most follow along a similar path: she's going to kill Master Chains.

As the pain in my chest grows, minutes on the clock tick by. Utterly exhausted from an emotionally draining weekend, the weight of my eyelids becomes too much for me to ignore. With Lexi's body heating my back, and her kind words warming my heart, I soon fall asleep.

By the time I wake the next morning, the sun is already hanging high in the sky. I lift my arms out of my comforter and take a long stretch. My muscles are still pulled taut from the exertion of sexual activities. It's a vindictive reminder of the day I endured yesterday.

My neck cranks to the side when I hear the padding of feet sounding down the hall. Lexi stands at my bedroom door with a mug of coffee in one hand and my cellphone in the other. She looks as exhausted as I feel. She stayed with me the majority of the night, not even leaving my side when Jackson arrived to whisk her away on a romantic date. Her dedication and love helped to soothe the hideous scars Marcus's betrayal caused to my heart.

Lexi paces two steps into my room. "I know this is the last thing you need," she says, nudging her head to my cellphone clasped in her hand. "But this has been ringing nonstop."

Immaturely, I roll my eyes and release an exasperated breath. "You'll have to show me how to block his number from calling me."

My eyes snap to Lexi when she says, "It isn't Chains who has been calling."

My heart kicks into overdrive, and shock smears my face. I guess I shouldn't be surprised, though. I was nothing more to Marcus than a silly little sub to play games with. His demoralizing games strengthen my belief of why he wanted me to sign an NDA. He would hate for any other naïve young lady to discover the tricks he's playing. It wouldn't be as much fun if they were prepared for having their hearts torn from their chests.

I scrub my hand over my tired eyes when Lexi sits on my bed. "Who is it, then?".

Lexi doesn't answer me. She simply hands me my phone. My swirling stomach kicks up a notch when my eyes drop to the screen. Lexi was right. This is the last thing I need. Before I can comprehend why I have eighteen missed calls from Delilah, my cellphone vibrates and rings in my hand.

Clutching my chest to ensure it remains in place, I swipe my finger across the screen and push my phone to my ear. Although wrangling an irate Delilah is more than I'm up for this Sunday morning, I'm too intrigued about why she's calling me with such urgency to ignore my inquisitiveness.

"Chloe, we need you in the office by noon," Delilah snarls, not bothering to issue a greeting.

"It's Sunday," I mumble, my groggy voice incapable of hiding my shock. "And my name is Cleo by the way," I add on, sick of being so disrespected.

A deep growl barrels down the line before Delilah barks, "When the story of the century is on the verge of breaking, it doesn't matter if it's Sunday or Christmas Day. If you're not in this office by noon, *Cleo*, don't bother arriving on Monday."

My pulse quickens, more from her declaration of the story of the century about to be broken than her snarky tone.

"What story?" My thumping heart is audible in my voice.

"The investigation into Chains has been reopened. Mr. Carson wants the story headlining every media outlet in the country before Christmas."

With that, Delilah disconnects the call. . .

To be continued. . .

*Like what you've read thus far? The story of Cleo and Marcus continues in the second heart-thrashing installment titled: **Links.***
Available now!

http://a.co/57dQZ25

Join my Facebook page:
www.facebook.com/authorshandi

Join my READER's group:
https://www.facebook.com/groups/1740600836169853/

Join my newsletter to remain informed:
http://eepurl.com/cyEzNv

My Amazon Page:
https://www.amazon.com/Shandi-Boyes/e/B01D8C13WU

If you enjoyed this book - please leave a review:
http://a.co/57dQZ25

ACKNOWLEDGMENTS

Thank you to all the wonderful people who have supported me in my new endeavor. I'm incredibly grateful to have been blessed with such wonderful family and friends.

The time and effort it takes in writing a book are immense. You sacrifice your family, your hobbies, and yourself to produce a book that you hope your readers will enjoy. If you have enjoyed this book, please leave a review. A review is the only way you can truly thank an author for all the effort they put in.

Not many people are aware, but I'm a mother of five. I have four boys and one little daughter. I'd never be able to produce these books without the support of my husband. He comes home from working ten hour plus days to shower the children and get them ready for bed, never once saying a negative word. He's my rock, my inspiration, and my everything.

Also thanks to my mum Carolyn, for reading and assisting me when I call you crazily saying a scene isn't working. I appreciate everything you do. And last, but not at all least, my editor, Krista. Thank you for making my manuscripts extra sparkly. I appreciate everything you do!

Once again, thank you for your support and messages. I read every single one received. Please leave a review, and I'll see you on the flip side.

Cheers Shandi xx

ALSO BY SHANDI BOYES

Links (Marcus and Cleo)

Bound (Marcus and Cleo)

Restrained (Marcus and Cleo)

Psycho (Dexter)

Russian Mob Chronicles

Nikolai: A Mafia Prince Romance

Nikolai: Taking Back What's Mine

Nikolai: What's Left of Me

Nikolai: Mine to Protect

Asher: My Russian Revenge

Infinite Time Trilogy

Lady In Waiting (Regan)

Man in Queue (Regan)

Couple on Hold (Regan)

Standalones

Just Playin' (Presley and Willow)

COMING SOON:

Skitzo

Colby